It happened one spring

A Novel

E.L DELIZA

It happened one spring (The seasons of love, book 4)

Published by E.L Deliza

Playlist

MELTING | KALI UCHIS

HERE COMES THE SUN | THE BEATLES

I LIKE ME BETTER | LAUV

LOVE LOOKS PRETTY ON YOU | NESSA BARRETT

DELICATE| TAYLOR SWIFT

FALLING IN LOVE | CIGARETTES AFTER SEX

BROOKLYN BABY | LANA DEL REY

NOTHING'S GONNA HURT YOU BABY | CIGARETTES AFTER SEX

18 | ONE DIRECTION

DELICATE | TAYLOR SWIFT

THOSE EYES | NEW WEST

I WANNA BE YOURS | ARTIC MONKEYS

TU JAANE NA | ATIF ASLAM, PRITAM

SUNSETZ | CIGARETTES AFTER SEX

Dicktionary

For those who wish to avoid or enjoy the spicy chapters, here they are:

Chapter 11

Chapter 14

Chapter 17

Chapter 23

Chapter 25

Chapter 29

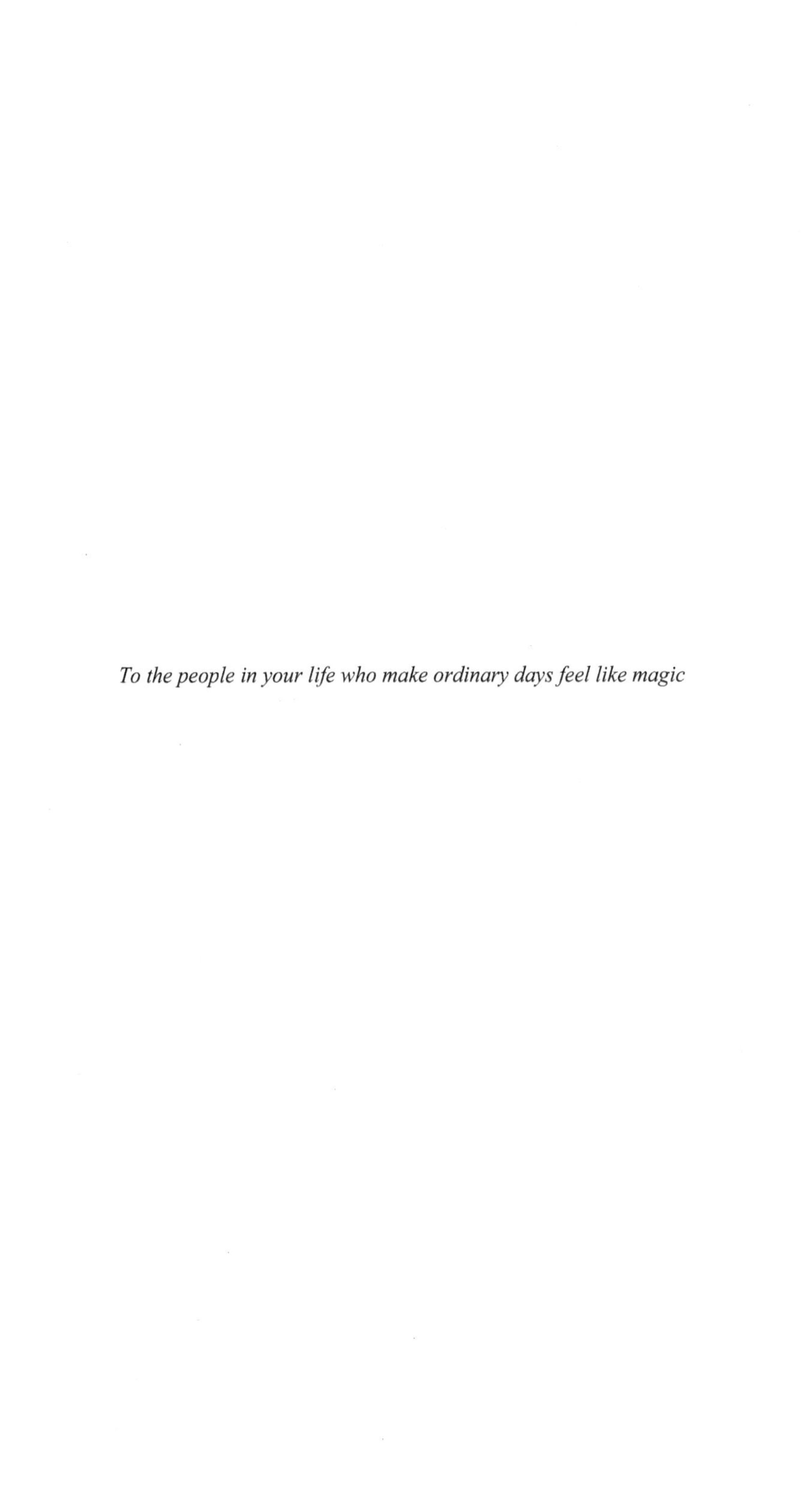

To the people in your life who make ordinary days feel like magic

Prologue.

Adam

Junior year was behind our backs—almost. My friends and I finished our exams. There was one day left before the departure of our summer break would come. Tonight, we were at Carter's for dinner and board games. Stella had made her famous spaghetti, Ibrahim and Darshini made their 'twin cookies special' which was basically a new recipe invented when the twins were bickering about what cookies to make, so they merged recipes.

I'm not complaining though, I loved my snickerdoodle, triple chocolate cookies. It wasn't healthy, but I didn't care. Summer was right around the corner. I knew it would be a night to remember as I looked among my friends and felt a deep seated happiness.

These are the same people I met my first year of DTU, my friend group had stayed the same. Our friendships blossomed, and I considered them family even. We've grown up together and soon we'd be heading into our last year of college.

I was lucky, I knew not everyone had such luck with finding great friends.

I picked up on the night shifting, the couple dynamics becoming apparent. Stella was leaning against Carter, his whispered words earning a smile from her. Ibrahim and Zaira shared secret glances, their intertwined hands hidden beneath the table—they assumed no one saw. Darshini and Dante seemed lost in each other's gazes, their smiles speaking volumes since

Ibrahim still gagged at the thought of his twin sister and best friend being together—he was dramatic.

I could see it all though, everyone's love was loud and clear.

Brooklyn and I, the odd ones out in the midst of these couples, exchanged knowing looks. We were familiar with this scenario.

"Do you guys want to head somewhere? We can continue our night," Carter suggested.

I knew they were tired and most likely wanted to kickback with their significant others. I didn't feel like heading out to be a third wheel, and by the looks of it neither did Brooke.

"Nah, it's fine," I assured him.

We all had plans this summer to meet up again anyways, it was fine. Instead, we cleaned up. Brooklyn looked at me and I could see a plan formulating in her eyes. I gave her a subtle nod, letting her know I didn't want the night to end either.

Our own little secret no one had to know about.

After cleaning up, I met up in the parking lot with Brooklyn while the others chatted. Often enough we'd talk outside of the group, head out to places they wouldn't like. I had a feeling tonight would be just the same.

"Hey," I greeted.

My eyes trailed down her body, admiring the short summer dress she wore when summer had barely even started. I noticed how she had her braids piled in a bun, a very rare sight since she almost always styled her hair—it was beautiful nonetheless. I was aware that lately I had been looking at her way too often but I tried not to think of that too often.

"Hey, what's the plan?"

"Club?" I asked simply.

We had our go-to spot right near a burger joint we'd visit after clubbing. This place would be packed after exams and quite lively. Just how we loved it.

"Definitely." She smirked.

"I'll swing by with an Uber around eleven," I promised.

"Deal."

Neither of us had to be designated drivers, perfect.

We were both excited, our idea of fun was quite the same. We loved the idea of dancing, drinking, and immersing ourselves in the lively crowd. It was a far better option than spending the night with our coupled-up friends that's for certain.

I was the first out of the Uber and extended my hand to Brooklyn.

"What a gentleman," she teased, placing her hand over mine as she exited the car.

Brooklyn never missed an opportunity to dress up. Her braids cascaded down her back with the ends loosened and curly, adorned with small pink and purple butterfly clips that matched her eyeliner, of course.

There's barely been a moment where she didn't have eyeliner on.

"I like what you did with the eye makeup," I commented, pointing to her face with a smile.

"Thank you, I only had four breakdowns because of how uneven it was," Brooklyn said in a joking matter but seemed to mean it.

"Is that... better than usual?" I frowned, leading us to the line.

"Definitely. Normally I give up after three attempts and wing it," she joked.

I stared at her winged eyeliner a little longer. It seemed difficult, I knew I wouldn't be able to replicate that twice. We began to talk about our summer plans, waiting patiently to be let inside. Brooklyn had her hand looped through my arm the entire time.

Once we were inside, she made a beeline for the bar, and I happily followed suit. We eyed the menu, contemplating our choices. The club had undergone a recent change in ownership, and the drink selection had expanded beyond their usual six options.

"I don't know what to pick," Brooklyn pondered aloud, tapping her chin.

"Caipirinha? I haven't had those in a while," I suggested, my mouth watering at the thought.

Between soccer, essays, and exams I never got much of a chance to drink. Tonight would be the perfect opportunity to let loose.

"Oh, yes," Brooklyn agreed. "Have you ever had whiskey?"

"Only with cola, but apparently that's not the right way to do it. How about you?"

I knew she hadn't. She preferred sweet drinks that knock you out by surprise.

"I've never had it before, but let's give it a try," Brooklyn decided.

Our drinks were served and we slowly nursed them as we waited for the dance floor to get a little more crowded. Once it called our name, I knew we had to go.

"Come on, Brooke." I took her hand and led us to the dance floor.

I expected her to break apart from me, but to my surprise, tonight she danced with me. The music became louder, the lights flashing more, and we swayed our bodies to the music till there was a thin layer of sweat coating our skin.

I wasn't sure who these people around me were, but they all smiled and danced in harmony, enjoying their night. Brooklyn turned around and took a step back 'til I felt the heat of her body pressing against mine.

This was new territory.

I was surprised at first, but then Brooklyn started swaying her hips. I sucked in a deep breath, feeling sober all of a sudden. I gently placed my hands on her shoulders, checking if she was okay with this. Brooklyn continued to dance, her hands finding mine. She slowly guided our hands down her curves, continuing to sway to the music, eyes closed with her head tipped back against my chest.

We've never danced this close before. But I certainly enjoyed every second of it till the song came to an end. Brooklyn turned around, her hand moving to my neck to pull me down.

"I think I need another drink," she whispered.

I nodded.

"Let's go."

On the way to the bar we saw a group of happy women cheering as they were served a bottle of fine tequila.

"I haven't had that in a while." Brooklyn laughed.

We should enjoy the night, right?

"Sir, could we each have two shots of that—"

"This one can only be sold by the bottle," the bartender cut me off.

"Fine, we'll take it."

Our bottle came with salt and lime, it rested right in front of us. Brooklyn and I stared at each other for a few seconds until I shrugged, undid the cap, and handed it to her.

"Open wide, bud." She grabbed my chin and pulled me down.

I laughed and complied, ignoring the salt platter we had. Brooklyn carefully held my jaw as she poured the liquid, just enough for me to swallow. I pulled away and grabbed the lime slice instantly.

The first drink had things rolling for us, one shot became two and soon it all blurred together. We even ended up sharing the rest with the group next to us. I knew for a fact I had a bit too much because I kept staring at Brooklyn, and I swore she looked at my lips like I did with hers.

"Watch out." I pulled Brooklyn towards me when the bartender walked past us with a tray full of glasses.

"Oops." She stepped away, hands landing on my chest for a moment.

I had my hand resting loosely on her waist when Brooklyn slid hers up to the back of my neck. We locked eyes, the soft light flickering across her face like something out of a dream. At that moment, something shifted. I stepped in closer, and she tilted her head up towards me.

Our lips met in a kiss—gentle at first, but it grew passionate almost instantly and unexpectedly. The urgency between us expanded. It was as if time froze around us, like it was just us two for the moment. Her hands travelled down my chest, sending shivers through me as she traced the shape of my muscles. I wrapped my arms around her hips and pulled her closer, not wanting to let go.

Then, someone bumped into us, pulling us out of the moment.

We finally broke apart, breathless. My lips tingled, and my heart pounded. I was sure I'd crossed a line—I half expected her to slap me. But instead, Brooklyn reached for my hand, laced her fingers with mine, and pulled me back towards the dance floor.

We danced the rest of the night without a single worry, as if nothing ever happened. But I knew no amount of alcohol could make me forget about this kiss. It had sobered me up.

The next morning came and I was in the kitchen. I nursed my lemon water, grimacing at its sour taste. This was bad. I heard movements from the couch and walked towards the living room. I sat down on the one-person seat and stared at Brooklyn.

She managed to roll around on the couch without falling once. It seems like the line of pillows I laid on the ground had no purpose.

"Dude, my head is killing me," Brooklyn groaned, blinking her eyes open. She must be grateful for the closed blinds and the dim lighting in the room.

"Shhhh, you're talking too loud," I groaned in agreement, gesturing towards the glass of water and Advil I had left on the table earlier.

"Wait, where am I? Did we come back to your place?" Brooklyn frowned, scanning her surroundings and noticing me.

"Don't you remember anything?" I could recall every detail of our night together.

I had woken up with a smile until my body reminded me of the consequences along with my head that played out a few scenarios of the kiss. I didn't want things to be awkward.

"I remember you picking me up and us sharing that bottle of tequila. I'm not sure, I think my mind went blank after the whiskey," Brooklyn admitted, sitting up and reaching for the water and medicine.

"That damn tequila always gets us." I laughed.

"I didn't mean to get so wasted. I don't know how it happened," Brooklyn apologised, looking at me with a slight pout.

"It's okay, next time we won't mix our drinks," I reassured her, the words sounding familiar from a previous outing during spring break. We made the same promise after a wild night—one where we hadn't kissed.

"Thank you for taking care of me last night, Adam. I really appreciate it," Brooklyn expressed her gratitude.

"I'd never leave you in such a state, Brooke. It's fine," I assured her, rising to my feet.

"Can I freshen up? I'll treat you to breakfast for being such a gentleman." Brooklyn stretched her arms out.

"I have expensive taste, but I'm sure you can afford me," I teased, pointing down the hallway. "Bathroom's down the hall to your right. There should be extra toiletries in the cabinet. Feel free to use whatever you like, but don't judge my toothpaste preference."

As Brooklyn walked away, I couldn't help but watch her. Closing my eyes, I tilted my head back and tried to push aside last night's memories. But even then, the sensations lingered—her body pressed against mine, the touch of her hand guiding mine over her curves, and that unforgettable kiss.

I knew it was best to forget, especially since Brooklyn didn't even remember it. Fuck, I never looked at her that way before. I couldn't shake off the guilt because a part of me wouldn't mind more.

I reminded myself it was just dancing and a kiss, hoping I'd forget it by tomorrow.

Chapter one

Brooklyn

|Senior year|

I swirled the ice in my drink, taking a sip of my iced tea as I walked alongside Darshini. The ride back had been silent, both of us utterly exhausted from everything. It was only January, yet we already felt drained. We were on the cusp of earning our bachelor's degrees, so close yet so far away. Like they say, the last miles are the longest.

"I think I might just collapse face-first onto the bed," Darshini mused as we approached the elevator. There was an eerie feeling about the place today, though I couldn't quite put my finger on why. Something just felt off.

"I'm so damn tired, I might just flop right at the door," I agreed, longing for a nap.

"What the hell?" Darshini whined as we reached the elevator, realising it was out of order. None of the buttons were lit up, and it was dead silent inside as if everything had suddenly stopped working.

"You've got to be kidding me," I groaned, realising this meant we had to walk up the flights of stairs. "Today? Really?" I sighed.

"No wonder there's no one around," Darshini remarked.

Darshini and I ascended the stairs as quickly as we could while complaining. We could have paused at each level to catch our breath, but the floors were sticky, wet, and disgustingly grimy. It was unusual, considering they usually kept the place clean, but I couldn't dwell on it too much since it was the first time.

"That's not right, why is it so wet?" I wrinkled my nose as we trudged along the damp carpet, the liquid squelching with every step we took.

"I'm not sure, let's head—" Darshini pushed the door open, and her jaw dropped. "What the fuck?!"

I gazed at our apartment, the floor submerged in water. With the door ajar, it spilt out, leaving us standing in ankle-deep water that flushed out.

"Did we leave something running?" I asked, struggling to keep my panic in check. The potential costs we were facing were daunting. We were definitely in trouble.

"Hey neighbour, packing to head out already?" a voice behind us asked. We turned around and saw Marik, he was kind and a college student like us. We mostly met in the elevator, and he always kept the conversations as short and kind as possible.

"What?" Darshini frowned, eyeing the multitude of bags Marik and his roommates were lugging down the stairs. What was going on in his mind right now? It was mid-January, and there couldn't be a single trip planned during the school season requiring that many bags.

"Don't you know?" Marik's frown deepened. Those three words rarely brought good news, so I braced myself for the worst.

"What happened?" I wondered.

"Some pipes burst—I'm not exactly sure what happened, but the building is being shut down. There's potential for electrical issues too, and... didn't they send you a notice?" Marik explained, his confusion mirroring our own. All I could hear was more problems added to our already full plate.

"No—Oh, our other roommate is the contact person." Darshini glanced at me, realisation dawning on us both. Dante was supposed to handle communications, but with his busy schedule of presentations and soccer training, I doubted he even had the chance to check his email.

"When did this happen?" I questioned, glancing at my watch briefly.

"This morning. The place was flooded due to faulty pipes—I literally have no idea. All I know is that they have a lot of repairs to do before it's safe for us to live here. There have been warnings and now they want us to move out for our own safety, of course," Marik explained, stepping aside to allow his roommate to pass with more bags. We would soon have to do the same.

"Oh, damn." Darshini sighed, and we exchanged a knowing look.

We thanked Marik and then stepped aside to call Ibrahim and Dante. Due to the emergency, they managed to leave practice early, and together we began to pack up what was necessary. It was infuriating with the property manager constantly reminding us to hurry as they didn't want to be liable for any injuries that might occur.

I stuffed my suitcase with as many clothes as it could hold, making sure to pack all my electronics and school books. Whatever hadn't suffered damage, I'd come back for more tomorrow. I tried to remain positive and thankful— at least my electronics were fine.

"Got all the necessary things?" Ibrahim asked, holding the door open for me as we piled everything near the front door.

"I think so, now we just have to bring all of this to ground level." I sighed, surveying the mountain of belongings. Shit, the elevator was out of order.

"Let's get going, people," Dante urged, taking Darshini's suitcase and allowing her to carry the lighter bags. In moments like these, I wished I had a boyfriend. A strong one.

Thankfully, Ibrahim helped out where he could. It was a true team effort to load up our cars, and we had to call in an emergency late lunch meeting with our friends.

So we went to lunch, where my car was parked with all my belongings. We were seated near a window though so I constantly looked out to make sure I wouldn't get robbed. The others planned and talked while I tried to figure out where I'd stay.

All I wanted was an evening with my latest romance book, some hot chocolate to accompany as I got lost in my book.

True love seemed nice, it was shown as something magical in art. It would perhaps be great to experience, but I knew that not everyone would ever get the chance to experience it. I was ok with being one of those people— that wouldn't stop me from consuming movies and books where love finds place though.

"Okay, so you managed to find a new place?" Stella pointed her fork at Dante.

Dante swallowed his bite before nodding. "Yeah, it's small, but it will do for Darsh and me for a few days." He placed his hand over Darshini's, and Ibrahim rolled his eyes. It didn't happen too often anymore, but he liked to be dramatic from time to time all because his sister and best friend were dating.

"It's nearly impossible to find good places this month. The available ones are far from school, and I can't manage that commute with everything on my schedule." Ibrahim sighed.

"You're staying with Zaira, right?" Adam asked.

"Yep," Ibrahim confirmed, with a goofy grin, while Zaira whispered "pray for me" to tease him.

"Brooke, just you then." Carter redirected everyone's attention to me. "I have extra rooms," he offered. I was well aware of his spacious apartment, but I couldn't possibly stay with him. Despite him being a great friend and Stella often being there, I still felt it would be awkward.

"No, no, I don't want to impose," I declined firmly.

"It's fine, literally—" Carter began, but I kept shaking my head, unable to accept his generous offer.

"Please, just let us help you. It'll be hard to find a place nearby this fast," Stella chimed in, her gaze softening.

I knew how difficult it would be, I had already searched without luck. All the spots near our university were taken, and the available ones were too expensive. I had managed to find an inn, and I hoped it wouldn't take more than a week for everything to return to normal.

"Yeah, you can take my room to my apartment if it'll make you feel better. I'll just stay with Cartie," Stella offered, and I could feel everyone's eyes still on me, urging me to accept.

That meant living with Zaira and Ibrahim—another couple.

"Guys, it's fine. I found a place for now. It's like a cute inn or something. They have a breakfast bar and all," I assured them, though I was convincing myself as well. "I'll stay there until we get some news about how long the renovation will take." I forced a quick smile.

"Okay, we'll drop you off first then," Darshini decided, winking at me.

"Guys, I have it covered, truly," I reiterated, turning to Ibrahim and Dante. "I'll go alone. I'm sure all of us are tired, especially with practice too."

That managed to change the subject—thankfully.

"Man, practice and carrying all those bags certainly made me tired." Ibrahim sighed, rolling his shoulders forward and backwards.

By the end of dinner, they had successfully forgotten about driving me to the inn. I grinned and waved as they all left one by one. My smile faltered when I noticed Adam still by my side.

"Aren't you going?" I glanced over at Adam as I pulled my keys out of my bag.

"You might've tricked the others, but you haven't tricked me," Adam said, swinging his arm around my shoulder and walking towards my car with me. "I'll see you at your 'cute' inn."

I liked Adam. We were both the single ones in the group and hanging out with him solo was often fun. We understood each other in a way the others didn't fully. Sadly, due to our busy schedules we haven't found time to hang out just the two of us.

"But it's the opposite of where you live." I frowned, pressing the unlock button on the fob.

"I don't care. We have to make sure you get there safely," Adam replied, holding the door open for me.

"We?" I raised a brow at him. The others had left, so who was this *we*? Was he about to trick me with a French joke like he had before? Last time I didn't do anything but this time I might resort to physical abuse after the day I had.

"Darshini is worried too," Adam explained, leaning down to close my door slowly. "She assumed you don't want a crowd, so I assured her I'd go," he continued, but all I could focus on was his cologne filling the air between us.

I inhaled deeply, a soft smile spreading on my lips. He smelled of the ocean, refreshing with a sense of cleanliness that washed away my worries like the soft crashes of the ocean against the shore. I took another breath, not yet having enough of it.

"Adam," I whispered, momentarily hypnotised by him. Men and their cologne, they'd be the death of me, especially ones like him.

"Nothing you say will make me change my mind, so you're just making us both wait for no reason," Adam decided, determination gleaming in his eyes.

"Let's go, I guess." I sighed, I knew that look and I didn't bother fighting it.

Adam closed the door and made his way to his own car. We drove to the inn, the GPS guiding me while Adam followed closely behind. I stole glances at him through the mirror. He seemed laid back, enjoying whatever music he was listening to and dancing to it while driving.

When the GPS announced we had arrived, I assumed it was a mistake. The last five minutes of the drive to this place had me questioning the directions. I thought it was wrong, I really did, but then I saw the dimly lit sign, reading Symphony Inn, the Inn flickering in and out.. I blinked in disbelief several times.

This couldn't be right. A trashcan was knocked over, and a furry creature was having the time of its life rummaging through it. The landscape was neglected, and the paint on the building's exterior was peeling, covered in specks of dirt.

A knock on my window startled me, and I looked over to see Adam. I unlocked the car, and we both stepped outside. The air smelled... questionable.

"You can't possibly—"

"We haven't even seen inside. Let's not judge," I hushed him, heading straight for the front desk. I could hear Adam's sigh as he followed behind me.

I dealt with the front desk and was given my key. I almost gagged when I felt how sticky it was. My first order of business would be soaking my hand in bleach followed by a deep scrub with alcohol.

I turned the key and pushed the door open. Flicking the light switch, my jaw dropped. The paint job inside was far worse. An odd mixture of brown and green peeked out behind a poorly applied white splatter that was supposed to cover it up. The bedsheets looked crunchy, and the room reeked of cheap air freshener that I knew would turn sour within hours. The supposed closet was open on one side, the hinge looking a bit broken. Discoloured splatters dotted the carpet here and there.

Had Dexter been here? No, he'd leave it spotless.

"You're not staying here," Adam scoffed, his eyes scanning the room, picking out each red flag.

"It's not that bad, Adam," I lied, trying to maintain a straight face. But deep down, I knew I wouldn't sleep well here. I'd be too worried. Is it a bad idea to sleep in a car in this weather?

"Don't you even dare attempt lying, Brooke," Adam retorted, gently wrapping his hand around my wrist.

"I can stay here," I insisted, eyeing the bed. I was sure I had clean bedsheets in one of my suitcases—or was it in a bag?

"Over my dead body." Adam declared being rather adamant about this. "We're going back to my place, and you can take one of my spare rooms," he decided, already pulling out his key with his other hand.

"Adam, I swear it's okay," I insisted, tugging on my hand, but he didn't budge.

"Brooklyn, it's okay to accept help sometimes," he spoke softly as if he could see right through my defences. "Let me do this for you, okay?" He placed his hand on my shoulder and rubbed it gently.

Chapter two

Adam

"But, but," Brooklyn began to stutter, and I could practically hear the gears in her head turning as she searched for an excuse. I've known her for over three years now, and I can confidently say I had her figured out, so I just waited, anticipating her excuse.

"What about your elderly women's sex dungeon?" she asked, her tone dead serious. Damn Carter, Ibrahim, Dante—everyone who started that ridiculous rumour about me loving older women.

I couldn't even help an elderly woman cross the road without them running that joke into the ground. All because I slept with a woman five years my senior once—it was completely legal, but the jokes had already started.

"So eager." I played along, smirking. "At least take me on a date first, then I'll take you there." I winked. Brooklyn was flustered, her mouth opening but no words coming out. She flipped me off with both hands.

Laughing, I grabbed her hands, pulling her out of the room before we caught some airborne disease. "Let's go home, Brooke. I don't mind having your company."

"We already have the same friend group, the same major, the same classes. We would be pushing our luck moving in together." She tried to give excuses.

"I made up my mind, I won't take no for an answer."

Brooklyn didn't object again. Instead, she followed me home. I sent her straight to the bathroom, promising to take care of everything. I quickly arranged the guest room for her, brought in all her bags, then went to find the spare garage remote.

Fluffing up the pillows, I heard the bathroom door open, and Brooklyn emerged in her robe.

"I'll wait for you in the kitchen."

I put two slices of chocolate ganache cake on a plate. I thought we both deserved this after a long day. I placed two small forks right next to it and waited patiently for Brooklyn to make her way down.

I heard footsteps and looked over to see Brooklyn in cute cow pyjamas, making her way to me. "You brought in everything?"

"Sure did. Here's the remote to the garage," I said, sliding closer to her. Brooklyn sat down beside me, her eyes fixed on the plate. Yeah, we both loved chocolate a lot.

"I lost the spare front door key, but this is the side door key in the garage that grants you access. I'll look for the front door key in the meantime or make a copy," I explained, watching as she dug into her slice of cake.

"Thank you, Adam, truly, for everything." She looked at me with those pretty hazel eyes, and I could only smile like a fool.

"You're welcome." I tore my eyes away from her and looked down at my plate. "This house is too big for one anyway," I said as I dug into my cake.

"I mean, you literally chose a house in a gated community, what did you expect?" Brooklyn pointed out, and I sighed dramatically.

It wasn't exactly my choice, but I did love it a lot.

"Hey, I would've loved an apartment, but my parents think this is better for safety reasons and such," I explained. "They also plan to retire in this house once I'm out."

"It's an incredible house," Brooklyn commented, scooping ganache onto her fork.

"Thank you, Brooklyn." I smiled, contemplating stealing that forkful of goodness. I shouldn't, she's been through enough for today. Perhaps being robbed of chocolate ganache will be her last straw.

"I promise I'll be out of your hair ASAP," she mentioned, but I paid no attention.

I wished her a good night and then headed to my room. After the long and tiring day of classes and endless practice with Coach Mendes, my bed looked so great right now, first class ticked to SnoozeVille.

There was a blaring alarm, one that wasn't from my phone, or I'd be ignoring it. Shit, that's the smoke alarm. My eyes shot open, and the light in the room indicated it was morning already. Right on cue, my phone alarm went off, mixing with the loud smoke alarm.

I put my phone aside and rushed down to see Brooklyn behind the stove, smoke in the air with the burned scent wafting around. What the hell?

"Brooklyn?" I looked at her and noticed steam billowing from a pan. The contents, presumably eggs and sausages, were now charred to crisps.

"Sorry, sorry, I–I messed up." She looked panicked.

"It's okay, hold on," I said, relieved to see no fire. I wrestled with the smoke alarm and managed to silence it. Taking a deep breath, I replaced it and turned to Brooklyn with a raised brow.

"I'm so sorry, Adam. I wanted to say thank you with some breakfast, but messed up," she began to apologise, but to me, it was all quite hilarious, and I broke into laughter.

It was the kind of laughter that had me tipping my head back, clutching my chest and stomach. The thought of Brooklyn behind the stove, and now that I knew there was no danger, I couldn't stop laughing about it.

"I don't know how to cook. It was a dumb decision," she said, sounding pissed as she started to leave the kitchen.

"Fuck, I didn't mean to make you feel terrible." I gently grabbed her hand and pulled her back. The look on her face wasn't pretty; my laughing must've made her feel like shit, and that had never been my intention.

"Hey, it's okay, Brooke," I assured her, rubbing her arms. "I think you're going soft. You despise cooking, yet you wanted to surprise me?" I teased, noticing how it brought a soft smile to her lips, followed by her rolling her eyes, of course.

"Shut up," she said, punching my arm gently.

"I mean it, it might not be edible, but the fact that you were willing to do that for me means a lot to me, Brooke," I said, now serious instead of laughing. Even when I laughed, these thoughts were exactly what was going through my head.

"This is embarrassing," Brooke groaned and walked away from me.

"I don't know how to cook either. I let the water evaporate completely once, burned the damn pot," I assured her with my most embarrassing cooking memory. It might not have caused the alarm to go off, but to me, 'burning' water is far worse than that.

Brooklyn laughed, an actual laugh, not just a quick little smile, but a proper smile and laugh that spread across her lips.

"We have to work on our cooking, then." Brooklyn sighed, grabbing some orange juice to pour.

"Tell you what, you and I will start watching those easy recipe videos and learn how to cook," I decided, rubbing my chin. This had been on my mind a lot, maybe she'd be my motivation.

"Really?" Brooklyn asked, suspicious of me.

"Yup, it's a deal." I extended my hand out to her.

"Fine." She shook my hand with a slight smirk.

"Oh, and Brooke," I called as I walked off.

"Yes, Adam?"

"I'm a simple man, some fruit smoothies with spinach for breakfast make me go feral." I winked, then went up to my room again.

I think I might just like having Brooklyn here. I would've gotten a roommate sooner had I known it would be like this.

Our schedules aligned today, so I drove us to school. Our friends awaited us by the bench near the pond. When we joined them, they were all there already, laughing about something.

"Oh, you guys made it—wait, did you come together?" Stella frowned, looking at the two of us. Everyone turned their attention towards us.

"Yep, I decided to stay with Adam," Brooklyn confirmed, taking a seat next to Stella. The bench had no more space left, so I continued to stand.

"Was the room not nice?" Dante wondered.

"It was horrendous," I interjected before Brooklyn could even say anything.

She shot me a glare. "Stop being so dramatic about it."

"Brooklyn, honey, I'm pretty sure there's a virus cooking up in that room, and you would've been patient zero," I continued with the drama, and the others gasped. It could be true.

"That bad?" Zaira frowned, looking at Brooklyn for a less dramatic explanation.

Brooklyn began to explain what she saw, and occasionally, I gave my input, still being dramatic about it, of course.

"That's not a disease layer, it's a killer layer. Maybe the carpet was never red, to begin with," Ibrahim joked.

"Thank you, I will forever think of that now." Brooklyn sighed and shook her head.

"What's important is that you have a safe place." Darshini smiled and patted her back.

"Get this, Zaira got angry with Ibrahim because he lied to her about waking up at 6:30 to get an early study session in," Carter successfully shifted the conversation, and I frowned.

"But you always get up at six." Brooklyn looked over at Ibrahim. "I wake up at six and he's already up, pacing around with his headphones and book in hand."

"Exactly! He's been lying. He's trying to throw me off guard," Zaira scoffed, removing Ibrahim's hand from her thigh.

"I need those extra thirty minutes just to be on the same level as you, angel," Ibrahim tried to say suavely.

"Ew, disgusting." Darshini rolled her eyes.

"I had to deal with you and Dante in one house," Ibrahim shot back.

And that covered our daily sibling squabble that usually ended up with all of us joining in and ranting about something else.

Man, I loved my friends.

Chapter three

Brooklyn

A week. It's been a week since our apartment shut down. I couldn't believe it. We waited for a response, and all we'd been told was that we could come by to pick up the rest of our things. Adam was a great housemate, but I didn't want to overstay my welcome.

I snapped back to reality, yet dinner day at Alfonso's with a large order everyone waited for impatiently.

"And when can we officially go back?" Ibrahim asked.

"Not too sure, turns out some inspections need to be redone and such, and they haven't even started reconstructing," Dante explained, leaning back in his seat with his arm behind Darshini.

"Oh, I asked my dad. I was right about the owner, he might consider selling because the fixing costs are too high," Carter shared.

I was hoping Carter would have good news, not this.

"You've got to be kidding me," Dante groaned and tipped his head back.

"What? You don't like your living arrangement?" I teased him, raising a brow. I would've thought being with his girlfriend without her twin present would be fun.

"I love it, it's just small for the two of us," Dante complained.

"Yeah, and I've gotten used to sharing a bathroom with you, Brooke." Darshini sighed. Both Darshini and Dante loved to be the first to use the bathroom, which I assume is the issue. I never minded being second since Darshini left the bathroom clean and smelling nice.

"I can ask around for a better place," Carter offered.

"Yes, please," Darshini said with a sigh of relief.

"I'm loving every moment of my new living arrangement." Ibrahim grinned and pulled Zaira closer.

"Of course you do, you're a clingy baby." Zaira smirked.

"You always rain on my parade," Ibrahim complained and removed his hand from hers.

"Brooky, you?" Zaira asked, and everyone turned to me.

Oh, I loved it. I had my own bathroom now and a chauffeur on some days.

"Oh, I'm great. I'm saving so much gas money riding with this one." I ruffled Adam's hair.

"A simple *Yes, I'm happy and Adam's an outstanding host* would've sufficed," Adam said. We paused the conversation as our drinks were served.

"Adam's an outstanding host," I said in a monotone voice, watching as he just sighed.

"Now it sounds as if you're forced," he groaned.

"Adam's angry because the new guy managed to score and he didn't," Dante teased.

"He and the goalie call each other brothers, they're helping each other, they're siblings!" Adam reasoned.

I knew he wanted to go pro I was sure some brothers wouldn't disrupt that. He was dedicated and talented.

After dinner came ice cream, and I looked among the couples. They would all come up with excuses to leave, and I always found it entertaining.

"I'm tired, we'll get going." Ibrahim stretched out, but it looked like an exaggeration.

"Yeah, super tired," Zaira lied without any semblance of believability. We all simply nodded as the two of them darted off.

"Yeah, I have to finish a paper," Carter explained, which was funny because he'd mentioned the same excuse yesterday.

"Mhm, he's my ride, so I'll be going." Stella rushed out, her hand clasped firmly in his.

"We're—" Darshini started, but Adam cut her off. "Just go, have a good night, and drive safely."

"They're all going to fuck," I remarked once the last two had driven off.

"Oh, 100 percent. We have an out-of-state match on Saturday, and we leave tomorrow. They have to make up for time that's going to be lost," Adam replied, and suddenly it all made sense. This wasn't the first time, but I'm impressed they couldn't come up with better excuses. If only the execution of the lies were just as decent.

One time, Darshini lied about having a paper to take care of. Stella takes the same classes as her and panicked, thinking she had one too. That was hilarious, and I never let them live that down.

"They could've just said good night, and we wouldn't assume anything." I shook my head and followed Adam to his car.

"They're so silly sometimes." Adam chuckled, unlocking the doors. "Cute together too."

"Disgustingly cute," I murmured, refraining from rolling my eyes. I was genuinely happy for my friends, they were all paired up perfectly together.

"Are we jealous?" A frown spread across his face.

"Nah, I'm sure we just need to get laid too." I grinned. Unlike our friends, we didn't really do relationships.

"Probably. Hey, you're okay with having the place to yourself on the weekend, right?" Adam asked as he got into the car.

"Are you okay with having me there alone?"

"Yeah, just don't burn anything and don't walk naked near the front and back door, there are cameras there," he teased, starting the ignition.

I rolled my eyes. "Wow, thank you so much. I definitely planned on walking naked around the house."

"Hey, I'm just telling you." He held his hands up as he shrugged. "Home?"

"Are you tired?" I wondered, before planning to answer his question.

"Not too tired, what did you have in mind?"

"We could grab a drink," I suggested. It was only Thursday, but hey, he was leaving for the weekend, so this would be our time.

"Sure, but just one, though," Adam decided and started to drive.

"Let's go then." I grinned.

As promised, we went to a bar near his house and each only had one drink. I enjoyed my passion fruit martini, and Adam enjoyed his dirty Shirley with four cherries. He loved the cherries and made sure to pay for extra.

"Check out the guy at the end of the bar. He's been eyeing you for the past ten minutes," Adam whispered to me, his eyes sliding from place to place. I looked over at the guy he spoke of.

He seemed tall, and was wearing an MIT hoodie. His eyes caught mine, and he smirked. He had dark hair and dark eyes with a charming look on his face, but... No, thank you.

"Really? I hadn't noticed... I've been too busy trying to charm the bartender into giving us free drinks," I whispered to Adam, who just laughed. I didn't know why he was laughing because we still hadn't paid for our drinks. The bartender kept smiling, blushing every time he looked at me. Most people there paid before they received their drink, so I believed my plan was working.

"You should do that giggle thing you always do when you're flushed," Adam said as he popped a cherry in his mouth.

"I don't do any giggle things." I frowned, eyes focused on his lips for a second.

"Oh, you do." He chuckled.

"You can't prove that," I scoffed, refusing to believe that I giggled. It takes a lot to even get me flustered!

"I bet I can make you giggle before the night is over," Adam whispered, offering me one of the cherries.

"Oh, you're on. But good luck with that, I'm not an easy target." I winked, taking the cherry and keeping my eyes focused on him.

"Challenge accepted. How about we make it interesting? Loser buys drinks next time?"

"Deal." I held my hand out to him, and he shook it, then pulled me closer to him.

Adam came closer and whispered in my ear, "Excuse me, but I think you dropped something: my jaw."

"Pick up lines? That's how you plan to do it?" I laughed loudly. Oh, the next time we go drinking, I'll be ordering the most expensive drink to teach him a lesson.

"Is it hot in here?" he asked, and I almost fell for it, almost. "Or is it just you?" He smirked.

"Pick-up lines won't work, buddy." I rolled my eyes.

"I guess you're right," he whispered in my ear, his fingertips sliding over my shoulder. "A pretty girl like you must've gotten dozens of those." He sighed, his voice a bit deeper and more serious than usual.

"Mhm," I simply confirmed, scared to move, but surely this won't make me giggle.

Adam leaned closer, his hand pushing my hair over my shoulder. His face came closer to mine, and I tipped my head back a little. His nose grazed my skin, and he breathed hot air on my skin.

Control. You need to prove him wrong, Brooke.

"Have I ever told you how great your perfume is, Brooklyn?" Adam asked, then continued in that sexy voice of his, "Every morning when you enter the car, it drives me insane."

I took a deep breath and turned to him, my eyes dropped down to his lips. I always wondered what he'd taste like. Reality tugged at me, and I shook off my thoughts. Not Adam, we can't.

I took a step back and cleared my throat. "Adam, it's gonna take more than that to get me," I lied. He almost got me, he was on the right track, even.

"Fine, I give up." He held his hands up, laughing.

The drive home, he spoke, and I tried paying attention—I was just elsewhere. All I could think of was my apartment. How unfortunate were we truly for this to happen to us?

Everyone else seemed to have their backup plan going, but I bet Adam didn't plan for me to stay so long. I wondered how long it would take him before he'd try to kick me out politely. No, I couldn't get kicked out. I didn't want to ask my parents for help.

I'd just continue to make him his fruit smoothies every morning, maybe that would put off his thoughts of potentially kicking me out.

When we got to the house, Adam went up to his room to get ready for bed, I assumed, and I did the same. I planned on sleeping, but all the thoughts of being kicked out still swirled in my head, and I couldn't settle down.

I now found myself in the kitchen with all the ingredients laid out in front of me to bake the most perfect chocolate ganache cake. I've been mastering this recipe since I was twelve, and I can now make it without needing to follow instructions. Cooking I struggle with, but baking was my forte

Adam came downstairs wearing some grey sweats and a thin white shirt. He saw me and raised a brow, giving me a questioning look.

"I'm gonna bake us a chocolate cake," I informed him, and looked around for a glass bowl.

"You sure you want to do that?" Adam asked, being careful about it, but I knew what he meant. I also didn't blame him for it.

"Would you believe me if I told you that I'm an excellent baker?" I wondered, watching as his brows furrowed.

He was truly thinking about this, and I took a second to look at him. His face was glistening, something about aloe vera moisturiser, he said once. His pink lips were covered with what I assumed were the lip balms I found in his car. His hair was usually neatly swept to the left, but without any products in it, the blond strands parted down the middle.

"Not really, but are you?"

"The best, in my opinion. Been baking since I was twelve." I smirked proudly. I left out the part where I should've mentioned that it was my coping mechanism. One that had a 75 percent success rate. If it failed, then at least I had cake, right?

"What's your best work?" Adam asked, his tone filled with genuine interest.

"Chocolate ganache cake, triple chocolate cookies, brownies of course, and if I feel fancy, pain au chocolat," I listed, watching as his jaw dropped with each dessert. Chocolate was his sweet spot, I knew that.

"Oh, I'd love some chocolate ganache cake, I think I have enough chocolate bars to make the ganache," Adam said with excitment, and I just laughed.

"Duh, why did you think I planned on making it?" I pointed to the counter where the chocolate rested for us to use.

"I love our love for chocolate," Adam said with a content look.

"Might just be the best thing about us," I admitted, pointing the whisk at him and then myself.

"I love it so much I'd like it right off someone's body." Adam took a step closer to me, his fingers dancing along the marble of his kitchen counter.

"Kinky, interesting, I will be thinking about that forever," I admitted, the words flowing out of my mouth without much thought.

"Let me know when you want to stop thinking and start experiencing it," he said in that seductive voice of his, a smirk on his lips as he passed by me to reach the chocolate.

I could suddenly picture it. Lying down flat, the thick chocolate trickling down my skin. Adam's flat tongue against me, devouring it like he did with that cherry in the bar.

A giggle left my lips, and I pressed them together to suppress my grin, but then it hit me. What I just did.

"I believe this means you buy the drinks next time?" Adam asked with a smirk. Fuck, he never gave up!

"I hate you," I scoffed and pushed him aside to reach for the carton of eggs.

"Sure you do, Brooklyn baby." He patted my back and leaned back against the counter. "Now what can I do to help?" he asked as if it was nothing.

I watched as he took off his shirt. I didn't blame him... It's a white shirt, but damn, I still wasn't used to the sight. His body was sculpted to perfection in my eyes. I knew how much time and effort he put into it, and it sure paid off.

"Do I make the ganache or?" Adam asked, looking at the chocolates.

"Okay... I think cupcakes will be easier?" There was nothing better than a cupcake that oozed chocolate filling.

"Oh yes, please," he said like a little child with hope in his eyes.

I began to instruct him, and we got to work in harmony. Adam was great at listening, but I ended up having him sit down. He helped with filling the cups and popping the tray in the oven, but he didn't seem to mind that I barely made him do anything.

It was almost as if he enjoyed just being here with me. The cupcakes had cooled down already, and we both had our makeshift piping bags.

"Okay, so you poke a hole like this," I instructed him, so we could fill the cupcakes. I looked over and saw Adam eat the cake hole he scooped out. "Adam, don't eat—" It's fine, it's just one. He looked me straight in the eyes as he brought the piping bag to his mouth and let it drip into his mouth. "You monster," I gasped.

"Try it." He licked his lips and brought the ganache bag to me.

"No," I scoffed. I was firm with my rules. You devour the leftovers, but never before decorating.

"Come on, you know you want to." Adam walked closer to me until I was trapped against the counter in the corner.

"You're ruining our hard work," I said, with my hand on his chest, maintaining a safe distance.

"I'm enjoying our hard work." He ate a bit more, almost as if he was rubbing salt in the wound.

"You're banned from now on, this is the last time you're helping me bake," I decided, and he pouted.

"As long as I still get to lick the bowl clean, I don't mind it." He winked.

"You disgust me," I said dramatically.

"Open wide, Brooklyn baby, you know you want some." His voice was so seductive. I swear, even the devil could make me sign my life away if it looked like Adam offering chocolate.

He was right. I did. Adam purchased the best of the best chocolate, rich and creamy. I sighed and folded. I couldn't pretend like I didn't do this when I was alone in the kitchen.

I opened my mouth, and Adam's hand gently held my chin in place. My head was tipped back a little, and Adam dangled the piping bag in place. I felt swirls of the chocolate on my tongue, and I hummed at the sweet taste.

"See, so fucking worth it," he commented and lessened the chocolate so it could stop. His hand left my chin, and I lowered my head, feeling some chocolate drop down my lip. "Always making a mess," he muttered, his thumb sweeping over my chin, gathering the chocolate.

"Stop stealing my chocolate," I warned.

"Do you want it?" He stuck his thumb at me, and I stared at it. I was about to take a step forward when he already sucked it clean. "Didn't think so."

"We have cupcakes to top," I reminded him.

Luckily, this time he obeyed, and by the end, we had all of them topped and filled with the ganache. The downside of baking was the mess it left, a mess we both had to clean up. There were flour and chocolate stains on our skin. It was wise of him to remove his shirt.

We cleaned up and met back downstairs to finally have the dessert we had baked. I had momentarily forgotten about my apartment issues. Instead, I was on the couch with Adam and enjoyed our chocolate ganache cupcakes with the TV on.

"Brooke, you're a great baker," Adam said as he bit into the cupcake, chocolate rolling down his chin.

"I know, Adam." I laughed.

"I like having you here. I don't care how long it will take for the apartment to get back to normal, but you can stay with me for as long as you're comfortable with," he said as he wiped his chin clean. He then went for a second bite, and I stared at him, wondering how the hell he was able to read my thoughts and soothe my worries so easily.

"Thank you, Adam," I said sincerely.

Chapter four

Adam

We finished our practice, ready for tomorrow's match. It was supposed to be easy. It was a home game against a team that hadn't figured out what teamwork truly meant.

We'd gone up against them twice already this year and won both times too. I was confident, we all were. This year was going incredibly well, and we hoped to make nationals again. So far, I was hitting all the goals I wanted and everything I'd planned out.

All but getting into a football club. I had everything riding on going pro. There isn't another job that would make me even a sliver as happy as going pro. Trust me, my parents took me to many conventions, and many on-hand experiences to see what other jobs would be like, but nothing brought the excitement football did.

The school year was coming to a close, and I still hadn't been approached by any football clubs, and it's starting to worry me. I've seen the work DTU does, the incredible players they've delivered to the pros, and I wanted to be one so badly. With the time ticking, however, I kept worrying it might not happen.

In my first year, Portland Spartans FC reached out. They wanted me, they were fairly new, and I was over the moon. However, my parents had their ultimatum. I was supposed to finish college first, but I was heartbroken. I had to wait four years because Portland Spartans FC didn't have a schedule that would allow me to move so freely.

In the end, it ended up being for the best, though. Two years ago, they were caught in a major scandal regarding doping and secret parties they organised, with both the management and some players, and now those who are innocent are tainted too. I do consider myself lucky, but I also never stopped wishing for more.

"Adammmm, you still haven't answered us," Brian's voice snapped me back to reality. I glanced over at him, then at the other guys on the team.

Right. A late lunch, they asked me to join. Carter, Ibrahim, and Dante were all worn out, usually my go-to lunch pals. The rest of the team was great, too, we had great chemistry on the field, but it ended there with them.

After lunch, I headed straight home and found the garage empty. I'm not too sure where Brooke went, but I showered and then went to nap right away. I should've planned out my dinner, but I was in dire need of a nap.

I was snuggled in bed under my blanket and in the dark with the fan blasting on me directly. My nap was going great till I heard a soft knock, but I ignored it, sinking deeper into my slumber. Then the blinding lights came suddenly, and I groaned.

I looked over to see Brooke standing by the door. How long was I out? Not nearly enough.

"Brooke," I whined and rolled over, burying my face into the pillow despite the restrained breathing it offered.

"It's dinner time. The last time you slept without dinner, you had a headache the next morning," Brooklyn reasoned as she walked closer to me. I could smell her peony-scented perfume as she leaned down to tug at my blanket.

I was bound by her spell, but when the cover was a quarter of the way down, I grabbed it tightly and rolled over. "I want to sleep."

"I know, but we can have a great dinner together," Brooklyn said sweetly. I did like the sound of that, and I didn't want to wake up with a headache tomorrow. The only meds that help me with that make me drowsy.

"Where were you?" I sighed, slowly waking up. I glanced over at Brooklyn and noticed how she surveyed the room. This might just be the longest she's ever been in my room.

"Coffee and study date with the girls, then I went to the animal shelter," she replied briefly. Right, the shelter. I bet all the animals love her there. She's far more gentle with them than she is with humans, and I think that's adorable.

"Oh." I stretched out and sat up.

"How was practice?" she asked, her eyes focused on the small collection of medals and trophies I had, particularly the youth soccer Olympics gold medal.

"It was good, coach went a little easy on us, I believe," I admitted, still watching her closely.

"What would you like for dinner? I'm ordering." Brooklyn turned to me, fishing out her phone from her pocket.

"Mexican?" I asked. I recently introduced her to my favourite local spot, and it was a hit for her.

"Your usual?"

"Yes, please." I grinned. They were located a bit far, but their food was worth the wait. "Now give me ten minutes to mourn the loss of the perfect nap, and I'll join you downstairs." I snuggled back into the warm spot on my bed.

"So dramatic." Brooklyn rolled her eyes as she walked away with the phone to her ear.

I did indeed take ten minutes. Tossing and turning, hugging my pillow until I had to go downstairs. I stared at the kitchen, damn it, we had to clean up. Without having to say anything, Brooke started washing the dishes, and I picked up the rag to dry and put them away.

"Did they say how long it would take?" I asked, feeling my hunger rising. I could eat cereal, but that would spoil my appetite. I carefully stacked the plates together and then put them away.

"Yeah, they're busy, so it might take an hour." Brooklyn sighed. The first time we ordered there, we waited a long time, and she complained until she had her first bite. I believe she mentioned something about love at first bite, but she always says that when something is good.

"An hour? That's fine, it's normal for them," I convinced myself, maybe some crackers would help with the wait.

"Can you last an hour, or will you go feral on the crackers?" Brooklyn teased, reading my mind.

"Crackers with cheese are good, okay?" I rolled my eyes, knowing how she felt about that combination. "I will not be judged by someone who drinks orange juice with pulp after brushing their teeth," I said when she made her judging face.

"You say that as if it's something bad," Brooklyn scoffed, turning the tap off and drying her hands.

"The fact that you say that shows me just how lost you are." I shook my head in disappointment, seeing the look on her face change. I was getting on her nerves—good, that would keep me a bit occupied.

"I—" She was about to speak when my phone rang, and I immediately picked up when I saw it was my grandmother calling.

"Vovó, Como você está?" I asked, my mood lit up entirely already.

"Oi, meu querido! Estou bem, obrigada. What are you up to, Querido?" Of course, I was her dearest one out of all the grandkids, and I'd do whatever it took to hold down that position.

"Cleaning the kitchen with Brooke," I replied with a grin. Avó was well aware of our living situation, and she was proud that I was so kind. I moved next to Brooke to show her the screen. "Brooke, say hey."

"Boa noite, Senhora," Brooklyn said politely, and her pronunciation was executed well.

"You took Portuguese too?" I asked, amazed. She never told me that, despite knowing I'm fluent in a few languages.

"I dabbled in it, but French was easier since we already had all the textbooks and such lying around the house," Brooke explained briefly. I guess that made sense. Her father was French after all.

"Is my grandson a good host? Are you fed?" Avó began to ask, ignoring me in the room.

"He's a great host, we just ordered food," Brooke said with a smile.

"You didn't cook for her?" Avó glared at me through the screen and shook her head.

"She's in my house, Vovó?" I frowned.

"And? I raised you better," Avó declared.

"How are you on her side?" I whined, shaking my head as I stared at the betrayer.

"Shh, tell me about practice," she changed the topic. She was one of the few people who took a great interest in the things I'm passionate about. I'm not even sure if she was ever that interested in football, but she did ask me to tell her.

So, I did. Brooklyn went up to her room after wishing my grandmother goodnight. I noticed the movie list on the mini whiteboard pinned to the fridge. I pressed my lips together as I listened to Avó tell me all about her trip to the markets. The movies were all classics, neither Brooklyn nor I had seen before, and we planned on watching them together.

She said the backyard would make the perfect place to watch a movie together, and I believed her because there was gear for a little projector screen. While I was still on the phone, I began to grab everything from the garage and put it together. Half of the fairy lights didn't work, but the half that did work made for great decoration. I'd have to get new ones before Christmas.

I adjusted the outdoor couches and threw in some extra pillows I had, and it looked decent. This always worked when the guys came over for gaming, so I didn't have to worry about that. Thinking about it, I couldn't believe we never had a movie night here before. I'm sure the girls would've loved it.

My call came to an end, and I went to the pantry to grab the many snacks we purchased. I'm pretty sure Brooklyn never had Guarana Antarctica before, so I took two cans and water for us both. Lately, I've noticed she always had three drinks, the third was usually a hot drink, though.

Weird, but hey, don't judge someone just because they sin differently than you. Or something like that.

I put the drinks and our chocolate bars in the cooler. I grabbed the bag of popcorn and chips and laid everything outside perfectly. The only thing missing was our blankets. I heard my phone chime and looked down to see Brooke was texting me.

Brooke

Where are you? The food is here.

I'm outside. I have a surprise.
Bring the food and blankets.

How many blankets?

Like four?

I'm not sure what
you've got planned, and
I'm not sure whether to
be scared or not.

The back door slid open, and I looked ahead to see Brooklyn with her arms full. She stopped in her tracks when she saw the setup, and her jaw dropped. I walked up to help with the blanket, and her eyes softened as she looked at everything.

"Adam, what's all this?" Brooklyn's voice carried excitement as she sauntered past me, heading straight for the setup.

"Welcome to the cinema, take a seat and get ready to be wowed." I flashed her a grin as I settled the blanket on a stack of cushions.

"You did all of this? You're amazing." Brooklyn's eyes sparkled with admiration as she absentmindedly placed the food on the table. I made a mental note to invest in more lights and perhaps spruce up the decorations a bit.

Taking my place in the corner, I leaned back.

"I know, but keep your cool, I've got more surprises." I reached to my side and placed the cooler in the middle. Flipping it open. "I've got water, your weird coffee, and of course, a soda, which I'm guessing you've never tried?"

Brooklyn snatched up each drink I offered, clutching them to her chest like treasures. "You always have it, but I haven't tasted it yet," she confessed, eyeing the guarana soda. I knew she'd love it. If she dared to speak ill of it, I might just kick her out.

"Today's the day for that," I declared, gesturing to the table.

"I'm going to devour all of this," Brooklyn said with a proud grin, rubbing her hands together.

"I know you will, Brooklyn baby," I teased with the nickname.

"Thank you, Adam honey," she teased back. I should've never told her that story, but it was better than being called Winnie-the-Pooh.

We got cosy in our own little corner, the couch was still plush and fairly unused, making it quite perfect for us. It was cold outside, but we were tucked in with our blankets and had our food.

"Look at us, two best buds chowing down on taquitos, sipping soda, and watching *Back to the Future*," Brooklyn said contentedly, taking a bite of her last taquito.

"This is the best. We should've done this sooner," I realised, feeling the warmth of our friendship wash over me. It beat mindlessly scrolling through my feed until I passed out.

"We can make it a regular thing. I'll whip up some snacks next time," Brooklyn suggested, and I eagerly accepted her offer.

"Deal." I grinned. "Hey, what did you think of the drink?"

"You shouldn't have let me try this." Brooklyn's serious tone made me frown. Wasn't it to her liking? "I'm going to raid your fridge for that drink from now on." She smirked, her empty can evidence of her newfound addiction.

"Oh no, I didn't think this through." I gasped, realising my mistake.

"Nope, you didn't." She smirked, returning her attention to the movie.

As we snuggled deeper into the blankets, we were three-quarters through the movie, having devoured all the popcorn. I still had my mini Reese's cups, so I savoured them. Suddenly, my phone rang repeatedly.

I sighed and grabbed it.

I read Kayley's message 'Are you seriously breaking up with me?' My brows pulled together in confusion. I thought that was what she wanted, a one time thing.
I typed my response. 'Kay, we both said we were just looking for a distraction.'

Kayley is typing...
'I know, but I thought it felt different, it feels like you led me on.'
Oh great, I need to stop getting myself in messes like these.

"You good over there?" Brooklyn asked, she must've noticed I wasn't paying attention. I hated when people tapped away on their phones during a movie, but this was an emergency.

"Yeah, almost," I replied, offering her some mini peanut butter cups. "Want some?"

"Deadly allergic to nuts," Brooklyn reminded me. Shit, I knew that. I just momentarily forgot.

"Right, sorry, I forgot," I apologised, glancing her way.

"What's wrong? Lady trouble?" Brooklyn teased, focused on the screen as she enjoyed her Kit Kat.

"Yeah, trying to avoid my name being dragged through the mud." I chuckled bitterly, shaking my head. I should've seen this coming.

"What happened? Did you tell her you use some weird toothpaste?" Brooklyn jabbed playfully, and I wished that was the reason.

"Again, I will not be judged by a pulp juice-loving girl," I scoffed with a smirk.

"Hey!" Brooklyn shoved me lightly.

"I've got to defend my honour. Fight me later." I pushed back gently, grabbing my buzzing phone. Kayley's messages were flooding in.

"What's going on?" Brooklyn's tone shifted, her concern evident.

"I'm being accused of stringing a woman along even after she, too, said it would be just once," I explained briefly.

I always kept it simple and made sure we both knew what we were getting into up front. Kayley, however, seemed to have had a change of heart and didn't appreciate my boundaries.

"I went through that yesterday," Brooklyn scoffed, shaking her head in understanding.

"You've been strung along?" I arched a brow at Brooke. Suddenly, our conversation became far more important and intriguing to me.

Brooke was someone you didn't mess with. She had a way of putting people in their place, making her the perfect ally in any battle you may have.

"No, I was accused of it," she retorted, her tone almost offended. She's right, I should've known better.

"Tell me more."

Brooklyn was now the only person I had to talk to about such things. All our friends spoke of buying cute gifts for their significant other or doing fun things with them. It was great to see them happy, but I realised some conversations could no longer be held with them.

I wasn't sure how Brooke would react, but her face lit up as if she'd been waiting for me to ask. Setting the popcorn aside, she took a deep breath.

"Before we got together, we agreed to keep it casual. I simply can't offer more than that," Brooklyn began her story. "We can talk, but it's mostly physical. He agreed, until over a week ago when he started acting distant. So, I finally asked, and it turns out he doesn't appreciate me spending so much time at the animal shelter. He wishes I'd spend that time on us instead." I listened attentively, and I've never related to anything more.

"Oh dear," I murmured. Nobody has to dictate Brooklyn's choices, especially when it comes to the animal shelter.

"So, I told him we're through, and he felt like I used him. I reminded him of our agreement in the beginning, but he assumed I was just playing hard to get or something," Brooklyn explained, making it sound easier than it probably was.

"And he's gone now?" I frowned.

"Yep, plus I blocked him, just in case." She shrugged.

"Good for you."

"I know, I'm a genius. Just remind her of your boundaries and part ways kindly," Brooke advised.

"I'm trying," I replied, letting out a sigh when Kayley stopped typing. "It's all fun and games until you meet someone who thinks boundaries don't apply to them." I chuckled, shaking my head. Luckily Kayley was being understanding after a few messages.

"See, we're on the same page." Brooke tapped my shoulder, her humour contagious. "We would've been perfect together."

"Would we?" I glanced at her.

"I like to think so if things were different," Brooke said, confidence easing in her tone. It was a thought that hadn't crossed my mind before, and now I was contemplating it a bit too much.

"Yeah, maybe," I muttered, looking back at my phone. Kayley expressed disappointment but understood.

I gazed at her. That would be crazy, right? Brooklyn's a great friend; we'd never cross that line. But I couldn't stop staring at her, wondering what that would be like. Then I remembered that despite us both understanding what casual means, I don't want to risk our friendship.

I stared at her for a moment. She tipped her head back, letting popcorn and M&M's fall down into her mouth. She looked so carefree right now, her curls were a mess and spilling down, but she was careful not to lie against them. She turned to me and raised a brow at me, and I just shook my head and turned to stare at the screen, but all I could think of were those hazel eyes full of mischief.

Brooklyn Armstrong alone could say something that would have me feeling lost, as if I were stuck in a maze.

Chapter five

Brooklyn

It's been three weeks now. Three weeks and still no update from the apartment, but we've officially moved all our things out. I had everything back at Adam's place, and he didn't seem to mind one bit. He even helped me arrange my mugs and rated them all. He liked all of them but the fish-shaped one for reasons I could not figure out.

I'm still surprised by how easy and enjoyable it is to live with him. He's a fairly simple man. I make him his fruity smoothie in the morning and occasionally whip up a chocolatey dessert, and he's happy. It's perfect since I love and need the dessert too.

Today, classes ended early for us all, and we gathered at our usual spot by the tree. Our bench had endured a lot but still stood with us. It's hard to believe it's been four years already since we first sat here. We all carved our names somewhere on the table. It could be considered vandalising, but there were marks far before we came, and no one seemed to care about it. The same can't be said about the furniture inside the building, though.

Truthfully, I didn't like the spot during this time of year. The dirt was a bit too moist, and the air was too cool. We all had our own conversation going on, but Dante and Ibrahim were busy figuring out what happened to a high school buddy. I'm not sure, but it involved social media stalking while Darshini and Stella were working on some chemistry issue. Carter and Zaira were just invested in Dante and Ibrahim's findings.

"Brooks, did you see the document I shared with you?" Adam asked, running his fingers through his hair. He looked at me with an excited grin and a twinkle of happiness in his azure eyes.

"Adam... soft drinks, chocolate, cheese, and bread don't make a complete shopping list. There's barely any proper grocery stores there." I laughed.

I was in the middle of an advanced international law class when I received the notification and saw his supposed grocery shopping list.

We attempted grocery shopping without a list yesterday, and we left with soda, crackers, grapes, protein powder, and chocolate. Nothing more and nothing less. It was a disaster, but crackers with cheese made for a great dinner.

"That's why you're a collaborator on the document," Adam sassed with a smirk.

"Let's fix our list right now," I decided, and opened the file on my phone. We had to prevent yesterday's incident from happening again. "We're out of cereal, so we need that for sure. Definitely need more milk and pasta. Oh, and fruits, or you won't have breakfast tomorrow."

"Oh, and eggs, cacao powder, and sweet condensed milk," Adam said, typing it in. "Oh, and cucumbers and tomatoes, we'll try that gyro recipe we found online," he continued

"You guys are gonna cook?" Darshini's voice cut through, and we looked up to see everyone staring at us. "Like together?" she asked for clarification.

"Yep, we'll go grocery shopping together, grab everything we need, and we'll make dinner later," Adam said with a huge grin on his face. "We are adults after all."

"We made sloppy cheeseburgers last night, it was heavenly," I raved, my mouth salivating at the memory of last night's food. "It was seriously the best I've ever had."

"Wait, that was homemade?" Carter asked, shocked.

"By yours truly." Adam grinned and pointed to both of us.

"Oh my god, you guys have been domesticated," Dante said teasingly.

I could tell the others caught on, and there was about to be some heavy teasing. I braced myself for it and looked ahead.

"Literally the cutest," Zaira began, and that's when I knew it was over. "Grocery shopping? Cooking together? Staying in? My, my, my, how the mighty has fallen," she said with a dramatic flair, counting the actions on her fingers. I looked at Adam, and he looked at me. We both shook our heads in disagreement with what Zaira said.

"That's not true," Adam spoke up, clearing his throat.

"Not at all," I added for extra measure.

"Tell me, do you bake for him too? That overly sweet chocolate cake with just enough bitterness?" Ibrahim asked.

It was the best way to release some stress, I couldn't just stop that.

"Hey, that cake is heaven on earth, and you should consider yourself lucky she makes it," Adam spoke up, making it hard to deny I ever even made him cake. No one loved my baking that much before.

"You guys are literally so cute," Darshini gushed, grinning widely. "Cosy and domestic, what's next?" There was a teasing edge to her tone.

"Me flipping you all off." I lifted both my hands, and they all just laughed.

"Mhm, now let's go." Adam got up when it was time for us to leave. "I bet they're jealous they don't have our great food," he said loud enough for them to hear, but they seemed unbothered by it.

"I think so too," I agreed with him, knowing Stella, Darshini, and Dante were great cooks. Perhaps Zaira and Ibrahim were jealous. "Now, where to?" I looped my hand through his and followed him to the car.

I was careful where I walked, campus wasn't exactly at its peak. It's right in between winter and spring, the awkward middle where everything was a bit muddy and the plants still looked a bit weird. I couldn't wait for the season to change, there was nothing better than a blossoming spring.

"Dida's, then shopping, right?" Adam guessed, stepping on the pavement now.

"You speak my language fluently." Darshini should watch out. I might make this man my first-place girlfriend. He's busy checking all the boxes.

"Let's go." Adam smiled and opened the door so we could stash our bags in the back. I'm not sure when, but Adam had been keeping his car spotless lately. He even cleared the extra cup-area so I'd be able to carry all my drinks.

At Dida's, we got seated at a cosy table.

Like always, there was some soft music playing in the background, and the air smelled sugary and tasty. The glow inside the shop was warm and cosy, and being there felt like being wrapped up in a soft fleece blanket on a rainy day.

I looked ahead at Adam. I watched as he focused on smearing jam on his pain au chocolat. His blond hair was styled to the left in meticulous waves, no doubt taking a lot of time this morning. It wasn't gel, though, I could tell it was something else, his hair looked incredibly soft. So inviting.

Then I stared at his eyes. God, his eyes resembled the ocean, not on a serene sunny day that matched his sunny character, but more like the tumultuous sea during a storm—captivating and dangerous to be caught in.

As our gazes met, he arched a brow at me, and I quickly diverted my attention to his lips grazing over the pastry instead. Dammit, not that either. I looked down at my pastry. I took a bite of my pain au chocolat, and the silence between us was dangerous to my mind.

Finally, gathering my courage, I raised the topic that had been weighing on my mind. "Hey, I have to ask," I began, clearing my throat and meeting Adam's focused gaze. "Since there's been no official word about the apartment, do you mind if I stay a bit longer?" I needed reassurance, despite his apparent happiness. I had to be 100 percent sure.

"Brooke, I love having you with me, I don't mind one bit." Adam smiled warmly. What a ray of sunshine this man was. I wonder if he brought everyone that same warm feeling with that charming smile of his, like he did me.

"Are you sure? I don't want to disrupt your life," I pressed further, pondering what his life was like before my arrival.

Now it was movie nights, late-night baking, and grocery runs.

"Not at all. You bring excitement to my life, Brooklyn." Adam winked, devouring his dessert with passion, a smear of jam adorning his lips before he swiftly cleaned up.

"Okay, just making sure. I wouldn't want to overstay my welcome," I replied with a smile.

"Are you kidding me? I love having someone to split chores with," Adam retorted with a teasing edge, though I sensed a hint of honesty beneath his joke.

"And here I thought you just enjoyed my company." I sighed for the dramatics of it, head tipping back.

"And smoothie and chocolate cake," Adam added ruthlessly, not caring about my feelings, apparently. Before I had the chance to be dramatic about it, Adam said, "Speaking off, I'll be making you a dessert tonight."

That sparked my interest. He was my foodie soulmate, and whatever he had in store would no doubt be perfect.

"So spill. How's the animal shelter going?" he replied.

"Want the full rundown or just the highlights?" I asked, appreciating his genuine interest. Some people only wanted the shortened version, but I still cherished those who asked.

"I want to hear it all." Adam smiled, sending a thrill through me. I always loved discussing the shelter and its furry inhabitants.

"Well, we had this stray mama cat, very pregnant when we first got her, but now she has given birth to her kittens. She's a tuxedo cat," I began, a smile spreading across my face at the memory.

"What's that?" He frowned, and I couldn't help but smirk. I knew the millions of photos I took would come in handy. Wiping my fingers, I grabbed my phone.

"Here, this is her, we call her Moo-moo." I showed him the best photos of her. Of course, all her photos were her best photos. "She gave birth to three little kittens, all super precious." I slid to the next photo where you could see the kittens snug with their mom.

"Is she friendly?" Adam asked, and I nearly burst out laughing.

"She's a mother... She scratched the shit out of Rachel, but she's warming up to us." I showed him yet another photo before taking my phone back. "We found her a possible forever home," I said, excitement brimming my voice.

"With her babies?" he asked, seeming worried. How cute.

"Yes! Someone already has another cat, a ginger female she rescued two years ago, and she's interested in Moo-moo and her kittens," I replied, glancing around the café. I had to break free from Adam's intense gaze. "We'll have to ensure they all get along, especially since the kittens are still young, but the other cat seems sweet," I reassured him.

"That's wonderful. Little Moo-moo and the gang will have a loving home," he hummed.

"She's super cute and the kittens too, but one is a bit uh... not so bright," I admitted, "He sucks his mother's face."

"I'm sure he's trying his best." Adam chuckled, shaking his head. Rachel found that amusing, too, which might explain why Moo-moo scratched her.

"We also have an old pitbull. He seems to have been mistreated, with some missing teeth, but he's as gentle as can be." I showed Adam a photo of the pitbull cuddled up with a blanket and plush toy.

For the next thirty minutes, we delved into tales of the animals I'd cared for. Adam's interest never left, his eagerness evident as he leaned forward, asking questions and looking at all the photos I wanted to show.

I could've spoken about it for hours, but we had to grab the groceries.

"Oh, by the way, some new lights and lanterns arrived. We're going to deck out the backyard and have the best outdoor movie nights," Adam informed me, passing me the lighter bags as we unloaded the car.

I could grumble and complain, but I wasn't foolish. I preferred this over the heavy bags and focused more on his new purchases.

"That will be perfect!" I looked at the delivery box, but it was wrapped up, so I couldn't tell what he had gotten. Regardless, I knew this was going to be perfect. The backyard was already cosy when he'd set it up, but with these new lights, it would be perfect.

Anticipation bubbled within me for our next movie night, but then a realisation struck. "Oh my god, we're choosing movie nights over going out... Our friends were right."

"We've been domesticated," Adam acknowledged, a wry smile playing on his lips. Our friends were right, but we'd never let them know that.

"I don't want to think of this anymore. Let's go." I sighed dramatically and took the bags inside. Adam followed right behind me.

"We'll plan a night out, we'll show them," he decided, and I nodded along.

After we had stowed away the groceries, I retreated to my room. Adam had practice, and I had spreadsheets to update for the animal shelter, along with social media content to post showcasing the adorable animals.

These posts helped us with getting donations and attracting potential adopters. Before my involvement, the shelter's social media presence was dry, barely getting any engagement, but with me in charge, it had changed, reaching thousands of views on a good day.

Once I finished up a bit of work, I put my phone aside and closed my eyes to get some shut-eye. I had a ton of homework to take care of, and I needed the rest badly if I planned on watching a movie with Adam later.

Adam was the last thing I thought of as I closed my eyes, and I couldn't help but smile as I drifted off to sleep.

When I woke up from my nap, I saw a message from Adam letting me know he'd be home soon. I sent a quick '*ok*' and then went downstairs to put everything out we'd need for our gyros.

I went ahead and set up the backyard like he usually does. I even opened up the packages and put out the new lanterns and fairy lights. While I waited for him, I returned to my room.

Joining the girls' group call, which was meant to be a study session but often devolved into gossip and laughter, I opened my laptop, eyeing my assignment with reluctance. Despite knowing what needed to be done, the allure of doing anything else was tempting.

"Well, I'm never setting foot in my own apartment again," Stella declared dramatically, and I could tell from her surroundings that she was at Carter's place.

"What happened?" I dared to ask and could see that Zaira was avoiding looking at the camera. She was busy writing away.

"Zaira and Ibrahim happened." Stella clapped her hands, and I laughed.

"Oh god, where?" Darshini dared to ask, she was already contorting in disgust. She shouldn't be talking too much, though. One time, I came home earlier than planned. I was barely through the door when I heard moaning from the two and decided to leave again. I could've been a menace and burst in, reminding them of their own no-sex-in-the-apartment rule, but I was rather benevolent.

"The couch for heaven's sake, my corner of it too!" Stelle scoffed, and Zaira finally looked up.

"We were making out!" Zaira defended herself.

"Try dry humping," Stella retorted, turning away from the camera.

"See why we enforced the no-sex rule in the apartment?" Darshini hummed, and I stared at her for a second. She had no idea what information I possessed, but she was my great friend, so I remained quiet.

"And poor Brooke got caught in the middle." Zaira whistled, shaking her head in disappointment.

"No, she wasn't, she was just doing it in solidarity," Darshini interjected before I could speak up.

"Yeah, because you decided to make it weird," I said dramatically. Truthfully, I never brought guys to our apartment. Felt too personal.

"What did I do?" Darshini scoffed.

"Date our roommate, aka your brother's buddy," I reminded her, highlighting the pieces I'd use from the current article.

"Oh, hush, did you come across any hot neighbours with Adam?" Zaira came to her defence. I suppose they might be sisters one day, so they might as well be on the same side.

"Haha, very funny... He lives in a gated community. Everyone there is either married or ancient," I scoffed, recalling my morning walks filled with cute elderly couples or committed individuals. “There was this creepy old married man who would stare rather sultrily, which gave me the creeps. I’m many things, but a homewrecker is not one of them.”

“You need to get out more,” Stella insisted, a far cry from her former self. Once a proud introvert, she now loved dressing up and hitting the town. Zaira and I must have done a stellar job pulling our friends out of their shells.

“We should plan something,” Darshini suggested, her finger tapping her chin in thought. Another converted introvert.

“This weekend, the guys are away for a match,” Zaira remembered, and I could already envision our weekend plans unfolding perfectly—just the four of us. No needy boyfriends.

“We’re definitely planning something,” I decided.

We chatted till I heard Adam’s car pull into the driveway. I bid my friends farewell and headed to the front door. Adam entered, looking as refreshed as ever. I’m not sure how he does it. No energy drink, no coffee, nothing, and still he looked his best.

“Don’t tell me you made the gyros without me,” he said, looking up from his bag with his cup in hand. This was the first ever cup he hadn’t lost, and I’m pretty sure he was gifted it during a secret Santa.

“I didn’t. I was just—” I muttered, avoiding his gaze, trying to distract myself from the sight of him in a compressed sleeveless shirt. Shit, what was I saying?

“My, my, is my presence having a certain effect on you?” Adam teased.

“Feeling special today, Adam?” I’m pretty sure I played that off well.

“Always, especially—” Adam began, then paused, clearing his throat. He glanced at me, a flicker of hesitation in his eyes. “Never mind, you’re a lady. I should be a gentleman.”

“Oh, absolutely,” I replied in the most sarcastic tone I could muster.

“I’ll go shower quickly and then I’ll join you downstairs, okay?” Adam chuckled.

“Mhm, I’ve already set up the backyard to save you the trouble,” I assured him, giving his shoulder a pat as I walked past.

"You're the best." He grinned.

"You know it."

A little later, we were both in the kitchen in our pyjamas, working together to craft our own gyros. We might have gone a bit overboard with the seasoning, but the aroma was divine.

Adam had been busy multitasking. I'm not sure what he was making, but it involved cacao powder and condensed milk, so naturally, I sat and waited for him. In the meantime, our steaming hot food cooled down a little, so our mouths wouldn't burn.

"What are you doing?" I asked. He was being super secretive, with his back turned to me, and I was too lazy to get up right now.

"I'm whipping up a small batch of brigadeiros for us," he announced, his back turned as he worked.

"Wait, you know how to make them?" I gasped, memories flooding back to the first friend dinner Adam had hosted. Pizza, wings, garlic bread, and those heavenly chocolate bites. Whenever he served them, I couldn't resist and always took leftovers. I'd hide it from the others in the apartment, and I had mastered that art quite well.

"Of course," he scoffed. "You like them?"

"Love them! They're the perfect snack, especially when it's that time of the month," I blurted out. To me, chocolate had a magical ability to alleviate at least 10 percent of my hatred and pain for those dreaded days.

"They're the perfect snack for any occasion," Adam agreed.

"True." I sighed, already yearning for those brigadeiros. As much as I knew I'd enjoy the gyros, the dessert now took the spotlight for me. "Did you make the grape-covered ones?"

"No, but I'll make them next time," Adam promised, placing the tray in the fridge. "Come on, they need to chill. Let's go watch that movie before our dinner gets too cold."

"Mhm, let's go," I agreed.

We settled into his backyard, the movie playing under the twinkling stars. Dinner was delicious, if a tad salty, but we savoured every bite.

Without wasting a moment, as soon as we finished, we retrieved the brigadeiros. Bundled up outside, we devoured them and enjoyed the movie with each other.

Chapter six

Adam

It was early March, spring hadn't officially begun yet, but the lush green grass and blossoming flowers in my area would beg to differ.

Friday morning was filled with training and exercise from the coach. I had a feeling we'd take nationals again. I just knew it. We had our last match for the round of sixteen tomorrow, everyone except Ibrahim was present on the field today. I bet he passed his test, his absence was noted, but we trained regardless, ready for the last match.

I was eager to keep training, to make sure I was more than ready for tomorrow's game. I glanced over at Carter. He seemed to consider my request for more time, but alas he shook his head and declined my request.

"Those guys need a break," Carter said, and I looked at the rest of the team. Almost everyone looked exhausted, their clothes drenched in sweat, fatigue evident in their eyes. I supposed they shouldn't be pushed too hard, especially with a game tomorrow.

One of our players had been scouted and offered a contract last month. He was hardly ever here now. I wondered if he'd even finish university. I couldn't help but feel a twinge of envy, but the guy had undeniable talent and deserved his shot.

"But I can stay with you for another thirty minutes, does that work?" Carter offered, and a smile spread across my lips. Thirty more minutes of training would help burn off all the pent-up energy I still had.

"That's all I need." I grinned, bending down to fix my laces.

"Great, let me text Stella quickly," he excused himself, running over to the sideline where his bag and water bottle were.

Rumours were floating around that there would be scouts at the upcoming games. I needed to be at my best for those. These moments were my final chances to get picked up by a club. The coach told me to be patient, and I was trying my hardest.

I grabbed my phone and texted Brooklyn. She was still putting up with me, never once complaining about living together. These past months have been incredible. Whether it was early morning car rides or late nights watching movies, she had a way of making every moment more lively.

Brooke

Hey, I'm staying an extra 30 mins

Fine, but don't stay any longer. I have a surprise for you

Movie?

Nope, something I haven't done in a while

Brookey, there are A LOT of things you haven't done in a while, be specific before my mind goes places

Adam honey, respectfully, get your head out of the gutters

I'm trying, but your statement isn't helping much

I hate you

I love your smoothie, the pineapple was a nice touch

Mhm, I know

I tucked my phone away and jogged back to Carter. We worked on some one-two passes. Carter was our striker, while I played our centre forward. I was great at it too, but this year I'd switched positions with Carter a few times. I scored some nice goals as a striker, but enjoyed centre forward better.

When I got home, I found Brooklyn stretched out on the couch. She was wearing a pair of pink leggings that hugged her curves, making her figure look even more alluring. The leggings came up to her waist, fitting her like a second skin, and she paired them with a matching tank top that left a small sliver of bronzed skin exposed.

Brooklyn had a book in her hand, her hair pulled up into a ponytail. I could tell she hadn't gone for her usual morning run, as it was already well past her usual schedule. Why was she dressed as if she were about to work out? She only wore that outfit when she needed to, those were her exact words.

"Any reason you're dressed like that instead of your usual black sweats and creepy smiley shirt?" I asked, tossing my duffle bag onto the table and catching sight of my dishevelled reflection in the mirror. I looked like a mess, but I ignored it and started unpacking my things.

"I don't always wear that," Brooklyn said defensively.

I laughed. What a lie. One of the things I strangely looked forward to after practice was coming home to find Brooklyn on the couch with either a book or her laptop. Her hair was always up, and she usually wore sweatpants paired with her favourite creepy smiley shirt.

I never realised how observant I was about her until now. I liked it, though. Discovering all these little things about Brooklyn made her even more interesting. There was more to her than just the carefree persona she projected. She genuinely cared. Deeply.

I wasn't sure who exactly she was hiding her true self from, or maybe I was just now noticing how incredible she truly was. But I was grateful to experience this side of her—the side I could live and laugh with without a single worry.

"Hmmm, maybe a little," I corrected her, hanging my bag. "Good thing you have that shirt in three colours, or I'd think you never wash your clothes," I admitted. Yesterday, she was wearing a lilac one. Two days ago, it was beige with green.

"Any reason you're being an annoying ass right now?" Brooklyn raised a brow at me.

Maybe I was a bit on edge. She didn't deserve snarky Adam.

"Hmmm, no," I hummed, giving her an apologetic look. I didn't feel like telling her about my worries about the future, not yet, at least.

"Go get ready, wear sporty clothes before I change my mind." She clapped her hands.

"Sure thing, boss." I rushed upstairs.

I showered only to sweat again, but I didn't want to ruin Brooklyn's plans. I got dressed as she told me to, pulling on a sleeveless dri-fit shirt and a backwards cap. I rushed downstairs and found her in the kitchen.

Brooklyn had two bags packed and handed me one, along with my water and Gatorade. Oh, this woman knew me so well.

"We're going hiking," Brooklyn announced, adjusting her ponytail and the straps of her bag before smiling at me.

"What?" I frowned. Hiking?

"I know you just came from soccer practice, but it's a short trail," Brooklyn promised. What was it about this woman that made it hard for me to say no? She could ask me to cosign a loan, and apparently, I'd sign it for her. It had to be some sort of magic, right?

"Where?" I simply asked, already knowing that even if the answer was the Himalayas, I'd still say yes. Witchcraft, I was sure of it. Her chocolate cake bewitched me.

"Right behind your backyard." She grinned and walked to the back door. "It'll be worth it."

I looked beyond the gate of my backyard. The area I lived in was surrounded by lush greenery and trees. There was a short hiking trail just beyond my backyard, slightly elevated with a decent view. I'd only been hiking once or twice before.

In our friend group, hiking was only considered in the fall, but in my opinion, the true beauty of nature showed itself in spring. The grass was lush and green, inviting, and though the sun was out, the mist on the plants created a cool, refreshing atmosphere after the winter chill. And the flowers—oh, the flowers were so colourful, so pretty. I wasn't a flower expert, but I knew damn well if one was pretty or not.

The path leading to the top was adorned with wildflowers among the trees. I was looking forward to this hike, though I wondered what Brooke had packed in our bags. I wasn't sure we needed that much for such a short hike, but I decided not to ask. It was a second surprise.

"Do you think it's a good idea? We can totally just go out for lunch, I'll have to change though." Brooke looked down at her outfit, god forbid my gaze followed hers.

"Shhh, it's a great idea. I can't wait—but go easy on me," I said, slipping my arm over her shoulder and pulling her with me as I headed to the back door. I glanced down at her.

Her lips tugged into a smile. "Of course, I can't let anything happen to you. Where would I stay?"

"Brooklyn Armstrong, destroyer of Adam's happiness," I said in the most serious, ancient-sounding voice I could muster. My eyes remained locked on her, and she still grinned.

"I love my title." Brooklyn sighed with a smile.

She reached over, unlocked the back door, slid it open, and walked past me, flipping her hair in my face. I took a deep breath—she was using the leave-in conditioner I recommended. I recognized that sweet scent from a mile away.

"You love it a bit too much." I cleared my throat and stepped out, helping with the gate.

"By tomorrow morning, when I hand you your smoothie, I'll be known as Brooklyn Armstrong, bringer of Adam's joy." Brooklyn shrugged and winked at me.

"That's... true," I relented.

Even if I tried to deny it, it would be of no use. Every morning, I went downstairs to find a fruit smoothie waiting for me. Every morning, it brought a smile to my face.

"I'm well aware." Brooke smirked.

We exited the property, making sure to lock the back gate before embarking on our journey. The long trail had brick stones, but they were deep in the earth, covered with dirt, grass, wildflowers, sticks, and stones.

We hiked our path up, following the dirt-cemented stones to the top. There was a mix of fresh scents in the air. It smelled clean and earthy with hints of the mist from recent rains. Our trail became more and more lined with wildflowers the further we went, and the sweet fragrance of the flowers wafting in the breeze. The sweet scent still was no match for the peony scent of Brooklyn.

I looked at the sky above us, which was clear blue with huge fluffy clouds drifting lazily. The sun shines brightly, casting many shadows through the trees. Man, it was an incredible idea to go hiking today.

I looked over at Brooklyn, and she had a smile on her face as she looked around the area. She only pulled out her phone once to take a photo of a pretty flower. We slowly reached the top. It wasn't that high, but you had a decent view of tall trees and ponds of water beneath us. It was stunning, and behind us rested an oak tree. It was large, broad, proud, and tall.

"What a majestic tree." Brooklyn's head tilted back as she tried to see the top, and I followed her gaze.

"I know," I muttered, listening to the birds chirping and the occasional distant critter.

"Unpack your bag. I brought everything we'd need for a picnic," Brooklyn announced, already shifting her bag to her front.

"You packed us lunch?" I asked, shocked.

I was instantly put in the greatest mood. The idea of sitting here under the oak tree, with the wind rustling the leaves , the blooming flowers dancing with the rain, and the birds singing in the distance—it was serene, and with her company, it would be a dream come true.

"Toasted BLT sandwiches with seasoned fries and chips." Brooklyn revealed two brown baggies with our names written in colourful markers. "Oh, and I made triple chocolate chip cookies." She pointed to the see-through Tupperware.

"Brooklyn Colette Armstrong." I cleared my throat and looked around before getting down on one knee. Adoration filled my eyes as I looked up at her. "Will you marry me?"

"No ring?" Brooklyn scoffed, looking down at me, a smile playing on her lips.

I looked around and spotted a thin, flexible wooden twine. I shaped it into a ring. "I have this for now. Perhaps when I make it big, I can get you whatever your heart desires," I said wholeheartedly, trying to be as charming as possible. It always worked on others when I was younger, and I like to think my charm has only improved since then.

"I want a golden ring with a teardrop-shaped ruby in the middle, with small diamonds encrusted around—lab diamonds by the way," Brooklyn spat out her answer so fast, I could only blink and envision it. I never knew she already had her dream ring picked out. "Can you handle that, honey?"

"Noted. Now, will you accept this?" I nodded, my gaze dropping to the current, cheap ring. "I'll get you the other one once I make it big."

"Fine, fine." She gave me her hand, and her soft hand rested in mine as I carefully slid the ring on. "I'll hold you to it, big shot." She held her hand up and admired it.

"I expect you to." I grinned, rising back to my feet, my knee hurting a bit from the pebble I had been kneeling on just moments ago.

I laid out the blanket Brooklyn had packed while she carefully pulled out the food from her bag. My mouth watered at the sight. All I had after practice was two granola bars.

"I made you an extra sandwich too. I figured you'd be hungry." She handed me my bag, and it looked heavier than hers indeed.

"Oh, trust me, I could eat a horse." I tore into the bag, taking a deep breath of the mouthwatering aroma.

"I always wondered why they say that." Brooklyn shook her head as she gracefully opened hers. "I mean, come on, a horse?"

I shrugged. How was I supposed to know?

We ate our lunch, and not a single crumb was left behind. Everything was demolished, and what Brooke couldn't eat, I finished for her. When it came to the sweet treat she made us, we devoured that as well. There was one final cookie left, and I could see Brooke eyeing it.

"You can have the cookie," I told her, pushing the Tupperware towards her.

"I can tell you want it too," Brooklyn replied, crumpling her napkin into a ball.

"No, I'm sure," I said, nodding reassuringly.

"Let's split it," Brooklyn suggested, picking up the cookie.

"Okay, that works."

Brooklyn broke the cookie in half and handed me one part. Within three bites, the cookie was finished, and I glanced over at Brooklyn to see that she had done the same. We just smiled and began to gather all the paper, tissues, and empty cans to take them back home.

Once the cloth was spotless, we lay back and stared up. The oak branches and leaves prevented us from seeing the sky, but there were small slivers of light peeking through, becoming dimmer and dimmer. I assumed it was probably a passing cloud.

"You truly outdid yourself this time, Brooks," I said, turning my head to look at her. She had both hands behind her head, staring up at the sky as well.

"Making sure you won't dare think of getting another roommate," she joked, teasing me with that look in her eyes.

"I just printed out posters, but I'll shred them when we get back home," I joked. I couldn't think of a single better person to be my housemate. Maybe my grandmother, but besides her, it was Brooklyn for me.

I was used to being solitary, but living with Brooklyn hadn't been a hassle once.

"Glad to know I saved myself there."

"Shit, I think it's gonna rain," I commented as I saw the sky darken.

"Oh, come on! I just did my hair routine this morning," Brooklyn groaned, sitting up. There was no use, though. We wouldn't be able to get home before the rain started pouring down.

"So, if I were to ask you to play in the rain with me—"

"I'd say yes because getting wet is inevitable." Brooklyn sighed, leaning over to remove her shoes and socks.

"I tend to have that effect." I smirked, following suit. These shoes were too good to get muddy.

"I'm gonna throw you off that cliff," Brooklyn scoffed, but I could tell she was left a little flustered. She was just incredible at masking it.

"I'll just drag you with me, baby." My smirk never once left my face.

The sky suddenly darkened, and raindrops began to fall, lightly at first, then steadily. Under the oak tree, there were open spots here and there, the rain seeping through. Neither of us took the first step into the rain.

Then Brooklyn grabbed my hand and dashed away from the shade and shelter of the tree. I inhaled deeply as the cold water dripped down my body. As the rain poured down, we just stood there for a few seconds. We both looked down at our feet, the rain coming down hard on us.

The cool rain cleansed away all my worries, all I cared about was the pure joy this moment brought me. Brooklyn laughed and started moving around. It poured down harder as we spun and twirled around. Our movement was fluid and playful as we danced around with spring showers.

"This is ridiculous!" Brooklyn shouted over the sound of the downpour, her voice full of exhilaration.

I grinned, feeling lighter than ever. "But it's wonderful, isn't it?"

Our clothes were drenched, sticking to our skin even more than before. Our hair was plastered to our faces. But right now, nothing seemed to matter. Just two friends caught in a spring shower and making the most of the situation.

"I couldn't think of a more perfect moment." Her lips curled into the purest, most precious smile ever. It was like nothing I'd ever seen before, and all I could think of was that crazy comment she made about us working out well.

Chapter seven

Brooklyn

I couldn't believe it was March already. That marks two months of staying with Adam. Initially, I was hesitant, but now? Now, I love every moment spent here. Baking and cooking were the highlights of it all—there were some failed recipes, but we learned from them.

We'd watched countless movies, tried numerous food joints, and, of course, hit up several clubs and bars together in the little time that passed. Our friends were great, but didn't share the love for nightlife, so it was nice Adam and I had each other.

There was no update on the apartment, but Adam enjoyed having me around. Even when I dragged him on a hike that ended with rain today.

I felt welcome here.

After playing in the rain, we returned home when the downpour had lessened. The rainy weather went perfectly with the chicken dumpling soup we ordered—Everything was going great until 8 PM hit, and I found myself curled up on the couch.

Of course, a day filled with fun, serenity, and great food had to be ruined by Mother Nature. Just my monthly reminder that my contraception was working perfectly fine, but in the cruellest, most painful way possible.

The first twenty-four hours were always the worst for me, and not even my favourite comfort shows could distract me from the pain. I shuddered at the thunder outside as it began to rain again, this time even harder than before. I lay on my left side, pulling my knees close to my chest. I wanted to turn up the volume, but that would mean sacrificing my comfortable position, and I wasn't willing to do that. The pain seemed less intense in this position.

Adam had been busy in the kitchen earlier, but I didn't bother asking what he was up to or turning to look. As long as the smoke alarm didn't go off, I felt safe in my cocoon of warmth.

I heard his footsteps coming my way. I looked over to see Adam making his way towards me with a plate full of brigadeiros. Is this what it feels like to be God's favourite?

"For you, milady," Adam said, moving my leg aside as he sat down, holding the plate of deliciousness. "The white ones are grapes covered with white chocolate, and those are the regular ones."

There were three of each, the perfect serving size for what I was going through right now.

"How did you know I needed this?" I sighed lovingly as I sat up. I picked the grape-covered ones and watched him as I took a bite. I hummed at the taste and gave him an approving nod.

"Well, uh, you mentioned they'd make the perfect snack for, uh, that time of the month," Adam said with an awkward expression , avoiding eye contact and focusing on the brigadeiros he made.

"How did you know?" I frowned and pulled my legs closer to my chest.

"I've been paying attention," he said with a smug expression.

I raised a brow at him for a moment.

"It's only been two months of you being here, but you get into a fetal position, you watch *Supernatural* on repeat, and devour every snack on the premises." Adam read me like a book. I could only stare at him with my lips slightly parted. "Oh, and you get super catty, which I assume I'll experience tomorrow morning," he added, ruining the moment. I rolled my eyes and stuffed another grape-covered brigadeiro into my mouth.

"I don't get catty," I denied, simply refusing to believe it could be true. I glanced over at the TV screen, frozen on Dean and Sam right now. Am I predictable?

"You do... just a smidge. But it's okay. Also, you left your period cramp meds on the counter," Adam replied, a teasing smile on his face.

"Give me that," I scoffed, grabbing the plate to hold it myself.

"Should I go now? Have I successfully fed the lion?" Adam teased, adjusting the end of my blanket since he had just sat on it.

"Call me that again and I'll bite you." I narrowed my eyes at him. Our eyes met, and I bit the brigadeiro harshly to prove my point.

"Baby, I love that shit." Adam's voice took on a slightly sultry tone as he rose to his feet.

"Adam," I warned.

"Brooklyn," he dragged out my name slightly, his voice sweet. Damn, that made me smile a little.

I cleared my throat and resumed my glare. "Go to sleep, you have a match tomorrow."

"I do indeed. Will you be there?" He sighed, running his fingers through his hair. It was adorable to see how nervous he got before every game.

"Duh, who knows, maybe there's a cute opponent." I winked and pressed play on the remote.

"How can I get you to sport my jersey?" Adam's silly question came out of nowhere, his arms crossed as he looked at me.

"Now, why would I do that?" I paused the show again. He might have made me the perfect snack, but he had interrupted my show twice already. "You have plenty already doing that," I reminded him. After all, he had a bit of a social media presence and a handsome face—also one of the few single DTU athletes. He had many fans.

"Yeah, but maybe if the scouts see more people in my jersey, it will make them even more interested in me." Adam and I both knew he just came up with that lie.

"Honey." I patted his cheek. "I'm pretty sure they're looking for talent, not how many girls you can attract."

"Don't you want to match with your girlfriends?" he teased.

"Nope, they're mushy, cheesy losers who wear their boyfriend's jersey," I joked. They knew I loved them a lot.

"Brooklyn, it's like you don't want me to reach my dreams." Adam sighed, tipping his head back for the theatrics.

"I do, I do. You did, after all, make promises." I held up my ring finger with a teasing smile.

"I'm going to bed, and I'll plot ways to get you in that jersey." He winked.

"In your dreams, Adam."

"You're already wearing it in my dreams. Everyone is, and they all love it." Adam's self-obsession rose up a little. You don't see it too often, but when it's there, he makes sure you know about it.

"Good thing it's just that, a dream." I smirked, watching as his smirk fell from his face.

Saturday morning, the girls and I were on the bleachers with our overpriced slushies and popcorn. Seriously, how much more money does DTU need? Isn't our significantly high tuition enough?

I've always loved school matches. In high school, I used to attend the school's football games religiously with my friends. It wasn't because I liked the sport in particular, but because my friends would be there, and we always made the best of it.

Like now, I'm here with all the girls. I'll admit, though, over the past four years, I have grown to love this sport and perhaps occasionally let out a few curse words here and there when I find something went wrong. Like right now, when the referee ignored the fact our opponent shoved Brian to the ground.

"Come on, Ref! Are you blind?" I snarled and threw my hands up. "Choke on your whistle!"

"Okay, Brooke, sit down." Stella stifled her laughter as she patted my back, gently trying to pull me back.

"No, I think she's onto something," Zaira scoffed, one leg over the other, shaking like crazy. She was just as furious as I was.

"No more bullying, sit down." Darshini tugged at the other side of me.

"Fine, but I'm only sitting down because my stomach hurts." I gave in, settling between Darshini and Stella.

I took the last sip of my slushy and continued to glare at the referee. He might not be aware, but it felt good enough for me to do just the glaring.

"Aunt Flo?" Zaira raised a brow at me.

"Yeah..."

"Same," Zaira and Stella said in unison.

"I just ended mine," Darshini said with grace, flipping her hair over her shoulder. I'm pretty sure we were scowling at her because she just awkwardly turned away to look at the field.

We continued watching the game, and for the first time ever, I found myself actively following Adam. Wow, this had to be one of his best performances ever. He scored two of the three goals near the end. The match ended with us winning three to one. It was an exciting match, and I could tell both the team and coach were quite happy with the results.

They were heading to the quarterfinals! One thing about these boys was that they were leaving their mark on the history of DTU sports.

They got cleaned up, and we all met up in the parking lot again, no doubt planning our lunch since that was our usual tradition.

Stella offered to make spaghetti, and everyone pretty much jumped on board. We all had our signature dishes that we made better than everyone else. Well, everyone but Adam and me. Adam always provided pizza and/or wings, while my thing was bringing an array of cookies since I could make them without a single problem.

We arrived at the apartment, and Stelle got to work on dinner with Darshini's help. Zaira and I lazily walked around and set the table. Dante and Adam made a quick dessert.

I filled the last cup, and Stella called everyone to the table. I took my seat and inhaled deeply, almost unravelling in the tasty aroma wafting through the air right now.

"Damn, Stella, you're spoiling us." Ibrahim rubbed his hands together, his gaze focused on the bowl as one was passed to him and the other came my way.

"Perhaps I should start charging per plate?" Stella joked, passing the tray of garlic bread to Dante.

"It's fine, name your price," Adam said, amused, then continued, "Your mega-rich boyfriend will pay for us all."

We all agreed with Adam, and Carter just rolled his eyes, but there was a smile subtly playing on his lips.

"You know," Zaira spoke up as she picked her bread pieces strategically. Her words got everyone to stare at her, waiting for her to continue her sentence.

"If Adam doesn't get scouted, Carter can just buy a football club, have them invest in Adam, and boom. Problem solved," she said as if all those things were done so simply.

I thought about it for a moment. I could vaguely remember Carter once saying the net worth of his family online was majorly inaccurate—it was a lot less than it originally was. Perhaps a football club wouldn't even put a dent.

"That's not too terrible," Dante agreed with Zaira and nodded along.

"Excuse me, I want to be accepted for my talent, not because of nepotism," Adam spoke up before Carter could interject.

Carter looked at Adam as he brought a towel to his face. He placed the towel back down and said, "I'm not sure how I'd explain to my dad that I want to purchase an entire team."

"No need to fret, the scouts had their eyes fixed on you the whole time," Ibrahim reassured Adam, giving his back a reassuring pat. "Well, at least I think they were scouts..."

"I certainly hope so." Adam sighed deeply before straightening his posture. "Shall we say grace, or can I start indulging?"

He was clearly deflecting. I decided against calling him out and instead chimed in, "Dig in. We've waited long enough."

"Hey, isn't your birthday coming up?" Stella inquired, her gaze fixed on the twins. Indeed, March tenth was right around the corner, coinciding with our spring break as usual.

"Wait, have you asked them yet?" Ibrahim turned to his twin.

"Oops, not yet," Darshini confessed, setting down her drink and clearing her throat.

"What?" I asked, wondering what party they could have planned this time.

"Well, with our spring break and everything, we found this charming local getaway," Darshini began, glancing around at all of us before focusing on Ibrahim. "We thought we'd spend the weekend celebrating our birthday."

"And I've already spoken to Coach, we're getting that weekend off from our Nationals prep," Ibrahim added preemptively before Carter and Adam could even ask. March was always a busy month, with finals leading up to nationals and, of course, the twins' birthday.

The schedule changed a while ago, nationals were now always held near the end of March after several universities complained about their students' academic performance suffering under the old schedule.

"Just the weekend? Count me in, we all need a break," Carter said, visibly relieved, both hands planted firmly on the table. If the captain was on board, that was good enough for everyone.

"Where are we going?" Adam asked, curious.

"There's this adorable place with plenty of cabins and outdoor activities, but there are also cosy indoor activity options," Darshini explained, reaching for her phone. "I'll send the details in the group chat."

"I'm in!" Stella said quickly.

A trip during our short spring break? Of course I was in. I might as well enjoy it before fully immersing myself in the last semester.

Chapter eight

Brooklyn

Nothing was going as planned—I couldn't find my sunglasses. I can't go without them, every outfit was planned around them, and they cost a fortune. The girls were at Adam's with me, the guys at Carter's.

We'd leave at 1 PM, stop for lunch, and arrive by 3. But I wouldn't go if I couldn't find my sunglasses.

"Brooks, what are you looking for?" Stella asked, her legs propped on the couch as she watched me rummage through the random cabinet.

I pulled out the tape, a hammer, and a red Sharpie—maybe this wasn't Adam's random cabinet, but it got treated as one. So far, I have found a hair bow, a butterfly necklace, but no sunglasses.

"The vintage cat-eye sunglasses. I have the perfect outfit—it will match my bow." I sighed and slammed the drawer shut.

"Mhm, one of your thousands bow?" Darshini teased.

Okay, so I had a huge collection of them. It's not my fault they looked perfect in my hair.

"Darshini?" I called out, looking over at her.

"Yes, dearest?" .he asked, faking innocence.

"Stop the teasing."

I walked over to the couch and flopped down, tipping my head back. Maybe I could do a faceless pose, no glasses needed then.

"I rarely get a chance, it's fun," Darshini continued teasing and sat down next to me.

"Ignore her. Ever since she's been staying with Dante alone, she has gotten more confident," Zaira tsked and shook her head.

"Must be all the praising," Stella teased, and that got Darshini to quiet down.

Darshini didn't blush, but you could tell when she was flustered.

"Well, you'd know a thing or two about that, wouldn't you?" I shot back at Stella.

We all laughed, though Stella tried denying it.

Thankfully, Zaira came to the rescue. "Consider me your saviour because I just texted Adam. He said you have two pairs of sunglasses in his car. I sent a reference photo, and he confirmed that one pair is in his car." Zaira showed me her chat, where Adam confirmed the whereabouts of my favourite glasses.

"You're a lifesaver," I exclaimed, wrapping my arms around her and giving her a gentle hug. Zaira appreciated short-lasting hugs, so I didn't overdo it.

"How's your dating life? Seeing any new athletes?" Stella then asked.

"Nope, nope, we agreed. I'm not dating another athlete," I reminded them. The last one was too clingy, and some were too self-absorbed. I had no wish to repeat those experiences.

"Is Brooke going through a dry spell?"

"By choice. It's just me and my Mr. O-giver," I admitted.

My girls smiled and shook their heads, used to me and my antics. I've had several friends, but these three right here are the ones I truly love and consider my girls.

The guys were great too, but I'd always craved the women's friendship bond—filled with laughter, teasing, female rage validation, and letting each other be who they are. The one thing I appreciated the most was the honesty to call each other out. I found that with these three.

"Maybe you'll find someone when we return from the trip," Darshini said, double-checking her bag.

"Better yet, maybe you'll meet someone there." Zaira nudged me.

I tried to picture the place from the images Darshini had sent.

"Oh, just imagine a rugged guy, with a rough beard, chopping wood shirtless," I exclaimed, translating my mental image into words.

"Why would he be chopping wood shirtless? That seems dangerous." Zaira frowned. Luckily, I wasn't the only one glaring at her right now. We all were. "What? I'm just figuring out the logistics here," she said, holding her hands up.

"Since when did you become a 'logistics' girl? What happened to the one who supported all my dreams?" I asked, leaning my head on her shoulder.

"Hey, I still support your dreams. I'm just not sure how lucky you'll be to see that," she said, patting my hair carefully.

"Well, we all know Brooklyn can manifest whatever her heart desires," Darshini said before taking a sip of her iced tea.

"Exactly," I hummed, and my phone buzzed with the timer. "Never forget I manifested your and Stella's relationship. So you're welcome."

"She did do that." Darshini pointed at me.

"Now come on. The cookies and cupcakes are done."

We spend a few minutes decorating them. Chances are, the guys wouldn't even care what they looked like, as long as they were edible. We carefully packed everything and placed it alongside the apple pie Stella made. Darshini had also brought some gulab jamun. Zaira had to study, so she opted for everyone's favourite chips and drinks.

I made sure to grab the twins' gifts. Ibrahim had a favourite coffee cup that broke during the hectic move, so I found him an exact replica. Darshini was so easy and lovely to shop for. I had found this adorable, whimsical dress that screamed Darshini's name in full caps. It was really hard to keep it a secret from them, but I was sure I could survive one more day.

The journey to Meadowview Hideaway was a mixture of car karaoke, laughter, conversation, and snacking. I took the first drive, and after lunch, Zaira took over and drove us all the way to our destination.

"I think I speak for everyone when I say I'm relieved this doesn't look like a murder site," Dante remarked, hands on his hips, his shades hanging low on his nose as he surveyed the surroundings.

"Yeah, I spotted the grill, people," Adam pointed out, and we all followed his gaze.

Dinner plans were saved. We had a whole food fest planned, one that included Adam's famous picanha on a grill, the only thing he claimed he could cook.

"Did you prep everything for the uh churrasco?" Zaira asked. She was a huge fan of it, like the rest of us.

"Hell yeah, I made sure the recipe is as authentic as possible," Adam said with pride, sliding his glasses up and closing the car door. The place wasn't too crowded, judging by the parking lot.

"Can confirm, his grandma gave him all the instructions," I chimed in, following Carter and Stella past the parking lot. "Nice lady," I added with a hum.

"You like her because she keeps complimenting you," Adam teased, swinging his arm around my neck and leaning his weight on me. I jabbed his rib, and he groaned in pain.

"Obviously." I smirked.

"Okay, check-in is in about forty-five minutes," Darshini said, checking the time on her watch. We stood in front of the front desk cabin. "Do you guys want to explore the area?" she suggested.

I looked around. Tall trees surrounded the place, and quaint cabins nestled among them with clear paths leading to each. There were blooms nestled between the green grass, some bushes bigger than others, but they were all pleasant to the eye.

"Yes! You mentioned there was kayaking too?" Zaira's voice interrupted my thoughts, and I looked ahead to see my friends gathered at the wooden sign with arrows.

"Yes, and there are several bonfire pits. There's also a lake we can swim in," Darshini confirmed.

"I read something about stargazing?" Carter asked, his hand sliding around Stella. Of course, those two would ask about stargazing.

"Yup, according to their site and the photos, the skies are quite clear here for a nice view," Darshini confirmed.

Carter and Stella grinned at the confirmation. Meanwhile, Dante, Ibrahim, and Adam were on the verge of fighting over something stupid, and I didn't want to stick around for that.

"Come on, we can follow this path," I suggested, stepping onto the trail. I followed the carved-out path with twigs and pebbles embedded in the dirt, and they all began to follow me. Honestly, I had no idea where I was heading, but that's what the path was for.

The warmth of the afternoon sun filtered through the leaves above us. Sunlight cast shadows onto the forest floor, dancing as the wind rustled the leaves. I looked ahead and smiled. Part of the group walked ahead of me now, another behind, and right next to me was Zaira, her hand looped through mine.

The sound of laughter and chit-chat filled the air as we hiked. I closed my eyes for a moment and could hear the nearby stream of water; the sound provided a soothing backdrop. I opened my eyes when I realised it was a terrible idea to walk with my eyes closed.

"Look at the flowers," Zaira marvelled.

I looked at the fresh spring flowers. Their scent hung in the air, paired with the earthy aroma of damp soil that we stepped on. I'm not sure what it was about spring, but I loved it so much. The birds chirping above our heads, the sound of water streams, and the chatter of my friends were the only things I heard as we walked our path.

It was all I needed to hear right now.

Each step I took washed away any tension I carried. Each step a reminder of how lucky I was with them. I made friends who would last. I knew that we were all set to graduate this year, but I had a feeling that what we had was going to last.

"Look at that lake, god, I can't wait to get in," Darshini marvelled at the sight of the peaceful lake in front of us.

The beauty of the nature surrounding it was perfectly vibrant greens with delicate blossoms amidst it, which only added more to the image.

One thing's for sure. We'll have great photos here.

"Did everyone remember to bring a floral swimsuit?" I asked, turning to the girls. They all nodded and smiled.

Our last group photo was far too long ago.

"We'd be fools not to." Stella winked.

"Absolutely, we're definitely having a group photo," Zaira confirmed, her arms crossed as she scanned the area.

"I can't wait." Glancing at the guys, I could tell they weren't looking forward to it. I didn't blame them, they were supposed to be trained photographers by now, but still lacked some skills.

A squirrel darted past me, and a loud shriek escaped my lips in surprise. Ibrahim and Dante burst into laughter, their voices echoing through the forest, while Adam bit back a smile.

"Are you okay?" he asked.

"Yeah, the little guy surprised me," I admitted, watching as the squirrel made its way up a tree.

"I think we can head back now. We'll be right on time to check in," Darshini said, her eyes focused on her screen.

If there was one thing I disliked about hiking, it was the trip back. I always got excited about reaching our destination, but the return journey made me want to flop down.

We reached the front desk, and each couple got their cabin. Adam and I chose to share one with two bedrooms. I doubted we'd use it for something other than sleeping.

Darshini handed me our key while Adam carried our bags.

We parted ways with the others, and I led Adam to our cabin, following the small map. I looked up and saw our cabin number, then glanced around. Another couple was heading to the cabin on our right. The one on our left seemed vacant.

The charming cabin we were going to call home for the next few days struck me with its delightful simplicity. Nestled among towering trees, it exuded a rustic charm with its weathered wood and sloping roof. A small but cosy porch welcomed us, adorned with various pots of plants hanging from the ceiling.

The moment we stepped in, a cosy warmth enveloped us. Streams of sunlight poured through the windows, casting a golden glow on the rustic wooden floors.

The cabin had been recently cleaned, and the scent of pine lingered in the air. Everywhere we looked, we saw the touches of rustic decor, from the knitted blankets draped over the couch to the vintage lanterns hanging on the walls. But then, we noticed the error.

A faint frosted glass caught my eye, and as I squinted, I realised it was the shower—out in the open. Worst of all, I spotted the singular bed. We both looked at the double bed adorned with towel swans. This was all one huge open space, besides the tiny room that was the toilet. This wasn't the two-bedroom cabin we had chosen.

I turned to Adam, and he took a deep breath, his duffel bag falling to the floor. I checked the group chat, and everybody had the right room. Adam and I had the correct cabin—just not what we wanted.

I glanced over at the shower. Even if I took a steamy shower, I realised Adam would be able to see more than enough. I pictured him on the couch, his gaze fixed on me as I stood in the shower. An electric shock ran through my body, and all I could think about was that night I had suggested we would have been great together.

I felt like I was losing my mind.

"Brooklyn," Adam called my name, snapping me out of my trance.

Chapter nine

Adam

The cabin was perfect until we went inside and discovered the error. We both seemed to be staring at the shower with our jaws dropped.

"Adam," Brooklyn replied and turned to me. Her eyes darted to the couch, and my eyes followed hers.

"Don't even think of saying 'not it'," I warned. There was no way I'd be sleeping there.

As cosy as the knitted blanket on top of it looked, I knew the couch would become uncomfortable after sitting on it for two hours. Sleeping on it would only be worse.

"Fine, we should go to the front desk then?" Brooklyn asked, her shoulders sagging at the disappointment.

"Yeah, I'm sure this is a mistake," I said with optimism in mind. I set my duffle bag down and was already out the front door.

"Of course it's my accommodation," Brooklyn pointed out, locking up the cabin after stepping out.

"Come on," I said as I began to lead the way.

The front desk wasn't far, but it was annoying to do this walk again. I held the door open and Brooklyn beelined for the front desk. I followed right behind her.

"Welcome to Meadowview Hideaway. How can I be of your service?" The woman named Lia, according to her name tag, asked. She had a gentle smile on her lips and beamed a friendly energy. I truly hoped she could help us.

"So, my friend and I have our cabin, but there seems to be a mistake," Brooklyn explained, placing down the key along with the tag it came with.

"You came with the group of eight, right?" she asked as she checked her computer.

"Indeed," I confirmed and explained the situation, "We have a couple's cabin. We were supposed to just have a two-bedroom cabin."

"Let me check." She tapped away on the keyboard. A few moments later, a frown etched onto her face. "Reservations were made under Dar-shy-ney Mirza?"

"Correct, our reservation was made under Darshini Mirza," Brooklyn confirmed and looked over at me.

"I'm checking..." Lia said clicking around and typing things in. She then looked up at us. "Well, I see here that she booked four couples' cabins for the weekend."

"That can't be right, we're not a couple," Brooklyn blurted out before I had the chance. The woman in front of us blinked once, then a second time.

"Oh... Oh, okay," Lia finally spoke up. "Let me double-check for a moment," she said, taking a deep breath as she began to type and click away on her computer. "Oh, dear."

That didn't seem like a good news 'Oh dear', it seemed like the complete opposite.

"Is everything okay?" I dared to ask.

"I see that the request was made for three couples and one two-bedroom cabin indeed, but there was a mistake made when it came to the booking," Lia explained, managing to find a way to avoid saying this was a mistake on their end.

"That's okay, can we get another cabin then?" I asked.

"I'm afraid we only have a couples cabins available," Lia said to our disappointment.

"Are there any—"

"We have people checking in tomorrow, so technically, we have no free cabins," Lia explained. "I'm terribly sorry for the inconvenience. I have these coupons for you. We can also bring in some extra cushions for a more comfortable couch if you'd like," she said as she pulled out a couple of vouchers and coupons for some of the activities here.

Brooklyn seemed a little pissed, but hadn't spoken a single word. I guess this means I needed to continue doing the talking for us.

"We'll take the coupons, hold the extra cushions." I grabbed the vouchers and coupons. I looked over at Brooklyn to see if she needed something, but she just shook her head. "And some extra pillows and a blanket would be nice too."

"Of course, I'll make sure it comes right away," she promised. "Again, I'm terribly sorry—"

"It's okay. Have a great day," Brooklyn cut her off and looked over at me. "Let's go."

We stepped outside together, walking down the path to our cabin yet again.

"What now?" Brooklyn asked, sounding annoyed still.

"Are you able to sleep without being all over me?" I teased and watched as her hazel eyes narrowed on me.

"You ask as if it's hard or something." She smirked with her jab taken at me. A small sacrifice to see her happy, I suppose.

"Are you comfortable with sharing a bed?" I asked in a much more serious tone. I didn't like the couch, I needed my body well rested. With all the training and preparation happening, I didn't want to be benched or play terribly because of a sore muscle.

"Yeah, we'll just put a divider," Brooklyn said confidently.

"Sounds good, I need an extra pillow though."

"What for?"

"I need a pillow to hug." I shrugged, watching as she stopped at the front door. She was in the middle of turning the key when she shook her head. "Unbelievable," she whispered.

"Some of us love physical touch. If anything, you're unbelievable for not liking it." I rolled my eyes and reached over to unlock the door. Brooklyn stumbled in, and I was right behind her.

"What's to like? Too much body heat, sweat, and drool." Brooklyn plopped down on the couch, sprawled almost as if she were a puddle.

"I don't think you're doing the cuddling thing well." I scrunched my nose. None of my cuddles seemed to be like that so far.

"What's next? You'll offer lessons?" She laughed outright.

I rolled my eyes and retaliated quite easily. "You wouldn't be able to afford me, Brooks."

"Sure, buddy... Also, can we not tell the others? Darshini will feel as if it's her fault."

"I agree, we'll just say it was the right cabin." I sat down on the fluffy poof. I didn't like it, my knees were practically against my chest. I got up and found a better seat on the couch next to Brooklyn.

The extra pillows and blanket were brought to us. We began to make our bed for later, placing a pillow-border in the middle. I had the biggest blanket on my side with three pillows, and Brooklyn had two on hers. It was hard to miss with the blue satin pillow cover.

The bed was fairly big enough, and even if I rolled around a little, I still wouldn't fall off the bed, so it was great.

We exited the cabin, meeting the others outside at the communal grill for dinner.

Ibrahim, Carter, and I took care of the meats on the grill while Dante and Darshini handled the fried rice. They also made the vinaigrette salsa per my instructions.

"That was so fucking good, if I didn't feel like a balloon already, I would've grabbed a fourth serving." Ibrahim rubbed his stomach and tried his best not to fall back.

We were all seated on a picnic table, none of us able to lean back without falling over.

"The beef was perfect this time, great job, Adam," Carter complimented the food, he, too, was so full, so much so that he was struggling with his last cookie.

"Yeah, it seems that you do indeed have some value in the kitchen." Dante smirked as he said the words.

I can tell Brooklyn was trying her best not to laugh right now. At least I didn't almost burn down the kitchen.

"Hey, I told you, my Brooks and I have been getting far better." I threw my arm around Brooklyn and pulled her close to me. "Tell them how you can make this brownie blindfolded." I lifted my chin towards the brownie. The very brownie that had many people losing their minds right there. She added a little cookie crumble in there, and everyone at the table raved about it.

When it came to desserts, the girls had outdone themselves. Everyone's favourite was present.

"Mhm, the crushed cookies within, pure genius," Zaira gushed, finishing her last piece of brownie. Unlike some of us, Zaira had planned and proportioned her plate correctly so she'd be able to enjoy a bit of everything.

"I try my best to be humble about it." Brooklyn flipped her hair over her shoulder.

"I think I need a walk. Perhaps it will help get the food down," Stella suggested, and everyone jumped on board.

We began to pack up everything and left the place just as we had found it. We regrouped in the middle, and soon our evening walk began.

Mini lanterns and fairy lights illuminated our path, casting a whimsical glow. Yet, with the vast darkness and the sound of critters in the night, it also felt somewhat eerie. We took a shortcut, and Brooklyn walked right next to me, occasionally stepping in my path and forcing me onto the grass instead of the paved walkway. After a while, it became a little annoying, and that's when I realised she was doing it to get on my nerves.

"Brooklyn, babes." I slung my arm around her and pulled her close to me, making it impossible for her to escape my grasp. "When will you learn not to poke the bear?" I teased, pinching the hand that reached my way.

"I'll throw you to a bear," she scoffed, attempting to jab me. But with her pressed so close to my side, her movement was strained.

"And that bear is going to love me so much, and we'll be the best of friends," I joked, and Ibrahim immediately turned around.

"I'm pretty sure the bear is going to maul your face off and dissect your body, which will ruin my birthday." Ibrahim rolled his eyes.

"Not everything's about you."

"Uhm, my birthday is?" Ibrahim scoffed.

Well, I couldn't argue that. I slowly let go of Brooklyn. With no more jabbing or attempts to walk in front of me, our walk became perfect. It reached an end once we circled back to the base, all of us heading towards our own cabin.

"I'll go shower if you don't mind," I said as we stood on the porch.

"No, go ahead. I, uh—" Brooklyn hesitated, looking around the porch. Her eyes landed on the cosy outdoor chair. "I'll be here. Let me know when you're done," she replied, but I could tell she didn't want to sit out here at night, and neither did I.

"Are you sure you want to sit out here? You can sit inside, just no peeking," I offered, opening the front door for her and waiting for her to step inside. I wouldn't take no for an answer.

"Aw, are you worried, Adam?" Brooklyn stopped in the doorway, leaning back against it.

Brooklyn wasn't exactly short, perhaps five six, about the same height as Darshini. Still, when she leaned against the door frame like that, without any heels, she looked short beneath me. I leaned towards her, my hand planted right above her head.

Brooklyn looked up at me, her hazel eyes shimmering in the moonlight, our only source of light. My gaze trailed from her eyes to her full lips.

"I just don't want to deal with the aftermath of a bear mauling your face or if you get kidnapped," I whispered, ushering her inside so I could lock the door behind us. However, she remained by the door, arms crossed, glaring at me.

"Kidnapped? You've got nothing to worry about," Brooklyn scoffed, her confidence giving way to annoyance. "My parents said my captors would always return me." She laughed bitterly, and I couldn't help but laugh along.

"That makes me feel 100 times better, but get your ass inside," I said, taking her hand and dragging her inside with me. I locked the door behind us, and when I turned around, Brooklyn still had her arms crossed as she looked at me.

"If I catch even the tiniest glimpse, I'll tell the whole world," Brooklyn teased, a smirk playing on her lips.

"It won't be tiny, baby," I whispered in her ear, then patted her shoulder and walked past her to grab her bags.

"Just be quick, I want to go to bed already," Brooklyn mumbled. I was sure if I were to turn around, she'd be a little flustered.

I chuckled and grabbed all the necessities out of my bag. In the small corner, there was a wooden divider where you could hang your towel. I went there and stripped naked behind the divider, wrapping the towel around my body.

When I stepped out, I spotted Brooklyn on the couch, her back to me, engrossed in a book. I headed into the shower and hung my towel. The bathroom was spacious but clearly designed for a couple.

The cold water cascaded down my body, and I took deep breaths, the coolness calmed me completely. I ran my fingers through my hair, relishing the refreshing sensation. I always preferred cold water over warm.

"How's the water, Adam?" Brooklyn's voice brought me back to reality. I glanced through the frosted glass, knowing she had looked over her shoulder just enough to hear me clearly but not enough to see much.

"Cold and perfect," I replied in a cheerful manner. God, I loved cold water. I ran my fingers through my hair, waiting for her response.

"You're taking a cold shower?" Brooklyn asked, seizing the opportunity immediately. "Are you sure you don't want your privacy?"

"Are you sure you don't want to join me?" I shot back quickly. I smirked, pleased with how easily that came out. She was quiet for a beat too long, meaning I won.

"I—" Brooklyn stuttered at first, then cleared her throat, composing herself. "You wouldn't be able to handle me."

"If that's your defence, then sure," I said, returning to my refreshing, cold shower.

Once I was dressed, we both headed to bed, each on our respective sides, of course. I was still fluffing my pillow when I noticed Brooklyn had already drifted off to sleep, tangled in her own blanket. I smiled and lowered my head back onto my pillow.

When the sun rose the next morning, its warmth filled the cabin, light streaks beaming through and illuminating the space. Despite my desire to sleep in, my body jolted me awake at the sound of chirping birds.

Slowly, I opened my eyes, but something tickled my face, and a heavenly scent filled the air. Dark, soft curls were scattered across my face, and I carefully brushed them aside.

The middle section of our pillow wall was intact, so how the hell did Brooklyn manage to get over it? Her cheek was pressed against my chest, with a leg thrown over my body. Her hand rested on my torso, fingers gently gripping my shirt, which I normally didn't wear to bed.

'I hate cuddling' my ass. Brooklyn was a professional. Right now, she was like a cute, clingy koala. Squinting my eyes, I realised it was far too bright to be considered early. This was supposed to be a getaway, so I doubted I needed to be up early. If I were needed, they'd find ways to wake me up.

I closed my eyes and gently placed my hand on Brooklyn's back, pulling her closer to me. It was wrong, I knew, but she had crossed the border, and I always preferred a human over a pillow to hold onto. Soon, I drifted back to sleep peacefully.

I heard water running, and this time, my chest felt a lot lighter. Rolling over to my left, I found no barrier, nothing. I looked over and noticed the left side of the bed was made up.

Looking ahead, I saw Brooklyn's silhouette behind the frosted glass. Steam coated the glass, but not enough to conceal the view completely. Immediately, I rolled over to my right, my heart racing in my chest.

I shouldn't be attracted to Brooklyn, I simply couldn't be. It wouldn't be right, we were friends. Whatever I felt towards her had to be lust, that wouldn't be fair to her... Even if her view on relationships aligned with mine, even if she once said we'd be perfect if given the chance, but I couldn't let that chance be given.

Neither of us would catch feelings, I knew that. But I didn't want our friendship to be at risk, especially when she was living with me. At the slightest inconvenience between us, she'd move out all on her own, and not even begging would get her to stay. She'd rather go to a moldy, creepy motel, and that did not sit right with me. She deserved far more.

She was my friend, a great friend. There was an undeniable comfort in her presence whenever she was near. It felt like coming home after a long journey, and her sight alone would bring a smile to my face. She made my dull moments at home much more lively, and I would do everything to keep it that way... As my friend.

Brooklyn and I were both in the mini kitchen, busy with breakfast. Neither of us spoke a single word about her cuddling me. I knew it would piss her off, and I preferred to start my morning with positivity surrounding me.

We heated some toast with butter and added some leftover meat from yesterday to make the perfect sandwich. Picking up the sandwiches, we went to sit on the porch to enjoy them and watch our surroundings like two old people.

For a moment, this tranquillity made me look forward to retirement. Of course, I was then reminded I wasn't even halfway there, and there were still a whole lot of things I wished to do. Maybe, just maybe, I'll get to enjoy retirement after everything.

"Let's walk?" Brooklyn suggested, picking up the steaming mug of tea.

"And sip our tea? I like your way of thinking," I agreed. It wasn't like any of our other friends were awake.

We walked the carved path, sipping our tea. We checked out all the other cabins, and they were indeed not vacant. We waved at one of the couples who did the same. Ahead, we saw Carter and Stella walking together, smiles resting on their faces.

"Good morning, you two. How was your rest?" Stella asked kindly. For a moment, I thought she knew that we had to share a bed, but then I noticed her tone, she was just genuinely interested.

"Perfect, good," Brooklyn and I said in unison.

"Yours? Was the lake noisy?" I asked, quickly moving on from our awkward, one-word answer.

"Nope, the lake provided a peaceful backdrop. It was good," Carter admitted, then looked over my shoulder. "The others are finally awake."

"We have a long day ahead of us, and Brooke and I scored some vouchers and coupons for kayaking. I'm not sure if you'll fit, but we are doing this," I said with a proud grin.

I left out the part about how we got the vouchers. If asked, we could always say we were charming—it was pretty believable after all, or we filled out a survey.

"We? As in... you and me?" Carter frowned, his pointed finger moving from me and back to himself.

"Yep, Stella, go find another partner," I said, looking over at Stella and offering her the warmest and fakest smile I could muster up.

Stella walked over to Brooklyn and looped her arm through hers. "If you were smart, you would've chosen Brooke. She's a champ at this," she said as she gently tugged her friend closer to her.

"Really?" I was quick to ask, Carter echoing my curiosity.

"No, but you should've seen your face." Stella laughed.

"This is a race," I declared. If Ibrahim and Zaira were looped into this, it would easily become a race. Darshini and Dante would join in due to FOMO or because Ibrahim and Zaira became too competitive and wanted different partners.

"Do I have any say in who I'll be partnered up with?" Carter asked, hands on his hips as he looked between the three of us.

"No," Stella and I answered in unison.

Chapter ten

Brooklyn

Kayaking didn't go as planned, Ibrahim and Zaira won the race. Adam and Carter, despite fighting the entire time, got second place, and Stella and I came in third. I was certain Darshini and Dante self-sabotaged, there was no way they failed so terribly. Third place wasn't a problem for me, Adam didn't win the race, and my pride was still intact.

The next game we played, however, was interesting. Victory at Uno for Adam was harder than herding cats. Somewhere during our first year of friendship, during one game, everyone decided to turn on Adam during Uno, and it hasn't changed.

Two hours of games, lunch, and cookies passed. We were all dressed to take a swim. We've done a lot, and Adam was still here bragging about his Uno double victory.

"I mean, seriously, mark this day. It is simply the best day of our lives," Adam said with a grin as we headed to the lake.

The girls and I had a shared Pinterest board with poses we all studied.

"Just because you won doesn't mean it's a great day for all of us." I rolled my eyes, though he couldn't see that beneath the shades.

"True friends support each other. I'm not sensing that right now," Adam scoffed and crossed his arms over his chest, holding his head high as he walked off.

I think it's cute when he pretends to be angry.

"There's no time to chit-chat if we want good photos," Zaira said in a stern manner.

If she told us to stand in a line, I'm pretty sure we'd all be lined up by now. There was a wooden dock wide enough for all four of us to sit down, matching our reference photo.

Carter took all the group photos from every angle we asked, patiently snapping away until we found the perfect shots. The breeze tousled our hair just right, the lake sparkled invitingly, and the lush greenery formed a stunning backdrop.

When the time came to plunge into the lake, the problem arose. It looked a little too cold. Jumping into that cold water required some serious contemplation.

"Ibrahim, I swear I'll—" Zaira started, but before she could finish, a flash of pink flashed by, and there was a loud splash.

Zaira and Ibrahim were suddenly underwater. Her boyfriend seemingly still held onto her like he did when he jumped in with her.

"Carter—no, Carter—" Stella tried to warn him, but it was too late. Carter scooped up Stella in his arms and leapt in.

Stella quickly swam away, likely plotting vengeance with Zaira.

Dante, ever the gentleman, walked in with Darshini by his side. Dante winced at the cold, and Darshini teased with a splash, sparking a playful water fight between them.

"Come on, Brooks, don't make me throw you over my shoulder like Ibrahim," Adam teased, gesturing towards the water.

I sighed dramatically and settled down on the dock, while Adam just dove in. The water was chilly around my feet, and I briefly considered making a run back to the cabin.

My contemplation ended when the guys decided to have a splash war, drenching each other and me in the freezing water.

I gave in, lowering myself. The cool water rose around my neck, and even though my hair was now up in a bun, I knew the others would mess that up.

"Now my hair is going to smell like lake water," Zaira complained as she swam around me. Stella and Darshini joined us.

"Tell me about it. I'm just hoping I won't feel the urge to dive in," I said, glancing over at Zaira.

"Good luck with that." Zaira chuckled, and we all watched as Darshini swam effortlessly. It was impressive, considering she couldn't swim when we first met. Now you could leave her unattended near deep bodies of water, and you wouldn't risk drowning.

"Look at her go," Stella said with pride.

"Oh, how she used to fear swimming." I remembered all too well.

"Now she's like a fish! I feel like a proud momma hen," Stella continued, and Darshini finally reached us. She had overheard our conversation and was now glaring at us.

"I mean, come on, we all know those 'lessons' she was getting were pretty exciting and motivating," Zaira said with a smirk. Yeah, I highly doubted that Dante's teaching methods were 100 percent ethical, but they seemed to have worked.

"Hey, my lessons were perfectly proper," Darshini insisted, but, of course, we were going to ignore that for teasing purposes.

"Sure thing, Darshini," Zaira said with sarcasm lacing her tone, patting her back.

"Let's have a race, men only," Ibrahim suggested, pushing Dante away without success.

"Oh, so what? Women aren't allowed to participate?" I raised an eyebrow at them. Was I actually interested in a race? No. But I was definitely interested in messing with them.

"We just thought... we thought you wouldn't be interested," Dante stammered, finally managing to stop pulling Ibrahim down.

Adam and Carter remained silent. Judging by the slight smirk tugging at the corners of their lips, I was pretty sure they knew what was going on.

"Now they want to dictate what we think," Zaira spoke up.

Dante and Ibrahim's faces changed completely. Panic settled in, evident on both of their faces.

"Hey, we didn't say that," Ibrahim said defensively, looking towards his best friend.

"You guys are doing this on purpose." Carter laughed, clearly not enjoying seeing his friends being tormented.

"Get in line and no crying about losing," Dante scoffed, gesturing towards the dock. His back almost touched it, marking 'the line'.

One race turned into three, and eventually Dante left the lake for a moment. He returned with a beach ball, keeping us entertained for quite a while in the water. We played and messed around until our fingers and toes got all wrinkly.

The next morning, we were up a little early, we all had our work cut out for us, it was, after all, the twins' birthday. For now, they only got simple hugs and handshakes as birthday wishes.

There was a planned surprise, but a slight error on Carter's side delayed the surprise. The cakes he ordered weren't going to be delivered on time. We could have continued without the cakes, but a birthday without a cake just didn't feel right to us. So, Carter found someone else to do the delivery.

Zaira was put on 'distracting the twins' duty, while Dante and Adam were busy cooking.

Stella, Carter, and I were on decorating duty. We chose the communal picnic bench with whimsical fairy lights hanging from pole to pole. With permission, we added some banners along the fairy lights.

The table was adorned with a nice cloth and balloons taped to the sides. Stella arranged the cake boxes, throwing a few candies on the table for decoration, along with some leftover desserts we had.

We laid out the presents on the table too, Ibrahim's on the right and Darshini's on the left, and enough space for our food.

Dante and Adam returned to the table with the biryani and chicken kabab. They arranged it nicely, and I texted Zaira to let her know she could stop whatever distraction she had going on.

A few minutes later, Zaira led the way with Ibrahim and Darshini. Excitement danced in the twins' eyes, and their lips curled into smiles.

"You knew about this?" Ibrahim turned to Zaira, and she nodded along. Darshini's eyes bounced to her boyfriend.

"You didn't think we'd forget the true purpose of this trip, did you?" Stella smirked.

"Oh my god, this looks amazing! Thank you, guys," Darshini gushed, her eyes moving around from the lights, banners, gifts, and the decoration on the table. It was safe to say that both Ibrahim and Darshini loved their party.

"Sorry, it took so long. I made a mistake when ordering your presents, but it finally arrived on time," Carter apologised and walked to the table.

"What is it?" Ibrahim asked with excitement brimming his voice.

We were all curious to know. Carter wouldn't let us even take a peek at the cake.

Carter finally opened the two boxes, revealing two cakes. One was a minimalist floral-themed cake with the prettiest pastel-coloured flowers and a beautiful candle. The second cake shared the same creamy white backdrop, but instead of flowers, there was a handsome Squidward made of icing.

"Carter, these look amazing. Thank you so much." Darshini's face lit up at the sight of her cake, and she gave him an awkward side hug.

"Carter, this is exactly what I wanted." Ibrahim grinned, admiring his cake.

Ibrahim... was just himself.

"Let's get this party started." Dante snapped a hat onto Ibrahim's head. Zaira did the same for Darshini, while the rest of us donned ours.

"Safari-themed hats, again." Darshini shook her head, adjusting the strap under her chin.

"I'm pretty sure it became a tradition after the first two birthdays we celebrated," Stella replied.

They were actually the leftovers from Adam's birthday when we accidentally ordered 100 instead of twenty.

We all sat down at the table. The twins opened their gifts swiftly, loving all of them. Finally, dinner started. We didn't waste time with it, savouring every last bite. I could truly see how Darshini fell in love with Dante after just one summer.

Once the plates were cleared, we sang "Happy Birthday" to the two, and that attracted two others who were staying at Meadowview Hideaway, along with a worker. They all sang along with us and got cake too.

Carter, Adam, and Dante waited patiently until the bystanders were gone. I could already tell what they were up to, just following tradition, so I stepped aside. Ibrahim didn't see it coming at all.

The poor guy was enjoying every bit of his strawberry lemon cake. Darshini knew the tradition and stepped aside.

Carter and Dante held Ibrahim down without giving him much of a chance to defend himself. Adam smeared the rest of his cake on his face. There was a muffled string of curse words when they finally let him go.

"Adam, that was the perfect slice with filling," Ibrahim protested.

"You smashed a brigadeiro slice of cake in my face last time. I smelled like chocolate for two days straight," he complained.

They always complained and went back and forth, only to do it again on each other's birthdays. All the boys did.

"Okay, well..." Ibrahim seemed like he was at a loss for words. He then looked between Carter and Dante, who were surely feeling the sting of betrayal.

Ibrahim pointed to Dante and turned to Darshini. "See? Is this the traitor you want to be dating?"

"You had it coming, Ibrahim." Darshini shrugged as she ate her coconut cake.

"Excuse me?" Ibrahim let out a dramatic gasp.

"You do it on their birthdays too." She shrugged.

There was a brief staring contest, then Ibrahim chased after Darshini, probably looking to even the damage done on his own face.

After three minutes or so, the twins returned. Both seemed tired, with coconut cake on both their faces, although Ibrahim bore more than Darshini. Not a complete loss for her. Before another fight could ensue between the two, Dante placed down a worn out box of Uno. That sealed our fate for the night.

With four rounds of Uno behind us, I could see that the others were starting to look at their significant others.

"So, I'm so tired, I think I'll be heading to the cabin." Ibrahim stretched his arms out, attempting to look convincing. Well, perhaps he assumed he was being convincing. He wasn't, not when I knew that most of us had napped earlier.

"Mhm, I'm gonna hit the hay," Zaira agreed, getting up with her phone and water bottle in her hands.

Carter held onto Stella's hand; she gave him a subtle nod. "We should go too. We still have tomorrow to enjoy."

"All those fun activities—"

I stopped listening and just nodded along. I knew what they were up to and waited until they had all left. The table was now empty, with only my cup, phone, and Adam across from me.

"Well, now that our friends are off to have the night of their lives, where do we go?" Adam got up as well, tucking his hands in his pockets and following me.

"Not another hike at night, that's for sure," I said quickly. I did not wish to become mosquito or bear food.

I led the way to our cabin, spotting Stella and Carter on the path ahead of us to their cabin.

"Cabin it is," Adam whispered, humming as we walked.

Stella and Carter stopped mid-track after pushing each other around and shared a kiss. Adam shook his head.

"Jeez, their room is right there," I pointed out as we climbed the stairs to our front door.

I got the keys out of my pocket and opened our cabin. Kicking my boots off by the door, I moved out of the doorway.

"Brooks, you sound a bit jealous," Adam teased, following behind me. As I switched the lights on, he locked the door behind us.

"No, I don't." Finally turning around to face him as he smirked.

"You do, just a little," he continued his teasing.

"You're projecting. Over two months and you haven't gotten laid," I said, confidently, spinning this on him.

"And how would you know?" Adam leaned back against the door, hands in his pockets, watching me. A challenge? I loved those.

"Hm, let's see." I took a step towards him. "All your time goes to practice, the guys, and spending time with me... Unless you sneak out early in the morning." I crossed my arms as I looked up at him.

"Fine, you're right... But the same goes for you, Brooke," Adam said with a smile as he tapped the tip of my nose with his pointer finger. He had turned it back on me. Of course.

"I'm not complaining?" I swatted his hand away.

"No?"

Chapter eleven

Brooklyn

"No," I repeated. "Because even if I did, you couldn't do anything about it." I confidently took a step closer.

I wasn't sure what it was, but something shifted between us at that moment. I wasn't entirely opposed to it, it had been simmering, and now it became undeniable. The look on Adam's face changed too. I wanted him to be flustered, but instead, he smirked, almost as if he had been waiting for this.

My brain was telling me to stop, but every other bit of me was screaming the opposite.

"I could." Adam took one step towards me, his voice a low whisper. "If you want me to."

I nearly forgot how incredibly gorgeous he was. From the way his blond hair was swept to the left in perfect strokes, to the slight smile, his perfectly sculpted nose, and jawline. Even his eyes.

God, his eyes. Locking eyes with him was dangerous, they drew you in. His deep blue eyes resembled the ocean during a storm. Mesmerising but entirely dangerous. They held such depths I yearned to explore.

Adam raised a brow at me as he caught me checking him out.

"Could what?" I cleared my throat, and a slight smirk formed on his face.

I knew exactly what he was saying, but was he messing with me right now?

"I think you know, don't you?" Adam asked, his eyes moving across my face. He reached out and carefully moved a stray curl out of my face. His fingers lingered on my skin, slowly caressing under my chin, forcing me to look up at him.

"There's nothing in our way," he stated as his thumb danced across my jawline.

"There's nothing in our way..." I repeated after him, my eyes trailing down to his lips. This was pure lust, and I was doomed to lose this battle, but not without trying to fight it at least. "What if you disappoint me, Adam?"

Adam didn't falter, didn't back down, or seem offended in the slightest. "Brooklyn baby, are you questioning my abilities?" he asked, a hint of confidence in his tone.

Brooklyn baby didn't usually do anything to me, but tonight... it made my heart skip a beat.

"Maybe a little," I replied.

Was I being truthful? I don't know. Something about Adam beamed the opposite, but what if he failed to do it for me in bed? What would happen to us? There it was, my rational thinking! I haven't lost it completely.

"We could give it a test trial," he replied, his finger lingering on my skin a little longer before he pulled his hand back. "You can decide afterwards, and there won't be any hard feelings."

He was serious. This wasn't Adam messing around, this was him being serious, and his offer sounded dangerously delicious to me.

"Are we seriously doing this?" I questioned out loud. I looked at him, not a single worry on his face. There was no pressure coming from him, whatever I'd pick, he'd be fine.

"It's up to you, baby." Adam shrugged off. This only made it harder for me to resist. I didn't want to resist, to begin with.

I should worry about this potentially ruining what we had going, but I didn't. I trusted him. No one understood the friends with just benefits better than him. I might as well, right? He said there'd be no hard feelings.

It might've been dumb of me to jump to this. Maybe he was right, it had been too long, and now my thoughts are clouded, but dear god, the moment my lips met his, I lost all rational thought. Thinking was no longer my strongest suit.

My lips met his, and a wave of heat washed over me. Adam didn't kiss back immediately, but once he caught on, I felt myself melting into him. His lips moving against mine jump-started an electric shock throughout my body. If he fucked half as good as he kissed, I might just end up having one of the best nights of my life.

"Is that yes?" he asked, his lips left mine, and I wanted to whine about it.

"Could I have been any clearer?" I pulled away just a little to look up at him, an ounce of sass found in my tone.

"Oh, sweet, Brooklyn." Adam laughed as his hand gently caressed my face. I closed my eyes at his gentle touch, then his hand went to the back of my neck, and he slammed my body to his.

His lips found mine again, and I immediately placed one hand on his chest as the other got lost in his hair. I struggled on my toes, and Adam seemed to have noticed. He scooped me up swiftly, wrapping my legs around his waist.

Our bodies pressed together, and I could feel the heat radiating off him. His lips moved with a hunger that matched my own, and I found myself clinging to him, lost in the sensation of his touch. Every brush of his lips against mine sent shivers down my spine, and I couldn't help but moan when I felt his tongue dancing with mine in perfect harmony.

Adam placed me on the table, his hands still on my thighs, slipping slowly. My dress wasn't exactly going to hide much from him. "Tell me, baby, what do you like?" Adam kissed down the column of my neck ever so slowly.

"What's wrong, Adam? Scared you can't impress me on your own?" I asked in a whisper, tipping my head back to grant him more access. "Scared you won't leave a good impression?" I teased, my tone confident at first, but then his lips brushed against that spot under my ear. I gasped as I felt his teeth graze against my soft skin.

I bit back a moan, my fingers tightening in his hair, a dead giveaway because I felt him smirking against my skin. Adam's hands left my thighs. One was now on my hip, and the other was placed on the back of my neck as he pulled his lips away from mine.

"I can sure as hell pleasure you better than that purple toy of yours," he promised, his eyes focused on mine as he pushed me back onto the table. He was mindful of my hair and had it floating above me rather than me lying on it.

That alone melted my heart, but then I realised what he said, and my eyes widened. How did he know about Mr. O-giver?!

Adam noticed how I froze and chuckled. "You should learn to close your suitcase, Brooklyn baby." There was no judgment, in fact, he seemed more intrigued.

"Do you always talk this much? You're not leaving the impression you wish to leave," I teased, watching as he still smiled. Was there no way to get under his skin? Adam didn't say another word, he hovered over me and kissed me once again.

I felt his fingers dancing along the thin strap of my dress. They were secured with knots, and I felt him tugging at the ends, the knot soon was undone. Adam broke free from the kiss, and his eyes immediately dropped down to my breasts, his fingers tugging the fabric down until my breasts were exposed to him.

"Brooklyn," Adam murmured, his eyes fixed on my breasts. His thumbs circled my nipple slowly, making me take laboured breaths in anticipation of what was to come.

"You're so beautiful," he whispered and lowered his head. I gasped as I felt his tongue circle my nipple, his hand squeezing the other breast. I closed my eyes and took a deep breath, feeling his other hand creeping under my dress, his touch sending shivers down my spine.

I couldn't focus on anything else. His tongue flicked and suckled my nipple, his finger pinching and rolling the other, while his knuckles brushed against my panties. I thought I was past the butterfly eruption phase of my life, but Adam successfully revived them, and he was barely getting started.

Adam let his teeth graze my nipple as he pulled away, my fingers tugging at his hair as my heavy breaths filled the air. Adam repeated his ministrations on the other side, only this time his fingers started rubbing me through my panties. It was teasingly slow and had me losing my mind.

"Adam," I moaned, bucking my hips up. "I need more, please."

Adam bit down on me, and I groaned at the delicious pain. He stood up and made quick work of my panties, which went flying somewhere, but I hadn't focused. Not when his lips were on mine again. I hadn't been greedy for kisses in years, but now I devoured every last one he had to offer me.

His fingers ghosted over my bare pussy as his lips left mine. He stood between my legs, preventing me from closing my thighs. His lips found their way to my ear again, hovering as he whispered, "Tell me, Brooklyn, can I taste this pretty pussy of yours?"

Before I had the chance to answer him, he ran his middle finger down my middle and then slowly circled my clit. "Do you want me down on my knees before you, Brooklyn?" he asked as he pinched my clit, and a loud moan was my mindless answer. I'd take anything he dished out.

I hadn't been given much time to register what was happening, but Adam lowered down to his knees. He could've easily taken a seat at the table, but he chose to kneel down, and that drove me mad. He threw my legs over his shoulders and pulled me towards him until I could feel his breath on me.

"I bet you taste like heaven," Adam said as he placed kisses along my inner thighs and mixed in gentle nibbles here and there. He stopped his kisses before he reached where I wanted them, and I withheld from groaning.

He spread my legs apart, and I shifted to my elbows to look down at him. His eyes were focused on the sight between my thighs with a slight smirk on his lips.

"You're practically dripping for me, Brooklyn," Adam marvelled.

"Don't get too confident, Adam. Things might change." I looked at him.

"Yeah?" He traced two fingers from my clit down my entrance. I expected him to just tease, and I was about to answer him when I felt those fingers sinking in. I moaned softly as he started working his fingers in and out, knowing exactly when to curl. "You don't sound too convincing right now," Adam teased and lowered his mouth down onto me.

My core tightened as his skilful tongue circled my clit, sending waves of pleasure coursing through me. Adam's strokes were no longer tame and slow, his fingers had picked up the pace. The tips of his fingers brushed exactly where I needed them as his tongue devoured me for all I had.

It was as if he knew exactly how to push me to the edge and keep me there, teetering on the brink of ecstasy. Every touch, every stroke of his tongue, sent me closer and closer to the edge until I was on the verge of falling apart completely.

"Adam, please, baby, I need to come," I moaned, slowly grinding myself against his face. My fingers were once again in his hair, trying to pull him closer as I begged for more. Adam let out a muffled moan against me, sending vibrations through my body. I couldn't comprehend completely what he said, but it seemed like my wish had been granted.

He no longer teased me, no, now he was a man on a mission. He wasn't tame anymore, he devoured me as if I were his last meal.

The tension within me was slowly reaching a peak again, he drove me closer to the edge with each movement. The sensation was overwhelming, consuming me entirely with pleasure.

My entire body tensed as the pleasure exploded within me. I cried out his name, my voice a mix of pleasure and desperation, as wave after wave of intense sensation washed over me. I was lost in a sea of ecstasy.

Adam slowly pulled his fingers out as I rode down from the peak of my pleasure. I expected him to come back up and kiss me. Instead, I felt his tongue still on me. Fuck, it wasn't over yet. Adam ate me out all throughout my orgasm.

I was chanting his name with curses in between, tugging at his hair. I wasn't sure if I wanted more or if I needed him to stop. I was rendered thoughtless, and he didn't stop until I was an overstimulated mess.

"You're every bit addicting, Brooklyn," Adam said as he finally got up. He wore a proud smirk on his face, one I admit he deserved. His hair was now dishevelled, even then, it was perfect.

I needed a few moments. Watching him pull his shirt over his head, I felt that spark inside me again. My eyes trailed down his body slowly, taking in the sight of his sculpted chest, the defined abs, and the path down to where I saw his bulge.

"My eyes are up here, you know," he teased and took my hand in his. Adam pulled me to sit up and kissed me immediately. He bent down to pick me up and carried me straight to the bed.

This was it. Our last chance to back out.

Adam kissed me gently, his hand stroking and caressing my body as he lay above me. I gently caressed his face and managed to pull him away from me so I could look into his eyes.

"Do you really want this, Adam?"

"Trust me, Brooklyn, there's nothing I want more." Adam took my hand and placed it on his covered erection. He was painfully hard, and I couldn't resist palming him through his pants.

"I tried to ignore it, the thoughts about you. I had been rather successful, but Brooklyn, one mere kiss is all it took for my restraints to shatter into pieces. I can no longer deny my desire for you," he said in a breathy tone, his hand on my wrist to stop me from teasing him any further.

"You're a great friend to me, Brooklyn. I don't want this to ruin things between us. Tell me if this would ruin things," Adam said sincerely, and I knew that if I stopped things now, he would've had the longest, most frustrating shower ever. Luckily, I didn't plan on ending things now.

He gave me his word, and I was hungry for more of him.

"The only way our friendship will be ruined is if you leave me unsatisfied tonight." I winked, and Adam laughed.

"Brooklyn, you were screaming my name several times just moments ago," Adam said as he moved around, and the sound of a zipper. "Do you really believe I'll fail?" he asked with a condom in hand, but also my vibrator. I didn't know whether to be mortified or excited.

"I thought you said you could do it better than that toy?" I watched as he pulled down his pants. Large, hard, throbbing, and so fucking divine.

Fuck, I couldn't wait to have him inside me.

"I did, and I stand by my point." Adam stood confidently there as he rolled his condom on. I bit down on my lip as I watched him. "United, however..." He grabbed my feet and pulled me closer. "I can make you see beyond the stars, and what man would I be if I withheld that opportunity from you?"

"Oh god," I whispered.

"God already answered your prayers, I'm here, baby." Adam kissed me hungrily, his throbbing cock pressed against my inner thighs, and I felt excitement bubbling within me. The need I had for this man was unreal. "Now tell me how you want it, Brooklyn." Adam kissed my throat next, teeth sinking into my skin.

"I want to see your face when I come," I moaned, grabbing his face to kiss him one more time.

I mostly preferred being the one on top. Adam, however, made me want to let go of that control.

"As you please." He smiled and kissed me briefly, then pulled away. He adjusted himself between my thighs, his hands smoothed over my knees and up my thighs. Adam spread my legs apart as far as he could and began to settle between me. He teased me by rubbing the tip of his cock from my clit to my entrance repeatedly. I closed my eyes and groaned.

"Eyes on me, Brooklyn." He squeezed my breast, the tip of his finger rolling over my nipple. "Let me see those pretty eyes when I fuck you." He tugged at my nipple, and my eyes opened to meet his.

"You talk more than I do," I whined, feeling him so close yet he wasn't inside me.

"God, I fucking love that mouth of yours." Adam laughed.

"You should fuck it sometime." I winked and watched as his expression changed completely, finally having a desired reaction from him.

"Fuck, Brooklyn." Lust danced in his eyes. His hand wrapped around my thigh as he entered me. I gasped at the feeling. Adam hadn't stopped until he had given me every last inch of him. I moaned at the size of him—he felt so fucking good and stretched me perfectly.

"Your pussy feels like paradise around my cock, Brooke," Adam moaned, his hands smoothing over my legs.

He guided my knees against my chest and started thrusting. He started off slow and deep.

I could only nod in agreement with him, my nails grazing up his arms. As Adam continued to thrust, I felt a slow, delicious heat spreading throughout my body. Every movement of his was building up that undeniably great pleasure. That sweet tension in the pit of my stomach soaring, and moans spilling.

His hands were firm as they roamed from my thigh to my hips, my breasts, and anywhere he touched made my skin tingle with excitement. I only now knew how large his hands were, how perfectly they cupped my breast.

"Fuck, Adam, more," I panted, my voice a desperate plea as he started picking up the pace. My nails dug into his skin, my fingers leaving marks as I held on tight, lost in a whirlwind of pleasure.

The room was filled with the sounds of our passion, his scent lingering on my skin. Each stroke and caress elicited a cry of pleasure from my lips.

Adam's thrusts became harder, faster, just how I wanted. His soft groans mixed in the air with the sound of our bodies moving together. He sounded so sexy, I could not think straight.

I felt Adam spreading my legs apart further, I didn't care what he did. As long as he continued this, I was so close—my eyes widened as I felt my vibrator against my clit. I looked at Adam, his smirk growing. He winked as he turned the setting higher.

"How's that, Brooklyn?" Adam asked.

How the hell was I supposed to form a coherent answer when the tip of his cock brushed against that sweet, perfect spot with each stroke, the vibrator buzzing against my clit.

"I love how you respond to me," he said with pride when there was only a moan that escaped my lips.

I could only nod, my cries of pleasure filling the air. Suddenly, a wave of ecstasy crashed over me. My legs shook uncontrollably, clenching around him as his name left my lips as a sinful 'thank you'.

Adam left me breathless and utterly spent.

It was as if every nerve in my body was on fire, and all I could do was ride the waves of pleasure, lost in the intensity of the moment. Adam's breathing became laboured, only lasting a few more thrusts. He buried himself deep within me, pressing against me as he kissed me hungrily. His tongue slid over mine, sharing a passionate dance as he came, his chest pressed against my breasts.

"My destruction," he whispered against my lips.

I wasn't given a chance to respond, he placed two more kisses on my lips. His lips lazily trailed down, a light tingle as we both came down the waves of our orgasms.

Adam went to clean himself up while I stretched out and rolled over onto my stomach, closing my eyes. I could fall asleep right here, right now. Blissful.

I heard footsteps, then I felt Adam tapping my back. I looked up at him.

"Come on, baby, let's get cleaned up and go to bed," he said, holding his hand to me.

Adam and I got cleaned up in the shower—as in together. I normally preferred to be alone in the shower, but I had no regrets. We laughed, kissed, and teased each other.

While I got dressed, Adam made the bed with the towel still wrapped around his waist.

"I think this arrangement might just work out, Adam." I yawned, stretching out my arms as I jumped onto my side of the bed. I adjusted our barrier. No cuddling, no touching, no nothing. Just pure bliss and sleep.

I meant to continue the conversation with Adam, lay some ground rules, but I felt my eyes flutter and his voice became distant. I tried to fight the sleep but ultimately lost.

Chapter twelve

Adam

The next morning proceeded as usual, and we got up and carried out our morning ritual. We even had breakfast as normal, just the two of us, sharing laughter and jokes.

The rest of our day unfolded with our friends. Despite the events of last night, we hadn't touched the subject, yet nothing felt awkward between us. Everything seemed normal, perfect even, but an important conversation lingered between Brooklyn and me.

I chose to be patient and waited till we got home. When evening came, I lounged on the sofa, awaiting our pizza delivery.

Finally, Brooklyn descended the stairs and settled down next to me.

"Okay, so..." Brooklyn began simply, pulling her legs up as she gazed at me.

"Are we finally going to talk about last night?" I asked, lowering the volume and setting the remote aside, leaning back. She sat across from me, her eyes tracing my form.

"Any regrets?" Brooklyn inquired, her face betraying no emotion. I couldn't read her.

"None at all," I confessed. She seemed relieved, or so I thought. Since when had she become so hard to read? "And you?"

"None at all," she replied with a simple smile, and I found myself letting out a relieved breath.

I wasn't ready to end things between us—we just had great chemistry. We understood each other and made each other happy. This arrangement seemed to suit us perfectly. It saved us both the trouble of finding someone else who shared our views on sex and attachment.

"So, shall we continue with this arrangement?" I proposed.

"Yes, but there need to be some ground rules, Adam," Brooklyn said, shifting in her seat and sitting up straight, pushing her hair over her shoulder.

"Oh, so, like, don't go and fall in love with you or something?" I teased, and Brooklyn initially just rolled her eyes.

"You couldn't, even if you tried." She laughed, shaking her head.

I knew I wouldn't, but she made it sound impossible.

"Hm, okay. What are the ground rules then?" I asked, hoping they were something I could work with. I tried to think of the worst possible rules, but nothing came to mind.

"Our friends can't know," she stated.

"Agreed. I don't want them trying to play matchmaker again," I added, remembering the not-so-subtle hints they'd dropped about Brooklyn and me giving a relationship a shot around a year ago.

We'd skillfully avoided that subject every time until they dropped it.

"Glad we're on the same page. Also, when I'm with someone, even if we're not officially dating, I prefer if we don't see other people," Brooklyn said, her tone serious.

"Awww, is Brooky getting jealous?" I teased, wondering what possessive Brooklyn would be like. The thought was kind of hot, actually.

"No, Adam," she replied, rolling her eyes and bursting my bubble. "The last time, some asshole got me in trouble by letting another girl think they were exclusive, and I was the outsider."

"I wouldn't do that to you. I agree with that rule," I said quickly. Having just one person was safer anyway.

"That's all. Oh, and no post-sex sweet talks and stuff. You can just leave," Brooklyn said, narrowing her eyes at me.

I noticed this last night. The moment we finished, it was a quick kiss and then I was sent on my way. I didn't mind, as long as we were both satisfied.

"Not even a cuddle?" I raised an eyebrow at her. I wondered if she was aware that she often cuddled me. I also wondered how long it would be before I could tease her about it without risking being beaten to a pulp. Maybe in another two days?

"Nope," she said, popping the 'p' in her answer.

"Fine." I sighed dramatically. Brooklyn smiled at me, my friend. I wondered for a moment if I had anything to add.

"I have just one rule," I realised and voiced my opinion. "No matter what happens between us, we will remain friends, and you won't move out until it's a good place," I asked of her. I was as serious as ever. If she moves out, it better be the old apartment fixed up or some new sparkling, safe place.

"Sure."

"I need your promise, Brooklyn," I said, narrowing my eyes at her, and she sighed.

"Fine, I promise, Adam," Brooklyn repeated, easing my worries.

"Then that settles it," I said, clapping my hands.

"Wait, are you into some weird kinky stuff?"

"Define weird." I frowned.

"I don't know, like toe-sucking or something." Brooklyn shrugged, and I burst out laughing.

"Toe sucking? No, that's not my thing. But if I come up with any weird, freaky ideas, I'll check with you first," I assured her, shaking my head.

"Oh, and just so you know, the girls might ask. If I'm seeing anyone, for anonymity reasons, I will have to alter your identity. Different names and sports, probably—so don't go thinking I'm breaking our 'no seeing others' rule," Brooklyn informed me.

I was thankful the guys never cared too much about that aspect of my life, unless I told them, of course.

"How dare you mess with the original?" I gasped, pretending to be hurt.

"You'll get over it," Brooklyn said, standing up.

"I don't think I will," I continued, watching as she sauntered over to me. The match playing on the TV had lost my interest a while ago.

"I'm sure we can arrange something to make you feel better," Brooklyn said as she stood between my legs. She leaned down, her hands trailing up my thighs, and I could feel my heart racing with excitement.

"I think so, yeah," I whispered, and her lips curled into a smirk. Brooklyn moved to straddle me, one hand planted on my chest and the other in my hair as she pressed her lips against mine. Yep, this would make everything okay. She could even let me play the disgrace of a sport called football, the American version.

|One week later|

It was surreal how great Brooklyn and I got along. We just fit together perfectly, like two pieces of a puzzle. I had never felt so understood and respected as I did with Brooklyn. I hoped she felt the same way because this woman had taken me to heaven and back several times in the span of a week.

Some days, we'd only kiss, but god, her kisses felt like they were from heaven. We were both busy, and she understood that. She understood my passion for soccer and why I gave it my all. She never demanded anything from me, and I didn't from her.

I loved our new morning routine, stolen kisses here and there. Nothing else had changed, we still cooked together, went out and watched movies—just with a few kisses here and there, and sometimes it led to more. But I didn't mind; what Brooklyn did to me was far more interesting than any wizards on screen.

I felt bad about tonight, though, we blew our friends off for plans of our own. Plans that required a lot fewer clothes.

I was still lying on the bed when Brooklyn returned from the bathroom. She had cleaned herself up already, wearing nothing but a thin dress. I watched as she stood in front of her mirror, slowly combing her hair. The ends of her dress rose up, exposing more and more of her bare thighs.

Damn, I had to look away before I got excited all over again.

"What's wrong, Adam? Did I tire you out?" Brooklyn asked as she checked out the products on the dresser, her fingertips ghosting over the surface. I could see her smirking in the mirror.

"I'm incapable of getting tired when it comes to you." I winked at her, slowly sitting up with the blanket sliding down my bare abdomen. Brooklyn's eyes trailed down before she turned around.

"You know all the right things to say, don't you?" She laughed and shook her head.

"It's easy when you're speaking the truth, Brooklyn darling," I replied, getting up, proud and naked.

"Nope, I will not fall for your sexy voice again." Brooklyn turned around to avoid looking at me.

"So you think my voice is sexy?" I walked past her, my hand squeezing her hip as I passed. I'd learned that she liked that from our mornings in the kitchen.

"No, you sound like a goat," Brooklyn scoffed defensively, but she wasn't very convincing.

"You should really reevaluate if you think my sexy goat voice turns you on."

"I never said that." Brooklyn rolled her eyes.

"More or less."

"You know, I didn't want to bring this up"—she cleared her throat and looked at me seriously—"but I'm starting to feel like I got the short end of our arrangement."

"What do you mean?" I frowned, instantly wrapping a towel around myself.

"Where's the part where I get food?" Brooklyn tilted her head. In my defence, I did bring her chocolate.

"Do you want to go out, Brooky? All you have to do is ask." I smiled.

"Mhm, I deserve some food, and you're paying," she said, getting up and walking to the door, holding it open for me. "You know, since you're leaving for your game tomorrow."

I sighed. I was looking forward to Saturday, but at the same time, I was nervous. The quarter finals were here.

"I'm well aware. What if you become my lucky charm?"

"Me having sex with you won't magically make you score three goals, Adam." Brooklyn rolled her eyes, but her words seemed more like a challenge to me.

"What if it does?"

"Remember that deal Stella made? Score a hat trick, and I'll wear your jersey?" Brooklyn asked, and I frowned, trying to recall Stella and any mention of a hat trick.

"Yeah?"

"Score a hat trick in your next game, and I'll wear whatever jersey you want me to," Brooklyn promised. My eyes lit up.

I knew I'd get my way one day. Seems like it will be sooner rather than later.

"Do you promise, Brooklyn?" I extended my pinky to her.

"I do." She locked her pinky with mine. I pulled her to me and sealed our promise with a quick, stolen kiss.

"I'll get ready, then we're heading out," I promised. "Also, quick question, why haven't you decorated the room?" I asked. The room was exactly as it was when she first arrived. The only difference was the bedding, and that the drawers and such were filled.

I expected Brooklyn to go all out with the decorations. She was free to do as she pleased, except for painting the walls a neon colour—that was my only rule.

"I, uh, just haven't gotten around to it," Brooklyn replied, her gaze following mine around the bare room.

"A nice pop of green here, some photos there, a nice wall decal—" I began to point, but when my eyes landed on her, I noticed she was glaring at me with her arms crossed.

"If I need an interior designer, I'll call you." Brooklyn shoved me out. "For now, go get ready. You owe me dinner."

When I returned downstairs, Brooklyn still wasn't finished. I responded to my grandmother's messages as I waited. Brooklyn descended the stairs, and my eyes were focused on her top. It seemed like crochet. From the front, it looked like a butterfly in soft pinks, purples, and blues. I'm pretty sure the back was just a few strings.

"Oh, shit, did I keep you waiting?" she asked, and before I could answer, she responded, "I don't care, though."

"Your top is beautiful. Did you make it yourself?" I asked, still unable to rip my eyes away.

"How did you know?" Brooklyn's eyes lit up as she looked down at the top too.

"I know you crochet, although you haven't done it lately." I remembered. I was aware of the flowers and other small things she crocheted, but I never knew it extended beyond that.

"Yeah, those Valentine's roses were the last. I just got too busy with books, my tbr was getting out of hand." Brooklyn shrugged and grabbed her water bottle. She was indeed more into books now. I remember one night I walked in on her little private book club with the other girls. I knew it was my cue to leave when they started talking about winged creatures being hot.

"You're good at it," I admitted and led the way to the garage, holding the door open so I could lock up after her.

"Thank you, I finally got to wear it," she said, lookinng over her shoulder with a grin. Her hair swayed aside when she whipped her head to me to wink.

"Come on, if you're nice, maybe I'll even take some photos of you," I hummed and unlocked the car.

"Oh, how benevolent you are, Adam Serra Valle."

For dinner, I took us to our favourite park, where there was a line of food trucks stationed. We had been there a couple of times before and had always loved it. This time wouldn't be any different, plus it had nice scenery if Brooklyn still wanted her photos.

"What do you want?" I asked, looking at the variety of trucks. There seemed to be a new addition to the lineup.

"Let's try the Turkish stand. Zaira mentioned their doner kebab is the best." Brooklyn pointed to the bright red truck. There was a rich aroma coming from it, with a short line ahead of us.

"Hm, okay, let's go." I led the way to the queue. "Do I still need to take your photo?" I looked around.

"Nope, this outfit is going to be better in daylight, on a picnic," Brooklyn said, smoothing her hands down her pants.

"I'm assuming yet another picnic where the boys are excluded?" I raised a brow at her, and she tried to remain stoic but failed when her lips curled into a slight smile.

"In our defence, you'll be out of town for the match." Brooklyn shrugged, hands tucked into her back pockets, giving me the fakest sincere look she could come up with.

"Oh, how convenient." I rolled my eyes playfully.

"I know, right?" She grinned.

We stood in the queue till we got our food, then got seated at one of the vibrant picnic tables. Our food was still steaming hot, so we sipped our drinks slowly. I looked around before my eyes landed back on Brooklyn.

"So, tell me about your shelter work recently. Any new animals?" I asked.

"Oh, yes." Brooklyn's eyes lit up at the mention.

These conversations always made her ten times happier. She immediately started telling me all the updates I had missed out on. I was rooting for a pitbull named Sparkles to get adopted, and it seemed like she did indeed find a new home and was living happily with her new owners. Brooklyn continued to tell me more, and I listened to every last detail.

Our dinner was long finished, the paper tray crumpled along with the tissue, and our bottles were empty, but the conversation kept going. I'm not sure how we ended up on the subject of school, but that's where we landed.

"I'll be right back," I promised, picking up all the items off the table that needed to be disposed of.

I threw our trash in the bin, then headed to the another truck. It was a little late, but luck seemed to be on my side because they were still open.

They sold desserts, and I knew we had to have some. There was only one slice of chocolate cake left, so I had to settle for the birthday cake for the second slice.

I returned to Brooklyn with the slices of cake. I handed her the chocolate and kept the other for myself.

"Dinner and dessert. This better get me off the hook."

"Consider yourself forgiven, Adam." Brooklyn grabbed the fork and dug in instantly.

"Make sure to remove the plastic wrap before eating, you little goblin," I teased, taking my time unwrapping mine.

"So funny." She rolled her eyes.

"Where did we leave off? Oh yes, after graduation," I recalled.

"I honestly can't wait. It's going to be the best summer break," Brooklyn said, a fork full of chocolate cake coming my way. I didn't hesitate to take a bite. The birthday cake was decent, but this chocolate cake—God, it was amazing.

"Don't you have to find a job afterwards?" I wondered, scraping the icing off the cake. Chocolate ganache might just be the only acceptable icing for me.

"Part-time, yes. I still want to get my master's." Brooklyn sighed, the fork pressed against her lips.

She seemed lost in thought suddenly. I could have changed the conversation, but I hesitated for too long.

"At DTU?" I asked. I suppose I'd be there too if I didn't get picked up by a club.

"I sure hope so." Brooklyn sighed. "That will give me an extra year to figure out what I actually want to do."

"I thought you knew?" I frowned. She always knew what to do; she had her life put together—this was news to me.

"Truth be told, I don't know yet. I know my options, but I don't feel pulled towards any of them just yet," Brooklyn explained.

"I mean, if all else fails, you can just live off your parents' estate and work for the shelters," I joked.

"Trust me, if I could earn a liveable wage off those shelters, I would do just that." Brooklyn laughed and shook her head. I didn't see the appeal of the animal shelters too much, but I could tell they truly made her happy.

"I assume the pay is bad?"

"It's mostly volunteering, and when they offer to pay, it feels terrible to take it when you see that they clearly need it," Brooklyn explained.

"What about those advocacy groups for animal welfare? I think they have a proper name, but I remember reading about them or something," I suggested.

I didn't pay too much attention when it came to those chapters in the textbooks, but I could remember a conversation like this between my professor and a student.

"It's high on the list. I'd be happy if I could do that. It's just very competitive," she replied with a pout, picking her nails to avoid having to look at me.

"I'm sure you'll earn it, Brooke. I've seen how passionate you are about it," I assured her, placing my hand over hers. "If anyone can do it, it's gotta be you." I squeezed her hand under mine.

"Thank you, Adam." Brooklyn smiled and looked down at our hands. She could've pulled hers away, but instead, she left it right there as if it belonged with mine.

We arrived late last night. This morning, the coach went easy on us for the preparation of the game. Now it was time for the game. It was time for Carter's usual pep talk that involved food bribing, then we'd run off to warm up.

"Alright, everyone, listen up! We've worked hard to get to this point. We've all made countless sacrifices, and now we show them what it was all for, what we're made of," Carter said. His voice was loud and clear as he stood at the door with his arms crossed, his gaze moving from member to member. "This is the first game in the quarterfinals. Let's remind them who we are," he continued to speak and brought his eyes to mine. "I'm proud to be alongside all of you."

"Remember, we've got the skill, we've got the passion, and we've got each other. Let's show them!" Carter got everyone amped up, even me. I jumped up once I laced my cleats. "Also, if we win, food is on me," he added, and that got every single one of us to whistle and shout.

"Any restaurant?" Kingsley asked.

"Anywhere your heart desires." Carter laughed as he exited the room. One thing about Carter was that he was a man of his word. Last year, after finals, we got a steak dinner.

My phone buzzed, and I looked over to see Brooklyn's text, *Good luck, Adam.*

A smile spread on my face. I got up, chucked my phone into the locker, and looked over at Ibrahim. He gave me a subtle nod, and we walked out together.

The benches were mostly full; these last few games would attract a much larger crowd. I knew there was a huge possibility several scouts hid among the crowd. But I didn't worry about it anymore, I knew I'd give this game my all.

The referee blew the whistle, and the game kicked off with an intense energy that electrified the air. I took my position on the left wing, feeling the familiar rush of adrenaline.

Carter, our reliable striker, was already making daring runs, keeping the opposing defenders on their toes. Ibrahim was right there with me, giving it his all.

I was determined to make an impact in this game. I pushed forward, looking for any and all openings to exploit. I passed the ball to Ibrahim, and he had a shot, but the keeper showed just how great he was.

A swift counterattack from our opponents caught us off guard, and soon the score was 1-0. The game intensified, but we never backed down.

It didn't take long for the breakthrough. A well-timed pass from Dante found me in space, and I made no mistake, slotting the ball past the goalkeeper to give us the lead. The crowd erupted in cheers, and it was one of the sweetest sounds.

The score was now equalised, but not for long.

Determined to regain the lead, we pushed forward relentlessly. This time, Carter left the ball to me when there were too many defenders on him. I didn't waste a single second, I struck with precision, and the ball hit the back of the net neatly. We erupted in celebration.

The halftime whistle blew, and as we regrouped, I couldn't help but feel the excitement coursing through my veins. We were halfway there, but the game was far from over.

I guzzled down my drink and stared at our opponents. Dante threw an arm around me and grinned. "You scored twice, dude, back to back!"

"Keep up the good work, Adam. Who knows, maybe you can score a hat trick in this game," Carter said, patting my back as he walked past me.

If he only knew how badly I wanted a hat trick. I wondered which DTU jersey would look best on Brooklyn. Lost in thought, I realised Carter was now calling for all of us to get into position for the second half of the game.

Chapter thirteen

Brooklyn

|Saturday morning|

I wrapped up my assignments swiftly as I ate my breakfast. I was excited to spend the day with my girls and checked out the group chat.

The girls

We're still on for later, right?

Zaira
Duh, did you find the cards, or do we have to ban you?

Nope, I found them. Both the friends and couples editions

Stella
There's a couples edition? You have that?

Darshini
Yeah, why do you have that?

Pardon me for wanting to add a little spice to the bedroom

Stella
Is it fun?

Yes. I can send you the link

Darshini
Can you send it to me too?

Zaira
Guys, we're planning a picnic here, not your next sexcapades

Stella

Since when did you become so uptight?

Zaira

Since I've been studying all morning and looking forward to a break

Darshini

Fair enough. I need to get started on our food.

I cleaned up a little, then baked the red velvet cookies and brownies I was tasked with. Afterwards, I headed straight to Tails and Whiskers shelter.

Outside, I spotted Rachel.

"What are you doing out here?" I asked, walking over with my hands full.

"Dealing with Marlene." Rachel sighed, rolling her eyes with a quiet sigh escaping her lips.

"She's back?" I groaned inwardly.

Marlene, Jake's girlfriend, was well-meaning but overenthusiastic, often ignoring the animals' boundaries and then complaining when scratched—unlike Mrs. Smith, Jake's mom, and the shelter owner.

"She's inside." Rachel shook her head, tucking her phone away.

"Did I miss anything important?" I wondered, peeking through the glass door, debating whether I wanted to deal with Marlene's presence or not.

She's sweet, just a lot to deal with sometimes, though.

"Nope, Toothless' new parents sent us some photos to show how well she's doing and how loved she is," Rachel gushed, pulling out her phone to share the pictures.

"Toothless?" I asked, trying to recall which pet went by that name.

"Sparkles," she replied, showing me the photos of the toothless pitbull who had recently been adopted. I gasped when I realised the name wasn't due to her dark fur.

"You're calling her toothless? That's so mean." I nudged her.

"Oh, come on, it suits her, doesn't it?" Rachel shook her head, scrolling through the images until she reached the last one, where Sparkles was nestled between her new owners, wrapped snugly in a soft blanket.

"Is this your version of tough love?" I teased.

"I only know tough love, Brooke."

"Who hurt you?" I joked.

"The woman who birthed me." Rachel rolled her eyes.

"Okay, let's head inside before all the animals start plotting Marlene's demise," I suggested, and Rachel's face lit up at the idea.

"And that's a bad thing?" she asked, and I couldn't tell if she was joking or being serious.

"Jake would be sad, Mrs. Smith would be sad, then everyone would be sad. So yeah, it's a bad thing," I reminded her, keeping my voice low as we stood by the door.

"Fine." She sighed, opening the door for me, and we headed inside.

Checking the daily task lists, I greeted Jake. I had my personal to-do list regarding social media, but wanted to see what else I could help with. I wrote my name under the restocking tasks, along with cleaning the kittens' area.

"Hey, I went through the last of the towels, so I put them in the wash," Jake said.

"Oh, then I'll dry them," I promised.

"Thanks, also I unpacked the new ones and put them on the shelf as requested," Jake informed me, going through his personal checklist before walking off.

Lila approached me, and from the look on her face, I knew she was about to ask me for a favour. I put down the clipboard and raised an eyebrow at her.

"Hello, Lila," I hummed, focusing on checking all the responses on the latest Facebook posts I made for the animals.

"Brooklyn, you look great. Did you ace that test?" Lila asked, leaning against the counter, her lashes fluttering playfully.

"I did, yes. How are you?" I asked while lining up the new posts for the upcoming weekend.

"I'm great," she replied.

"What favour do you need this time?" I asked, finally giving her my full attention. Lila had her nails and eyebrows done, which was unusual for her. She's going somewhere.

"Please don't tell me you need first-date suggestions. You know you're asking the wrong girl," I joked. Our interests outside of the shelter differed widely.

"I learned my lesson the first time." Lila rolled her eyes and grabbed a lollipop from the snack jar.

"Hey, that date did score you a second one." I shrugged.

"I'm only teasing. I'm going to be unavailable for the next two weeks, and I spoke to Mrs. Smith, but she hasn't found anyone yet to take over the financial work," Lila began to explain, and I internally groaned. "I could leave it as it is, but after two weeks, it will be a big mess for me to sort through. Could you cover it?" she asked batting her lashes at me. We always tried to have each other's backs, but two weeks was a lot.

"It won't have to be in full detail. I also have some tips to navigate the wonky app, and I'll be available through texts if you need any help," she added.

"It's okay, I can cover it," I told Lila.

"Are you sure? Aren't you super busy with college?" Marlene asked. She was truly sweet, but I knew Lila preferred me to do it.

"Yes, but this is straightforward work. Plus, she'll leave me the notes, and I've helped out before," I assured her with a warm smile. "If I need help, I'll be sure to let you know."

"Okay, I'll be going then." Marlene waved at the others and then turned to leave. "Goodbye, Gorgeous."

Gorgeous, the cat, hissed at Marlene, and she just pouted as Jake led her outside.

"Thank you so much. I'll owe you two weeks of work," Lila said the moment the door closed.

"I'll be sure to cash it in." I winked.

"I know. I just hope this vacation is worth it," Lila said as she scooted next to me and started up the laptop to get her work done.

"Ah, so that's why you have the pretty nails, lashes, and brows," I realised and smiled at her.

"Duh." Lila flipped her hair over her shoulder. "Did you think I'd wax my eyebrows just to rot away at home?"

"What if she finds someone abroad and doesn't come back? How will you get your two weeks of work compensated?" Rachel asked as she returned with the brush gloves that the dogs loved.

She was saying it to stir up some drama, and I was totally here for it.

"Rachel, don't put ideas in my head." Lila smirked, then turned to me with her sweet look. "Even if I find a gazillionaire, I'll be sure to do my two weeks' duty."

"That makes me feel so much better. Make sure the gazillionaire donates to us."

I straightened up and focused on my tasks, joking with the others here and there. There was a slight window of free time that I spent with a kitten in my lap as I finished up my last college assignment for the weekend.

Finishing up my shift, I made my way to the cats first.

"Hey, Millie girl, I'll be going now, okay?" I petted the little ginger, feeling her rub her face against my hand. I continued to gently scratch her head, her soft purring making me smile.

"Okay, girly, I have to tell the others goodnight too," I explained, scratching her head one last time.

I said my goodbyes to all of them, including the dogs.

Once I was dressed, I packed up the desserts, grabbed the sparkling wines from the fridge, and then went to pick up Stella. The entire car ride was filled with our terrible singing to break-up songs we didn't even relate to, but it was everything I could have wished for.

"The others are there," Stella pointed out.

I spotted Zaira's silver car. The parking lot was less vacant than I thought it would be, but then again, it was the perfect day and weather to be outside.

"There's an open spot near them. I'll park there," I said, turning off my blinker and driving towards the others. "Don't jump out while I'm driving," I warned Stella.

"I don't jump out while someone drives. I jump out when they take too long to park," Stella mumbled.

"Not everyone's boyfriend has a self-driving car, Stella." I smirked as I parked the car.

"Not everyone has a boyfriend either," Stella said so fast I had to pick up my jaw from hell. What a damn shock.

"I hope you bite into a ball of allspice when eating," I scoffed, and Stella gasped at my words.

"You evil little cursing witch," Stella said as she already had the door open. I didn't even get a chance to put the car in park.

Darshini stood at the side, removing her sunglasses as she looked between the two of us.

"What did she do?" Darshini asked and moved aside further.

"She wished for me to bite into allspice," Stella was quick to say, and Darshini looked at me in horror. You'd think I put a curse upon Stella's firstborn, but perhaps it's close to being the same.

"Oh, that's cruel. What did she do?" Zaira finally asked, understanding that a story has two sides.

"She said 'not everyone has a boyfriend' after talking smack about my parking," I defended myself, putting the car in park, then turning the engine off.

Zaira and Darshini shared a look, then their eyes dropped down to the ground.

"Well, you don't have a boyfriend, and you just parked rather close to the line," Darshini pointed out. I looked at my side and noticed I was indeed almost touching the line.

"I don't listen to people who don't drive," I decided, looking at Darshini.

It was no secret that Dante had a dual role as a boyfriend and personal chauffeur.

"Come on, my fellow passenger princess, let's walk away from the jealous ones." Darshini reached for Stella's hand. I smirked, knowing she couldn't say anything to defend herself in this case.

"I think everybody's just hangry." Zaira rolled her eyes, taking a step back as the other two passed her.

The spring sun shone brightly over our heads, and we spread out the pink chequered blanket on the green grass. Colourful flowers in full bloom surrounded us and painted the meadow quite vibrantly. There was a gentle breeze in the air that carried the scent of the fresh flowers.

We set up under a nice tree that provided just enough shade for us to enjoy the sun as well. Our food and drink were all laid out nicely. The stack of card games on the sides and empty wine glasses with a little heart in the middle of the stem. The birds were chirping in the distance, and there were others on their own picnic that chattered—all that created a nice soothing sound to the scene.

Zaira was kind enough to take pretty pictures of me with my butterfly top. It was far better during the day with the spring flowers blossoming and the gorgeous sky as my backdrop.

Zaira was right, we were all hungry. The moment we finished our first plate, everyone was smiling again, and life felt good.

"What shall we play first?" I asked, plating my snacks like the others did.

"Truths, more truths, and dares." Darshini pointed to the middle of the stacked games.

"You brought the couple edition too?" Zaira frowned as she grabbed both versions.

"Yeah, you can take a look before buying," I said, looking at Stella. Zaira and Darshini opened the box and started reading the cards.

Darshini laughed, showing Stella the card that read *Act out your first kiss with me*. They continued to shuffle through them.

I noticed Zaira was acting less enthusiastic than usual, so I asked, "How are you?"

"It's really stressful when your rival also happens to be your boyfriend." Zaira responded.

"I can only imagine, but I've seen the time and effort you put in. I'm sure you'll get what you deserve," I assured her, bringing my hand to hers and squeezing.

"Thank you. You will join us for the finals, right?" Zaira asked, and the mention of the finals got the other girls' attention.

"Yeah, you have to come," Darshini said, leaving no room for me to even consider it. "We already made our list of stores we'll visit and food vendors," she continued.

It might be the boys' big night, but we always made sure we enjoyed the finals weekend as much as possible. We always attended together, and I wasn't planning on breaking tradition.

"Oh yeah, and I found the perfect place for us to stay. It's the break we deserve before our finals," Stella continued, and I was already seduced.

Stella and Carter always picked the best spots. Any trip planned by them required very little thinking for me.

"What do you say?" Zaira nudged me.

"Of course, I'll go. FOMO will get the best of me if I don't," I said, picking some green grapes.

"You can say you love us, we already know." Stella rolled her eyes.

"Of course, I love you girls, always seeking my love and validation." I nudged her back.

We soon started our games, but it led to us just ranting and snacking. It made our picnic all the better. We spoke and laughed so much, it was lovely. I cherished days like these, especially when I knew I didn't have any chores or assignments waiting for me. Once this was done, I'd go home, shower, and plant my face down onto my bed.

I noticed my mom was calling as we were packing up. I excused myself, and once I was out of their earshot, I answered the phone.

"Hello, Mom."

"Hello, Brooklyn. It's like you forget you have parents sometimes," Mom scoffed upon my answer. It was a two-way street. For a while, I had always been the one reaching out, but they would never see that.

"I was busy with school and the shelter. How have you been?" I answered shortly, crossing one arm over my chest as I listened. They never called without a reason, so I wondered what it might be.

"Great, your dad and I have some free time with the whole renovation and all, so we were thinking of visiting you," Mom responded.

Shit. I never told them about the apartment—we just didn't talk often.

"Oh, uh, now is not—"

"You always complained we didn't have time, so we figured we'd come by now," Dad added, joining the call. It was a little too late now.

"Oh, uhm, well..." I stuttered, trying to think of how I could get them not to come, but I couldn't figure out anything. "Yeah, I can't wait to see you guys. Let me know when you're coming," I lied.

"In two weeks," Dad replied and immediately asked, "You graduate this year, yes?"

"Yes, Dad," I replied, trying not to be hurt by the simple question.

"Have you given our idea much thought?" Mom asked.

"Yes," I answered, feeling bitterness take over.

"And?"

"We'll talk more when you guys come." I ended the conversation shortly. "I'm out in public, so I have to go now. Enjoy your evening," I added politely before ending the call and taking a deep breath.

Fuck, how was I going to explain my living situation to them without them throwing their bribes in my face? No, I could show them I could do it without them. Two weeks was enough time to mentally prepare for them.

"Are you okay?" Darshini's hand rested on my shoulder, startling me. I turned to her and nodded.

"Was it your mom?" Darshini asked. Over time, I had told her about my situation with my parents. She didn't know the full story, but she knew more than anyone else.

"Yeah." I sighed, tucking my phone away.

"Did they ask you about the clinic again?" Darshini asked, rubbing my back as she looked at me, her amber eyes softening.

"More or less. They'll be coming to town in two weeks." I sighed, noticing the others had packed everything up and were walking towards us.

"What for?" Darshini frowned.

"I'm not sure, and that worries me."

"I'm sorry, Brooks." Darshini gave me a quick hug.

"Everything okay here?" Zaira asked, holding the basket by her hip.

"Yes, in two weeks I'll have two people questioning everything about my existence," I muttered, taking my bag from Stella.

"Your parents?"

"Yeah," I confirmed, leading the way back to our cars before it became too dark.

"I'll be sure to send you cute cat videos," Stella promised. Of course, those would cheer me up. Stella could be sweet like that. She even made Pinterest boards for each one of us, and I've been looking at mine quite often, especially when I can't figure out what to wear.

"Come on, two weeks is far away. Let's all enjoy our Saturday night." Zaira threw an arm over my shoulder and pulled me closer to her. "We're grabbing ice cream on the way home."

"I like the way you guys think." I laughed. It might be temporary, but I felt better about the situation.

"We happen to be quite intelligent indeed," Stella quipped, kicking a pebble out of her way.

"Should we address the alien po—smut book Brooke suggested or not?" Darshini asked, and the two others refrained from laughing. Of course, the one time I suggest a book without reading the synopsis, this happens.

"Hey, I didn't know it was an alien romance story," I swore, but it was no use. They never stopped teasing, not even after we had gotten our ice creams. "It was still a good book, though."

After dropping Stella home, my night went exactly as planned: crackers with far too much cheese, a hot shower, and my comfiest PJs. I read my book, even as my phone buzzed distractingly. I stared at it for a moment, the curiosity getting the best of me. I opened Adam's message *'scored a hat trick, baby'*

One photo.

I opened the photo to see the scoreboard. There were three timestamps next to his name. Hat trick.

Let me know which colour and size you prefer. My personal favourite is the second one.

Adam sent three photos of the different jersey options DTU had. Fuck, he actually scored a hat trick.

I had to hold up my end of the deal. I groaned and threw my phone to the other side of the bed. I closed my eyes, but my phone kept vibrating.

Adam

Can't ignore me, Brooklyn baby.

Can I counter this offer by promising not to remind our friends about your Winnie-the-Pooh phase?

No. My name and number will be on your back, Brooke.

Fine. The second option is to do a size small. I'll be cropping it. I might as well make it as fashionable as possible.

|Sunday evening|

My plans to stay home were disrupted because I added the wrong address for the cat food to be delivered. I meant to have it delivered to the shelter, but instead, it came to Adam's house. Adam had just gotten back home and was in the garage with me.

"Congrats on the game," I said, walking to the back of my car.

"Thanks," he said, watching as I arranged my trunk.

"I thought you'd have my shirt already," I teased, looking over to see him smirking now.

"I know you're extra, so I put in a special request for the number and such to be in golden glitter, so I will have to wait an extra day." He might just know me too well, then.

"Of course, I spoke too soon." I laughed and walked over to grab the bags of cat food. I started off with the lighter bags, praying to everything holy that my back wouldn't act out in the morning.

"Where are you going with those?"

"Tails and Whiskers," I answered and walked to the rest of the pile. "I put in the wrong address—it's a whole thing, but I have to drop these off."

"You're gonna pull a non-existent muscle, Brooks," Adam teased, walking over to me. I held onto the bag as he tried to tug away. "Let me help you," Adam said and pulled the bag, but I still didn't let go.

"I can handle it." I narrowed my eyes at him.

"I know, baby," Adam said, and I felt something melt inside me, my grip loosened. "But why work hard when you can have men doing it for you?" He winked and lifted the bag effortlessly.

He had to show off and carry two.

"You make a compelling case," I muttered, watching as he carried the bags for me.

"Damn right." Adam smiled and shut the trunk. "Grab the keys and let's go." Adam circled around to the driver's side.

"Where are you going?" I frowned, pressing the unlock button on the fob.

"I'm going with you so I can help you put those wherever they belong," Adam said, already climbing into the car.

"Oh, you don't have to."

Why would he bother? He had a game last night, he should be resting.

"I want to. Maybe you can show me the cute little kittens," Adam said sheepishly.

"All the kittens are adopted or grown," I said, watching as he rolled his eyes at the bad news.

"The one time I can go there isn't any," he scoffed and shook his head. He pulled the seatbelt over his body, making it clear to me he wouldn't budge.

"Come on, there's a cute golden retriever, though." I sighed and got into the passenger's side.

I put in the directions to the shelter, and when we arrived, we greeted Mrs. Smith. Adam brought in all the bags of cat food and was given a tour by Mrs. Smith. Adam petted all the animals that allowed him to.

He was gushing about the animals, and of course, he loved the mischievous golden retriever, Oakley. They shared the same personality after all. Mrs. Smith rewarded us with a lollipop each, then we returned to the car.

"What are your dinner plans?" Adam asked.

"I don't know, probably takeout. Yours?" I replied, putting my lollipop in my bag for later.

"The new movie from *The Enchanted Isles* is out," Adam mentioned, showing me the announcement on his phone. We finished catching up on the series just a week ago. "We can go watch it and grab some dinner afterwards," he suggested.

"Is it my treat for being your lucky charm?" I teased, hoping to score a free dinner. I think I deserve it just this once.

"Oh, so now that it can be in your favour, you'll accept that you're my lucky charm?" Adam put down his phone and raised a brow at me.

"Business, Adam, business." I winked.

"What's next? My wallet?" he scoffed and started the engine.

"It was a hat trick... Three separate favours in return for me."

I kept my eyes locked on his blue ones and extended my hand out to him. It was meant as a joke, but Adam sighed and retrieved his wallet, placing it in my palm.

"What now, Brooke?" he teased.

I stared at his wallet, and I saw a neon colour peaking out. I couldn't resist. I looked past the bills and paid attention to the several cards he had and multiple punch cards to a frozen yogurt place, but what caught my attention was a credit card that had a cancelled Uno card cover. No, there were two of them!

"Who needs this many cards?" I raised a brow at him.

"One's for using, one's for savings, one's for travelling, and the rest is just for existing purposes," he explained, pointing to each one of them.

"These all have separate pins?"

"Nope, 0-6-2-4 all of them," Adam answered, surprising me.

"Do you have no sense of security?" I asked him to stuff his cards back into his wallet. It was a damn surprise he even locked the doors at night at this point.

"I do, but I trust you." Adam smiled.

Hearing him admit he trusted me brought a smile to my face. I never would've thought those words would sound so nice, but they did. Adam had a kind heart and a charming smile with dimples—that was all I needed.

"0-6?" I asked, referring to his choice of PIN. I knew the 24 was for his birthday, but the 0-6 seemed random.

"Lucky number." He shrugged, watching me.

It surprised me that his information never got stolen. As I slid his credit card back in place, I found his student card and laughed at the awful photo.

"Hey, no, give that back." Adam reached over as I pulled out my phone.

I tried to take a photo of the card, but Adam kept fighting me for it. When he was about to lose, he started to tickle my side till my grip loosened.

"You're so mean. You want to ruin my perfectly polished, handsome man identity," he complained, hiding his card.

"Come on, you looked so nice with the poofy hair and the four-strand chin beard." I laughed, and Adam narrowed his eyes at me.

"I suggest you put on your seatbelt if you still want me to treat you to a movie and dinner."

"Fine," I obeyed, not because of his tone, but because I actually did want to spend time with him.

"In my defence, it was an old photo."

Chapter fourteen

Adam

Monday's practice was as intense as ever, and Coach yelling at us more than usual. With the semi-final and final coming up, we had a week off to prepare. I lost count of how many times he blew his whistle to scream at us.

By the time we finished, it was already 6 PM. We were lucky Coach forgot about the extra fifteen laps he had threatened us with. Dante, Ibrahim, and I stayed on the field for cleanup duty. It would have been quicker if Dante and Ibrahim hadn't decided to kick the ball around, but I didn't mind watching.

"We should go out to dinner," Dante suggested, picking up the last few cones.

"Yes! Just the four of us," Ibrahim added almost immediately. Lately, we've only been spending time on the field. It had been a while since the four of us had gone out together.

"Think Carter has plans with Stella?" I wondered, glancing between the two of them. Practice seemed to be running later these days, sometimes, we all had plans of our own.

"I don't care. We'll emotionally blackmail him if we have to," Ibrahim said proudly, and I couldn't agree more. We deserved a break and a night out together.

Dante laughed, turning to me. "Sounds perfect. Are you in? Or do you have to go play house with Brooke?"

I rolled my eyes. "Yes actually, we need whiny toddlers, and you two would fit that role perfectly."

"Fuck you." Dante threw a cone at me.

"Time and date? I have a busy schedule, but I can make time for you." I winked, dodging the second one he threw at me.

"What's going on here?" Carter stepped out, eyes narrowed on all three of us.

"Adam and Dante are gonna hook up," Ibrahim said, amused. Carter just shook his head, but he didn't seem too surprised.

"Your sister still makes me very happy, especially since we don't live with you," Dante said, wearing a shit-eating grin. I remember when this was all new, when Ibrahim would accidentally shoot the ball onto Dante's body.

"You're saying this shit on purpose," Ibrahim muttered.

"We're going out to dinner, and you're coming with us," I told Carter.

"It has to be burgers."

"Big fat ones." Ibrahim smiled.

"Let's hurry."

We finished cleaning up and then headed to the locker room. Once we freshened up, we met up at Ibrahim's newest burger spot. I wasn't sure how he kept finding these places, but we were all thankful for it.

"Look at this, smothered in caramelised onions, oozing with sauce," Ibrahim said as he smashed his burger a little, the sauce spilling out. "Just perfection between two buns." He smiled happily and took a huge bite.

"Excuse him while he makes love to his burger." Dante shook his head, handing Ibrahim a napkin.

"I had a shitty lunch. Let me enjoy this as intended," Ibrahim mumbled.

"Okay, Silver Lions won. It's them we're up against," Carter said as he picked up his burger.

"Yeah, they didn't qualify the past few years," I recalled and frowned. "What changed?"

There were ten teams that always came to the top, Silver Lions hadn't been one of them.

"According to the coach, they have a new leader and the new group is just that good."

"Anything we should be worried about?" Dante asked, stealing Ibrahim's fry sauce.

"Nope, but Coach will discuss strategy with us tomorrow," Carter explained, putting my worries at ease. Coach always scouted the other team well, and so far, the strategies he and Carter came up with hadn't failed us yet.

Coach might be a hardass sometimes, but he knew what he was doing. "If we keep playing with the same determination and stay humble, we'll make it to the final."

"Enough soccer talk, all I see now is Coach Mendes and his red face when he yells at us," Dante said.

"Hey, at least we don't have the women's basketball coach," Ibrahim said, using the napkin.

"What's the drama there? I heard something happened?" I asked. Curiosity was in our nature, and any sports drama on campus was meant to be heard.

"Yeah, he was a menace. According to another classmate, he yelled too much and was borderline verbally abusing them," Ibrahim said.

"Is he fired or something?"

"Oh, of course, DTU can't afford scandals. I heard the new coach is nice, though." Carter shrugged. "Good for them, the DTU women's basketball team did far better than the men's."

"Hey, how's living with Brooke?" Dante nudged me, shoving fries into his mouth.

"Really great. She bullies me from time to time, but I like it. I should've gotten roommates sooner." I wondered what she was up to right now.

"Yeah?" Ibrahim asked, narrowing his gaze.

"Yeah. We're learning how to cook together. I love takeout, but I have to be careful about what I put in my body," I continued and felt their heavy stares. I was aware of what I said as I currently devoured a greasy burger.

"You would eat an entire triple chocolate cake in one sitting, don't come talking about 'being careful' what you put in your body," Carter said, laughing with the others.

"See, this is exactly why Brooklyn is better than all of you." I rolled my eyes and chose not to flip him off due to a mother and two children passing by. "She understands my reasoning and knows that chocolate is the only piece of heaven we'll ever know," I scoffed.

"Adam, being a Brooklyn supporter was not on my list of things happening this year," Ibrahim said, amused.

"I'm a changed man," I said proudly.

After dinner with the guys, we parted ways. I returned home, preparing for the night ahead. The house was quiet, but Brooklyn had left some croissants with a small note threatening my existence if I dared to devour them all.

Ignoring the warning, I settled on the couch with three croissants on my plate—less than half of what she made—I liked to think I'd live to see the next day.

Hearing Brooklyn's arrival, I turned the volume down and looked towards the garage door. She let out a long sigh, keys clattering as she made her way inside. She looked tired.

"Rough day, bud?" I teased, earning an eye roll from her.

"Too rough." Brooklyn sighed again, sinking into the seat at the other end of the couch, her hands behind her head.

"What happened?" I asked, concerned.

"I was helping a girl at the shelter with her tasks for the next two weeks. Everything was going smoothly until someone logged in on the computer and accidentally deleted the financial statements and other important data," Brooklyn explained, frustration evident in her voice.

"What? How did that happen?" I frowned, trying to understand the gravity of the situation.

"Mrs. Smith clicked the wrong button, and suddenly I had to play tech support!" Brooklyn groaned.

"Is everything okay now?"

"We couldn't recover the lost data, but thankfully, the other girl had copies of everything. I had to re-enter her data and mine that wasn't backed up," she responded, relief evident in her voice despite the exhausting day.

"Oh, you poor thing." I shook my head, earning a pillow thrown in my direction.

"I need a drink," she mumbled.

"I think there should still be some vodka and our dear friend Jack," I suggested, nodding towards the liquor cabinet. Though it wasn't as stocked as it had been in December, there were still a few bottles left.

"I start class late tomorrow, you?" Brooklyn asked, her expression indicating that we would both be indulging in a well-deserved drink.

"Same." Only one class and a boatload of practice awaited us tomorrow. "Jack?" I asked, already heading to the liquor cabinet. Turning back to her, I awaited her response.

"Sure." She shrugged. "How was practice?"

"Same old, same old. I brought burgers, they're in the microwave," I said, grabbing the bottle.

"I'll freshen up quickly, then I'll have that drink with you," she promised, heading upstairs.

Returning to my seat on the couch, I noticed the last half of my croissant was stolen. Damn, she's fast. I set the bottle down with two glasses next to it.

I patiently waited for her, knowing I left a small gift on her bed.

A few minutes later, Brooklyn came back downstairs. My jaw nearly hit the floor. She was wearing one of the gifts—I got her two jerseys with my name in two different sizes.

She wore the oversized jersey, curls up in a bun, skin dewy from the shower—she was effortlessly beautiful like this. She had that confident, proud smirk on her lips, leaving me speechless.

"What do you think?" Brooklyn struck a pose with one hand on her hip, smiling.

"Twirl around," I said, moving my finger in a circular motion. Brooklyn rolled her eyes but still obliged, giving me a full 360. My eyes trailed up and down her body. "Absolutely stunning," I complimented.

"Thank you." She smiled, taking a seat next to me.

I leaned over to grab the bottle and poured our whiskey.

"Oh, and Adam?" Brooklyn called my name so sweetly.

I knew this meant trouble. Nothing good ever came when she called me like this. I almost spilled some whiskey.

"Yes?" I looked over at her, handing her one of the whiskey-filled glasses.

"I'm not wearing anything underneath this, you know," she informed me, bringing the brim of the glass to her lips.

"God have mercy on me," I whispered to myself, my eyes taking in her bare thighs. I knew just how soft they were, and I loved how they'd quiver when I was between them. Brooklyn cleared her throat, and I stopped staring. "That's good, Brooke, so good," I said, avoiding eye contact and focusing on sipping my whiskey.

Brooklyn sipped her drink, eyeing me. I knew that look in her eyes. Her gaze lingered on my thighs in particular. She had commented on the muscles more than once. Her eyes were still glued on them. I hoped I read her eyes right and that it was desire swirling within them.

"Interested in a ride of some sort, Brooke?" My tone was casual, watching as her lips parted for a moment.

"What?" she asked, her tone was excited, but I could tell there was some scepticism in it. Lucky for her, I never joked about these things—especially when it comes to her.

"Take your panties off and come sit that pretty pussy on me." I patted my thighs as I looked at her.

"I'm not wearing any, remember?" She smirked and put her drink aside. She swayed her hips as she walked over to me.

I sank into my seat, spreading my legs as I looked up at her.

"You came prepared."

Brooklyn straddled me and placed her hands on my chest. The jersey rode up a little, my eyes lingered down, but Brooklyn placed a finger under my chin and forced me to look into her eyes. The gold and hints of green dancing in those eyes, every glance of hers left me enchanted. This moment wasn't any different.

Brooklyn leaned over and kissed me, the whiskey from her last sip was faint as I kissed her back. It didn't take long for the hunger and passion to overtake us, her fingers were in my hair, guiding me through the kiss as she pleased. I opened my mouth, allowing her to do as she pleased while my hand snuck under her jersey.

"Fuck, Adam," Brooklyn moaned against my lips when I stroked her clit. She rolled her hips, seeking friction from my fingers, and I let her.

I pulled my hand away, and Brooklyn glared at me, "What?"

"Ride my thigh instead, baby," I murmured, guiding her.

Brooklyn didn't resist, not once. I slid my hands under her shirt, feeling the warmth of her skin, tracing the curves of her body. "Take what you want, Brooklyn," I whispered, leaning in to kiss her neck.

Brooklyn moaned, tilting her head back as I continued to kiss and nibble at her skin. Her hands gripped my shoulders, nails digging into my skin as she slowly began to move her hips. I could sense her initial hesitation, but as she found her rhythm, any trace of shyness vanished.

"Oh, fuck," she breathed as she found her perfect rhythm, her movements growing more urgent. I cupped her breasts under her shirt, my thumbs teasing her nipples, eliciting sweet sounds from her.

With a need of my own, I lifted her shirt just enough to expose her left breast, bringing my lips to her nipple. My tongue swirled around it, and I felt Brooklyn's nails dig deeper into my skin. Brooklyn started moving faster, one hand in my hair that held my face buried in her breast—not that I wished to be elsewhere right now.

Her body trembled against mine as she reached her peak, her breath coming in ragged gasps. I held her close, feeling the heat of her skin against mine, savouring every moment of her release as she chanted my name in a soft whisper. Her movements slowed down, and her head tipped back, her fingers grazing the back of my neck in a gentle caress.

Brooklyn took a deep breath and gently pushed me away from her chest, her hands caressing my face as she looked at me. She kissed me briefly, my fingers threading through her hair as I guided her through the kiss.

"You made a mess on me, Brooke," I whispered against her lips. Brooklyn pulled away and sat right next to me, her fingers tracing a path down my chest.

"Do you want me to clean it up?" she asked sweetly as her hand continued down. "Or would you rather I take care of this, Adam?" she asked, cupping my rock-hard dick through my pants, giving me a gentle squeeze.

Fuck.

"Definitely that." I nodded desperately.

When it came to this, Brooklyn was incredible. She knew just how much it affected me, and understood the power she and that perfect mouth of hers held.

"The cleanup?" she asked, moving to sit between my legs. I narrowed my eyes at her; she knew damn well what I wanted. "Oh, you mean you want me to take this perfect cock down my throat?" She palmed my cock once again and looked up at me.

"Yes, please," I asked, not hesitating to express my desire. A smile curled on her lips. I tossed my shirt aside and then helped her tug down my pants.

"What do I get in return?" she asked, slowly pumping my cock with her soft, perfect hand.

"I'll pleasure you wherever you want, however you want," I offered, tracing the path down her jawline, then tipping her chin forward. I leaned down and kissed her, her fingertips grazing over my tip, eliciting a soft groan from me.

"Get to work, Brooklyn," I whispered against her lips, then pulled away.

Brooklyn kept her eyes on me as she darted her tongue out. I groaned softly as I felt her tongue circling around my head, her hand continuing the slow pumping motion. She wrapped her lips around the tip completely, and my hand moved to her hair.

As Brooklyn went down on me, I felt a surge of pleasure ripple through my body. She let her tongue tease my tip while her hands caressed my thighs. Her mouth and touch were electrifying and sent shivers down my spine. I tangled my fingers in her hair, urging her on as she took me deeper. Her tempo picked up, and with each movement, she took more of me until her nose brushed against my abdomen.

"Fuck," I whispered, throwing my head back as she continued to take me deep and fast.

Every flick of her tongue, every gentle suck sent waves of pleasure coursing through me, building higher and higher. I could feel the tension coiling within me, the sweet anticipation of release.

Brooklyn moaned with my cock in her mouth, her nails grazing over my abs and down my thighs. It didn't take long for me, not when Brooklyn was the one driving me insane right now.

With a guttural groan, I gave in to the overwhelming sensation. My body trembled with ecstasy as I came. It was like a wave crashing over me, intense and all-consuming. I closed my eyes, lost in the moment, and Brooklyn continued to work her magic, prolonging the pleasure until I couldn't take it anymore.

I looked down at her, gently tugging at her hair. She pulled away and swallowed every drop I had to offer. A proud smirk on her lips.

"You're so fucking incredible," I said as I pulled her up and slammed my lips to hers. She wrapped her arms around me and kissed me with just as much hunger. I switched our position and placed her under me, breaking the kiss so we could breathe.

"I'm well aware." She winked, looked around, then pointed to my left. "Can you grab my drink for me? Wouldn't want to waste it."

I stared at the glass, a mischievous smirk playing on my lips. I picked up the glass with deliberate slowness, my eyes never leaving hers. As I brought the glass to my lips, I took a sip of the whiskey, savouring the rich, smoky flavour that flooded my senses.

Without breaking eye contact, I leaned in closer to her, one hand gently wrapping around her neck, pulling her towards me. My hand then moved up, my thumb teasing at her bottom lip.

With a wicked grin, I pressed my lips to hers, sharing the taste of the whiskey between us. Then, with a playful twist, I pulled back slightly, my lips parting as I continued to let the whiskey spill from my mouth into hers.

She made a quiet sound, surprised at first, before the excitement took over. Without hesitation, her mouth opened a little wider, eagerly drinking up every last drop of the whiskey I had to offer her.

"You're so fucking weird." Brooklyn laughed and pulled me over to kiss.

"You're even weirder for allowing me," I muttered against her lips, groaning when she bit at my lip.

"Your bed, from behind," she said as she kissed down the side of my neck. Her tongue swirled over the spot under my neck.

"What?" I tried making sense of what she said, but she then sank her teeth into my skin. I closed my eyes and let out a soft moan as she did it again.

"My requests," she repeated, and I finally understood I still had a price to pay.

"Oh yes," I hissed and slowly got up, holding her in my arms. "The shirt stays on, yes?" I asked as I wrapped her legs around my waist.

"Fine, just fuck me already," Brooklyn whined.

I chuckled and placed her on my bed. She looked good sprawled over my bed, wearing only a shirt. Her pussy glistening, a warm welcome just for me. I climbed on top and kissed her briefly, then pulled away.

"Quit stalling, Adam," Brooklyn whined against my lips, my fingers tugging at the hair tie until it freed from her hair.

"Yes, ma'am." I chuckled. I flipped her around, my hands trailing down to her hips. I pulled her hips up, my knee sliding between her legs to part them further. I reached for her hands and brought them behind her knees. "Keep these here."

I smoothed my hand over her ass, admiring the sight in front of me. She bared it all to me in this position, her sweet cunt begging for it. I dragged two fingers down to her clit and began to rub her at a leisurely pace. Brooklyn moaned and pressed herself against me, wiggling to get more.

"How much longer will you make me wait for your cock?" she asked, pressing her cheek into the mattress.

"Is this not enough?" I teased and started rubbing her clit. That got her attention for sure; she moved with need against my fingers, desperate for more.

"Do it or I'll find someone else, Adam," Brooklyn whined.

"Fuck, I love your empty threats. Tell me more." I chuckled, settling behind her and slowly pulling my fingers out.

"Next time I—" Brooklyn's rant was cut off as I entered her. Her curse soon turned into her chanting my name, her voice filling the room with desire.

I had both hands on her ass, massaging her soft flesh as I gave her every last inch of me. Her pussy wrapped around my cock so perfectly that it almost felt as if we were made for each other. The way she surrounded me, the way my name rolled off her tongue—it was almost too much to bear, but I held back. I savoured every last moan and cry of hers.

I pulled out till she only had the tip, then slammed back into her, giving her everything she was able to take. I repeated, and with each movement, I picked up the pace.

"I'm not hearing much from you, Brooklyn darling," I teased, spanking her ass.

"Sh-shut up," she sassed, and I'm pretty sure she was rolling her eyes at me. There was just something about her that filled me with pride when I had her stuttering and a mess beneath me.

"Do you want me to stop too?" I asked, slowing down the thrusts. She whipped her head to me and narrowed her eyes.

"Don't you fuck—" I interrupted her again by picking up the slack. I started thrusting into her with more urgency, the desire burning hotter and hotter. Her moans grew louder, more desperate, driving me to go faster, harder.

Her release was building up little by little. In the short time we've spent together, I've learned so much about her body already. I learned what every little cry, moan, and whimper meant, and right now I was on the right track.

"Fuck, Adam, don't stop," she begged, her voice filled with need.

I kept the pace just the same for her, everything remained just the same, and her moans were my green light. I struck my hand on her ass, a soft "oh god do it again" followed from her lips, and I fulfilled her wishes.

I trailed a finger to her other hole, her body tensed, and squeezed me so hard I could barely control myself. My finger circled her hole, my thrusts continuing at the same speed. "Tell me, Brooke, has anyone ever been here?"

"N-no," Brooklyn replied, stuttering as she pushed herself further against me.

"Do you ever want anyone here?" I asked out of curiosity, my thumb continuing to trace the circles.

"Maybe, you?" she said in between deep breaths.

"Fuck, Brooke," I moaned. Her words were enough to push me over the edge, but I tried to prolong this for both of us. We'll revisit this conversation another day. I took one hand of hers and placed it between her legs. "Rub your clit, baby."

I quickened my pace, thrusting into her harder and faster, lost in the rhythm of our bodies moving together. The sound of our skin slapping together filled the room, mixing with her moans of pleasure.

Brooklyn cried out as she reached her own climax, her body trembling with pleasure beneath me. The sensation of her tightening around me, her walls gripping me so perfectly, was almost too much to bear.

I couldn't hold back much longer, not when she was squeezing the sweet life out of me. With one final thrust, I felt the tension within me snap. I released, and every muscle in my body tensed with the force of my climax as a flood of pleasure drowned me. It was pure bliss for me.

I slowly pulled out and went to lay down next to her, my breaths were laboured as I tried to calm down. I looked over at her, and she just smiled and leaned over and pecked my lips.

Once Brooklyn calmed down, she sat up and winked at me. "Good job, bud."

"This bud thing is starting to annoy me," I complained, placing my hands behind my head as I looked at her.

"That's the meaning of it, bud." She smirked and walked off. My jersey was on her body, and my name and number on her back.

"Hey, where are you going?"

"Shower and sleep?" she replied as if I should've known that already.

No cuddles, no hugs, no sweet talks. Those were the rules.

"Of course," I replied and watched as she walked away.

After getting ready for the night—again, I put on my clean PJs and went downstairs. I made two mugs of hot chocolate, added some marshmallows, and a drizzle of caramel syrup. I stopped by Brooklyn's room and knocked on the door.

"Come in," she hummed. I stepped into the bedroom, and Brooklyn stood by the mirror, braiding her hair for bed.

"Here you go." I placed the mug on the desk next to her.

"Thank you," she said and looked over at the mug, her face lit up immediately. "Aww, you remembered the caramel, thank you."

"You're welcome, have a good night," I said, and without thinking, I kissed the top of her head. That wasn't part of our routine—not at all. It was weird for a moment, but the good kind.

"Yeah—uh, you too," Brooklyn replied, her brows furrowed a little.

Chapter fifteen

Brooklyn

I was up far too early only because the girls guilt-tripped me last night into baking them doughnuts. Now I waited in the kitchen for the doughnuts to cool down so I could continue with them.

I tasted a bit of the fresh raspberry jam filling—Perfect. The entire house was enveloped in a sweet, fruity aroma. I even made Adam's morning smoothie. His rested in his cup while mine was in a bowl.

"Why are you up so early? We don't have to leave for like another hour," Adam asked, rubbing his eyes, followed by a yawn and a stretch.

He looked adorable in the morning. His slightly puffy face, messy blond strands, and groggy voice—it did something to me.

"I promised the girls doughnuts last night," I explained as I sprinkled some granola bits mixed with cacao nibs into my smoothie. I left out the part where they emotionally blackmailed me into it. He can't know I have a soft heart.

"Just the girls?" Adam asked, jealousy evident in his tone.

"Of course, I automatically made some for the rest of you too." I rolled my eyes. "Here's your smoothie." I scooted his glass towards him.

"Thank you. Did you add the new protein?"

"Mhm, right after I poured out mine," I assured him. I tried it with the protein before, but I didn't like it. Adam keeps saying it's great. I'm sure he's just lying to himself, though.

"I'll go get ready, see you soon."

I finished my smoothie while watching an episode of my comfort show. By the time the episode was finished, I was back in the kitchen, filling the doughnuts with the jam and brushing a sugar coating on the top.

Once the doughnuts were all packed up, I sent a drool worthy photo of them in the group chat, then ignored every following message afterwards. It's fun leaving them in a little suspense.

I was running late and had to rush, but still, I wasn't done yet. I adjusted the sage coloured shirt to tuck into the beige cargo pants. It felt like I was copying *Shaggy*, but it was too late to go back.

I pressed my lips together as I did a final evaluation in the mirror. Perhaps some butterfly clips to hold back my hair on the sides.

There was a knock on the door followed by Adam's voice, "Brooklyn, we've got to go."

"I'm coming," I said as I hastily put in the clips.

"Baby, I haven't even touched you yet," Adam said smoothly. I couldn't see him right now, but I knew exactly what smirk he had on his face. I smiled and shook my head at his words.

"You're too old for those jokes, Adam," I shouted back.

"I'm serious, though, are you ready?" he asked.

I didn't answer him verbally, instead, I just stepped out. He looked at me from head to toe, then gave me a subtle nod.

We drove straight to campus and went to our friends at the picnic table. Ibrahim was talking about something intriguing because he had everyone's attention. When his eyes darted over to us, he grinned. "Look who finally came."

"With treats too." Zaira rubbed her hands together, her loving gaze no longer reserved for just Ibrahim but the box in my hand as well.

I placed the box in the middle of the table and sat down between Stella and Darshini. Stella wrapped her arms around me in a tight hug. "Brooklyn, you are the best."

"I love you so much right now, the cafeteria shut down," Darshini said and leaned over to grab a doughnut.

"What? Why?" I frowned. This explains why we came across three students complaining about being hungry.

"I don't know! The one time I didn't pack any food, they decided to shut down." Darshini rolled her eyes.

"Oh my poor child, the horrors you've faced," I teased, pulling her to me as I wrapped an arm around her and patted her head.

"You guys have your tickets for the flight and game, right?" Carter asked, mouth dusted with sugar from the doughnut.

"Yep, we arrive Friday, so you better win the semi-final so our Saturday final tickets don't go to waste," Zaira answered, swatting Ibrahim's hand when he tried to steal her doughnut.

I'm glad the doughnut was worthy of starting fights between partners.

"It won't go to waste," Adam said self-assuredly, and Dante agreed with him.

"Good, because I got a new jersey because of you guys," I said.

"We should get you girls some pom-poms," Dante joked. "More cheering, more motivation to win," he gave his supposed logic behind it.

Ibrahim seemed to think of it as anything but a joke because he was looking at Zaira a certain way.

"Buy me pom-poms and I will shove them down your throat." Zaira narrowed her eyes at him.

"There are people at the table. Why are you dirty-talking to me right now?" Ibrahim smirked as he looked at her. Zaira opened her mouth to speak, but was unable to utter words.

"You guys disgust me," Dante disapproved with his nose scrunched up.

We changed the conversation soon, enjoying every last doughnut till the box had been neatly disposed of. We all parted ways when classes started, but Darshini and I already made plans to meet up after class. We were out the earliest out of them all.

Once the last class was over, I rushed out to meet Darshini in the parking lot. It was funny to see her in the driver's seat, she was rarely there.

"Should we grab lunch first?" I mentioned, pulling the seat belt over my body. Perhaps I'll need it extra.

"Yeah, I don't like that the cafeteria is still closed," she said as she adjusted the AC.

"I hope it doesn't shut down, I still have lunch credit from that quiz I won," I groaned.

I knew I shouldn't have saved up all those credits. I mostly used it for our popcorn and slushies on game days, but lately, the guys have been away from games.

"Really? Those expensive slushies haven't taken it all?"

"No." I laughed.

As planned, we picked up lunch and then headed back to Adam's. We had our food and school supplies laid out for our study session. The first thirty minutes went without getting off topic once. Then one innocent question about a song derailed us.

"We should focus, this internship report isn't going to write itself," Darshini groaned and hit the backspace button several times.

"Did you include the part where they kept praising you?" I raised a brow at her. She and Stella did their internship at the same company with positive results.

"No, but I did put the things I fixed that they couldn't," she said and winked.

"Good," I responded and stared at my own screen. "This presentation will be the death of me," I groaned and gently leaned over until my head rested against the table.

"It can't be that hard. You've made so many great ones already." She leaned over my shoulder and stared at my screen. I was already on slide ten, which was barely 50 percent of what I needed.

"We have to summarise a thirty-page essay. I got feedback on the essay, it was good, but we're not allowed to have a too long presentation," I complained. I then straightened up, "The sooner I hand this in, the sooner I can get back to my book." This was my usual self-motivation, and it tended to work.

"I can't believe we're graduating this year," she muttered.

Time had flown by, and what seemed like a sudden, short time had been filled with so many memories I hoped I'd get to cherish forever.

"I remember being here the first year, whining that these years would take too long." I thought this would be like high school, where I had to be bribed by my grandmother to get to school.

"Mama said that college years would be the best and most carefree ones. I'm not 100 percent sold on the carefree part, but I do believe these were some of my best years." Darshini reached for her iced tea. "High school was such a mess."

"The angstiest years. Thank god my grandma was still alive to hold me back from embarrassing myself." I shuddered at the memories.

"She should've let you wear that tux to prom," Darshini teased, and I knew it was a mistake to show her my initial prom outfit. Luckily, my grandma had my back. It was one of the last fondest memories I had with her. I lost her shortly after, and that dress she picked out with me was carefully wrapped.

"I thought it was cute!" I said defensively, despite knowing I was wrong. I was willing to die on that hill.

"You looked as if you got lost in your father's closet." Darshini laughed.

"Keep talking, and I'll tell everyone how you almost fell into the fountain." I smirked, her clumsiness never failing to save me.

"Hey, that's mean," she scoffed.

As a reward for finishing our assignments, we grabbed ice cream and watched a movie. We didn't get to finish the movie, though, because we both had places to be. Mine was a nap followed by heading to the shelter for some photos.

There were two new cats, Shadow and Misty. I needed to make some content for them, but focused on the photos and petting every dog and cat I could tonight till they got bored with me.

I walked up front where Jake and Marlene were busy on the ancient computer.

"Guess what," Marlene said excitedly, looking at me with a huge grin on her face.

"What's up?"

"I just spoke to my boss and he's interested in donating!" Marlene revealed. Marlene worked at a top-tier art gallery that constantly donated large amounts of money.

This money could help us a lot—I don't even care how they truly got their money.

"Really? Marlene, that's incredible," I admitted, filled with excitement. "The animals will appreciate that!" I looked towards the door that separated us from the animals.

"I'm just glad I can help!" Marlene squealed and hugged Jake.

Marlene's heart was in the right place, always had been. She's just utterly new to these things and can't properly read the animals' feelings just yet. But she was making an effort for them. Over half of these babies were rejected by their owners or lost their owners, taking proper care of them and making them feel loved wasn't as easy, but she'd learn.

"That's truly amazing. I'll be going now, have a great night, you two," I said to them both. Jake looked up for a split second and gave me a subtle nod before he went back to click-clacking on the keyboard.

"You too, Brooklyn." Marlene smiled.

When I got in my car, a pounding headache persisted. I tried to ignore it, but it got worse with every passing second. My phone rang with a notification. When I saw it was my parents, I instantly swiped it away. I wasn't trying to make my headache worse.

All I wanted now was to go home, curl up on the couch.

Chapter sixteen

Adam

I slung my bag over my shoulder, feeling the weight of the exhausting day of practice. Glancing back, I observed some of my teammates, who were messing around on the field. I didn't have cleaning duty tonight, thankfully, and was prepared to leave. With the semi-finals nearing, both Coach and Carter had already immersed themselves in analysis. Tomorrow, we'd meet to dissect their findings.

Carter, already packed up and waiting to lock up, caught my attention. His fatigue mirrored my own.

"Any plans for tonight?" he asked.

"None, man, I'm utterly drained," I answered, shaking my head.

Ibrahim emerged from the changing room, nudging me aside gently as he passed, Dante trailing behind him.

"I'm starving," Ibrahim declared, his hand grazing his stomach.

"Guess what Darshini made for me? Samosas. Warm, filled to the brim, samosas await me at home." Dante smirked, boasting.

"How dare you! I'm tagging along home with you, Dante. I demand my fair share! I'm her brother, I have rights!" Ibrahim's protests continued as he walked behind his friend.

Carter and I exchanged amused glances as Ibrahim followed Dante, his protests fading into the distance.

"Take care, Adam." Carter gave me a nod.

Settling into my car, I checked my messages, disappointment settling in as Brooklyn remained unresponsive. Not even a reply to my offer for dinner.

My calls led nowhere, her phone was set to Do Not Disturb. I was redirected to voicemail.

I sighed, giving in.

"Brooklyn, it's the sexiest man alive speaking, Adam Gabriel Serra-Valle. Who the hell even listens to voicemail in this day and age? Anyway, I can't believe you're ignoring me when I would've bought you whatever dinner you wanted. I'm picking the spot myself, and when I get home, I'm telling you off for being so absent—unless you're not doing okay. You'd better be doing okay. Please tell me you're doing alright."

Ending the voicemail, I put away my phone. Before going home, I made a pit stop to grab us dinner. Arriving home, a sense of relief washed over me at the sight of her car parked in the garage. Perhaps she was indulging in a deep slumber, hence her radio silence.

I pushed the door open. The living room TV was on, and judging by the actor's voices, I knew it was her favourite show playing. I put aside everything and walked over to the living room.

Brooklyn lay there completely curled up, and she wore her beige-coloured shirt. The look on her face wasn't too pretty, she seemed drained. It could be that she was tired, but I had a feeling that wasn't the case at all.

"Is there a reason you're cosplaying as an armadillo?" I teased, marvelling at her tightly wound and curled form.

"Are you in pain? Should I bring you some Ibuprofen and chocolate?" I offered when I realised it might be that time of the month. I noticed she hadn't replied. "You know what, we just bought those chocolate wafers, I think we can finally open them," I continued about the chocolate topic. Let's face it, we both love our chocolate.

"I'm not having my period, Adam." Brooklyn's voice was laced with exhaustion, but she finally turned to face me.

"Oh. Okay." I scratched the back of my head, trying to figure out what to do next. I knew she wasn't having a great time.

"But I wouldn't say no to that chocolate," she conceded softly.

I smiled and went to grab the chocolate.

"Did you lock the door when you came in, Adam?" Brooklyn asked with a hint of worry in her tone.

"I think so."

"Just make sure everything's locked up completely," Brooklyn urged, her concern evident in her tone. Without protest, I gave in, understanding that her peace of mind needed me to do this.

I locked up the house as she asked, then returned to her. I sat down next to her. I gently moved her feet onto my lap and handed her some chocolate. "Your chocolate, madam."

"Thanks," she murmured, tearing into the blue wrapper instantly.

"Brooke, are you okay?" I asked, watching as she took a bite from her chocolate. "I had been texting you like crazy, I even left a voicemail," I told her. I saw her phone on the table. She was obviously ignoring my messages. I didn't demand replies, but after her absence, I was worried, and her behaviour right now wasn't easing that worry.

"Who even bothers with voicemails these days?" she scoffed, wrinkling her nose in disgust.

"That's what I said!" I chuckled, relieved to lighten the mood, if only momentarily.

"Of course you did, I'll have to listen to that voicemail." She finally offered me a bite of the chocolate.

"Mhm, now, care to tell me what happened?" I asked, running my hands up and down her shins, occasionally squeezing her gently.

"Just a headache and a stupid text message," she said. Her eyes never met mine, she only ate her chocolate.

"I'm so sorry that happened to you, Brooklyn," I said sincerely. She sat down next to me, and I moved my arm around her and gently squeezed her shoulder. "Is there anything I can do to make you feel better?" I asked.

I knew she wouldn't tell me who it was, but in the past, it happened twice where she received a message and her mood was soured. I assumed she'd tell me once she's ready.

"I don't know," she said, fidgeting with her hands in her lap.

“Mind if I freshen up?” I asked, the lingering scent of grass and sweat clinging to my skin. “Once I’m back, we can enjoy dinner together and unwind with a movie, or simply sit in blissful silence. Your call.”

“Movie. Thank you.” Brooklyn nodded in agreement, her gratitude palpable.

After a shower, I walked down the stairs and found Brooklyn still engrossed in the show.

“I’ve brought us dinner. Assuming you haven’t eaten yet,” I remarked, retrieving plates from the cabinet. Our collection had transformed since Brooklyn’s arrival, a vibrant array replacing the formerly mundane white dishes. Knowing her preference, I selected the ones adorned with a chequered pattern.

“No, I haven’t. What did you get?” Brooklyn inquired, turning to face me.

“Noodle bowl, with spring rolls on the side,” I confirmed, gesturing towards the familiar bag. Her smile brightened at the mention of her favourite dish.

After reheating our takeout, I brought our meal to the coffee table, steam rising from the tasty food. Fetching two cans of guarana soda, I joined Brooklyn on the couch. She smiled so beautifully, I wished that it was for me and not the food.

“You remembered to ask them to skip the shredded carrots,” she gushed, expertly handling her chopsticks.

“Duh, you whine about it constantly,” I teased, feeling her gaze harden on me.

“You sure know how to ruin a moment, Adam.” She rolled her eyes, her sass hadn’t left—luckily.

“I am the moment, Brooklyn.” I winked, and that earned me a pillow being thrown at me.

“I hate you,” she muttered.

“Lying is a sin.” I carefully booped her nose.

"Do not lecture me on sins, Mr. Walking-talking-sin." Brooklyn laughed, falling back against the plush couch.

"I'm regretting being so benevolent to you." I rolled my eyes and turned my attention to my food. I think it was safe to eat without burning my mouth.

"You learn one word and you abuse it," Brooklyn mumbled, shaking her head.

"That's it, I'm getting extra carrots next time." I smirked. "Also, I found a show to watch. It's about two neighbouring big farmers, and they have a feud."

"Of course, and let me guess, their kids are secretly in love?"

"Even better, the kids loathe each other, but there are hints they'll fall in love." I grinned and began to look for the show.

"What are you waiting for? Put that show on!"

As the show progressed, we shifted position. I sat in the corner with two blankets draped over me, but I was kind enough to hold them open for Brooklyn to scoot under.

She hesitated for a moment, her gaze softening as she gave in. She nestled next to me, and I savoured every moment of it. I wrapped my arm around her, pulling her as close as possible. I caught her subtle yet captivating scent, it was like a garden in full bloom. Reminiscences of peony.

I think that might be my new favourite scent.

"Adam, are you going to play the next episode or not? You're already getting the luxury of cuddling with me," Brooklyn teased, playfully poking my stomach. Shaking myself from my thoughts, I reached for the remote as she nestled closer.

Brooklyn hated cuddling, yet she fit so perfectly with me. She shifted until her head rested on my chest, one hand of hers draped over my torso. Her fingers went up and down my side, and I looked at her, and I noticed her gaze was fixed on the TV. I carefully moved my hand to settle on her lower back, tracing shapes.

It was only cuddling, yet it felt far more intimate than sex—was this why she hated cuddling? Was this comfort terrifying for her?

When the second episode ended, we decided to call it a night, and I turned the TV off, but neither of us wanted to move from the couch. Brooklyn only moved closer to me, her face buried in my chest and her leg entwined with mine. Yep, there's no way we're leaving this couch tonight.

"You looked so giddy when you came in. How was your practice?"

"Practice was hell as usual. I was happy because the coach mentioned someone called for information about Carter and me," I replied, and she whipped her head up to me immediately.

"Really?" Brooklyn's amazement was evident in her tone, her eyes widening with genuine surprise. I nodded to confirm the news, and a radiant smile graced her lips. "Adam, that's amazing!"

"It'll truly be great once I receive an offer," I replied modestly, attempting to temper my own excitement. I didn't want to get excited for nothing.

"Well, this is you coming one step closer to it." Brooklyn had both hands planted on my chest, her chin on top.

"Perhaps." I shrugged, though her unwavering faith in me warmed my heart.

"You're destined for success, Adam, you just wait."

"Thank you," I murmured gratefully, closing my eyes briefly to savour the moment.

"Hey, Adam," Brooklyn said quietly, and my eyes fluttered open to meet hers.

"Brooklyn?"

"Thank you... How can I repay you for everything?" she asked, her voice still soft.

"I sent you a new chocolate croissant recipe. A dozen of those will make me happy."

Brooklyn nodded and reached for her phone.

"Not now." I grabbed her phone from her hand and put it away. "You're tired, close your eyes," I reminded her.

"I'm not tired... but I'll close my eyes for a few minutes," Brooklyn said, trying her hardest not to yawn, so she buried her face in my chest again. She wiggled her body against mine, getting comfortable.

"If you need anything at all, don't be scared to ask, okay?" I said, looking down at her on my chest.

"Just hold me and hush," she whispered, and a chuckle escaped my lips.

So I did. I held her close to me, carefully playing with her curls. It hadn't taken long for Brooklyn to fall asleep. I marvelled at the sight of her in my arms, the lights were dimmed, but I could still see the contours of her face, she seemed utterly relaxed and at peace. Like she found solace in my arms, and I was just happy to have helped somehow.

I wasn't sure what this meant for us. I technically knew where we stood. I told myself I knew the rules, nothing more than a no-strings-attached situation. Yet the tug in my chest told a different story, her warmth against me made me feel like I wanted something I wasn't allowed. When Brooklyn stirred, I froze, holding my breath until her soft, steady rhythm returned, wrapping me in a calm I didn't know I craved. With her so close, I slowly closed my eyes and drifted off to sleep.

Chapter seventeen

Brooklyn

Lately, Adam and I have been spending more time together. Surprisingly, I didn't mind his constant presence. We ran errands together for the shelter, he joined me on trips to the store, and even picked up packages without complaining. It felt nice to have someone there, sharing the load and encouraging me to take things at my own pace. His patience was admirable.

Patient. Attentive. Encouraging. Compassionate. Those were the words to describe him, yet I felt like this was a dangerous combination, dangerous for my feelings.

He'd leave for the semi-final game soon, and instead of resting, he insisted on driving me to the mall. I needed some last-minute items for the trip this weekend.

"How much would I have to pay you to wear this pretty skirt?" Adam asked, and when I turned to him, I saw a skirt in his hand. It was a sky-blue miniskirt that would barely cover much.

"To an event?" I stared at the skirt. It was pretty...

"Mhm, to the game." He grinned and looked at the skirt, then at me.

"After the game," I countered. That blue wouldn't match the jerseys, and I had already pre-planned my outfits.

"Fine, now what will it cost me?"

"I don't know, Adam, this is going to take a lot of convincing. It's super short and the colour won't match any of the ideas I had in mind," I teased as we strolled through the aisles.

"You've worn shorter, Brooke," Adam reminded me casually, and I stopped in my tracks, realising he had a point.

Fuck, he was right. I couldn't deny that, not with all the mini dresses in my closet.

"What if I'm a changed woman?" I asked, a playful glint in my eye. His lips curved into a suppressed smile.

"I'll foot the bill for everything in your basket," he offered, gesturing towards the pile of clothes I'd collected.

My eyes widened at first, surprised by this offer. I couldn't turn that down!

"You've got yourself a deal...But I just remembered I'm not quite done shopping yet."

"Of course, you're not." Adam chuckled, falling into step behind me as I circled back to the jean overalls. I picked out two different pairs and turned to Adam, raising a brow at him.

"Get that one, I love the little embroidered flowers," he pointed out, and I studied the option.

Adam picked the light-washed one, the pants stopped above mid-thigh. Around the front pockets were delicate flowers embroidered. One last thing to go, I might as well take advantage of this opportunity. Right?

Adam helped me pick yet another skirt and a beige maxi dress with a high slit—all his idea. I wasn't paying, so I added it to the cart.

"That's the one, it will go well with the pink top you got." Turned out he was a fashionista all along.

"Thank you, my basket is now complete," I said.

Adam glanced down at the basket, then back at me.

"You'd better wear that skirt," he muttered.

"I'll do you one better." I walked closer to him, then rose to my toes. My breath ghosted against his ear. "When I wear it, I'll let you bend me over and take me wherever and however you please."

"Fuck, Brooklyn," Adam groaned lowly, his eyes narrowing on me.

I smirked and walked towards the counter. Adam followed behind me and rested the basket on the counter. As promised, he paid and carried the bags too.

"Where to next?" he asked.

"I got my skincare, outfits..." I said as I went down the mental list I created.

"And notebooks," Adam remarked, lifting the stationary store bag a touch higher.

"Then that's all. We grab a snack," I said, feeling relieved that our shopping trip was winding down.

"Mhm," Adam inquired, his gaze shifting to his hands as he held the bags. "Do you think I need a manicure? You know, with the shiny polish on top?"

"A topcoat?" I clarified.

"Whatever that means." He shrugged, inspecting his fingers. "I think I need one."

"Do you want to go?" I asked, looking at my nails. They needed to be redone.

"Yes, let's." He smiled.

I texted Stella for her go-to spot in the mall and received a response within two minutes. Adam and I were fortunate enough that they had spots available for walk-ins. Adam opted for a clear topcoat, and I chose a nude shade.

"I'm surprised by how much you're enjoying this," I said, glancing over at Adam. He sat with his hands extended to the manicurist, watching in awe as she meticulously applied the clear coat.

"Well, I used to do this often before college," Adam said simply, leaving me wanting to hear more. He had always been impeccably groomed, his clothes never had a wrinkle or lint, for that matter—even his dark clothing. His nails were always pristine and not a single hair out of place. The only time he'd be dirty was after a match, but he always cleaned up instantly.

"Adam, I'll need more than just that."

"Of course." He chuckled, adjusting his position. "My mom's work was hectic, and my schedule was always filled with either homework or soccer practice and such. To spend time together, she'd take me to her salon trips, and we'd chat, have fun, and grab snacks afterwards. I participated in one of her activities, and she did the same for me. It was our special bonding time."

"What activity of yours did she participate in?" I asked, intrigued.

"Soccer practice at home. She'd help me." He grinned.

"Is she any good?" I noticed a mischievous glint in his eye.

"Nope, she tripped over the ball once and hurt her arm badly. Dad and I still like to remind her of it." Adam laughed. He sank back into the chair, but the lady doing his nails held his hands firmly.

"Of course you do," I said with a gentle smile.

He had a great bond with his parents. I envied that.

"What about you? Weren't there rumours that you helped your parents with their work?" Adam asked.

I sighed at the mention of those rumours, a reminder of one of the reasons why I yearned to escape Brentwood. My parents, renowned in their field, had close ties with a few celebrities, and they made sure people knew.

"Adam, that would be highly unethical—especially since they took great pride in maintaining the integrity of their clinic," I responded, my voice laced with a hint of resignation. My parents' cosmetic surgery clinic meant everything to them.

"Hey, I'm just curious," Adam said gently.

"Yeah, I obviously wasn't qualified to help with the surgeries, but I did help with some administrative tasks once. It seemed to only make me see them less," I confessed, recalling a brief stint where I assisted at the clinic. "So, I eventually stopped. The pay was decent, though."

"Yeah?"

"Mhm. Did you know there were rumours in high school that I used my parents' services?" I brought up, feeling a need to confide in someone. The two ladies who were doing our nails seemed lost in their own world.

"You're telling me all that beauty is natural?" Adam gestured towards me with his chin, his hands occupied with the manicure.

"You're lucky I don't want to mess up my gel polish," I teased, rolling my eyes as he chuckled.

"I'm kidding... I've seen your old photos, you've always been beautiful," he remarked. "But also, isn't there an age restriction?"

"My parents don't operate on anyone under eighteen, unless it's an emergency," I confirmed, glancing at my nails. The colour was perfect.

"How did you handle the rumours?" Adam inquired, genuinely curious.

"Two teachers both got pregnant by the same person, so that pretty much overshadowed everything else," I revealed, reminiscing about the dramatic days of high school.

"What the hell?" Adam's mouth hung open, clearly eager for more details.

"Yeah, my grandmother wanted to pull me out of that school, but they managed some solid PR, and it wasn't like the father of the kids was a student or teacher—just a student's father." I recounted the story as vividly as I could, and Adam's astonishment mirrored that of the girls when I shared it with them.

"Brooklyn, holy shit," Adam exclaimed, still processing the shocking revelation.

"Right? Never a dull moment." I shook my head, a wry smile playing on my lips.

"Clearly." Adam chuckled, settling back as the nail technician finished oiling his cuticles.

With our manicures complete, Adam and I grabbed our mall snack and then returned home. As I busied myself putting away our new purchases, I heard Adam moving around. My curiosity piqued, and I went to see what he was up to and found him in the lounge area, packing his bag at the last minute, as usual.

I looked around the lounge room as he tried to stuff his rolled-up pants in the bag. The wall facing the street had a huge window covered with sheer curtains, under the window was an ottoman, and on both sides were nice bookshelves, but they were empty except for a crystal dolphin on one side and a painted tile with Portuguese scripture.

Just as I was about to say something, Adam walked past me and went back into his room. Only a few seconds passed, and Adam emerged with a small brown package in hand.

"Hey, I got you a gift and forgot to give it to you earlier," he said, offering me the box with a warm smile.

"Yeah?" I arched a brow at him, slowly accepting the gift. As I held the box, I couldn't help but wonder what could be inside. It wasn't too heavy, yet it wasn't light either. I couldn't recall asking him for anything recently.

"What is it? Oh my god, you didn't buy me some bizarre sex toy, did you?" I asked, narrowing my eyes at him. Adam burst into laughter and shook his head, dispelling my concern.

"Maybe next time, but for now, just open this," he urged, tapping the box in my hand. I nodded and eagerly opened it. Inside, I found a stunning, blue bedazzled taser with matching pepper spray, along with a small, round device whose purpose confused me.

It was perfect—after a few intruder movies and him going out of town, I certainly had some worries.

"I'd get you a small knife too, but I'm not sure if you can be trusted with a weapon," Adam quipped, his playful tone laced with affection.

"Good call." I chuckled, looking up at him with admiration. His gift was incredibly thoughtful, a testament to the depth of our friendship. Lately, I had found myself viewing Adam in a new light, but I knew now that our bond was simply that of great friends—friends who shared moments like this.

"It's not much," Adam suggested, his gaze lingering on the pepper spray in my hand.

"Thank you, Adam," I said sincerely, stowing the gifts on the table before turning to hug him.

"I hope you never find yourself in a situation where you have to use it," he murmured, returning the embrace with warmth.

"I hope so too," I replied, closing my eyes briefly. "What's the tiny round thing?"

"If you pull the pin, it emits a loud alarm," he explained, gesturing towards the open box. "But don't test it. I already did, and I almost went deaf," he confessed with a sheepish grin.

"You wouldn't be Adam if you didn't test it." I chuckled, taking a step back. Adam simply smiled and resumed packing his bag. After a moment, he left the room briefly, returning shirtless but holding two hangers—one with our university sweater and the other with a simple T-shirt featuring the embroidered logo.

"Should I wear the sweater? It has a tiny stain on it. I purchased a new one, but it comes in tomorrow," Adam explained, stuck in a dilemma, and sadly, my focus couldn't be there.

My eyes trailed down his abdomen. I've seen the view many times already, beautiful and stunning, and worth looking at each and every time.

"You look at me as if I'm a piece of meat," Adam said, narrowing his gaze on me. He was trying to make me handle this in a serious manner, but I wasn't prepared to just yet.

"You look at me just the same when I wear anything that exposes a bit of cleavage," I reminded him.

Sure, I sometimes wear more revealing clothes around him to get a reaction out of him. With a subtle shift in posture, I leaned forward ever so slightly, allowing the V-neck of my dress to dip lower. My movements were deliberate, calculated to captivate him, and his eyes already dipped down.

"Or ass, I do love yours," he said proudly, and his eyes trailed down my body.

I refrained from rolling my eyes at him, instead, I tilted my head up a little, and a coy smile danced upon my lips. I twirled a strand of hair between my fingers, my gaze moving to his lips. "And stop looking at me like that," Adam said, judging by his tone, I could tell he was trying to restrain himself, which meant I definitely stood a chance.

As his gaze lingered on me, I knew that I had succeeded in planting erotic thoughts in his head. Thoughts he'd certainly want to make into reality. Maybe I can give one last nudge.

"Like what, Adam honey?" I took a step forward, and he inhaled deeply. "Like I want you to push me against this wall and fuck me?"

"Brooklyn sweetheart, we don't have that much time," he stated, looking down at the watch on his wrist. His eyes then met mine again, slowly going down.

"Am I not your lucky charm, Adam?" I whispered with a mischievous glint in my eyes. My finger traced a delicate path along his jawline. He leaned into my caress, his eyes darkening with desire.

"Fuck it, we'll make it work," he declared, his voice laced with a hint of defiance. With swift movements, he chucked his shirts.

In one fluid motion, he scooped me up into his arms, effortlessly lifting me off the ground. My legs wrapped around his waist immediately, and my arms went around his neck. There was a soft thud as my back was slammed against the wall, his body pressing against mine with urgency.

As our lips met in a passionate kiss, the world fell away, leaving only the intoxicating heat of our desire. His hands roamed hungrily over my body, he tugged down the straps of my dress, and his lips descended down my neck to my breasts, a path of kisses and bites left behind.

"Think you can make us both come before they pick you up?" I asked as my fingers threaded through his hair. A loud gasp escaped my lips as he unclasped my bra, his tongue instantly swirling around my nipple.

"Guess we'll find out then, yeah?" he said in between the caresses of his lips on my skin, each kiss towards my other breast filled me with longing and desire. I wanted more, and I was going to voice it, when I felt his hand slip between us.

Adam adjusted our position better, his hand right between my thighs and his lips back on mine. He pushed past my panties and stroked me leisurely. He wanted me to plead, but I was trying to stay strong, even when his forefinger circled my clit.

Adam's fingers entered me in a slow, deliberate manner, and I moaned softly into our kiss. My fingers tugged at his hair, trying to deepen the kiss, but he pulled his lips from mine.

"Your pussy is weeping for me." He kissed my chin, his fingers finally moving at a much more desired pace. "So cock hungry."

I'd give anything right now to have his lips on my clit, that man knew how to use his tongue, but we didn't have time for that.

"Adam, we don't have much time, please," I whined desperately.

"Okay." He didn't tease, he couldn't. Not when I could see his restrained cock, needing me just as much as I needed him.

Adam's resistance faltered too, his own need mirroring mine as he swiftly removed my dress and threw it to the side while I got busy with his pants. He bent down to help me with my panties, his lips placing butterfly kisses down my stomach. He rose back up and slammed his lips to mine as he helped me discard the rest of his clothes.

I didn't want us to waste a single second, we didn't have much time, and this thought had been lingering on my mind for a while.

"Wait." I held onto him. My eyes met with his, and I could feel my heartbeat in my throat. "You passed those screenings?"

"Yeah, I'm clean and I've only been with you since the last screening," Adam said as his hand caressed my skin.

"I'm clean too."

"Birth control?" Adam asked, a soft groan escaping his lips as I palmed his hardened cock.

"Yes, Adam, fuck me already," I whined, hoping he'd want it as much as I did.

"Fuck, Brooklyn, I can't ever get enough of you," Adam said. His lips then crashed with mine, and he pushed me against the wall again, his hands on my legs as he spread me and entered me slowly.

"My destruction." He groaned. I felt waves of pleasure crashing through me as he entered me in one fluid moment, his throbbing cock buried within me. He hadn't stopped till I took every last inch of him. I felt deliciously full. His lips found my neck, sucking, biting, and licking. I tipped my head back against the wall, giving him all the space he needed to drive me fucking insane.

"Adam, you feel so fucking good," I moaned into his ear as he started thrusting into me.

His pace became more urgent. I wanted it hard and fast, and Adam was delivering. One of his hands was planted on my hip, pinning me to the wall, while the other was tangled in my hair. A primal fire burned within us, each thrust sent shockwaves of pleasure coursing through my veins, and the loud moans that escaped my lips were proof.

I clung to him with my nails, digging into his skin. He called me his destruction, he stated he couldn't ever get enough of me, but Adam possessed me completely. He made me feel things no one ever had. I never wanted this arrangement to end between us.

Each movement drew me closer to the edge of euphoria, he slowly pushed me beyond the brink. When he started rubbing my clit I lost the last shred of my control. I tipped my head back against the wall, not caring about the thud.

Adam's lips found the sweet spot right under my ear, and he sucked at my skin, shooting shivers straight down my spine. "Do you have any idea how perfect you are, baby?"

"Adam, I'm so close," I moaned as I clenched him.

"Come for me, Brooklyn baby, let me feel that sweet pussy come on my cock." I surrendered to his command, losing myself to the overwhelming raw sensation.

His name was chanted by me, repeated constantly with devotion and joy. I grabbed his face and slammed my lips to his. Adam thrust into me with one last hard stroke, and my walls pulsed around him as I felt him come, his moans muffled by our kiss.

That was... everything I had hoped for. Adam never once disappointed, even when he was given less than ten minutes.

Adam pulled out slowly, and I sighed softly. He carried me to the ottoman. He was about to kiss me again when a loud honk startled us both.

His eyes went to the curtains, and I'm pretty sure that the school bus was waiting outside.

"Shit," Adam cursed. He threw my dress my way and then disappeared into his bedroom. He was there for at least five minutes, and I could hear the water running.

There was another honk followed by the constant ringing of his phone. Adam rushed back from his bedroom. I was still seated on the ottoman with a satisfied smirk on my face as I watched him scramble around.

"Hello? Yes, Carter, I know, I'm running down right now," Adam said as he picked up the phone. He multitasked, juggling the phone while putting his pants back on, then he tucked his phone in his pockets and narrowed his eyes on me. "You. You are dangerous to me, Brooklyn Armstrong."

"I don't know what you speak of," I said innocently as he put on the T-shirt.

"Stay out of trouble, okay," he said as he walked over to me. I kneeled on the ottoman as he leaned down. He kissed me briefly and then spanked me. I wasn't given a chance to say much because he already had his bag and ran downstairs.

I was still kneeling on the ottoman, turned towards the window, and peering through the curtains as Adam walked towards the bus. Right before he boarded, he turned around and our eyes met. It only took a simple, playful wink for him to send a storm of butterflies fluttering through my stomach. I gently trailed my hand down my neck and breasts, feeling the ghost of his touch, reminiscing about the way his hands explored me only moments ago. The trail of kisses he left on my skin, the excitement it had brought me.

Taking a deep breath, I closed the curtains and turned away from the window. My phone was vibrating constantly, pulling me back to reality. I reached for it, my heart still racing from the memory of him.

The girls

Stella

Hello? @Me where are you???

Zaira

She's probably busy with a guy who she refuses to tell us about

Darshini

No, I think she has a dry spell

Stella

Ten more minutes then I'm showing up at Adam's

Guys, relax. I'm alive and well and I never have a dry spell. It's me we're talking about

Zaira

We don't believe you, maybe if you tell us a bit about him

I knew I had avoided telling them about this for long enough already. Any longer and they'd get suspicious. This part of my life was never kept a secret before and I couldn't start now. Adam and I couldn't afford to get caught. Not when things we're getting this good.

The girls

Fine... He's a jock, blond hair and he might just be normal

Stella

Glad to know this one won't steal your panties

Zaira

Didn't you say you were done with jocks?

Darshini

Is it someone from DTU?

I said I was done indeed but then he came and he was just too good to resist. He may or may not be from DTU

Stella

We're not gonna get more info from you are we?

Nope

Darshini

Does he make you happy?

I stared at my phone. Darshini's question made my heart skip several beats. Yes, he made me happy but that wasn't anything new. It was perfectly normal. All my current friends made me immensely happy. Adam wasn't any different from the rest of the group, he was part of that friend group too.

It was after all no-strings-attached.

Chapter eighteen

Adam

The referee's whistle marked the end of the match, and we secured a triumphant 3-2 victory for DTU. We were off to the finals! Coach Mendes couldn't contain his joy, shouting out in celebration and tossing his cap on the floor in excitement.

The defeated opposing team looked disappointed, but I had to admit, they put up a fair match. I glanced around, smiling as Ibrahim launched himself at Dante, both cheering our win.

Gathering in a circle, we soaked up the atmosphere of the night, still buzzing with adrenaline. The crowd was big, but a large part supported the underdog, Silver Lions. Didn't bother us. On Saturday, the bleachers would be filled with DTU fans, just like the past three years.

One of the new guys got caught up flirting on the sidelines. Catching Dante's eye, I raised an eyebrow, and he just shrugged. "Can't blame them." He chuckled. "We were probably just the same in our first year." We were.

"Adam, that last ball was great. Really saved our asses." Carter patted my back as he joined me.

"Thanks for the assist," I replied. It was a team effort.

"It was that or risk getting a dirty tackle by that bulldozer," Carter said, nodding towards the big guy from Silver Lions. I looked at the guy, Miller.

He was definitely new and intimidating. He was great on the field, but far too aggressive with a yellow card under his belt already.

"True, I thought at least one of us would return with a broken leg," I admitted, and Ibrahim just shook his head at me.

Their new coach seemed more supportive, genuinely trying to lift his team's spirits.

"Yeah, let's celebrate!" Dante exclaimed, barely getting the words out before the rest of the team whisked him away.

"Voss, Serra-Valle," Coach called out, making us freeze in place. Oh no, this couldn't be good. Coach never summoned us after a win; he usually allowed us to bask in the moment.

"Coach?" Carter called out.

"Did you guys pull off that prank?" Carter narrowed his eyes at me, referring to the infamous prank we had planned.

This had been planned for years now, but we hadn't gone through with it yet, knowing we'd be stuck with Coach still—but not for much longer.

"No, absolutely not," I scoffed, nudging Carter away. He continued to scrutinise me, and with a sigh, I relented, "We'll save it for when we get back to our base."

"Adam," Carter warned, his tone bordering on an annoyed whine.

"It's a parting gift. This is our last year with him," I reminded him. Four years together, and the most mischief we had managed was giving him a birthday cake with a photo of him with his stern coach face. "Come on, he deserves something to remember us by."

"Winning three times in a row would suffice, but the prank works too," Carter conceded, a smirk creeping onto my face. If the captain was on our side, we'd sure as hell get this done.

We caught up to Coach Mendes, standing before him. "Yes, Coach?" Carter inquired, while I studied the man closely. He didn't seem angry; rather, he appeared to be still basking in our victory. I couldn't recall any illegal moves made on the field, so clearly, this wasn't a reprimand.

"I was pondering when to share this with you. Initially, I planned to wait until after the finals, but I suppose I could tell you now," Coach

Mendes spoke cryptically. I had an idea about what this might be about, but I didn't want to let my hopes soar prematurely.

"What's going on?" I finally asked.

"I've recently been contacted by scouts from Liberty FC, possibly even Seattle Sounders FC, and New York Cosmos. These are reputable teams, and they've expressed genuine interest in your performance. However, I want you guys to hold off on any offers for now," Coach explained. My heart raced with excitement, it was finally happening. My shot at going pro, and with such esteemed teams showing interest, this could be my big break. The teams were great for a start.

"For now, keep up the stellar work. If your performance in the finals continues to impress, I have no doubt that more will come." Coach's tone shifted, becoming more serious as he fixed his gaze on us both.

I glanced at the other players on our team, some were only doing this for their full-ride scholarship, like Ibrahim, others played for the sheer love of the game, like Carter and Dante, but only a handful did it with the intention of going pro like me.

"There's more, but I don't want you guys to start celebrating too early. We still have finals." He was right, many of us on the team were prone to letting success go to our heads, especially the newcomers. "I need you two at the top of your game tomorrow, understood?" Coach patted my shoulder.

"Yes, Coach. Thank you," Carter and I replied in unison. Carter shot me a proud look, and I smiled at him.

"You both performed admirably. If you ever need advice about those offers or what to do next, my door is always open."

I stared at the man for a moment. He had been our coach since day one. I couldn't believe it'd been four years already, and I sure didn't think someone's beard would have so many grey strands so fast.

"Yes, Coach," Carter affirmed, nudging me to snap me out of my thoughts.

"Now, go on and make sure your teammates don't do anything stupid before the finals," Coach commanded in his customary drill sergeant tone.

"So, after the finals..." I trailed off with suggestions.

"Don't push it, Serra Valle." Coach narrowed his eyes at me.

"Oh, come on," Carter intervened, pulling me away by the shoulder.

"Seattle Sounders, that's close to home for you," I remarked to Carter, expecting him to be more enthusiastic about going pro.

"Yeah, I'm just not certain anymore," Carter confessed.

I was a little surprised. I didn't think he'd change his mind. Not when he had so much talent, he was great on the field. The four years we played together were some of my best.

"About going pro? You did speak to your dad about it, right?" I asked. I knew he mentioned taking over Voss Holding.

"Yeah. He's fine with it, but as I started handling more and more of the business, I truly fell in love with it," Carter explained, and I could tell he meant it. "It's also best since I still want and require my master's," he added with a soft sigh.

"Whatever brings you the most happiness and fulfilment," I reassured him. As much as I'd miss his presence on the field, I understood that our paths might diverge at some point.

"If I take over the business, I'd have more flexibility in my schedule," he reasoned, and I empathised with his perspective. I knew his family meant the world to him, and spending time with them would always come above all else. "But at the same time, soccer has always been a part of me, I started playing the moment I was able to walk—I can't imagine life without it."

"There are always non-competitive clubs you could join and still manage the business and family," I added, offering a potential compromise.

"Oh yeah, you're right," Carter realized. He then patted my back. "Hey, but I'm so proud of you, I told you it would all work out."

"Alright, mother hen." I chuckled, though I appreciated his support.

"Don't call me 'mother hen,'" he retorted with a playful glare.

"So, what happened?" Dante inquired, shrugging off Ibrahim's playful antics.

"You didn't rat us out, did you?" Ibrahim teased, shaking his head in mock disappointment.

"I didn't, it was unrelated. He just told me to make sure you don't do stupid shit. No alcohol for you, Fernandez," Carter cleared the air and pointed to Fernandez. He just nodded with a slight smirk. "I mean it," he continued, using his captain's tone this time.

"After the finals, when the trophy is in our hands, you can all go do whatever the hell you want," I declared.

"For now, behave," Carter added.

"Fine, let's go then." One of them sighed dramatically. A bunch of kids.

The team piled into a nearby diner, still buzzing with excitement from our victory. We settled into our seats, and laughter and chatter filled the air. Our celebratory feast consisted of a perfect blend of carbs, protein, and fats.

Our night didn't last long with tomorrow's scheduled training, so we returned to our rooms. I used to share a room with Carter, but ever since Dante started dating Darshini, Ibrahim, I had always complained that I didn't want to hear the couple on the phone, so now I shared a room with Ibrahim.

I put down the hair dryer and stared at my reflection. I could hear Ibrahim on the phone on the other side of his door, no doubt talking to Zaira. I ran my fingers through my hair when my phone buzzed three times in a row. I picked up my phone immediately when I saw it was Brooklyn.

There was a photo attached. I double-checked to make sure I locked the door, then opened the photo. Brooklyn wore that blue miniskirt I picked out for her. She sat on the edge of the bed, her legs on display in the photo. She wore a thin tank top, and I could see the outline of her nipples. Fuck me.

I went to check her other messages instantly.

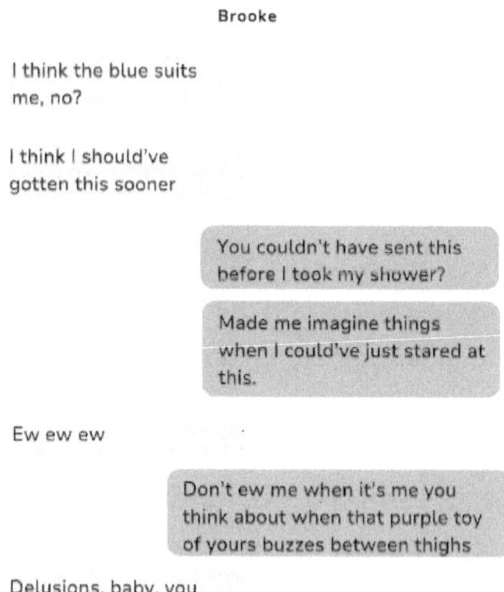

I chuckled, staring at her message. Fine, two could play this game. The bathroom lighting was already flattering. My skin was still damp and hair tousled, so I took a quick photo.

'Just in case you need some inspiration later.'

I messaged her along with the photo and waited for her response.

Damn Brooklyn, she had me wrapped around her finger without even realising it. I had never once felt the need to seek approval. And yet, here I was, craving her praise and validation.

Sudden banging on the door snapped me out of my thoughts.

"You done wearing your panties? I've been waiting for hours already," Ibrahim complained. I rolled my eyes and went to unlock the door. I'm pretty sure he barely even put down the phone, but I decided not to say anything and kept it classy. I flipped him off on the way out.

A little later, I was still in bed, phone in hand. Ibrahim's bed was vacant since he decided to go grab us some snacks from Dante and Carter's room. I returned to Brooklyn's message.

I was drawn to her photo, a photo she took just for me. The picture captured her radiance, the shimmer in her hazel eyes, and the thick dark curls that danced around her face. With the sly smirk on her face, she knew she was out-of-this-world stunning. I wonder if she also knew what effect she had on me.

I didn't bother taking a second glance, not when I knew she'd follow me into my dream like she had this past week. I was close to crossing a dangerous line. The problem was that I didn't see the danger. I wanted the prize at the end, but I knew I couldn't have it all. That was never the deal.

Brooklyn was intelligent and driven, with passions and ambitions that didn't include me in the equation. And that was the unspoken agreement we'd made from the start.

"Okay, I got chips, apple juice, applesauce, and cookies," Ibrahim announced, returning with a bag brimming with snacks.

"Apple juice and sauce?" I raised an eyebrow, placing my phone on the nightstand.

"You know how Carter is about his apples." Ibrahim shrugged, beginning to distribute the snacks.

"Weirdo," I mumbled.

We snacked and then bickered over who would brush their teeth first.

The next morning, we attended our light recovery training, followed by video analysis and discussing the game for tomorrow. Coach didn't keep us for long, we were free to enjoy the rest of our day, so long as we didn't get in trouble.

The girls had plans of their own, and so did we. I would have much rather stayed inside and played games, but Carter convinced us to go outside, claiming "It would be good for us."

Outside led to lunch, followed by shopping. I didn't plan on getting anything until I saw a sleeveless shirt that said *Suns out, guns out*. It was perfect for Dante, and I couldn't resist getting it.

I also found the perfect shirt for Ibrahim. I knew Zaira would agree. It said *I'm the reason we can't have nice things*.

"What did you buy?" Ibrahim asked, his eyes flickering to my bag.

"Just some shirts and those adorable pens with little cats and dogs on top for Brooke." I was casual about the shirts—they would be a surprise. I even picked up one for Carter.

"Please, spare us the sight of whatever ugly shirt you got," Ibrahim pleaded, eyeing my bag with a hint of dismay.

"Jealous you won't rock them like I do?" I teased, a playful grin tugging at my lips.

"I'm so jealous I won't get to embarrass myself," Ibrahim retorted sarcastically, rolling his eyes.

"No bickering or there'll be no ice cream," Carter interjected.

That got us to shut up—until the last bit of our ice cream was done and we were back at the hotel. The bickering only ended when the guys went to visit their girlfriends. I, on the other hand, revelled in the freedom to blast my music and delve into my essay. The blank page taunted me, but I was determined to make progress tonight.

And I did.

In two hours, I had managed to draft and refine 30 percent of my essay. A well-deserved break was in order. Without hesitation, I went to Brooke's messages.

'I'm gonna cry'

A frown creased my brow as I immediately dialled her number, my heart was racing with concern. Had something happened?

"Hey, what's wrong?" I asked as soon as she picked up.

"I didn't expect you to actually call," Brooklyn said. "I was just being dramatic because I wanted food from a specific place only to find out they don't do delivery."

"Is it far?" I asked, checking the time.

"No, but..." Brooke trailed off, hesitating.

Silence hung in the air. Was she reluctant to go out alone? Glancing out the window, I noticed the darkness outside. While the other girls enjoyed the company of their boyfriends, Brooke was alone.

"Anyways." She sighed. "What were you up to? Dreaming of how you'll kiss the trophy?"

"Send me your address," I requested, brushing off her teasing with a smirk.

Chapter nineteen

Brooklyn

The girls and I arrived in New York just after 1 PM. Thanks to Stella's magic, we checked into an apartment that somehow managed to be both within our budget and spacious enough for our quartet. But there was no time to lounge inside—we were ready to dive headfirst into the bustling city.

Bags barely dropped, we headed straight out. A day filled with retail therapy. From chic boutiques to glittering jewellery stores, our shopping spree ended with a visit to a renowned bookstore. Despite my self-imposed book ban—I found myself seduced by the displays of special edition copies and signed treasures. I could not refuse, the book ban ended today.

"That's gonna leave a dent," Darshini whispered as she took her two bags of books. I didn't bother saying anything, I felt just the same.

"Okay, let's go before I buy another set of books I already own purely because of the special cover," Stella muttered, hooking her arm through Zaira's.

"Come on, guys." Zaira took charge and led us outside. "Next stop is that doughnut spot Stella found," Zaira continued to say.

We were back at the apartment, staring at the box of doughnuts. There were many scents coming from it, and we stared at each other for a moment. We split all of them into four ways and began to eat them.

The thing that made Alchemy Donuts Co. special was its bizarre selection of doughnuts. The only normal doughnuts they had were glazed ones. It was a viral doughnut shop that remained on our itinerary for a while.

"Not to be biased, but we all agree that the chai spice goes first, right?" Darshini asked as she ate the last of her chai doughnut.

"Absolutely, and the lavender blueberry comes in a close second," Stella concurred, a smudge of blueberry adorning her cheek. I leaned in, carefully wiping it away with a gentle gesture.

"Don't lick my thumb, I'm not Carter," I teased.

"I am well aware." She rolled her eyes.

"This one tastes like the baklava you made," Zaira gushed and gave Darshini her prettiest look. Those baby browns are working overtime for homemade desserts from Darshini. I, for one, do miss living with Darshini and Dante because they made the best food. But on the other hand, splitting apart did push me to finally learn how to cook.

"I just need us all to collectively agree that matcha coconut is the worst," I said with a disgusted face.

"Oh yeah, there is coconut shaving stuck in my mouth. I need to brush my teeth again," Zaira complained. She swept her tongue across her teeth, trying to remove said coconut shaving.

She wasn't lying, but I still couldn't admit any of them deserved last place. "Don't blame the doughnuts for this. You plan on seeing Darshini's brother, possibly make out with him, so of course you'll brush your teeth."

Darshini groaned the same way Ibrahim groaned when Dante would do something romantic for Darshini.

"He has a name. Also, he kissed me several times after his games, covered in sweat, grass, and dirt. I'm sure he can handle coconut shaving," Zaira defended Ibrahim, something that would've never happened three years ago.

Sweat, grass, and dirt. I could picture Adam coming home after his game, his scent close to me as he'd sneak a quick kiss.

"Are you even listening?" Zaira swiped her hand back and forth in my face.

"No, if I wanted smut, I'd pick up Darshini's current read." I smirked and looked at Darshini. Stella sat in the background with a grin, loving every moment of this.

"A lot of judgment from someone who reads alien porn," Darshini was quick to say, my smirk flattered.

"You guys read it too! Loved it even," I groaned. One mistake and I'm still not living it down. The girls laughed still.

"Mhm, but you're the odd duck who picked it." Stella laughed.

"Try building a stronger case." Zaira winked and patted my back.

This back and forth continued until the girls had to get ready to leave—plans with their boyfriends in the city, of course. Stella stopped by the door.

"Want me to grab dinner with you?" Stella offered. How sweet, but I'm sure Carter would brood around if he found out I stole his girlfriend.

"Nah. You go out and make sure to tell Carter to win that game tomorrow," I said, patting her shoulder. She looked at me for a second longer, and I just gave her a subtle nod.

"Okido. Call me if you need anything."

"She's probably gonna sext with that jock of hers," Zaira said loudly from the bathroom.

"I paid attention to those digital literacy classes in high school. I will not be sexting." I rolled my eyes.

Okay, so I sent Adam some questionable photos, but I hadn't done it before, and in my defence, I wasn't naked.

Once the girls left, I went back on my phone to order my dinner... only to find out they don't do delivery at all.

I gazed out the window, the darkness of the night enveloping the city. The destination wasn't too far, and I could have gone out alone, yet a sense of unease lingered within me. I didn't go out alone in cities I wasn't used to. With a resigned sigh, I went to look at all the other sad options for dinner. They were decent. I was well aware I was being dramatic, but I truly wanted food from that place.

I took a break from swiping on food and went to Adam's messages. We chatted till there was a knock on the front door. I froze for a moment. The girls wouldn't be back so soon, the knocking became much more frantic.

Heart pounding, I cautiously made my way to the kitchen, my pulse quickening with each knock on the door.

"Brooke? Are you there, or have I made a mistake with the address?" Adam's voice echoed through the door, causing me to freeze in disbelief.

Adam had actually come? I gave him my address because I thought he'd send food, not come over. I abandoned the idea of grabbing the sharpest knife and went to the door.

"Adam? You came?" I exclaimed, swinging the door open to reveal his familiar face, my brows furrowed with confusion.

"You needed me," Adam stated, his gaze sweeping the room to make sure we were alone before he planted a tender kiss on my lips.

"I didn't say that," I muttered. I'm sure the happiness on my face told a different story, though.

"I know you well enough to understand," Adam replied with a casual shrug, stepping inside. "But let's not waste any time. Grab your things, we're going to that restaurant you've been craving."

"You don't have to bother," I said quietly. My chest betrayed me, fluttering at the thought of how far he'd gone just to be here. His kindness stirred something deep inside, emotions pressing against my heart—emotions I wasn't ready to acknowledge.

"Brooklyn baby, if I didn't want to bother, I wouldn't have fought a couple to get a cab so I could get to you." Adam's laughter wrapped around me, and my resistance melted under the sound of it, and before I knew it, I surrendered to him completely.

We headed out together, joking on the way over. When we arrived, I placed my order and then settled at an outdoor table with Adam. The evening breeze cooled us, and I noticed Adam glancing around, taking in the surroundings. The scent of cotton candy from the shop next door drifted through the air.

Above us hung strings of lights with green leaves wrapped around them as they cast a soft glow. The yellow lights gently illuminated Adam's face, adding a warm glow to his features. My heart fluttered as his eyes found mine.

"Are you sure you don't want anything?" I inquired, my gaze lingering on his nose now. I didn't want to risk getting lost in his eyes.

"Nah, I'm good with just the ranch chips," Adam replied, sensing my disappointment with his choice. "One time before an important game, I had takeout and ended up with a stomach bug. Now I wait till after the games to try new places."

"Oh... I understand now."

"If the food's good, we can grab some after the game," Adam suggested.

"Is that an invitation, Adam?" I teased, leaning in as he reached across the table to intertwine our fingers. It felt strangely natural, though we were in public. I should have pulled away, but the warmth of his touch was too inviting and normal to resist.

"Mhm, it will be on me."

"You do too much already. I need to stop that," I pointed out.

I wasn't feeling guilty yet, but I knew myself. I knew that soon enough I'd wake up and feel as if I had taken advantage of his generosity, or worse, he'd come to that realisation and it would cost us our friendship.

"Why?" Adam's expression shifted.

"Because you never let me repay the favour," I replied, arching a brow at him.

Despite my attempts, there were times when he adamantly refused any gesture of repayment, leaving me with only one option—making him his beloved smoothie and baking desserts, but that didn't hold a candle to everything else he did for me.

"You want to repay me? Fine, I accept handwritten notes," he bargained.

"Should I pack them with your lunch?" I joked, but then his face lit up.

"Yes! How did you know? I love those so much, unpacking my lunch and reading the little notes," Adam spoke with such excitement. I thought he was kidding at first, but as he continued to talk, I realised he was not kidding. At all.

"I was kidding," I mumbled.

"I'm not. I expect handwritten notes," he said with some sass.

"Okay." I laughed. I brought this upon myself. I heard my number being called and looked towards the counter. "That's mine."

"I'll go grab it for you."

I couldn't take my eyes off Adam as he walked over to the counter and back. When he handed me my food, his smile radiated warmth, a sight that never failed to stir something within me. That freaking smile made my heart flutter and opened a zoo in my stomach. We were just friends, or so I kept telling myself. Friends with benefits, to be exact. It was a simple arrangement, one that we both enjoyed a lot without any complications.

But somewhere along the line, I messed up. I broke the one rule I swore I wouldn't— catching feelings. I couldn't deny it any longer, not with the way my heart raced whenever he was near. It was frustrating that this realisation hit me now, right at this moment. Fuck, why couldn't my brain wait to tell me this when he wasn't around?

Should I tell him? Confess the truth about my feelings? There was a nagging voice in my head, whispering about the possibility that he might feel the same way. And what was the worst that could happen, really? Maybe we'd just laugh it off, chalk it up to a momentary lapse in judgment.

Adam cared about me, took an interest in my work at the shelter, and indulged my love for chocolate without hesitation—that might be bad, but I appreciated it. He was sweet in every sense of the word. He was like no one I had ever met, no one had ever cared for me like he did, and it scared the living hell out of me.

It was an odd twist of fate to find him when my heart wasn't seeking companionship. I had never longed for any of it before. I loved reading romance books, I loved reading about characters falling in love, but I never sought to experience it myself.

Too many risks. But what do I know about this? I've never touched the subject.

Then he smiled again and carefully reached over to tuck my hair out of my face. That's it. I couldn't shake the feeling that there was something more between us, something worth exploring. It was scary, sure, but it was also exhilarating—or it could be.

"Oh, I forgot to tell you, great news." Adam's face lit up. He screwed the cap back onto his bottle and focused on me.

"What's up?"

"There are clubs that called for me, nothing's official yet, but after the game tomorrow, I can expect some calls," Adam said as a huge grin split across his face. "The best part is that they are from the area. There's a really great one in New York, I hope they call after tomorrow," he continued, and I smiled back at him. I was happy for him, all his hard work would pay off, and his dreams would soon turn into reality.

His dream awaited him in New York. Chances were that I'd have to move back home to LA. Even if I told him how I felt, we'd still part ways when we graduated. I didn't even want to dare think about long distance.

Things might have just been better if I kept it to myself. I was sure the feelings would dissolve soon.

"Brooke? Are you listening?"

"Yes, I was just processing it." I cleared my throat. Suddenly, my hunger had disappeared. I still forced myself to take a few bites of the tacos or he'd know something was wrong. "So this is good, right? This means that after you graduate, you can go there?"

"Yeah, depending on their contract, of course, and my performance tomorrow. Things should go great. I'm so excited, Brooke, I might not have to get suited up every morning to do a nine-to-five in a cubicle," Adam said, all excited, but all I could picture now was him in suits. He didn't wear suits too often, but when he did, it was a stunning sight.

"Too bad, I love my men in suits," I joked.

"I can make you change your mind, Brooklyn baby." Adam winked. Oh, Adam, if only you knew you already did.

After dinner, Adam got us a ride back to the apartment. He walked me back to the door, stealing a quick kiss from me before having to go. He had to rest for the game tomorrow, and frankly, I was tired too.

The next morning was a flurry of all four of us running around. Zaira had the perfect winged liner on one eye, and the other was wiped twice already. She was seated at the dining table with her mirror in her hand because the lighting was far better there than it was in the bathroom.

Stella didn't like her pants at all, she kept trying on different pants only to take them off. Darshini couldn't find her shirt and was parading around in her bra. I looked over at her suitcase, which was inside out, and no sign of her shirt.

I struggled with my hair. I was crazy to think I could maintain waist-length thick curls. I should've put it in a protective hairstyle last night, I was paying the damn price for it now.

"You know, if we were smart, we would've laid out our outfit last night," I pointed out smugly. "But nooo, you guys were too busy getting laid," I continued and winced when the comb got stuck in my hair.

"I give up, I'm going like this." Stella's voice was laced with frustration as she walked out. The jersey she wore was cinched a little and stopped right under her ass. Voss was perfectly printed on the back; this was all custom work, of course.

"Stella, you have great thighs, truthfully, but I don't think you should go like that," I said, stealing a glance at her toned legs. She was well aware of their beauty, almost always picking a skirt to show them off.

"I can't find anything," she whined, rummaging through the pile of rejected outfits. It seemed her suitcase held an entire wardrobe. I'm not sure how many outfits she carried.

"I have these light-washed jeans that do wonders for your ass. They're on my bed, try them on," I offered.

Stella didn't object; she went to try them on. Moments later, she was admiring herself in the mirror, a radiant smile gracing her lips. I managed to make someone happy today, so I can already call it a day.

"These are perfect!" Stella gushed, the bootcut jeans fitting her like a glove. "Come here, let me help you," she said, turning her attention to Zaira's makeup. Stella had mastered the art of winged eyeliner long ago.

“I physically cannot watch you torture your hair any longer,” Darshini intervened, snatching the brush from my hand. “Sit down,” she instructed, taking a seat herself. I complied, though I made sure to sulk about it.

With careful and skilful hands, Darshini carefully transformed my hair into the reference photo—two braids cascaded from the front to the back, meeting in a sleek ponytail.

“Is there anything she can’t do?” I marvelled. Dante was certainly a lucky bastard.

“Mhm, finding her shirt—luckily I remembered she pulled it out yesterday while searching for her headphone charger and left it by that table,” Zaira chimed in, tossing the shirt to Darshini.

“Guys, are we really going to gloss over the fact that Brooklyn is wearing a shirt with a guy’s name on the back?” Stella teased. I let out a soft groan.

“Shut it. I won’t have any of that, and if one of you brings it up, I’ll send your numbers to telemarketing centres,” I warned, effectively silencing them. A great threat I could repeat several times with a hundred percent success rate.

We managed to snap some pictures before heading to the stadium. The bleachers were filled with fans for both teams. I spotted a lot of people from our university, here to support, but most likely to enjoy the school spirit. There were many people here for the excitement of the game, and the opposing team wasn’t lacking fans either.

I pulled out my phone to text Adam.

Adam

No lucky charm magic this time, you better win this game, Adam

No need to worry. Seeing you in my jersey will be motivation enough. I won't let you regret having my name on your back

Good. Give it your best performance and secure your spot

I will, Brooke, thank you

Don't thank me yet. I haven't even rewarded you yet

Don't excite me for no reason

Have I ever disappointed you?

Not one damn time

Good. Now good luck

Chapter twenty

Adam

As I step out onto the field, the air is charged with anticipation. The scent of freshly cut grass calmed me. The stands were filled with passionate fans, their cheers echoing through the stadium. It hadn't taken long before I spotted the girls, a smile forming on my face instantly.

The sun hung low in the sky, casting a warm golden glow over the field. I just prayed it wouldn't rain today. I could handle the sun, I could handle cold weather, but the rain disrupted our game and held us back from our full potential.

All the guys from my team had determination and focus etched on their faces. The tension and pressure of the game were quite clear, even as we went through our warm-up. It was only a reminder of how close we were to our last game of the season.

Soon, the sound of the referee's whistle pierced through the air, signalling the start of the match. Adrenaline coursed through my veins as I took my position on the field, my heart pounding with excitement and nerves. I could do this, I'd been waiting for this.

The first half of the game started, and I sought out any and all opportunities I could to score. There were many attempts, but all failed. After fifteen minutes of dealing with a null-to-null score, Dante passed the ball to Carter. Carter carefully and skillfully managed to pass through the defences and kicked the ball straight into the goal. The keeper jumped in the wrong direction, and it was thrilling to see the score change from zero to one.

Less than five minutes later, the ball was passed to Ibrahim, but he lost control of it. I seized the moment, the ball rolling off my cleat, and with one final movement, I kicked the ball. One of their guys tried to divert the play, but it rolled right through the opening between his legs. The keeper had been unable to stop it as well. Our score now turned into a two, and the crowd erupted.

It was all going well until our opponent decided to dive.

"I didn't lay a finger on him!" Rylan exclaimed, frustration boiling over as the referee flaunted the yellow card in the air for him.

Carter pulled Rylan back before things could escalate.

The penalty led to a 2-1 score for DTU. We were still in the lead, but I knew it took only a few minutes for the game to change completely.

We gave it our hardest, but their defence line became harder to infiltrate, and the score remained the same all the way to our break.

When the second half began, Carter found the moment to pass me the ball. I struck it instantly. I calculated shots like those many times before, and it hit the right corner perfectly. The keeper's glove grazed the ball, but he wasn't able to stop it. The guys on the field and the crowd shouted cheerfully as the ball hit the back of the net.

The game continued with the score remaining just the same. There were attempts on their side to equalise the score, but the defence line and keeper made sure to give them a hard time.

Three extra minutes passed, and the piercing sound of the whistle filled our ears and ended the game. Nationals belonged to us once again.

"Three times in a row, national champions! Our legacy is imprinted in DTU history," Ibrahim declared, his overjoyed embrace surrounded Carter and me, with Dante and the rest of the team joining in the celebration. For our college soccer division, it was quite a win too.

Coach, beaming with pride, joined the celebration. "You've made history for the school," he exclaimed, the pride evident in his eyes.

"That last ball, Adam, it was shot with precision, dude!"

"Yeah, I noticed the keeper had a blind spot despite being tall." I grinned.

I was so fucking happy the ball went in. We would've won regardless, but that shot was impressive and showed the teamwork that went into it. All the things agents loved. There was a lot more excitement being shared on the field while we waited to be given our trophy and such. It wasn't anything fancy, but it sure was nice to see the logo of our school enlarged.

The podium was all set up, and the coach almost had to smack us to get us in line. We were given our medals and then it was time for *Man of the Match*. The last two years that went to Carter, and our freshman year, it went to our keeper for the outstanding performance he did.

"Adam Sierra Vall," the man announced. Carter and Ibrahim were on either side of me and began to shake my arms, tugging at me out of the shared happiness.

I was shocked and filled with sudden excitement I didn't care that the man butchered my last name. I got the trophy! I immediately accepted it with the biggest grin on my face. Luckily, my name was written correctly.

"He is going to sleep with that reward," Dante yelled with a grin.

"Oh yeah, I'd put on some noise-cancelling headphones if I were you, Ibra," Carter went on with the joke, and I just rolled my eyes and admired my trophy.

"First the snoring, now this," Ibrahim whined, and my jaw dropped. The damn audacity.

"You want to talk about snoring?" I asked, jabbing Ibrahim's chest. That man's snoring took me by complete surprise. I was close to muffling him with the pillow when he started snoring last night.

"I'm a pre-med student at an athletic scho–"

"If you guys don't shut up right now, I will make the off-season extra hard on all of you," Coach Mendes whispered sternly and glared at us.

We scoffed but didn't dare to poke the bear further. We remained still until our trophy was handed to us. The trophy was shiny, perfectly polished, and our school's name was nicely engraved. When we were ready for our photos, the cannons erupted with gold and purple snippets shooting out.

After multiple photos and conversations, we were finally off to the changing room. There were many plans for the night, plans we were all overly excited about. I took a photo of myself with my trophy and sent it to my parents first.

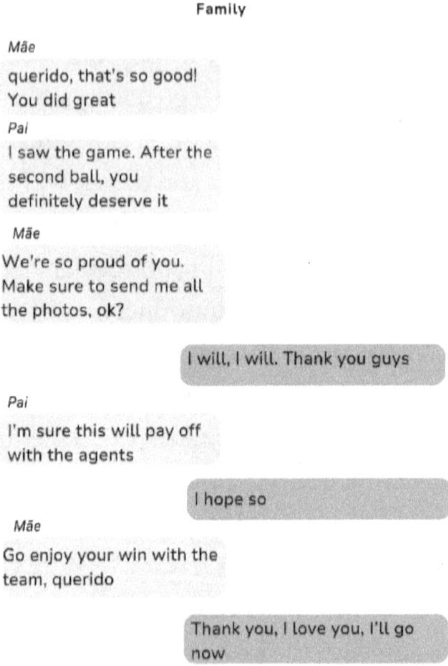

I smiled at their messages, their support. All my life, till high school, they had attended all the games they could; even if they were tired, they'd still sit there and cheer for me. Since university, there had only been a few games they could attend, and I understood, I didn't expect them to just take a plane to come watch a game when they had so much going on. Instead, they watched the live stream on TV, they paid extra for that access, and supported through messages.

Everyone exited the locker room one by one. I grabbed my bag and deliberately moved slower to be last. I messaged Brooklyn to meet me outside, and I hoped she'd come. For now, I was finishing up my call with my grandmother, who hadn't been able to stream the match, so I had to let her know I won.

"My precious boy, you did so great!" she cheered, followed by many other praises in Portuguese to show how happy and proud she was. "I bet you have big plans. I'll end the call now, okay?"

"Boa noite, vovó," I said politely, then put my phone away.

I could already see Brooklyn coming towards me. I cocked my head to the side, signalling for her to follow me, and she did.

"Where are the others?" I asked, looking at our surroundings. Not a single soul in sight, but I still wanted to be sure. We did have a van shielding us from others right now, though.

"Up front with their boyfriends," Brooklyn replied, her hand landing reassuringly on my shoulder. "You really nailed it out there, Adam."

"I did, didn't I?" I smirked proudly. I knew how great I had been out there, but it felt thrilling to hear from her.

"Mhm, you have plans to go celebrate with the team, don't you?" Brooklyn asked, already knowing the drill.

"Yeah, Carter promised steak dinner and such." I smiled and finally admired her in my shirt. Oh, my jersey was perfect on her, but all I could think about right now was the first time she wore it.

"Go enjoy your night, Adam, you deserve every bit of it," Brooklyn said, rising to her toes to kiss my cheek. She then attempted to walk away, but I took a step towards her.

"Come here," I whispered softly, pulling her close with a gentle touch on her wrist. Her breasts pressed against me, her warmth enveloped me, and I couldn't help but cup her face tenderly.

In the dim light of the night, her hazel eyes glistened, but the golden specks faded into the shadows. I didn't need the light to see her beauty, every detail of her was etched into my heart. The subtle green hues that danced with the gold in her eyes, the way she rolled her lips when she tried not to smile, the rich scent of peony when she'd enter the room, the confidence that she carried in her voice—god, that was a sound that calmed the rhythm of my heart.

I knew them all by heart, as if they were a part of me, ingrained in my very soul.

Brooklyn was dangerous to me, but I was addicted to her and unwilling to break free from this new addiction.

"Adam?" Brooklyn's voice pulled me out of the train of thought I was lost in. I flashed her a quick smile, her hand snuck up my chest until she yanked me down.

Her lips touched mine, and it felt like home. The sweet taste of strawberry on her lips rolled against mine and had me craving more. Our kiss grew with a fiery passion, her fingers digging into my skin as she held me close, almost as if she feared having to let go.

Each kiss swept me away and had me needing more. I explored her mouth, her tongue rolling with mine in harmony. My hand slipped down her back slowly, squeezing her ass. She giggled and squirmed in my touch.

Even when we parted, breathless and exhilarated, I was left with the lingering taste of her.

"We'll get caught," she whispered as she fixed her hair, a strand moving between her fingers.

"You're right, pick this up when we get home?" I asked. There was no way we'd get time alone during this trip, we were set to fly home tomorrow.

"Certainly, go celebrate your win." She patted my shoulder. "We'll celebrate another time."

I waited till she ran off to be with her friends, then slowly walked to the guys. They hadn't noticed me missing, luckily, they were too busy figuring out where we'd go for dinner.

Luckily, the first stop was the hotel. Everyone got cleaned up. This was the one time everyone was dressed so nicely that we didn't pass up the opportunity to take photos with our trophy in the hallway. We had the restaurant dress-code to thank for that.

We went out for our celebratory dinner, which consisted of all the food we avoided for the sake of the game, now we indulged in it—even with Coach right there. It was Carter's treat after all. We all enjoyed our dinner, and luckily Coach left after. I'm sure he left because it was better he didn't know what we had planned for the rest of the night.

Our next stop was a bar. Carter and Ibrahim were the only ones who planned to remain sober, while the rest of us made the most of the night. I was smart this time and stuck to just two drinks—of the same kind.

The night involved a lot of singing, dancing, and chatting about every detail of the games we had this season. We recalled all the moments we were in our A game, all the moments where fate was on our side, moments where we could've been better. All in all, it was a busy night for the bar, but around 1 AM, Carter and Ibrahim hauled our asses back to the hotel.

"Come on, guys, be quiet," Carter said sternly, but one of the guys on the team giggled a proper loud giggle that took everyone by surprise. Others joined in on the laughing, and another even rolled on the floor.

"Coach is on the same floor as us. If he comes out, I will claim I have no idea what you guys were up to," Carter warned.

"Snitch," Brian groaned and helped his roommate off the floor.

After a bit of hassle, we were all in our respective rooms. I stripped down to my boxers and then dove straight into bed, the cover snug around me.

"Good night, bud." Ibrahim yawned and turned off the lights.

|Almost a week later|

I now had to focus on my last exams. Or try to at least. I had the chance to do an internship and write my paper based on that—it would've counted for two classes—but I didn't take the opportunity. There would have been conflicts with my schedule that I couldn't afford.

I carefully pulled out a box from my shelf and removed the lid. Inside rested four crochet roses, gifts from Brooklyn. She gave all of us one every Valentine's Day, and over the course of the year, I could tell she had honed her skills. I had collected them and was unable to throw them away, when I knew it took her time and effort. I pulled out today's and yesterday's hidden notes from Brooklyn to store away.

Today was *Roses are red, Violets are blue, Your singing voice could use a retune or two.*

Yesterday was *No pen, no paper, but you still drew my attention*.

I assumed she was referring to my singing voice she heard when she walked into my room while I was in the shower. Singing. It's an incident we shall not mention again. I thought I was home alone.

There had been a note every school day of the week since we returned from Nationals. All of them went in the box along with the roses. My personal favourite was *Roses are red, violets are blue, kiss me on the lips and I'll open my legs for you*. The handwriting, the humour, it was all magnificent, I'd pick her poems over the motivational messages for sure.

Okay, no more distractions. I had to work on that paper. I put the box away, then went to sit at my desk.

There was a soft knock on my door. I hummed and looked over at Brooklyn, her gaze finding mine immediately. I raised a brow at her, waiting to see what it was she needed.

"So uh, I have to tell you something," Brooklyn said, her hands were behind her back, and she nervously moved from her heels to her toes. I haven't seen this side of her, ever. I'm not sure if I liked it.

"What's up?" I studied her closely, and she seemed nervous.

"My parents are coming over this weekend," Brooklyn explained, and suddenly her chest seemed a lot lighter. That was it? I thought—

"Tomorrow's Saturday," I said out loud, realisation hitting me right away.

"Yes," Brooklyn muttered, well aware of the date. "They obviously won't stay here. They just want to visit me, and I never told them that we lost our apartment," she rambled.

"You can have your parents over if you want, Brooke, just make sure they leave their shoes at the door, and we won't have an issue." I shrugged. I was happy this was all. I was worried something terrible had happened... like her finding a place of her own.

"Thank you. One thing though... They don't know that we lost the apartment. I told them I'm staying here temporarily because of a gas leak," Brooklyn continued, and I just nodded.

I noticed how little contact she had with her folks, she never once spoke positively about them unless it was about them being renowned surgeons. I didn't think she liked them very much, and I didn't think their trip would be fun for Brooklyn.

"Of course," I finally said and flashed her a quick smile. "If you need anything, I'm right here. I'm a master with parents." I winked. Parents loved me.

"Thank you, Adam. I'll be sure to remember." Brooklyn smiled, then exited my room.

Chapter twenty-one

Brooklyn

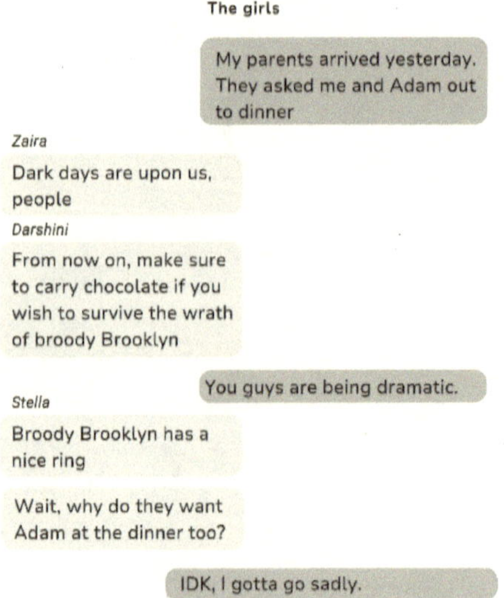

Putting aside my phone, I fastened my robe. I thought over the sudden interest in Adam. They'd never shown concern for my roommates before, their curiosity was a little peculiar. Were they up to something?

I fabricated a story about moving in with him last week due to a gas leak in my apartment, and they believed it. Their insistence on meeting him left me uneasy. Were they trying to 'vet' the man their daughter was living with? It was unlike them to care, and I doubted they would start caring after so many years.

I went to Adam's door, knocking till he let me in. He was fresh out of the shower and looked the part. His damp hair had the colour of wheat, a stark difference compared to the spun gold-like tone when it was dry and styled. Droplets of water rolled down his bare torso, and I was caught in a daze.

"Brooklyn?" Adam's voice broke the spell, his hands resting on his hips.

I cleared my throat.

"Yeah, I just wanted to let you know it's not mandatory for you to go."

"Do you not want me to go?" he asked, frowning.

"I... I'm not sure. I just don't want you to feel pressured," I confessed.

I wanted him to come, but I dreaded my parents' inevitable judgment. Adam had been so kind to me, the last thing I wanted was for him to be hurt by the things my parents would say.

"I don't mind going. Do you?" Adam asked as he began selecting his outfit.

My parents had chosen a high-end restaurant, of course. Adam picked out black slacks and a matching black button-up shirt, looking effortlessly sophisticated.

"I guess not," I admitted.

Did I say that just because I wanted to see him in that outfit? I'm not even sure at this point. "But I need to warn you, I can't control what my parents say, and I apologise in advance."

"It can't be that bad. I can handle it," Adam said with confidence and winked.

Oh, but it can be, Adam.

"I'll finish getting ready, then," I muttered, returning to my room.

My parents were always critical, so I had to make myself as presentable as possible. I didn't feel like getting picked apart. I made sure my makeup was perfect, fought with the damn strappy heels, and straightened my posture.

Finally, I went downstairs, catching Adam's eyes trailing down my figure slowly.

"Wow, you look like a million bucks," Adam complimented, his gaze filled with genuine admiration.

I felt the same way. Perfecting every curl in my hair was no easy task, and these heels? They'd be the death of me, but they complemented my champagne mini-dress perfectly.

"I'm well aware. You look quite dashing too," I returned the compliment, and Adam's lips curled into a smile.

On the way over, I read the menu aloud so we'd know what to order. Normally, I wouldn't decide until I got there, but my parents aren't very patient people.

When we entered the restaurant, we were greeted by a dimly lit ambience that oozed sophistication. A long silver chandelier hung from the ceiling, casting a soft glow over the room. The walls, painted in dark tones, provided a dramatic backdrop to the elegant decor. On one side, there was a golden gleaming bar. The atmosphere radiated luxury, which was exactly how my parents preferred it.

The receptionist greeted us politely and then led us to the table where my parents were already seated.

Dad got up and extended his hand to Adam almost instantly. "Adam, so lovely to meet you."

"Lovely to meet you both, thanks for the dinner invite," Adam said politely, then shook my mom's hand. He then pulled out my chair before sitting down himself.

"We had already reserved for four, so we might as well," Dad replied.

A frown spread across my face. Mom jabbed him, trying to be subtle but failing. Adam and I shared a quick look of confusion.

"Yes, thank you for helping my daughter with a place to stay," Mom said, smoothly changing the subject. Her eyes scanned every detail of my appearance—my hair, jewellery, makeup. She scrutinised everything but didn't complain, indicating her approval. Yay...

"Speaking of, any updates from your apartment?" Dad asked.

"Not really, they expect it to be fully safe next month," I lied. Adam sat still. I was surprised he never asked why we were lying. He had just simply said *Okay*.

"Yeah? That's good." Dad smiled and reached for his sparkling water.

"So, have you looked into med schools then?" Mom asked Adam. I turned to him, and he looked at her with a frown etched on his face.

"Med school?" Adam repeated.

"Don't you want to become a neurosurgeon?" Mom asked. "Personally, I would've done it, but cosmetic surgery was my calling," she continued, and I refrained from rolling my eyes.

"You're confusing Adam with Ibrahim. Adam doesn't want to attend med school," I clarified. Mom and Dad both looked shocked, their expressions quickly shifting to disapproval.

"No?" Dad asked with a hint of disgust in his voice. He looked at Adam, who remained calm and unfazed.

"No, it sounds lovely and a great challenge for the mind, but it's not what my heart desires," Adam confessed wholeheartedly. Bless his soul, he must truly think they'd be okay with what he just said.

"Oh, you're the son of the diplomats," Mom recalled, surprising me with her memory. She barely remembered these things. "Will you take after your parents?"

"No. If all goes well, I'll be playing professional football," Adam said with pride. I placed my hand on his knee under the table, preparing to comfort him against my parents' inevitable criticism.

In their eyes, any job based on skills was merely a hobby, not a legitimate profession. And something like entertainment? It's like you slapped them across the face.

"Sports? You–You want to play games for a profession?" Dad's face resembled that of distaste. Mom glared at him for a moment and nudged him.

Before Adam could respond, Mom swiftly changed the subject. "Anyway, have you heard much from Liam lately?"

I froze at the mention of Liam, my hand squeezing Adam's knee hard. He placed his hand over mine, and I released the tension. Liam Dineen, the son of my parents' business partner. Liam was the child they wanted me to be, and when they realised that wasn't happening, they kept pushing me to date him.

"No, why would I?" I asked, trying to keep my voice steady. After one date, I had expertly avoided Liam.

"He graduated Summa Cum Laude. He actually came with us, but he was tired from the flight," Mom explained in such a gushing tone that it was evident how proud she was of Liam. Dad shared the same bright smile, and that made me simmer with jealousy. "We helped him get settled in, but we'll do more tomorrow," she continued, and now Adam was the one squeezing my hand.

"What is Liam doing here?" I asked as calmly as possible.

They couldn't read me, not like Adam, who was now tracing shapes on the back of my hand. He attempted to calm me down, but I was close to imploding.

Our conversation was briefly interrupted by the waiter to take our order and then my attention returned to my parents, waiting for their answer.

"Liam is going to attend Harvard Medical School, so we came to help him get settled in," Dad explained. Great, I'll be in the same state as that guy again. "Can you believe it? He'll be a surgeon too and take over his parents' share of the clinic," he continued, speaking so highly of Liam.

"Good for him," I said bitterly.

"We want that for you, too, Brooke. It's not too late," Mom said. "Don't you think these childish games have gone on long enough?" she asked, her tone laced with annoyance.

This was it, the beginning of a terrible night.

"Childish games? Not too late for what?" Adam interjected, no longer pleased with the half-given information. He was missing a lot.

"Brooklyn was meant to become a surgeon too, but she decided to defy us," Dad explained, not caring to disclose my personal matters at all. "I'm sure your grandmother's fund is running dry now. We decided to still be kind, we'll pay for your studies completely if you go down the surgeon path now—it's not too late," he continued. I'm not quite sure if he thought he was a salesman, but he was failing terribly. All those words did was anger me.

"Enough," I muttered, trying to avoid causing a scene despite my dwindling patience.

I looked at Adam, and he was repulsed by what my father had said.

"Don't fight it, just think about it," Mom continued, where Dad left off. "Liam is going to be in town too, so you can show him around and maybe give your relationship another shot," she added with a suggestive smile.

That was the final straw for me.

"Oh, for the love of everything holy, I do not want to date that pompous jerk, and I do not want to become a surgeon, I do not want to take after you. I am my own person, is that so hard to understand?"

"This is what I'm talking about. All you ever do is fight us on everything," Dad scoffed and shook his head.

"How about we talk about something else?" Adam asked and instantly changed the subject, "What do you think of the city?"

"It's fine. It's not home, but there are some lovely places around," Mom answered truthfully. I knew how much they loved home. That place is their solace, but to me, it was the opposite.

"I think we love the West Coast a little too much. Where are you from?" Dad laughed, looking over at Adam.

"I'm from Bethesda. I lived there my entire life until college," Adam replied, and the mood seemed to lighten. I eased up a bit.

"So, after you graduate, will you follow in your parents' footsteps?" Mom asked again.

"I hope not. It's not my main plan." Adam shrugged it off. I admired him. I walked around on eggshells with these two, but he simply remained who he was and answered everything as he pleased.

"Right, soccer..." Dad sighed disapprovingly. "I still can't believe you want to participate in some games for a living."

"Soccer, which happens to be the most popular sport in the world and is rising within the country too," I said, coming up to Adam's defence. I didn't even know why I was so protective all of a sudden.

"I know what soccer is. I just don't see how someone could find their life fulfilling by just kicking a ball around," Dad argued, narrowing his gaze at me.

"I don't see how that's an issue. I've wanted to do this since I was a boy, and my parents supported me." Adam shrugged.

"Your parents are diplomats, and they thought this was a wise idea?" Mom asked incredulously.

This was why I didn't want Adam to come. I didn't want them to treat him the way they treated me.

"I, of course, have a backup plan, hence why I pursued political science," Adam explained, but I could already tell they disapproved of his life plan.

"Right, I was looking forward to meeting that Ibrahim boy," Mom scoffed rudely.

"Seriously? What is your deal?" I asked. I was fine with them coming after me constantly, but judging my friends? That's where I drew the line. My friends have been there for me more than them.

"I'm sorry, you just surround yourself with terrible people. I mean, someone who counts on playing sports for the rest of their lives? What else does he have going for him?" Mom pointed her finger at Adam, looking up and down at him. I didn't dare look at Adam, not wanting to see the impact of her cruel words.

I had simply had enough. Before Adam could say anything, I interjected, "Adam speaks five languages fluently, his grades have always been above 75 percent, and if he wanted, he could easily get a job that's far better than just filling lips and doing silly facelifts."

I knew they took pride in their jobs, I knew they loathed it when it would be compared to some measly thing, and right now, seeing the shock on their face made it all worth it.

"Brooklyn, do not disrespect us like that!" Dad warned, his voice raised but still mindful of his surroundings.

"Oh, but it's totally fine for you guys to come here and insult my friend, try to financially manipulate me?" I asked, feeling Adam's hand on my thigh, but that wouldn't calm me anymore. "Oh, and your poor attempts to pimp me out to your partner's son, I mean, seriously? Since I was little, you spoke of how great Liam and I would be together, but can't you see I don't want that?"

Their faces went through many emotions, but they settled upon anger.

"You are one ungrateful girl," Dad snapped, throwing his napkin on the table and pointing a finger at me. "We're trying to give you the world, but you always fight and rebel."

"I never wanted any of that!" I shouted, not caring if I caused a scene. "All I ever wanted was supportive parents." The anger and hatred consumed me, my hands shaking. I could feel the tears welling up because I never knew how to handle anger well.

"You never once visited me. I had to beg you to come to parents' weekend just so my friends would think I had great, supportive parents like them. The day I graduated high school, you didn't celebrate. When I left for college, you were at work and didn't care. I had to drive myself because you simply did not care. But for dearest Liam? You took time off from work to help him get settled in?" Everything I promised myself to keep buried, but dear god, I failed miserably because I realised all the things I wanted, they gave to Liam.

Their faces changed to embarrassment, and they briefly looked at Adam.

"Brook—" Mom reached over.

I got up and stormed out of the restaurant, heading straight for the parking lot. With my angry stomping, it was a miracle my heels didn't snap. I couldn't stay in that place a second longer. I didn't even care that we hadn't gotten our food yet.

I tried breathing techniques to calm my anger, imagined adorable kittens snuggling with dogs, but nothing worked. That was until I felt a familiar hand wrap around my arm, and the soothing oceanic scent filled my nose. I turned to Adam.

"Brooklyn baby." Adam's voice was gentle as he enveloped me in his arms. There was no space between us, and he moved my cheek to rest against his chest. "I'm sorry," he whispered, as if any of this was his fault.

"You haven't done anything." I sighed, feeling my anger slowly dissipate. His tender words, gentle embrace, and calming cologne worked.

"I may or may not have told your parents off. I didn't mean to, but I was angry," Adam confessed. I stepped back and looked up at him. There was not a single trace of regret on his face. I didn't know what he said in there, but he meant every word.

"They deserve it."

"Let's go home, Brooke," Adam said, opening the passenger door for me.

Adam didn't say a word during the drive, thankfully. I needed the silence to sort through my thoughts and memories of all the times my parents had disappointed me. They were countless. Adam made one stop on the way home, at a drive-thru ice cream shop. He got my usual milkshake, trying to cheer me up a little.

I grabbed my phone. I had muted Liam on social media to avoid seeing his posts. I checked out his account and saw the photos of his graduation. My parents were alongside him, carrying the same happiness on their faces as if they were his parents. I felt a bitter aftertaste in my mouth, and my stomach felt messed up with the churned jealousy and disappointment I felt.

"We're home," Adam announced. I locked my phone and looked up to see we were in the garage.

I didn't want to cry here, but everything was bothering me. The hair clips, the earrings, the necklace—every damn thing I wore just so they wouldn't pick on my clothing— I was suffocating. It was only a reminder that no matter what I did, I was never who they wanted me to be.

I struggled to remove the fucking strappy heels.

"Let me." Adam pushed to sit down on the entryway bench.

"I can handle it," I said, and leaned over, but Adam already kneeled down.

"I know you can, but I can too," he decided, placing my feet on his knee. He was a lot more gentle than I was moments ago. His touch was gentle, and I couldn't help but stare at him.

I shouldn't be letting him do this, it would only confuse my heart more.

"There." He stood back up and extended his hand to me.

I took his hand to get up, and Adam was about to say something, but I waited long enough to cry. I stormed off to my room after uttering a broken, "Thank you."

Tears started spilling the moment I closed my bedroom door. I didn't even try to hold them back, it needed to happen. I paced around the room, wiping my tears constantly. I hadn't bothered putting anything away, the entire pile of jewellery and my purse were scattered on my desk. My dress was pooled by the dresser.

I put on some comfortable clothes and sat down to remove my makeup, feeling at ease finally. Everything my parents had said and done was cleared from my head. I closed my eyes for a moment and practised some calming breathing techniques.

"Dinner is served," Adam announced, his voice projecting up the stairs.

I frowned and headed down. Adam walked towards the couch with two bowls. I peeked into the bowls and saw he had made his famous cheesy ramen with eggs. I loved it when he made it because he scrambled the egg before adding it to the ramen.

"You made dinner?"

"Mhm, didn't feel like eating out anymore," he said, handing me chopsticks while he held his fork.

It was the little things like these that made my heart flutter.

Chapter twenty-two

Adam

We were on the couch, bowls of homemade sundaes in hand. I wasn't sure how many treats it would take to make her feel better, but I was willing to find out.

"You're probably wondering what exactly happened all those years ago, aren't you?" Brooklyn asked, lowering her spoon.

I studied her face for a moment, despite her best efforts, her puffy eyes still betrayed that she had been crying.

"Of course, I want to know," I said, not wanting to lie to her. "But I don't want you to talk about something you don't feel like talking about."

"What did you tell my parents?" Brooklyn then asked, and I couldn't bear to look at her. Not after what I had told them.

"Hm?" I played dumb, hoping she wouldn't press further.

"You said you told them off. What did you say?" Her tone made it clear she wouldn't let it go until I confessed.

"I told them they're the most arrogant, heartless people I've ever met, and I don't know how their patients even trust them. I, uh, told your mother she's pathetic and disgusting for pushing that guy onto you. Among some more stuff..." I knew better than to mess with family, but I didn't appreciate the way they spoke to her.

"Adam," Brooklyn gasped, her lips curving into a small smile, her eyes widening with what seemed like happiness.

Seeing that I hadn't overstepped in her eyes, I decided to tell her the rest. "I also told them it's a good thing you didn't inherit their hideous manners because no amount of surgery could ever fix that."

"I was rude, out of line, but at that moment, I was angry," I confessed. I knew they were still her parents.

I didn't want to behave poorly in front of them, but I felt like I had no choice.

"Thank you for saying all of that. I don't mind a single thing you told them. I guess I owe you an explanation about everything." She smiled.

"It's okay if you don't want to... but I am curious about your grandmother's story," I admitted. She could sidestep the family drama, but I was genuinely interested in her inheritance and current financial situation.

Brooklyn took a deep breath.

"Well, you see, I did receive some merit-based grants and some private organisations grants, but they don't cover everything, you've seen DTU's tuition. Some scholarships I couldn't apply for because of my parents' annual income. They were aware of this and thought it would give them power to control me after high school. My grandparents owned an architecture firm and were quite wealthy when they retired. Grandma left all of that to me since I was the only grandchild," she began to explain, and the story was much more dramatic than I could've imagined. I knew my parents didn't always approve of my choice to put going pro first, but they had never tried to control my future like that.

"You mentioned having cousins?" I recalled being stuck on the only grandchild part.

"Yeah, from my great aunt and great uncles, but my grandma only has me," Brooklyn clarified.

"Oh, okay continue." I crossed one leg over the other as I looked at her.

"Yeah, so my grandma promised to help me with college funds and left everything to me, including her house," Brooklyn continued. Then her face turned a bit bitter. "I used most of that money for uni, but also because I had lent my cousin some when she needed extensive surgery. She promised to pay me back, and I know she will, it's just taking longer than we thought, and I don't want to pressure her, she's been through enough already."

She never told me any of this. I wasn't entitled to it, but she usually told me all the little things that stressed her, like rants about professors and the shelter, and I just thought this would be one of the things we'd talk about too.

"The money is running low, and I thought I'd be paid back. All I have left is the house, but I refuse to sell it. It means too much to me, and now I'm stuck." She sighed, tipping her head back.

"And your parents are aware of that?" I asked. They had used money as leverage before; what was stopping them from trying it again?

I felt a pang of guilt for all the times we'd teased her about her parents' wealth and her supposed inheritance. She'd always laughed along, playing the part convincingly.

"I think so. They always wanted me to become a surgeon like them," she said, rolling her eyes before revealing a surprising detail. "I wanted that once too."

Brooklyn? A surgeon? Wow.

"You mentioned your grandma's house. Did you spend a lot of time there?" I asked.

"Adam, I was practically raised in that house," Brooklyn scoffed as if I should've known this already. Then her eyes drifted off, and she began to tell me about her childhood.

|Brooklyn, Age Six|

Brooklyn sat on the bench with her legs crossed as her fingers toyed with her tie. She despised her school uniform and would have torn it off if she could. She watched every car that passed by to pick up students, her frustration growing as one by one, her classmates left, and she remained in the pickup area. The adults in the office around were visibly annoyed. Brooklyn was always picked up late. Finally, a candy apple red car appeared, one she recognized instantly.

"Hello, angel," Hazel greeted her granddaughter with a sweet smile.

Brooklyn adored her grandma, but had expected her parents to pick her up. They had promised to make up for missing her recital by getting ice cream. That's all she wanted, but once again, they hadn't shown up. This was the third time that week.

"I know you're upset, baby. I'm sorry," Hazel said, cupping the little girl's face and smiling warmly. "I do have a plan to make it up to you," she added with a mischievous smirk.

"Okay," Brooklyn mumbled. Her grandma's surprises were always fun, perhaps better than her parents' broken promises.

"I've got some fancy chocolates from Belgium at home, but before we head there, we'll stop by the animal shelter. Susie told me they have new kittens, and maybe you can help take care of them," Hazel explained, opening the car door.

Susie, Hazel's old friend, ran the shelter. Hazel often helped out there and had taken Brooklyn along before. Brooklyn loved every moment of it.

"Really?" Brooklyn's face lit up. The idea of all the cute kittens and dogs excited her, they liked her! There was this old golden retriever who was very lazy but loved her a lot.

"Yeah!" Hazel smirked. The mission succeeded.

Brooklyn's grandmother always did her best to make her as happy as she could. She tried talking to her mother so she'd become a better parent, but was threatened with not being able to see Brooklyn, so her grandmother had to back off.

Brooklyn's grandmother became the one to always care for her until her parents would come pick her up, but they always worked late and arrived when Brooklyn was asleep, carrying her out to the car.

|Now|

"So yeah, I was pretty much raised there. This continued until my grandma passed away. She'd pick me up, we'd run errands together or visit the animal shelter. My grandma's best friend always called us, and we'd care for the animals together. Sometimes my parents wouldn't even bother to pick me up on their way home from work. But my grandma was always there for me," Brooklyn reminisced, a warm smile lighting up her face.

Hearing about her grandmother touched my heart. It seemed we shared a deep love for our grandmas. Hers sounded like an angel, too, and I couldn't help but wonder what embarrassing stories about young Brooklyn she might have shared with me.

"She sounds incredible," I said sincerely.

"She was," Brooklyn agreed, her voice filled with affection. "She taught me how to bake and crochet and so much more. She was freaking smart too, you should've seen the buildings she helped design."

"Were you close to your grandpa?" I asked, seizing the opportunity to learn more about her past.

"He passed away five years before I was even born," she said with glossy eyes.

"I mean this in the most respectful way ever, but why did your parents even have a child if they didn't want to properly raise one?" I asked, and that seemed to light a fire within her.

"I was wondering about that too." She pulled one leg under the other and got comfortable. "So let me tell you what I discovered..."

|Brooklyn, Age 14|

Brooklyn was beyond furious. Her parents had persuaded—borderline forced—her to take violin classes and ballet, which she had to fight for because they initially wanted her to do fencing. Lastly, there was Model United Nations, which she actually enjoyed, so that didn't feel like a chore.

She remembered their words: "Your college application needs to be perfect. You are to be a surgeon like us, and you need to get into an Ivy League university."

Now, she ripped off the pink lint from her hair and threw it on the floor, her bag sliding across the floor, and the door slammed behind her. Her parents missed her dance recital, the biggest show the dance school had every year, the one where she had to give up so much to impress them.

"Brooky, honey, I know you're upset—" Hazel began, but Brooklyn cut her off with a fierce glare.

"Upset doesn't even describe what I'm feeling," she retorted, her voice raised. She had never spoken to Hazel this way before and left her momentarily stunned.

The teenage years had their challenging days, but the good days always made up for it.

"At least I was there, right? You did so perfectly. I even videoed the whole thing!" Hazel gushed, pulling out her phone. Brooklyn had convinced her to get a fancy phone, talking about megapixels and how much she could capture with it. Now, Hazel's phone was filled with photos of animals and her beloved granddaughter.

Brooklyn scoffed and rolled her eyes.

"What—"

"I didn't want you there. I wanted my parents there. They're never there!" she screamed, tears streaming down her cheeks. "It's always you, never them," she sobbed.

"Is my presence and support not enough?" Hazel pouted, walking over to her. She wrapped her arms around Brooklyn, feeling the tears soak through her shirt.

"No," Brooklyn replied, her voice muffled. "But—"

"They're your parents, and you wished they were there," Hazel finished her thought for her. A soft sigh escaped her lips.

"I'm taking all these stupid classes, making sure I get perfect grades—I even hang out with their partners' weird kids. I do everything they want, and they can't even be there for my recital!" Brooklyn wiped her tears as she looked at her grandmother. What was all the hard work for then?

"I know, angel, I know," Hazel whispered, wiping her tears and pulling her closer to kiss her forehead. "This is why I tell you to do what you want, not what they want," she spoke gently, hoping Brooklyn would listen before it was too late. "Become a vet or anything else, but don't become a surgeon just because they demand it."

"No, if I become a surgeon, they'll have more time for me. We can work together and—" She had been chanting it in her head several times, believing her theory. It would work, it should work according to her, but Hazel was appalled by what she was hearing.

"For Christ's sake, Brooky, that won't fix anything," Hazel interrupted her words.

She couldn't bear to listen to it much longer. She knew her granddaughter was smart, but she also knew how much she craved validation to the point she'd break herself, and Hazel wouldn't sit and let that happen. Not while she's still alive.

"How do you know that? They had me for a reason, they love me, and they want me to be as great as them," Brooklyn replied with the words that she had convinced herself of.

"That's not—" Hazel swallowed her words.

"You don't know anything."

"They never had you because they wanted you." The words slipped from Hazel's mouth and she regretted them instantly. She hoped Brooklyn would shrug it off, but instead, Brooklyn froze, and her brows furrowed.

"What?" Brooklyn tried to make sense of it.

"Shit," Hazel cursed. Brooklyn knew that face.

"W-what do you mean, Gam?" she asked.

Her heart was racing against her chest, she had a gut feeling this night would end on a far worse note than it already was.

"Nothing, forget I said anything. I'm just angry, I didn't mean anything, sorry," Hazel rambled and walked off to the kitchen, but she could hear Brooklyn's footsteps right behind her. Her husband had always told her she was different when upset—she never thought she'd let those words slip.

"No, tell me," Brooklyn demanded, but her voice was already cracking. "Please," she then pleaded, on the brink of crying. Hazel was never able to stand Brooklyn's cry, it broke her heart to pieces.

Hazel turned to her and carefully cupped her chin. "I shouldn't tell you this, Brooklyn, no child deserves to hear this," she whispered. She shouldn't tell her a thing, she believed that it would only make things worse mentally for Brooklyn.

"You know something, please Gam Gam," Brooklyn continued to plead, and Hazel stared into those eyes that reminded her of her husband.

She considered lying, making up some story that would put Brooklyn's mind at ease, but she had never lied to Brooklyn before and didn't want to start now. She mentally justified her following actions by convincing herself that Brooklyn needed to hear this, or she'd keep doing things to satisfy others rather than making herself happy.

"Your parents had you because your dad's mother called your mother infertile and insulted her because she didn't give her son a child."

Brooklyn's lips parted, processing the information. She wanted to deny it—but it made sense to her.

"So, it was all for pride? To prove a point?" Brooklyn asked, swallowing the lump in her throat. She was angry and upset and hugged her grandmother tightly as she began to sob in her chest.

The worst part of it all was that her paternal grandmother asked for a grandchild but still didn't love her. She just tolerated Brooklyn—all because her son left home for a woman. Her paternal grandmother hated Brooklyn's mother, and that hatred extended to the child.

She was disappointed and let down by reality. Never would she ever put someone's happiness before her own.

|Now|

"I'm so sorry," I said, feeling my heart ache. I couldn't even imagine going through something like that. When she told the story, I could tell she still harboured that resentment within her.

"Yeah... Since that day, I changed my mind, I no longer wanted to become a surgeon. I wanted to become a vet before changing my mind to settle on political science." Brooklyn brushed it off as if it were nothing. I just now realised how great she was at putting up a facade. "I think it was around that time I had to deal with the Liam drama."

"Tell me more about this Liam guy," I asked.

|Brooklyn, Age 16|

Brooklyn found herself trapped at one of her parents' clinic parties. Normally, they wouldn't force her to attend, but this time they had been adamant. She regretted not fighting harder to stay home, the room was filled with people she didn't like.

Moments like these made her miss her grandmother dearly. Just one call, and Hazel would have come to pick her up. Instead, she was stuck here, forced to mingle with the kids of her parents' colleagues and partners.

"I mean, have you seen Amanda and Josh? Coming to school with shoes like that? I know they're on a scholarship, but they bring down the school's name and reputation by wearing those knockoffs," Brayden, some associate's son, complained. Over half of them attended the same private school, and Brooklyn looked around as they all laughed at Brayden's comment. It wasn't her responsibility to teach them decency, she'd met their parents and knew it was a lost cause. So, she excused herself.

Brooklyn wandered over to the dessert station, trying to decide what she wanted. A strong scent of cologne filled the room, too overpowering, pricking her nose. She turned to see it was Liam.

Puberty had treated him well, according to the girls who watched the lacrosse matches. Liam's body had developed some toned muscles, and his hazel eyes, similar to hers but with more green, had a certain allure. He had grown his hair out, keeping the sides shorter. Many found him attractive, but Brooklyn felt no pull to him.

"The cookies are here. Your parents said you liked the chocolatey ones," Liam said, clearing his throat and pointing to the cookies. He was almost right.

"I do... but these have Reese's cups in them," Brooklyn noted, glancing at the cookies and the sign disclosing that.

"And... that's not delicious?" Liam asked, stepping closer. All the years they'd known each other, and he still couldn't remember one tiny, crucial bit of information.

"I wouldn't know. Last time I tried something with peanuts, I choked, my ears swelled up, and I'm sure I was close to seeing the other side," Brooklyn replied, watching as his lips parted and the tips of his ears turned red. He was embarrassed.

"Brooky, you're being silly," her mother's voice cut through the moment. She gave Brooklyn a subtle glare as she walked past them. "Now, don't mind me. I'm just grabbing some pudding, then I'll be out of your hair," she said, forcing a soft laugh.

Brooklyn sighed internally. These gatherings were always the same—full of superficial conversations and criticisms. She longed for the warmth and authenticity of her grandmother's company.

Brooklyn loaded some cheesecake shots onto a plate along with some other treats. Liam stood there awkwardly as he waited for her mother to leave, and when she finally did, he sighed in relief.

"Wow, that's a lot," Liam muttered, then cleared his throat when Brooklyn glared at him. "Listen, uh, we have that dance coming up and I'd love to take you—maybe we can go out on a date next week first?" Liam asked, tucking his hands into his pockets.

"Uh... I'll think about it," she answered, then hurried out of there.

She managed to avoid everyone until it was time to head home.

"So, did Liam finally ask you out? His parents spoke to us about it." Her mother's words caught her off guard.

"He did," she said suspiciously.

"You said yes, right? I think we should go shopping for dresses, a super cute mini dress with some nice shoes, and—"

"I haven't answered him yet," Brooklyn stopped her. She had a feeling this was her plan, her and Liam's mom. Liam's mom would often comment on how pretty she was, how she'd make a great surgeon, and how perfect she and Liam would fit.

"What do you mean? You'll say yes, right?" Juliana asked, looking at her through the rear-view mirror.

"You've known him all your life, and his parents are good people," Thomas spoke up.

Brooklyn could tell it would end badly if she turned Liam down. In fact, she made a quick calculation. Liam would be very busy with lacrosse and studying for his SATs, they'd have to spend very little time together, even in the summer, since her parents had plans to go to France and she'd be going with them. After that, Liam was set to graduate early and head off to college, then she'd be rid of him.

So, for one last time, she accepted something she didn't want just to avoid a war.

|Now|

"You went out with the pompous dude?" I asked with a disapproving tone.

"You don't even know him." Brooklyn rolled her eyes.

"Okay, is he not pompous?" I then asked.

"He is. He's such a self-absorbed asshole, he truly thinks he's the smartest in a room and disrespects anyone who's not from the same class as him. Our dates were awful, he'd talk about himself so much, then he'd try to explain shit to me I already knew," Brooklyn ranted, it was quite clear Liam was not liked at all.

"Your parents didn't care?" I wondered. My parents were actively invading my privacy when I was that age.

"Nope, I fooled them into thinking it was going great. Liam had to leave for college, and we broke it off. I think we had a total of six dates?" Brooklyn replied with a shrug.

"That's six too many," I muttered without thinking.

"Tell me about it." Brooklyn sighed. "My mom tried to make me attend his college."

"How did they react when you told them you wanted to become a vet?" I asked. Dinner tonight sure showed me what type of people her parents are.

"They were disgusted, but they also thought that I was throwing some sort of fit—I never told them I knew the truth, and neither did my grandma," Brooklyn replied, and all I could wonder was why the hell would she even go to today's dinner when they treated her like that.

"I see."

"I think my grandma knew she was going to pass away because two weeks before she died, she told me about my inheritance and how she wanted me to do as I please, but to never do something or become someone I'm not. So I waited patiently and applied for colleges," Brooklyn said, mindlessly toying with the pillow in her lap. "My parents knew DTU was on my list and thought I'd go pre-med and then DTU med school, but when I showed them what I was going for and all hell broke loose."

|Brooklyn age 17|

Brooklyn showed her parents her acceptance letter. Soon she'd graduate and be off to DTU. It was quite an accomplishment, and she knew her grandmother would be so damn proud of her.

Juliana and Thomas were proud to know she got accepted into DTU. Then her mother read the letter further, and her face fell, "Esteemed Political Science program?" she read the sentence loudly.

"Brooklyn, is this some sort of funny joke?" Thomas asked, his eyes narrowing on his daughter.

"No, I want to do political science, and I got accepted for the program." Brooklyn shrugged and continued to make her chocolate croissants. She had been waiting to tell her parents the whole day, and she needed something to calm her nerves.

Brooklyn figured that if she became a vet, she might save dozens, maybe even hundreds of animals. But through political science, she could advocate for change, help shape and enforce laws, and protect countless more. She knew with absolute certainty that she would thrive in that world.

"You will not do that. We told you your route," Juliana said with a slightly raised voice.

"And I do not want to become a surgeon." Brooklyn shrugged yet again and hadn't bothered looking up at them.

"You are to become one so you can take over our half of the clinic, that's what we agreed upon," her father said as he circled around.

"No, that's what you guys agreed upon." She looked up at her father.

"I'd like to know how you'll pay for college then," Juliana said, her lips curling into a smile.

"What do you mean?" Brooklyn asked. They had set money aside for her college fund, and they always told her about it. She knew her parents were desperate for her to follow in their footsteps. Part of her was prepared for this, but she still hoped they'd prove her worries wrong.

Her parents' high income made it much more difficult, and she only ever volunteered, so she didn't save up much money on her own, but all the social work did earn her a few small grants, just enough for the high tuition DTU demanded.

"We will not be funding this," her dad then said and earned a subtle nod from Juliana.

"The only way we'll pay is if you agree to our terms," Juliana decided on the spot. That should teach her daughter a lesson, right?

"I'll use grandma's money then." Brooklyn tugged her apron off. "I'll be eighteen by that time and I can access it."

|Now|

"So you paid your way yourself?" I wondered. I knew how expensive our school was. Incredible university, but expensive.

"Yeah. Had some grants and award money too. I had enough money, but then my cousin's surgery happened," Brooklyn explained. "I think they know I'm gonna be in need of money."

"Why do you say that?"

"They always remind me of their offer, but lately it's gotten worse. They offered to pay for everything for me, to take the classes necessary until I'm let into med school. They promised to give me half of their share of the clinic. I think they know I can't afford my master's here and might have to leave," Brooklyn replied, annoyed.

All I could think about was her leaving. I didn't want her to leave.

"You'll do your master's elsewhere?" I asked without thinking.

"I think I'll have to go home. I'll stay in my grandma's house rent-free since my cousin stays there. She has to take care of all the bills and such to stay there. I couldn't sell the house, and my cousin figured she could look after the house," Brooklyn replied with a smile, but now I can tell she didn't mean it. She was trying to convince herself she'd like it. "I'll get into a cheaper college there. There's a cheap master's program," she continued, and the 'happy' tone was annoying when I knew she was the furthest from happy because of the situation.

"Is that what you want?"

"No, Adam, I know my parents will haunt me, but I can't be here unless I get accepted into the Animal Rights Education Program. It's what the dean suggested for me since they usually accept DTU students. They'll pay for half, and I can pay the other half myself, and on top of that, I'll work part-time for them so I'll also get some experience."

"You never told me about this program," I mentioned. I didn't know much about it, and I'd research them later, but it sounded like something she'd love.

"I'm kinda waiting on their response so I can break the good news," Brooklyn said shyly, and I could tell she was nervous about it.

"I understand." I smiled. "I guess I held back on you too. I'm currently negotiating some terms, and I think I might accept Liberty FC's offer."

I didn't want to say anything yet, even though my grandma didn't know a single thing. I was waiting until the ink on the paper would dry, but the news was so exciting and I couldn't contain it much longer.

"Adam, that's incredible, that's the one you were eyeing, right?" Brooklyn said excitedly with her face lit up.

"Yep, them or one in Miami, but I think I'll have to work my way up to that one," I replied.

"You did great, and uh, thanks for listening to me rant. I think I needed it," Brooklyn said on a much softer note.

"I'm glad to be able to help, and thank you for trusting me with your story." I winked, then scooted closer to her. "I never knew about all of that, but I'm quite proud of everything you achieved. Do you have photos of your ballet years? And also, did you have to wear a suit for your violin recitals?"

"I will not give you my embarrassing photos," Brooklyn scoffed and pushed the pillow into my face.

"Show me pleaseeee," I whined.

"Adam, no, I have a reputation to uphold," Brooklyn said as we fought over the pillow.

"I'll show you a photo of where I had earrings," I promised, hoping her old photos would be worth it.

"Fine," she groaned and gave in. She pulled her phone from her pocket. "What did you think of today's note? I forgot to ask."

"*My dearest Adam honey boo-boo, my results are in and the doctor said I'm lacking vitamin U,*" I repeated the words as best as I could. That letter was already added to the box. Brooklyn smiled at me when I repeated it. "I know it by heart already. Perhaps poetry should've been your running career choice," I joked.

"Of course, but I don't want to put the others to shame." Brooklyn laughed. "Grandma did want me to take some poetry classes along with self-defence."

"Really?"

"Mhm, grandpa wrote her poems in high school—she loved it all. The self-defence, she said, was because I don't know how to shut up, so she'd much rather I learn how to defend myself physically since I can handle myself verbally."

"I think she was onto something," I said, watching her look through her phone for the photos.

"Yeah, but the classes are so expensive." She sighed.

I got lost in thoughts, staring at her, wondering if it was her financial situation that stopped her from decorating her room. I'll see if I can change that.

"Hello?" Brooklyn called my name.

"Right, sorry—" I snapped out of my thoughts, and my eyes immediately widened at her photo. Brooklyn in a tutu, I never thought I'd see this. "This is so precious. Look at your make-up." I laughed.

"Hey, the make-up artist was a seventy-year-old woman, we couldn't get her fired because she had a tragic story and needed the money," Brooklyn whined, and when I tried to forward the photo to myself, she slapped away my hand. "No cheating, Adam."

"Fine, I'll show you the photo now, but please remember I was thirteen." I found the photo in my cursed gallery and showed it to her. I expected her to laugh, but not as loudly as she was right now, and non-stop. Well, I made her laugh, but at what cost?

Chapter twenty-three

Brooklyn

A week went by and Friday finally arrived. I hadn't heard from my parents until yesterday, and I hadn't heard from my parents until yesterday. They sent some messages, but I had their notifications muted, not bothering to hear what they had to say.

I mixed in Adam's protein powder for his share of the smoothie. I think this mango-pineapple blend was his favourite. He'd always devour it in the car before even exiting the neighbourhood.

While the blender was going, I grabbed a pink heart-shaped sticky note and a glitter gel pen. I thought for a moment.

Witty, naughty, or a pun... Naughty it is. He could use the boost.

Roses are red, Violets are blue, my dearest Adam, I love your cock.

I stuck it on some crackers and tossed that into his bag along with a mini pack of wafers. I tried to hide them, or he'd read it the minute he grabbed his lunch.

I turned off the blender and could hear loud footsteps descending the stairs.

"Okay, so we danced around the idea a lot," Adam said as he came down.

"What idea?"

"You're getting some self-defence classes," he decided, sitting behind the counter while I poured his smoothie into his takeaway cup.

"Mhm. Okay?" We had talked about it, but nothing had come of it. It's an additional expense, and I'm not sure about that right now.

"I found some classes near Tails and Whiskers. Flexible schedule too. I called, and there's a beginner class starting in two weeks. The days matched with your visits to Tails and Whiskers, so after the shelter, you could go," Adam explained, and all I could do was stare at him in awe.

He was actually serious about this? I hadn't expected him to do so much for me.

"You called them?"

"Yeah, called a bunch till I found one that was good and fit your schedule." Adam shrugged.

"I like the idea a lot, Adam, but I'm trying to save up a little," I admitted. I didn't have to shy away from that topic anymore, now that he knew the truth.

"I know. They're affordable, and I can cover the first few lessons," Adam offered. I was already taking so much from him, it felt as if I were freeloading. There was no way I could accept more.

"I cannot let you do that." I shook my head, walking away with the blender to clean.

"You have to," Adam said, getting up. I heard him move until he was behind me.

"No, Adam, you can't do that for me too."

"Why?" Adam asked, hands settling on my hips as he turned me to face him.

"It's not fair, you already do a lot, and you'll get nothing from this," I reminded him. There were so many things he did for me without him ever getting anything back in return. I valued our friendship a lot. I didn't want him to wake up one day and feel as if he was taken advantage of.

I could've gotten a job, but working at Tails and Whiskers looked a lot better on my application for the grants.

"Yes, I will, I'll have you protecting me, duh?" Adam said with a teasing smile, his fingers still lazily on my hips. "It's smart, you can be like my bodyguard. It's like that romance book you're reading," he reminded me. I regretted leaving my books out in the open. I didn't know he'd look through them.

I turned back around and rinsed the suds from the dishes. "They fuck in that book."

"We fuck too, no?" Adam whispered in my ear, only coming closer to me with his front pressed against my back.

"Adam," I warned, but his hands on my hips slowly smoothed down my sides.

"Brooklyn, come on, just got to one class to test it out," he begged.

"Fine," I gave in, hoping he'd take a step back. I had a hard time denying myself of him.

"Good," he whispered and started kissing the side of my neck very slowly.

"We have class, Adam, we can't be late," I reminded him, finding the strength within me to resist.

"Not even a few minutes?"

"Adam."

"Fine," he pouted.

"Come on, lover boy." I laughed and took his hand to lead the way, grabbing his smoothie on the way. "Here's your smoothie."

"You mentioned yesterday you won't be home for dinner tonight?"

"Yeah, so... Liam asked to go out for dinner—platonic, I think," I confessed. I wasn't planning to hide it from him, I was hoping that my lack of enthusiasm would give Liam a clear message, but he was set on reconnecting, claiming "He missed his old friend."

"And you said yes?" Adam asked, a hint of hurt in his tone.

"Knowing those people, he'll keep insisting, so I said yes. I plan to be as boring as ever and also make it clear to him that we've both changed," I assured him. Liam could never hold a torch next to him, Adam had nothing to worry about.

"What if you fall in love with him? It has been like four years—" Adam began to tease, and I shoved him out the door.

"He's far from my type, and I have a feeling he doesn't want to go and is being forced by our parents." I rolled my eyes and slipped on my shoes.

"So, dinner then? Somewhere fancy?" Adam asked, throwing our bags in the backseat, then opened the passenger door for me.

"Same spot my parents picked, which is why I think he's being forced by my them," I replied, and he just nodded and circled around to get in the car.

"Are you bothered by this? I know we have rules and such," I asked.

The rules were set to keep the peace, and I didn't want to disrupt it.

"It's fine, he's not your type anyway. Blond guys with blue eyes who play football are." Adam winked, starting the ignition.

"Exactly, you've got nothing to worry about." I smiled and leaned over the middle, my lips almost touching him as I whispered, "Nobody fucks me as good as you do."

"Brooklyn," Adam groaned and sank in his seat.

I smirked, watching him.

I arrived at the same restaurant. This time I wore what pleased me, a nice sky-blue dress compared to the dull-tone one I wore the last time, and my heels weren't killing me.

I spotted Liam, who sat with his back to me and was busy scrolling down social media and liking every photo he came across. I got closer and saw him zooming in on a photo Stella posted—I didn't even know he followed her.

"Your date is here, sir," the hostess said, stopping me from spying on him and causing him to scroll away from my friend's profile.

"Oh, Brooklyn, how are you?" Liam asked, tucking away his phone. He only stood up to shake my hand, then went to sit back down.

"I'm good, Liam, you?" I asked, pulling my chair out and sitting down across from him. This table was only one table away from where I sat with my parents.

"A waiter will be with you in a moment," the hostess promised, then walked away.

"I'm good too," Liam hummed, and his eyes took me in. I looked around and stared at the wooden plant boxes to my right. It was completely potted with greenery for more privacy, I assumed.

"Wow, you look good," he continued to say. Then he ruined it with his following sentence, "All that chocolate luckily didn't affect you."

"What the fuck?" I asked genuinely. I didn't see any reason for him to speak that way.

"It's a joke." Liam shrugged it off.

Jokes are meant to be funny, he was no Adam. I could tell him off, storm out, but chances are he'd just try again another day. I needed to sit down and properly tell him we would never happen.

"Right, well, how have you been?" I asked.

"I've been great, actually amazing." Liam smirked, leaning back against his seat with pride radiating from his face. I braced myself. "I got this fine new apartment really close to school," he boasted. "I visited the campus, spoke to a few professors, and they were rather impressed with my track record."

Then came more bragging. He went on about his stellar grades, varsity lacrosse achievements, and the lavish trips he had planned.

Once he was done flaunting his own accomplishments, he moved on to belittling other students he had only met for a split second. Moments like these made me thankful to my grandmother for not making me turn out like him.

"And then the professor practically yelled at them, but to be honest, I don't think the professor himself knew much," Liam said, proud of himself. I wasn't even following half of the story.

"Isn't the guy in your group as well?"

"Yeah, but he's stupid. He got there on an athletic scholarship," Liam dismissed. "They're not my favourite to work with." "Honestly, it's like he barely even paid attention and did the bare minimum."

"Right, but why would he care about a class that's an elective for him?" I mumbled.

"Let's just order," he scoffed, grabbing the menu. "The chickpea salad looks great. They have salmon too, I heard that's excellent," he pointed out. Salad and salmon? I knew that order—Juliana Armstrong.

"Then you can try it. Maybe the smoked salmon even." I rolled my eyes, opening the menu out of courtesy. "I'll try the steak frites," I decided, since I didn't get to have it last time.

"Oh, uh, okay," Liam mumbled with a weird expression. "I think I'll have the rib-eye steak," he finally chose, still flipping through the pages one by one.

"Sounds good."

"We should try their satays. Your mom said the sauce was perfect," Liam suggested, and I just sighed.

How many times is he going to attempt murder on my life? Was this his way of securing 100 percent of the company? He could just ask my parents, and I'm sure they'd give it to him.

"The sauce that contains peanuts? The thing that would make me asphyxiate?" I asked and watched as his face turned red.

"Fuck, I keep screwing up with you, don't I?" He sighed and pinched the bridge of his nose. Something told me that he didn't like any of this.

"Listen, Liam, I'm trying to be as polite as possible about this. I'm not interested in you," I ripped off the Band-Aid.

Liam looked shocked at first, then he seemed... relieved?

"Truth be told, neither do I. I just figured we could be great partners. Your parents sent me to come convince you to go down the same route."

"I figured." I looked at my glass of water.

"So, where does that leave us?"

"We can enjoy our dinner—no satay or satay sauce," I replied, then shrugged. "Then we part ways."

"Sounds perfect." He smiled.

The waiter came to take our order, and we went back to just staring at each other awkwardly.

"So uh, by saying you're not interested in me, is it me? Is there someone else?" Liam broke the silence with a rather interesting question.

"You've never been my type," I answered truthfully.

"Wow, so careful and mindful of my feelings," he joked, finally something I could smile about.

"Honesty is key," I replied. He didn't need any ego boosts, he did that himself.

We actually had a great dinner, it was a lot easier when I didn't have to worry about him making a move. With the air cleared between us all, all I had to do was refrain from rolling my eyes when he'd brag about himself.

Before dinner came to an end, I ordered some molten chocolate cake to go, then headed straight home. I tried calling Adam, but he wasn't taking the phone. I hope I didn't screw things up. On the way to the house, I spotted a familiar white car and jeep—Boys' night? That's probably why I wasn't getting a response.

Everything seemed normal, and his car was parked inside. I barely turned the ignition off when the garage door opened widely. Adam stood there with a grin and his hat on backwards.

"I just saw your messages. I was busy," he told me as I barely got out of the car. "Two things, firstly, how was the date?"

"We both agreed we didn't like each other and we're out of each other's hair for good," I said, and a smile spread on his face. "Second thing?" I asked, curious to know what he'd say.

"Second thing, close your eyes and follow me." Adam held the door open for me, a red bandana in his other hand.

"If I close my eyes, how will I follow you?" I teased.

"Don't get smart with me, put these on and I'll guide you." He threw the bandana at me.

I swear, one of these days he'll drag me into some weird kinky thing. For now, I trusted him and wore the blindfold. Adam took my hand and carried me upstairs, then led the way. I'm not 100 percent sure, but I think we should be in my room; there was a clean cotton scent in the air. My favourite candle? It can't be, I finished it already.

"Ready?"

"Yes, Adam," I said anxiously, and he removed the blindfold.

My jaw dropped. This was indeed my room, but it was different.

The wall where my bed was supposed to be had been painted a soothing sage green, with a faint hint of paint still lingering in the air. The generic bedside tables were now replaced with light wooden ones that matched the other furniture perfectly.

A fake jasmine plant sat on the bedside table, adding a nice touch to the room. I finally had a proper vanity instead of just a random desk with a mirror on top, complete with a small chair that matched the sage green walls. My old rug had been swapped out for a fluffy, pale green one that tied the room together.

Photos I'd collected over the years with friends and from memorable occasions were hung on the wall by a short string instead of stacked on the dresser. This place felt like an upgraded version of my old room at the apartment, the one I had carefully crafted into a little heaven I loved.

My favourite candle lit in the room, along with a new comforter on the bed. Before, I was thankful for my room. I was comfortable in it. Now? It's perfect and I can't ever imagine leaving it.

He even added a small bookcase for my collection with small trinkets on the shelf.

"Adam, what did you do?" I turned to him immediately, my brows furrowed. He was grinning like crazy; it was quite clear how proud he was of everything.

"I knew you'd never decorate your room, so I did it for you," Adam said, entering the room. He grabbed some loose screws off the desk and tucked them into his pockets as if I hadn't seen them already.

"Adam, this must've cost a lot, I don't—" I wanted to protest, but he cut me off.

"I know what you're going to say, but, Brooklyn, you deserve this. You make my morning routine easier, you listen to my football rants when I'm pretty sure you have no clue what I'm on about, and you're a really great friend. Doing this felt like an honour," Adam said. His words were so sweet and kind. I couldn't help but smile at him.

So fucking sweet. How did it ever take me so long to realise how incredible this man was? That's it, I was making him dinner as a treat. I didn't care how long it took. Speaking of time...

"How did you do this in under three hours?" I frowned and looked around. The paint wasn't completely dry yet.

"The girls came to help. I know you admire me, but baby, I could never have come up with this design myself. Darshini helped with the wall, Stella worked on the bookshelf, and Zaira and I worked on the rest of the furniture and rearranging your room," Adam explained, and I felt my heart warm.

It wasn't a boys' night he had, it was the girls who came over and gave their free time to help him with this. For me? Now I had to make them brownies as a thank you.

"Don't worry, your Mr. O is still in his rightful place, no one meddled with him." Adam winked and patted my dresser.

"You're insane for doing this."

"Your room should feel like your room, Brooke. I should've done this a long time ago." Adam smiled and leaned against the door frame with his arms crossed.

"The paint scent is a bit heavy," I muttered, staring at the pretty colour. It was the exact same one from the apartment.

"Yeah, I think you might have to sleep in another room for the night."

"That's totally okay, thank you for all of this, Adam." I smiled and walked over to give him a hug.

"Surgeon boy wouldn't be able to do this." The hug was ruined. I took a step back and raised a brow at him. "He'd plaster his face all over the wall," Adam continued to say— he probably had a point.

"Are you seriously comparing yourself to him?"

"Let me have this moment." Adam rolled his eyes and hugged me again.

"Fine, step out. I'll change, then I'll make you dinner."

"Oh, I have some seasoned yuca and fish that's waiting to be fried. Can you make that?" Adam asked, pulling away just enough to look into my eyes.

"Sounds tasty. I'll do it," I promised. He could ask me for a five-course meal and I'd treat him to it. Adam was doing things to me that no man had ever done.

"How was dinner by the way?"

"Decent, the fries were heavenly, but I didn't like the steak." I sighed.

"Bummer," he muttered and shook his head. That's exactly how I felt about it, luckily, Liam's ego wouldn't allow me to pay for it.

"Yeah, it really was." I finally pulled out of the hug and urged him towards the door. "Now, chop chop, let me make you some dinner."

I changed into some comfortable clothes, then I stepped outside. Adam sat in the kitchen while I treated him to his dinner. Once dinner was served, we went outside and Adam set everything up so we could watch a movie together. Tonight was, all in all, perfect.

Another day at the shelter for me meant wrapping up the quick tasks. Having taken enough photos and videos for content and assisted with minimal chores, I almost called it a day. I then saw the food supplies and snacks needed to be restocked, so I picked those chores up.

"Thanks so much, girl. If Mrs. Smith returned from her trip and saw I was slacking, I'd be in trouble," Lila said, hands on her hips as she looked at me. She still had scooping duties ahead, but I wasn't sticking around for that.

"You were studying. You should've asked me earlier, and I would've helped sooner," I replied while packing up my bag.

"Your help is appreciated and more than enough," Lila said, sitting behind the counter and checking items off her list. She had three days' worth of tasks piled up. "Also, the art gallery donation—oh my god. That girl just became one of my favourite people. I don't care if she's bad at helping out here, she secured a nice donation," Lila gushed.

Marlene really did.

"Marlene sure did. I think the animals know it too. The dogs are letting her pet them, and most of the cats don't hiss at her anymore," I replied. It might also be because we taught her how to be gentler with them, but both reasons worked fine for me.

"With that sizable donation, I think a long-awaited revamp is coming." Lila clapped her hands.

We had been longing for some renovations. The last time we had some money to spruce up the place, we had to spend it on one of the cats that needed surgery. Even with the vet's discount, it cost a lot, and we had to start all over. Marlene's donation can help tremendously with decorating and leave us enough for a rainy day.

"I truly hope so," I muttered.

If that's the case, I hoped I could convince Mrs. Smith to let me run point on the project. That would boost my application since I'm sure they'd call her for a reference, and she could put in a good word with clear proof of my efforts.

"I'll be heading out then. Take care," I said, tapping the counter and grabbing the hard candy Lila gifted me straight from the public candy jar.

I headed home straight away, eager to rest before making brownies for the girls. We planned to study for our finals. Adam had plans with the guys, so the house would be ours for the evening.

Barely parking the car, I noticed Adam waiting in the doorway with the same mischievous grin he had last night. This can't be good, can it?

"Adam honey, why are you looking at me like that?" I asked, stepping out of the car.

"Because I'm literally a genius," he bragged.

"What did you do?" I frowned.

He called himself a genius when he made a grilled cheese sandwich with eggs and ham, or when he managed to stack all the pillows in the closet without them toppling over.

"Go put on some athletic clothes and meet me in the gym room," Adam instructed. I frowned at him, puzzled. The so-called gym room was originally a bedroom, but he'd made a few changes and added some workout equipment. However, he rarely used it, preferring to train outside on the patio.

"Excuse me? Wear athletic clothes? Gym room?" I asked, probably looking as confused as I felt. What could he possibly have done to make him consider himself a genius?

"Do you trust me?" Adam asked.

"Sadly," I groaned dramatically, suspecting today might be the day I get roped into one of his weird ideas.

"Chop chop then." He clapped his hands, his glare focused on me.

I sighed and went up to my room. Changing into shorts and an athletic crop top, I made my way to the gym room. Adam leaned against the door frame, watching me approach. His eyes slowly trailed down my body, and he took a deep breath.

"So, what did you do this time?" I asked.

"Tada." Adam opened the door to the room. "These are for you." He handed me some boxing gloves, but I was too focused on the room I always avoided.

The room had a foam black mat covering the floor, along with a treadmill, a leg press machine, and a pull-up bar. There was a rack of dumbbells, but half were missing since he kept them outside for his workouts.

The treadmill likely only got used when the weather kept him from running outside. The room was quite tidy, with even the wall of mirrors spotless. The room even smelled like citrus from his new cleaning products.

"Why?" I asked, looking between him and the gloves.

"Since you're not sure about the self-defence classes, I thought I could bring you the cheap version till you're ready for more," Adam said and patted the punching bag. "I'll teach you."

"Do you know what you're doing?" I frowned.

"Nope, I watched YouTube videos and did some research, so I'll just be your trainer," he replied, and I just hummed and nodded.

"I don't know about this." I looked down at the gloves, squeezing them in my hand.

"It's just punching, imagine it's your worst enemy's face," Adam continued, and I stared at the bag. I imagined that one pesky teacher from middle school. Yes, he lived in my head rent free.

He called me stupid in front of everyone, so my grandma, in return, showed up in class and told him off in front of everyone—Gam Gam wasn't one to fight hate with love, she spat back what you threw at her.

"Okay... maybe that could work," I muttered, then turned to Adam. "Did you really buy this for me?"

"No, I bought it when my parents first got the home. I never got around to putting it up, though." Adam stroked the punching bag. "The gloves are new, though."

"Let's do this," I decided. He was right, I had to start somewhere, and this might be a good idea.

"Great, let's start with some cardio to warm up," Adam said, and I hoped to never hear those words ever again.

I thought warm-ups were five minutes, but Adam kept me going for what felt like forever, but according to the clock, it was fifteen minutes. I slid the gloves on and started showing what I could do, which was close to nothing.

"Okay, first of all, your stance is a bit off." He circled to me. "Your feet should be like this, bend your knees just a little, your arms like so," he explained and adjusted me like I was a puppet.

"I thought you didn't know anything." I looked over at him.

"I did some intense research." He shrugged and grabbed the punching bag again, "Now, let's try again. I also thought I'd be the next Rocky Balboa when I was younger."

I pressed my lips together to suppress my laughter.

"Let me see your hook," he asked, and I delivered, but then he just blinked at me, confused. "That's an uppercut which was actually quite decent."

"Ugh," I groaned and wanted to throw in the towel.

"Don't let this demotivate you, it's far from what the self-defence class would be like. They focus more on specific cases and situations. This is just to get you into the rhythm," Adam spoke gently, leaning against the bag as he held onto it.

"I think the gloves are the problem," I muttered, feeling them slip.

"They're huge. I wasn't aware these things were sized differently, but we can get you proper ones if you want to continue this," Adam offered and fastened them tighter once again.

I stared at Adam, then at the bag. He put this thing up for me, he was trying to find me a solution, and this was only in my best interest. I should give it a proper shot, so I removed all negative thoughts and got back into position.

"Let's go again. Focus on rhythm, form, and balance. Strength will come later."

I nodded. "Let's do this."

"That's my girl," Adam said with a grin, and I felt those pesky butterflies in my stomach again. He could certainly call me that again.

Adam would constantly correct my stance, but as we continued, I slowly started to enjoy it. I was nowhere near decent, but I could see myself doing this for one to two hours a couple of days a week. It felt nice... Grandma was right yet again.

"Okay, I'm letting go of the bag. Try to punch it now," Adam suggested. I nodded and punched the bag poorly. So poorly that it came back to me and caught me off balance. I went down on my ass, and Adam's loud laughter filled the room.

"Damn, Brooklyn, it's a good thing you'll practise here first." Adam laughed as he walked over to me. I shot him a glare. "You are downright bad at this; you would have let me get kidnapped," he continued to tease, extending his hand to me.

I was petty, and he knew it. Yet, he still taunted me. I took his hand, but as soon as I was up, I swept my foot under his and tugged him forward, causing him to fall on top of me. The expected impact never came, he caught himself with his hands, inches above me.

"You couldn't let me have it, could you?" Adam groaned, adjusting himself between my legs.

"Of course not, it involved you laughing at me."

"Or maybe you got hot and bothered with me mentoring you and now you want me on top of you," Adam teased, his finger tracing a line from my collarbone down to the top of my breast.

"You're full of yourself." I slapped his hand away. Adam leaned closer, his lips hovering just below my ear.

"And you could be too if you play your cards right," he whispered, his gaze dropping to my lips. My eyes shut as he leaned closer, his breath warm against my skin. He brushed his lips against mine, teasingly, briefly. A surge of excitement ran through me, only for him to pull away with a chuckle.

I grabbed his collar and yanked him back down, our lips crashing together with a longing that left no room for hesitation.

"Don't tease me again," I demanded between kisses.

"Noted," he muttered with a slight smirk.

Our kiss deepened, growing hungry and desperate. My hands tangled in his hair, pulling him closer, craving every inch of him. His hand slipped down to my throat, and I moaned against his lips when he applied pressure.

His kisses trailed down my jawline and neck, leaving a path of wet, heated desire. My heart fluttered, anticipation building with every touch. I yearned for more, far more. Tugging at his shirt, Adam quickly discarded it, revealing his sweat-slicked body. I reached out, running my nails down his abdomen, feeling his muscles tighten under my touch. He captured my hands and pinned them above my head.

"Is this what you wanted, Brooklyn?" Adam murmured, his lips attacking my neck with fiery kisses. He found my sweet spot and nibbled on the soft flesh, eliciting a string of moans from me.

"Yes," I whispered breathlessly. Adam's kisses trailed down to my breasts as he swiftly pulled my sports bra over my head. He released my wrists, his hands moving to cup my breasts, his thumbs expertly rolling over my nipples. I moaned, arching my back into him, craving more.

Adam tugged at one nipple while his lips captured the other. He grazed his teeth over the sensitive peak before biting the soft flesh above, leaving a mark for me to admire later. I moaned his name, desire consuming me. I needed him right fucking now.

"Adam," I breathed sweetly.

"Brooklyn," he replied in a teasing tone, his open-mouthed kisses descending down my stomach.

"Are we doing this?" Adam asked, looking up at me, desire dancing in those pretty eyes.

"Yes," I replied desperately.

"How'd I get so fucking lucky?" he muttered before leaning up to kiss me again.

Adam pulled away, flipping me over with a swift motion. His hands gripped my hips, pulling them until my ass pressed against his clothed cock.

"Look to your right, Brooklyn, you'll enjoy the show," Adam ordered, tugging my shorts and panties down.

I turned to my right, meeting the wall-covered mirror. We were close enough for me to see our reflection clearly. Adam winked at me through the mirror before his hand struck my ass.

I gasped, jerking forward.

"This ass, Brooklyn, it drives me crazy," he said, gripping both cheeks. He leaned down and bit me. I must have gone insane because I loved what he just did.

My eyes widened as his tongue circled my clit. My nails dug into the foam floor as I watched our reflection. His face was buried between my legs, his tongue working me until I was a moaning mess.

Adam pulled away, parting my cheeks and spitting. My toes curled as I felt it slick down. His thumb circled around my ass, teasing.

"This okay?" Adam asked, his eyes locked on mine through the mirror. The gentle pressure of the pad of his thumb against my entrance, our newest trick—only tried it twice, but enjoyed it.

"Mhm," I answered, and Adam gave me a nod. He swiped his thumb over me until it was slick with my desire.

He leaned down again, his mouth descending on my pussy like a starving man. I felt his thumb circling around my ass, slowly entering me. I tensed up at first.

"Relax your body for me, Brooke," Adam murmured between butterfly kisses on my pussy. I took a deep breath, letting go of all the tension. The sensation was strange at first, but as he slowly started moving his finger in a delicious pattern, a moan escaped my lips.

"Is that good, Brooke?" he asked.

"Yes, yes," I answered mindlessly, pushing back against him.

Adam resumed eating me out, his thumb matching the sweet rhythm of his tongue. It hadn't taken long for me to become a mess yet again, pleasure overwhelmed me. His tongue, moans, and fingers all built up my release rapidly. I didn't even realise I was close until I screamed his name and my nails dug into the foam of the floor.

"That's it, baby, come all over my face," he whispered, still devouring me as I came. He licked one last strip from my clit to my entrance before placing a final kiss on my ass. He pulled away, pride etched on his face.

Adam pushed his pants and boxers down, his cock springing free—hard and dripping, ready for me. He palmed my ass, tugging me closer so I could feel him. "See what you do to me, Brooklyn baby?"

"Yeah, yeah, I make you hard. Fuck me already," I demanded, taunting him by moving my hips and pressing myself against him. I wouldn't last long, but I needed him badly.

"Bossy," he muttered, his grip on my hips so tight I knew it would leave beautiful bruises. Adam slipped the tip of his cock in, and we both moaned softly. He didn't ease in, he slammed into me, filling me completely.

"Fuck, Adam," I moaned, looking into the mirror again. His gaze was fixed on me, watching as he began to thrust.

"Put your hands on your back," he ordered, following his command with a sharp spank.

"What do I get if I do that?" I asked, each slow thrust leaving me aching for more.

"Always bargaining." Adam shook his head, his hand striking my ass once again.

I bit back a moan even as he started slamming into me faster. "I'm waiting... for an answer," I said between deep breaths, unable to resist moaning when he pulled out to the tip only to slam back into me. Each thrust sent sparks down my spine, and I grew hungrier for more. The tension in my stomach was building rapidly.

"Be a good girl and put your hands on your back," Adam ordered again, palming my ass. "And I'll fuck you like the desperate little thing you are," he bargained, his eyes locking with mine in the mirror.

"Fuck," I whispered. He knew me so well, knew exactly what to say to bend me to his will. Desperation overtook me, and I placed my hands on my back.

"That wasn't hard, was it?" Adam held my wrists down with one hand while the other snuck to my clit.

I chanted his name, eyes closing as I savoured the pleasure. Maybe I liked working out with him after all.

"Open your eyes, Brooklyn." Adam spanked my pussy, making me jolt. "Watch while I fuck your brains out."

And he did. Adam tugged at my hands as he started thrusting faster and harder into me without a single care in the world. Each movement was more intense than the last. I watched him in the mirror, a pleased smile on my lips. I was close, so damn close.

"Tell me, Brooke, where do you want it?" Adam asked, but all I could think about was coming. "Should I blow all over your back?" The image sent shivers down my spine. "Or maybe in this sweet pussy." He pinched my clit, making me buck forward. "Or should I wait and cum all over your face like last week?" His filthy words were the cherry on top.

"Fuck, Adam," I moaned, my walls quivering around him. "Don't stop!"

Adam obeyed, fucking me into madness. The tension snapped, and euphoria filled every last sense as I came all over his cock. He continued to thrust throughout my orgasm, drawing it out for as long as possible, and I couldn't form a coherent sentence.

"Answer me, Brooklyn," Adam groaned gutturally, his face twisting with pleasure.

"In me, please."

Adam leaned over, kissing and biting my shoulder as he came.

"You're so fucking perfect," he whispered into the kiss. I squeezed my thighs together as his cum trickled down.

"I'm well aware." I caressed his face and kissed him back.

See, I knew he brought me here for some weird kinky thing of his.

Chapter twenty-four

Adam

Coach called me in on Monday, and I was worried it might be about what we did on Friday.

|Friday|

"Everything set?" Ibrahim asked, juggling three water balloons.

"Yes. Ready?" I glanced over at Carter.

We were all in position, waiting for Coach.

"I can't believe I'm being dragged into this," Carter muttered. He had the most crucial task: getting Coach inside.

Carter went outside while Dante and Fernandez set up the water ambush. We had been begging Coach to take us to a local water park for team bonding, but he always rejected the idea. While we didn't have any slides here, we did have a ton of water balloons and water guns at our disposal.

"What the hell is—" Coach barged in but stopped right before the trap could be activated. "There's no fight?" He frowned. Carter had to lie about a fight to get him to come in.

Coach took one step forward, pushing the door further. "What the—"

A bucket of water fell down, drenching him completely.

"Go!" Brian yelled, stepping forward and launching all the balloons he had. The rest of us emerged from hiding and began ambushing Coach, who looked both dumbfounded and furious.

"You knew about this?" Coach turned to Carter, who shrugged and threw one of the water balloons at him, sealing his fate like the rest of us.

We had more bins filled with balloons behind the building, but before we knew it, Coach wrestled one of the boys for their weapon and began to spray us. We expected him to retaliate, but not this quickly. We all scrambled outside, with Coach, like the fool he was, chasing after us into another ambush behind the building.

"I was bragging about how great you guys were yesterday," Coach said as he chased us. "Four years in a row, no pranks," he continued, grabbing a few balloons to throw at us and using his water pistol again.

"Come on, Coach, we had to give you a going away present," Ibrahim said, jumping away when Dante turned on him.

"What the hell?" Ibrahim gasped.

"This is for the torment you put me through." Dante threw several more balloons.

The main target was Coach, but that soon changed. Everyone became a target, launching water balloons and spraying until the guns ran dry. Laughter and cursing filled the air as we soaked up the fun.

Eventually, we calmed down, but we had one final prank up our sleeves—not a harmful one.

"Coach, we got you this new whistle," Carter said, pulling a box from his locker.

"Wow, guys, this is incredible," Coach said, admiring the whistle. It looked fancy, with his name and old jersey number engraved on it. "Thank you." That smile was precious.

Once he blew that whistle, he'd be surprised with a quacking sound. We wouldn't witness it, but we'd hear about it at some point.

"I'm letting this slide just this once, but if it happens again, expect to run laps nonstop for two hours," he warned sternly.

|Now|

"Good morning, Coach," I greeted politely as I entered his office.

"Morning, Serra. Take a seat," he said, pointing to the chair across from him. Behind him, his whiteboard listed my name at 8 AM and Vos at 9 AM.

"I have great news for you," Coach said, walking to the small printer and retrieving a document. "Grimes called," he announced.

My heart did cartwheels.

Grimes was from Liberty FC. After the finals, we had a few meetings, and they were certainly the team I dreamed of joining. Coach guided me through the process, and I was anxiously waiting for their invitation to tryouts.

"And?" I asked, leaning forward. I tried to peek at the document, but he held it to his chest as he approached me.

"You've been invited to the tryouts, Serra," Coach said with a smile, handing over the document.

"Seriously?" I read the paper. I had a week to prepare—more than enough time.

This was it. I was so close to achieving my dreams.

"Yes, and even better, Cosmos has invited you as well," Coach said, placing another document in front of me. "I checked the dates, they don't overlap, so you can give both of them a shot."

He had advised me to have a backup plan. And while Liberty FC was my dream, I had Cosmos as second best.

"Thanks, Coach." I grinned, carefully placing the sheets in my notebook.

"Listen, about those other two teams—are you sure you're not interested?" he asked, leaning on the desk.

"I'm certain," I replied confidently. Maybe it was a bit cocky, but I knew I had what it took to make it into Liberty FC. The other clubs were good, but they weren't my dream.

"Then that's all," he said. "I'm really proud of you, and I hope to see three players off to the pros this year."

"Thanks, Coach," I replied, my excitement barely contained. "I'll be going then. Have a great day." I grabbed my bag.

"Yes." He nodded. "I'll see you on the field."

While most of us would graduate and leave, we still had a schedule to practise and help the new team formulate and witness tryouts. There were friendly games here and there, but it was more to keep us in shape.

I remembered my first day there. I fell in love with the university immediately. I gave my all during tryouts, even met with Dante and Ibrahim. After the tryouts, they told me they'd stay in contact, and they did. I got officially accepted onto the team.

I headed home. Brooklyn didn't have any classes today, she mentioned finishing up a project. The drive home was meant to be peaceful and thoughtless, and it was—until the radio played a particular song. It was the same song that played in the club the night Brooklyn and I first kissed.

I never told her about that kiss. I never thought it would matter, but now I couldn't stop thinking about all the kisses that followed. Every moment after, every laugh, every lingering glance—they all came back to that spark. Brooklyn was constantly on my mind, and I knew my thoughts about her were no longer platonic—they hadn't been for a long time.

This wasn't fair to her; I had promised there wouldn't be any feelings involved, but how do I do that when every part of her left me restless and aching for more?

I never anticipated unravelling every intricate layer of Brooklyn. Each one was so beautifully interesting, and there was nothing about her that could ever bore me. Getting to know the real Brooklyn had been an honour, and I would never do anything to ruin that.

She meant too much to me to risk.

By the time I snapped back to my senses, I was already in the garage. I parked the car and went inside.

"No, Liam, what the hell?" Brooklyn's voice was hoarse and loud. Her eyes met mine as I walked through the door. I raised an eyebrow at her.

It had been a little over a week since her parents left, and honestly, Liam should've left with them. California surely had great schools for him, right?

"No, I will not marry you, Liam," Brooklyn groaned in exasperation. Her voice was strained, her eyes puffy, and there was a pile of tissues next to her.

She ended the call, threw the phone onto the couch, and sank down beside it.

"Do I even want to know?" Why the hell was Liam talking about marriage? He didn't deserve her. If Brooklyn were to walk down the aisle, it shouldn't be to him.

"I thought Liam and I had a clear understanding, but no. He's being pressured by our parents, and apparently, he thinks now that I don't want to become a surgeon, we should get married. He'll handle everything at the clinic, and I'll get my share of the money monthly," Brooklyn explained.

"Is he insane? Why would he jump to marriage? A simple business deal would suffice," I pointed out. All of this for a share of the clinic that Brooklyn wasn't even interested in.

"Exactly! But his reasoning is that he doesn't believe in love, and he thinks I don't either. So, in his head, that means we can get married, get our parents off our backs, and everything will be fine. Can't he grow a spine and stand up to them? Jeez," she said, massaging her temple with her eyes closed. "He astonishes me."

"You don't believe in love? How did he come to that conclusion?" Now wasn't the time, but I had to know where she stood on the matter.

"I said it when I was an angsty teen," she mumbled. God, I would've loved some photos of angsty teen Brooklyn, I could've teased her endlessly.

"And now?" I asked, hoping something had changed her mind.

"I don't... I don't know," she stuttered, breaking eye contact. "Maybe? All I know is that I'm not marrying him. There's no way he'll be the father of my child," she rambled and would've continued if I hadn't gasped loudly.

"Child? Love? Brooklyn Colette Armstrong wants the white picket fence life?" I teased.

"I want what I never had." Brooklyn laughed, sniffling slightly. Her tone was light, but I could taste the bitterness beneath her words. Despite joking about it, I knew she meant every word.

"For the wedding, may I propose satays with peanut sauce as an entrée?" I said, trying to lighten the mood. "And perhaps a Reese's buttercup cake?"

"Ha-ha, very funny." She rolled her eyes, but a slight smile played on her lips as she toyed with the pillow in her lap. "What about you? Marriage? Kids?"

"Obviously, these awesome genes have to be passed down," I joked, though I meant it.

"And I do hope to find a partner, my best friend. Something like what my parents have," I said sincerely.

My parents shared an admirable love and support for each other, true soulmates. They encouraged each other to pursue their dreams, always protecting each other. They had been friends long before they started dating, and my mom often said that was the reason it worked so well. They had built a strong foundation.

"My parents love each other deeply; they even have an epic love story. But I'm scared of loving like them. What if I love someone so much that I push away our child?" Brooklyn's voice was filled with vulnerability.

"You'd never let that happen, Brooklyn," I said, moving closer and placing my hand over hers. "You're incredibly attentive and caring. I could never see you repeating that cycle."

"Thanks, Adam." Brooklyn leaned her head against my shoulder, our hands resting in her lap, and she didn't let go.

Loving Brooklyn would be so easy, there was so much about her to admire. I wonder if I'd be able to give her the life she desired. I knew how wrong it was to even think of that.

"Also, are you sick?" I finally asked when I heard her sniffling constantly.

"No?"

"Brooklyn." I scooted away to look at her.

"I have a teeny tiny cold," she replied and showed me her thumb and forefinger touching. That's not a 'teeny tiny.'

Brooklyn didn't let me lecture her, she got up.

"And where do you think you're going?" I followed her, quickly taking her car keys from her hand. Crossing my arms, I waited for her answer.

"I have to," Brooklyn said, but was interrupted by a series of sneezes. "Bring this to the shelter." She pointed to the manila folder.

"Like hell you are."

"They're important—" Brooklyn was yet again interrupted by a series of sneezes, "Documents, I promised to get it to them."

"Brooklyn, you've sneezed so much your eyes are barely even open," I told her, walking over to grab my keys now. "You are in no condition to drive. Did you even eat?"

"I was finishing up my project, which I handed in by the way." She avoided answering my question.

"Good girl." I booped her nose, then grabbed the folder from her hand. "But that doesn't mean you get to not take care of yourself."

"Adam, I have to go." She sighed. "They need these today."

"I'll bring it for them," I decided. I'm sure I'm saving people on the road by not letting her go out and drive in this state. "You go sit down, and when I come back, I better not catch you working."

"You're so mean!" Brooklyn whined and sniffled yet again.

"How am I the bad guy in this?"

She shrugged.

I shook my head and went on my way. I headed inside, finding a woman behind the counter. Her demeanour changed when she saw me and seemed a lot friendlier.

"Good evening, welcome to Tails and Whiskers, are you here to bring home—" she started to ask, but when I held up the folder, she sighed. "New mail guy?"

"Nope, Brooklyn, sent me." I extended the file to her. "Adam Serra Valle."

"Rachel, thanks for these," she said, taking the folder and putting it aside. She assessed me from top to bottom. "I didn't know Brooklyn had a boyfriend."

"We're not together together," I said awkwardly.

"Good, Mr. Borris would be mad and possibly attempt murder on your life," Rachel then said and began to open up the folder.

"Mr. Borris?" I frowned. Who the hell was Mr. Borris? That's a grandpa's name!

"She hasn't told you about Mr. Borris?" Rachel gasped, a hint of devious dancing in her eyes. "The ninety-pound lab?" she continued to say, and I felt my heart settle.

This fucking girl. Chaos, I can tell her and Brooklyn must be friends. I tried thinking of one of the labs Brooklyn showed me.

"Is it the one that's greying?" I wondered.

"That's the one," Rachel confirmed, smirked. "Mr. Borris, who has jealousy issues."

"Well, she asked me to take a photo of Pen-pen, then I can head out," I mentioned, already pulling out my phone.

Rachel took me to Pen-pen, and I took several photos. I don't think this dog likes being photographed because she did everything in her power to avoid looking good on camera. Once I had had enough, I said goodbye to Rachel.

When I walked through the door, I found Brooklyn curled up on the couch, asleep with the TV still playing in the background. I went up to my room quietly. I texted my grandma back and forth.

After a while, I went back downstairs, and Brooklyn stirred around before finally sitting up to cough. She spotted me and coughed yet again.

"Coughing is new. Did you drink meds before napping?" I asked, unpacking the groceries.

"I was too lazy to get up," Brooklyn admitted, eyes closed as she rubbed the sides of her head.

"Unbelievable," I muttered. Maybe I wasn't cut out to be a nurse.

"I didn't know it would get worse," she whined and gathered her strength to get up.

"Just lie back, I'll take care of you," I replied, walking over to her.

"I'm fine."

"Brooklyn, you're hot and I don't mean it in terms of looks right now," I said. Brooklyn glared at me. "Your face is puffy and your nose is runny. You are anything but fine, and you will let me help you." I poked her cheek. She truly was sick because she didn't slap my hand away or bite my finger.

"Now hush, my grandmother is calling. She has a great recipe for battling colds," I said when I heard my phone ringing.

"Don't shush me." Brooklyn narrowed her eyes at me as I answered the phone. I placed a finger over her lips.

"My sweet baby, are you sick? Must be that damn weather," Avo gushed. The one time she had to speak Portuguese, she didn't. "If I were there, I'd spoon-feed you and tuck you in."

Even when she's sick, she's still smirking about the endearing name my grandma calls me. I glared at her, but she just stifled her laughter, followed by a cough and frankly... she deserved it.

"Vovó, it's not for me, it's for Brooklyn." I stopped her before she could embarrass me further.

"Oh, that poor thing," Vovó said sincerely.

"She's coughing too."

"Make her some chá de alho," she suggested, and I looked over at Brooklyn. Oh boy, she will not like this.

"What's that?" Brooklyn frowned

"Garlic tea," I responded, and her nose scrunched up. "Don't make that face, I'm making it and you're drinking it," I warned her.

"Oh, and chicken soup," Vovó hummed. Perfect, it's her chicken soup that always heals me. That and an ungodly amount of freshly squeezed orange juice.

Avo then started to explain how I should make the chicken soup with some dumplings in it, of course. She explained everything thoroughly. I didn't have the heart to tell her I had store-bought dumplings, she might disown me over it.

"Brooklyn, you better tell me if he messes up the recipe," Avo said, and Brooklyn took this as her invitation to steal my phone from my hand.

"I will, ma'am," she promised and looked at me with a devious look.

"And if he acts up, you should just call me, in fact, have him give you my number," Avo decided. My jaw dropped, I'm fucked. I should've never let them speak to each other. "I will fly down there to pull on his ear if he doesn't behave," she promised Brooklyn, who was still grinning despite being sick.

"He's still good for now, but if you must know, I haven't been given any brigadeiros for three weeks already," Brooklyn said. There it was, my screwup.

"Outrageous," she gasped. "Give me him again."

I took the phone and spent the rest of my phone call having to fight for my life just because I didn't make the chocolate-gobbling lady her brigadeiros. I started to prepare everything for the soup and tea while Brooklyn put on our show.

I served her some tea first, I put in some extra honey in hopes to sweeten it, but she was still disgusted by the taste of the tea.

"All of it." I narrowed my eyes at her.

"I don't like this nurse," she scoffed, refusing to drink more.

"Do you want me to call one of your girlfriends?" I asked, knowing damn well that if it was any of those three girls, they'd be a lot more overbearing.

"I'll drink all of it," she said immediately and drank more of the tea.

"Good."

After tea, we sat down for dinner.

"It looks good, it pains me that I can't smell anything," Brooklyn pouted, stirring around her spoon in the soup. The steam was still coming from it.

"Can you taste?" I wondered. That's the worst part about being sick for me.

"I tasted that god-awful tea, I'm sure my taste buds are still intact." She shuddered as she relived the memories of the tea. I hated it too. I was forced to drink it many times, but it always helped.

"Great."

After another serving, I made sure that she drank her medicine and cleaned up after us. She didn't feel like going to her own bed, so I tucked her in on the couch, added some tissues, and refilled her bottle of water for her.

We were watching the last few minutes of the show, she had lain down in position already, and I rubbed her back lazily. When I looked over at her, I noticed she was barely awake.

"You're truly the greatest at putting up a facade," I whispered, running my hand along her back. "But you don't have to do that around me, you can be yourself, Brooklyn, I can handle it," I promised.

"Good night." I kissed her forehead, and she just smiled and snuggled closer into her pillow.

Chapter twenty-five

Brooklyn

I, Brooklyn Colette Armstrong, am embarrassed that it took me three whole days to recover. Thanks to Nurse Adam and his freshly squeezed orange juice, vegetable soups, and, as much as I hate to admit it, his garlic tea.

It's a week later, and I'm finally back on track with everything. I still had to study for my finals, but I was nearly finished. The last item on my to-do list was to convince Mrs. Smith to let me run the shelter's remodelling project.

This was the first time in a while that we sat down for a one-on-one meeting. The last and only time before this was when I wanted to volunteer.

"Are you sure you can handle it, Brooklyn? Aren't you graduating this year?" Mrs. Smith asked with worry dancing in her eyes.

Every student who volunteered asked for shortened shifts around this time of the year. But I knew what I was doing.

"I am, Mrs. Smith. I can handle this project," I assured her, hoping to convince her.

"Well, you are the only one so far to show interest. I'll give you the project, but you have until this Saturday to tell me if you change your mind," she decided, and I felt a smile creeping up my face.

"Thank you so much, Mrs. Smith. You won't regret it."

"Of course, I know you'll do well, but remember, you can quit until Saturday," she reminded me.

I assured her that it wouldn't be necessary, then packed up.

I arrived at the bakery and was presented with the cake. It was a classic black forest cake with an edible print of Adam holding his first contract with Liberty FC, along with his new jersey.

After his successful tryouts, he was offered a contract. The boys took him to get his contract signed along with his manager, while the girls stayed behind to help me organise the party. Really, they chose to stay so we could discuss our long-overdue book club book.

I headed home with the cake. The girls and I had our work cut out for us. Although it wasn't going to be big, I still wanted Adam to feel celebrated. I was genuinely happy for him, even if his success meant he was one step closer to leaving me. I couldn't blame him for that.

He deserved to chase his dreams. I just never expected him to become one of mine—one so close I could almost touch it, yet elusive enough to slip right through my fingers if I tried to reach for it.

"You can be yourself, Brooklyn. I can handle it."

I never told him I heard those words, he thought I was sleeping. However, I heard them, and they still echoed in my mind.

Arriving home, I put the cake in the fridge just as a honk came from outside. Peeking through the curtains, I saw the girls had arrived. I immediately opened the door, and they came piling in with their bags.

"Oh, good, you didn't decorate yet. I got the perfect banner," Zaira announced, rummaging through a paper bag.

She pulled out a banner.

Game Over - He Said Yes! the banner read, adorned with small rings on each side.

"I'm pretty sure this is for a wedding," I said, glancing over at Zaira, who groaned in response.

"Yes, but we can cover the rings with these," she replied, holding up tiny soccer ball stickers.

"Duh, where's your creativity?" Darshini teased.

"Keep talking and I'll spoil the second book for you," I warned, narrowing my eyes at her. These girls with their STEM majors were behind on their reading for once. Yes, I was gloating about it because usually, I was the last to finish the book in the group.

"You wouldn't dare." Darshini narrowed her eyes back at me.

"Test me," I challenged, but she just walked off smiling.

Stella and I prepared apple pie and brownies together, and I assisted her in making spaghetti. Meanwhile, Darshini and Zaira took charge of decorating the place with streamers, banners, and a few balloons.

It was coming together perfectly. We were pleased with our work.

"Should we become professional party planners?" Stella mused, rubbing her chin. Her knack for these types of things was impeccable; no event ever went uncelebrated under her watch.

"Maybe as a side gig, definitely not as a main job." Zaira pointed to the few balloons we accidentally popped.

"Fair enough." I laughed.

With just over an hour before the others would arrive with Adam, we scrambled to get ready. We met up in my room after freshening up and continued getting ready. I opted for a blue miniskirt I hadn't worn in public yet.

"That's a super cute skirt. Where'd you get it?" Zaira gushed, running her fingers over the soft fabric. It was short, pretty, and sparkly—just our taste.

"The mall. There was a perfect, pale pink one too," I replied, glancing at her. "You have to get it."

"Please, I need it," she pouted.

"I'll send you the details. Their catalogue is online," I promised, looking it up on my phone to send to her.

"Thank you." Zaira grinned.

"Come on, let me do your cat eye," Stella offered, holding a baby blue eyeliner and a fine-point brush.

I sat down, and Stella tipped my chin up as I closed my eyes. She carefully drew the lines for me. We never needed a reason to get dolled up, even if we'd stay in.

"All done." She patted my cheek, and I went to look in the mirror. The double lines were flawlessly executed, and the cat eye was even on both sides.

"You never cease to amaze me," I muttered, still admiring her work.

"It's what I do," she said with a playful flip of her ponytail. "Now, let's talk about that book," she added, looking between the three of us and tapping her brush against the palette to dust off the excess powder.

"I first need to know if I'm messed up or not... What did you guys think of that dagger scene?" Darshini asked. We all exchanged glances, not saying a word. The message was clear. "Okay, so we're all messed up in the head. Got it." Darshini sighed.

The boys were here, the door barely opened before we erupted into cheers.

"Congratulations, Adam!" I said, offering him a hug. He held on much longer than he should have, his face lighting up with excitement as he took in the decorations and preparations.

"This is amazing, guys. Thank you so much," he said, his eyes sparkling with gratitude.

"You did well, bud," Zaira said, giving Adam a friendly pat on the arm.

"Oh my god, the banner! I love it," Adam exclaimed, pointing to the decorative sign. Zaira turned to me with a triumphant grin, offering me a high five that I gladly accepted. "All of you were in on this?"

"Mhm, congrats, Adam," Stella confirmed, glancing over his shoulder to find her boyfriend in the crowd.

"Thank you guys so much," Adam said, his happiness palpable.

Everyone settled as Adam proudly showed off the cool gear and merch he received from the team. It was clear how proud he was of himself and how excited he was for his future. All his hard work had paid off.

We set up some board games and gathered around to enjoy the snacks and play. After two rounds of Go Fish, we decided to turn things up a notch to Monopoly.

Adam kept glancing my way, and I had to force myself not to look back too often. If I did, I'd start smiling, and right now, this was a serious game.

My phone vibrated, and I glanced down to see Adam's message telling me to throw the game. I put my phone away and glared at him.

His eyes then darted upstairs, trying to send me a signal. I hoped I wasn't misreading it. After a few minutes, Adam declared bankruptcy and headed upstairs. Before disappearing, he cocked his head to the side, and I gave in.

I slowly tucked away my game money and declared bankruptcy. Zaira and Ibrahim were debating the rules, while Darshini and Carter were arguing about rent costs.

Their chaos kept them unaware of my absence. I walked up the stairs and looked around for Adam. I barely knocked on his door when it swung open. He pulled me inside, a smirk playing on his lips as he looked at me.

"I see you finally wore the skirt?" Adam asked, pinning me against the door. His hands settled on my hips, thumbs slipping under the small sliver of exposed skin between my skirt and blouse.

"Mhm, remember our deal?" I asked with a smirk, my hands trailing up his arms. I dragged them slowly, my nails gently scratching his skin, causing goosebumps to rise under my touch.

"You wore this on purpose?" His hands now smoothed down the sides of my skirt.

"Of course, I did, Adam." I winked. "Seemed appropriate for the celebration, right?"

"You're the best." He gazed into my eyes.

"I'm well aware." I pulled him down towards me. Our breaths mingled between us. "Now, do something about this skirt," I whispered before pressing my lips to his.

Adam sighed lovingly into the kiss as I traced the outline of his jawline, and the other hand slowly slipped up into his hair. I felt his hands go up the globes of my ass, slowly pulling down my panties.

Our kiss grew more urgent, his lips so hungry and eager against mine. Each kiss of his was met with the same energy, my fingers tugged at his hair as I needed him far closer. Adam's tongue swept over the seam of my mouth.

I denied him access till he cupped my pussy, eliciting a moan from me and offering him the right chance to slip his tongue into my mouth.

His fingers circled my clit, and waves of pleasure crashed through my body. It's like I came back to life with an uncontrolled hunger, a hunger only he could satisfy. I had gotten so used to Adam that I was sure no other man could ever give me what he gave me.

His kisses trailed down my neck, sending shivers through me. I could feel the heat of his breath on my skin, each touch of his was electrifying. His free hand roamed down, tugging my blouse and bra down with a desperate urgency he was never afraid of displaying. So much for wearing strapless ones, I thought, then his mouth found the sensitive skin of my neck again. He sucked and bit gently, each sensation making me gasp and yearn for more.

I began to tug at his shirt, and he took it off instantly. His hand moved to my breast, tugging and rolling over my nipple, sending jolts of pleasure straight to my core. When his other hand moved to my entrance, excitement filled me.

Two fingers slid inside me, and I couldn't hold back the soft moan that escaped my lips as I tipped my head back against the door. His fingers moved deeper and faster, making come-hither motions that had me on the edge almost instantly.

I closed my eyes, my hands burying themselves in his hair to anchor myself. One hand slowly slipped down his back. He couldn't get enough of me, and neither could I. I didn't think I ever would. His lips continued their assault on my neck, his fingers still buried deep within me, and he tweaked my nipple roughly, eliciting a sharp gasp from me. There wasn't a part of my body that he didn't give attention to.

The pleasure was overwhelming; every touch, every movement sent me spiralling.

He began kissing his way down my body, and each kiss brought him down south faster and faster. He slowly lowered himself to his knees, and my breath hitched in my throat. He's not gonna—He did. Adam kneeled before me, guiding my thighs over his shoulders. He looked up at me, mischief glittering in those beautiful blue eyes, a smirk tugging at his lips. "Make sure to be quiet, okay?" he murmured between kisses that trailed down my pubic bone.

The anticipation was almost too much to bear, when his mouth finally found me, I couldn't help the cry that escaped. He worked his magic with his tongue and lips, each stroke sending me higher, closer to the edge.

My fingers tightened in his hair, my body trembling with need and the overwhelming pleasure that he so expertly knew to deliver. Every flick of his tongue, every gentle nip and suck, brought me closer and closer to my end. The pleasure I felt before intensified ten times, my breathing became shallower, my fingers fisted in his hair.

Adam knew where and how to touch me, what to do to be my undoing. The pleasure built up with each action of his, and my thighs closed around him. The tension coiled within my core until I became undone, my hips moved against him. My mouth fell open as I rode out the waves of pleasure. I knew Adam enjoyed every moment of it.

Adam kissed my inner thighs as he gently pulled away. He placed me back down on my feet but held onto my hips, thankfully. I'm sure I would've toppled over if he hadn't. I wrapped my arms around him and kissed him hungrily. There were so many raw emotions he brought out of me, emotions I was scared to explore, so I just kissed him, my taste lingering between us.

"Can you handle more?" Adam asked, gently caressing my face as he looked into my eyes.

"Have I ever turned down more?" I asked, running my hand up his leg until I felt his erect cock under my touch.

I helped him take off his pants and boxers. The sight of his cock so hard and dripping for me shot pleasure straight to my core. If we had all the time in the world tonight, I'd be going on my knees for him, but we didn't have all night.

His hands roamed all over my body, each touch sparking anticipation within me. I was ready and yearned for more yet again. I could sense his need, his want, it matched mine, and he caught onto that.

Adam lifted me and aligned himself with me as I wrapped my legs around him. My hands went around his neck immediately, holding him close to me. I moaned softly as he entered me at once. So perfect.

Adam pulled out till only the tip was in, then entered me again, and a loud moan spilled from my lips. He froze for a second, his hand covered my mouth, and a wicked smile played on his lips.

"I told you to be quiet, Brooke," Adam said as he started thrusting into me. "Quiet, Brooke. Or do you want everyone downstairs to hear exactly what we're doing?" His eyes focused on mine. I shook my head uncontrollably, fearing he'd stop. "Good."

Each thrust of him came quicker and harder, filling all the needs and wants we had. Each movement of his drove us closer and closer to the edge. He kissed and bit wherever he could, his hand teased my breast again, but slowly roamed down to my thighs.

My moans became muffled against his hand as he fucked me. I lost all control when his fingers brushed against my clit. He rubbed me hastily and matched the pace he ploughed into me. I clung to him, nails digging into his back as I held him.

I chanted his name as I came, the sound was all muffled but matched the guttural groan he suppressed. I felt my walls closing in on him. He stopped moving, and his cock twitched within me. He removed his hand and slammed his lips to mine as he came.

"Fuck Brooke," he whispered, trying his hardest to capture his breath.

"Yeah." There wasn't any need for more words.

"I bought this skirt to tease you, but instead that backfired on me," he said and shook his head.

"All your plans seem to backfire." I smiled and played with his hair, trying to put it back in place.

"They do." He laughed and slowly pulled out and settled me on my own feet. "But I don't regret it for a second." He kissed me once more.

"I don't regret any of it," I replied, emphasising any.

By any, I meant everything that happened between us. I wondered if he thought about it like I did. If it kept him up at night, wondering what more could come from it.

"Need any help? I can wait to head down together," Adam asked, already brushing down my skirt and adjusting it back into place. It's nice of him, but I still had to get cleaned up in the bathroom. I could feel his release still trickling down my thigh.

"No, you go first, I'll be there in a minute," I promised and brushed down my shirt. "I think it's time we cut the cake. I think you're gonna love it." I readjusted my bra underneath my shirt. Adam's eyes were focused on my breasts.

"I already had my favourite cake." Adam winked at me and stole a quick kiss from me.

"Ew, get out." I rolled my eyes and pushed him away, but it was too late, he had already seen the slight smile on my lips.

"Thanks for the party, by the way."

"It wasn't just my idea."

"Well, then let me go thank the others too," he decided, stepping out of his room.

"Hopefully not the same way you thanked me," I joked, and he went downstairs laughing.

Chapter twenty-six

Brooklyn

Shit.

"What do you mean you cannot come? We have a contract," I asked, struggling to keep my voice steady. This conversation had been a frustrating loop.

"We had a clause stating we could cancel within fourteen days, today is the last day, so that clause is still valid," the man replied. Greedy bastard. "Miss Armstrong, we've been over this yesterday, and our decision is final."

"I hope every dog you come across bites you," I spat out before hanging up. Unprofessional? Yes. Necessary? Absolutely.

I sank to the floor, leaning my head back against the wall. This was bad. Everything had been going so well. I was acing my finals and managing the shelter renovation project efficiently.

It was all going perfectly until last night.

I didn't have an extra week to wait, Mrs. Smith was stern with her deadline. I couldn't afford any missteps, even if it wouldn't be my fault. I needed her to speak highly of me when the Animal Rights Education Program contacted her.

I heard someone at the door, persistently knocking. Oh god, this better not be Mrs. Smith. She'd be devastated by the news. The knocking continued, it couldn't be her, she had a key.

Please don't be burglars. I got up and cautiously walked to the front door, gripping a wooden post for safety.

"Brooklyn?" I heard Zaira's voice.

"Her car is here, so she must be too," Dante added.

"What if she fainted?" Stella gasped.

"She skipped breakfast this morning," Adam pointed out, his voice laced with panic.

Before they could think about breaking in, I opened the door and found all seven of my friends standing there. "Guys?" I asked, confused.

"Oh, she's alive," Zaira said, relieved. "Thank god."

"What on earth are you all doing here?" I asked.

Stella briefly took photos of the flowerpots caging the doors, they wildflowers within them were in full bloom during spring.

"We're here to help." Ibrahim had one arm draped around Zaira's shoulder as he leaned against her.

"Overalls?" I questioned.

"He calls them his work clothes," Zaira said, clearly annoyed and disapproving of his choice.

"Wait, what are you—how did you guys even know?"

"Adam." They all pointed at him. Of course. I had ranted to him about the contractors last night.

"To be frank, we're offended you didn't think to ask us, but we'll let it slide," Stella said, narrowing her eyes at me.

"Tell us what needs to be done," Carter said, finally closing the door, the taped newspaper fluttering in the breeze.

"Uh, the list is long," I replied. While it was great that they were all there, it felt strange. I didn't want them to feel obligated.

"And there are eight of us," Darshini pointed out.

"Lay it on us, Brooke," Adam encouraged.

I grabbed my clipboard.

"Reception area and adoption room need to be painted, several lights need to be replaced, and the flooring needs to be secured in the main area," I listed, one by one. I continued, "The fences outside need to be swapped out, the grooming station has many tasks of its own, and the main area will get new cages and beds."

"Is that all?" Carter asked.

"No, we also need to make new signs since the old ones are discoloured and peeling." It was a lot.

"Dante and I can handle the painting and replacing the light fixtures," Darshini offered. Dante nodded in agreement.

"I'll design a cute mural on the wall, but I think we'll need more colours, so I can do that tomorrow with non-toxic paint," she stated.

"For now, I think Stella and I could do the flooring and outside work," Carter said, and Stella nodded in agreement.

I was a little surprised at how well they were already dividing the work without my help.

"Ibrahim, do you want to handle the grooming station and related tasks?" Zaira asked, looking up at her boyfriend.

"I swear, if you make one Wookiee joke, I will restrain you right there in that room." Ibrahim narrowed his eyes at her.

"Guys, keep it in your pants, we're here on serious matters." Adam snapped his fingers in front of Ibrahim's eyes several times.

"Zaira and I will handle that," Ibrahim confirmed and looked between Adam and me. "Will you two manage the rest?"

"Of course," Adam assured them.

"Wait, are you guys really going to do all of this?" I asked, frowning.

"Of course, Brooklyn. You're our friend, and you need us," Stella said, patting my shoulder.

"Now chop, chop, people." Darshini clapped her hands. "Also, Adam said food is on him."

"I only give food to those who make progress, so get to work," Adam said sternly. I handed them the plans that were written down, and everyone split to tackle their agreed-upon tasks.

"Adam, you didn't have to do all of this."

I couldn't believe he had orchestrated all of this.

"Are you kidding me, Brooke? You're always there, you listen, you care, you make us feel heard—even when you don't have to. Of course, we want to be there for you. You have no idea how much it means to me to have you in my life." Adam kept on talking, and I was lost for words. Truly. It was so good to hear how he felt about having me in his life.

A smile spread across my lips.

"Besides, the guys are more than happy to help. You attend almost all of our games and provide great jokes afterwards, so in return, we can help you out." He winked.

"Thank you, Adam."

"Next time, all you have to do is ask, Brooke," he said, putting his phone aside. "It's a damn pleasure to be of your help."

"Let's get to it then. We have our work cut out for us." I felt accomplished knowing the renovations might just work out after all.

Adam and I sat down and started peeling the decals to stick on the new signs. We then cured them with a glossy layer as instructed. We still had to assemble the new crates, furnishing them with beds and a toy for each animal because every animal had one toy that was completely theirs. Even when they're adopted, it went with them.

All the parts for the cages were dumped in the box. Adam and I looked at each other.

"Let's sort first," I decided, trying to be positive.

"Yes, ma'am," Adam replied, and we got straight to work.

Adam and I managed to build the crates and sort them. There were some screws, pins, and such left over, but we couldn't seem to find out where those belonged. All the crates were tested and deemed stable with zero chances of them caving in.

Adam had taken his role seriously and went out to buy popsicles for us, which we enjoyed during our break. After our break, we went back to work and we only stopped when it was 7 PM.

Outside was pretty much completed, and the old, unstable gates were swapped out for the new ones. The grooming station looked sparkling new, and they even managed to fix the leaking faucet. The tiles inside needed to set in, and while some were a little wonky, it was far better than what it was once. The paint job wasn't finished, but Darshini and Dante came close to finishing it up, and they even managed to fix all the new lights.

By tomorrow, they would've done all they could do for me already, and frankly, it's far better than what the constructors had promised. The electrical work will still be checked by a professional by the end of the week. This was all easy work, and I'd be meeting the deadline with two days to spare and three grand saved.

"We'll finish the paint job tomorrow," Dante said, wiping his hands with a towel soaked in some sort of chemical thinner.

"I'll do the mural, and he'll take care of setting up the backyard," Stella said, referring to Carter as she dusted some grass off his arm.

"Ha, we finished all our tasks today," Ibrahim said with a smirk, wrapping an arm around Zaira's back and pulling her closer.

"And we even spruced up the bathroom a little," Zaira added proudly.

"This wasn't a competition," Darshini reminded them before I could.

"It couldn't be, we smoked you," Ibrahim said smugly, holding up his hand. Zaira high-fived him, looking just as proud.

"I give up, everything's a competition with you two." I laughed.

"Where do you guys want to go for dinner?" Adam asked, rubbing his stomach. We were all starving. I had told them to stop working a while ago, but they were determined to keep going until seven.

"We look like a mess, and we're all tired," Darshini pointed out. "Let's go somewhere close."

"Alfonso's?" I suggested. It was less than fifteen minutes away, and they served food quickly.

"Sounds perfect," Carter agreed, already grabbing his keys.

"Let's go. You're still paying, right, Serra Valle?" Zaira asked as we exited the shelter one by one.

"Wouldn't dare lie about that," Adam said, holding the door open.

I waited for Adam to exit and then began to lock up the door.

"Oh, by the way, I came with Darsh and Dante, can I drive with you?" Adam said, already waiting by my car.

"Did they flirt too much?" Stella teased.

"Too much hand-holding and longing looks."

"Yuck." Ibrahim shuddered and gagged physically.

"Come on, I'm hungry and I can't survive a pending Mirza twins fight on an empty stomach." I unlocked the car.

We drove over to Alfonso's Kitchen and were taken to our usual booth. We didn't need a second to think, we instantly placed our go-to order.

"Hey, good news! We checked your schedule, and we'll still be able to make that graduation trip!" Stella said, pointing to Adam. With his new contract, he wasn't going to have much of a summer break.

"Stella has planned everything, it's going to be amazing," Carter gushed, pulling her closer to him.

"I can't wait to take my last final and be done. I'll start packing for that trip immediately." Darshini sighed, taking a sip of her iced tea.

"Mhm, I have two important presentations, and I'm praying I get the sub-professor because he's a lot more chill," Adam said, crossing his fingers.

"I'll practise mine soon," I replied, making a mental note to revise my presentation.

"I think we're set to finish tomorrow, right?" Dante asked.

"Yes." I smiled and thanked them again. "Thank you so much. I'll be able to meet the deadline."

"Hey, why is there such a tight deadline?" Stella asked.

"For starters, all the animals have been temporarily sent to other shelters, and we can't keep taking up their space for too long," I explained. The distance was also inconvenient and time-consuming for the volunteers.

"The fastest contractors within the budget wouldn't be able to start for another week. I can't afford that extra week, and I really want to impress Mrs. Smith," I added with a sigh. I needed to blow her socks off, and given the work these amazing friends of mine had done, it was likely to happen.

"Oh, that makes sense," Stella said.

"Why impress Mrs. Smith? You already do such an outstanding job," Zaira gushed.

"There's this program I want to get into, and I know they'll contact her for a reference. I need to make sure she can speak highly about me," I explained.

"Ah, that makes sense," Ibrahim said, stuffing his face with more breadsticks.

"Program? What program?" Stella asked, brows furrowed.

"It's an internship for Animal Rights Education. They'll partially fund my master's, and I'll get to work alongside them in the organisation," I replied.

"Oh, that sounds perfect for you!" she responded.

"She's incredible, isn't she?" Adam poked my side, focusing all the attention on me. "She had it all planned out, and managed this renovation project so her boss could put in a good word, which she will because you did impressive work."

He spoke with pride about me, something that rarely happened for me, and I could only blink at him with a slight smile.

"It was all thanks to you guys." I cleared my throat and looked at the rest of them.

"I hope you get that spot," Zaira wished.

"Yeah, no one deserves it more than you," Adam continued, his smile warm. "You've been working incredibly hard for it."

"Look at you two, the best of friends," Carter teased. If he hadn't spoken, I might've forgotten our arrangement and held Adam's hand in front of everyone.

"Yeah, she is," Adam confirmed, his eyes softening as he looked at me. "She's incredible."

We lingered in that moment, just gazing into each other's eyes. Adam then cleared his throat and shot a playful glare at Carter. "And she doesn't put honey on my fries."

"It was an accident, let it go already." Carter sighed.

The rest of the night was filled with more friendly banter, but all I could focus on was the way Adam spoke about me. The way his eyes sparkled and his lips curved into a genuine smile. It consumed my thoughts, and I mindlessly answered the others as they spoke.

When Adam and I got home, he turned to me before rushing up the stairs. "I'm tired, so I'll wash up and head straight to bed," he explained.

"Goodnight and sweet dreams, Brooklyn," Adam said, then pressed his lips to my forehead before heading upstairs.

"Goodnight, Adam," I replied, watching him go.

Things hadn't been platonic or casual for me for a long time. His actions, his appreciation, the morning and goodnight kisses, the way he'd look at me when he spoke about me. I had fallen for Adam without being assured that he'd catch me.

Chapter twenty-seven

Adam

I finished up a call with my agent, still celebrating the acceptance from Liberty FC. It all happened so fast. I remembered Brooke and I were hiking the trail in the backyard when I got the call, and I nearly fainted from excitement.

To make things even better, I wouldn't have to miss our graduation. The schedule was solid, and I'd have some time to myself before having to move to New York and being thrown into the deep end.

"Sounds great. I'm okay with everything but orange cleats," I said. I hadn't even expected to discuss this. DTU had great sponsors, and our budget allowed us to have good cleats, but Liberty FC's catalogue was on another level.

"This is the beginning of something great, Serra Valle. We'll stay in contact," my agent replied.

"Have a good day."

That was one phone call down. Now for the second. My parents and grandmother. I clicked on the group call. I wasn't sure why they took their sweet time answering when they were the ones who picked the time and date.

"Ah, you guys finally decided to pick up the phone," I scoffed, leaning back in my seat.

"Don't sass us now, Adam," Dad mumbled.

"Tell him the good news, tell him," Vovó said, her enthusiasm infectious.

"Tell me what?" I asked, eager to know more.

"We made arrangements, and we're all going to come for your graduation," Dad replied.

"All three of you?" My dad wasn't sure at first since he needed to get his time off approved, and Vovó lived in Brazil.

"Yep, we know you have plans with your friends, so we'll only stay a few days to celebrate," Mom explained, but I was already envisioning them there, watching me accept my degree.

"We'll also be there to help you move into your new place," Vovó added sweetly. She had been there to see me off to college, and now she'd watch me join the football club of my dreams.

"This is the best news ever! I can't wait to see you guys." I smiled warmly. "Vovó, I can't believe you're coming."

"I wouldn't miss my baby's graduation," she said in her endearing voice.

"Stop babying him," Dad groaned good-naturedly.

"Stop being jealous," Vovó retorted, and a proud smirk graced my face. He used to be her favourite until I came along—according to him.

"We're proud of you, meu amor," Mom chimed in. "I'm so glad everything worked out as planned."

"Thank you, Mãe," I hummed. "I can't wait to see you guys."

"We've gotta get going now. Have a good day, Adam," Dad wished.

I ended the call and looked ahead to see Carter finally making his way out of the building. Finally, we both finished our last presentations.

"How'd it go?"

"Perfect. I even nailed the questions," he said with a smug grin.

"Great job," I complimented. "My parents called. They're coming to my graduation, and so is my grandma!" I couldn't contain my joy, even if I tried.

"That's awesome. Didn't you say your grandma hates flying?" Carter asked.

"Exactly. She's coming just for me." I grinned. "What about your folks?"

"Are you kidding? They wouldn't miss it. In fact, Stefi made a huge glittery card for me and Stella. Carter pulled out his phone to show me a picture of it. Stefani was clearly creative.

"That's adorable."

"She thinks I'm moving back home already." Carter sighed. His little sister, Stefi, always tried to convince him to stay home every summer, but she failed every year.

"You haven't told her about the master's program yet?"

"Nope." He sighed. "Before we grab lunch, I need to stop by the post office for Stella's graduation gift."

"What did you get her—wait, is it something bedroom related? Never mind, I don't want to know." I shuddered.

"I got her a personalised planner. God knows she loves her planner books," he said proudly. "I also put together a scrapbook filled with her best college memories and a ring she had been eyeing."

"A ring? An engagement?" I teased. They had become serious over time.

"A promise. Engagement comes later." Carter smiled.

"Really?"

"Absolutely. I will marry Stella one day," Carter stated with confidence. "She's the love of my life."

"How did you know?"

"It's simple, really, no one knows me better than she does. She brings out the best in me and has always supported me. There's no one who makes me happier than her, and I feel like the luckiest person alive to know that I make her feel the same way. I can't imagine my life without her in it. The bond we have is special and unbreakable, it feels as if we're made for each other. She's not just my best friend, she's my soulmate," Carter spoke mindlessly as he drove, his gaze softened, and he was smiling.

Carter spoke about himself and Stella, but all I could think about was how perfectly that aligned with what I felt for Brooklyn. My feelings for her had been on my mind for a while, and I tried to shake them off, to remind myself this was strictly for pleasure, but I couldn't deny it much longer.

I loved Brooklyn, I fell in love with her since that day she took me on a hike in the backyard and surprised me with a picnic.

I was thankful for all the time we got to spend together because it made me realise how mad I am for this woman. I was confessing my love for her today.

I had never felt more comfortable with anyone. I was tired of watching others experience love while denying myself. I knew she felt something too, and I was determined to show her we could be more than friends. Brooklyn brightened my world and made life more exciting. I would be foolish to let this opportunity slip away.

Brooklyn was out. I'm not sure if she was distancing herself because we had plans to go hiking yesterday, but she bailed at the last minute. With our schedule freed up from finals, we had planned to go out to this new club, but she just texted me to let me know tonight wouldn't work for her.

Fuck, she's distancing herself already.

I had to confess, and I had to do it tonight before it's too late.

I called my parents again for a little favour as I prepared dinner and dessert. I even went into the backyard to pick flowers. My bouquet wasn't professional looking, but I added a bow to it so the bright colours should count for something.

I heard her pulling up and rushed to the door. A smile formed on my face as she stepped inside. Brooklyn's eyes went around the room swiftly before coming to mine.

"I need to tell—"

"I want to end our arrangement," Brooklyn said without showing any bit of emotion.

I'm fairly certain I felt my heart shatter into pieces.

Chapter twenty-eight

Brooklyn

I stared at my email, disbelief mingling with excitement. I had been accepted into the Animal Rights Education Program, a dream come true. But as I read further, my heart sank. They were moving downtown, significantly farther. The distance was a major disruption in the meticulously crafted plan. Fuck.

I had calculated everything down to the last detail. They were covering a large part of my tuition, which was an incredible relief, but I still needed to handle my living expenses. With a part-time job, I could just about manage to live in this expensive town by watching my pennies closely and taking the subway would work out much better.

But now, with the change in address, the commute would take up any free time I had for a part-time job. Every solution I thought of fell apart. It felt as if the universe was pushing me to leave Massachusetts, to abandon the only place I had ever truly felt at home besides my grandmother's house.

I had been foolish to believe I could make this work, that I could stay close to the only family I had ever known, and to Adam, the only person whom I adored in a way I did for no other. All my friends would continue to live their dream life, I was happy for them, but I just wished I could've been a part of that.

With a few weeks left until graduation, Adam and I had grown closer with each day. Every joke, every smile, every thoughtful gesture from him made me fall deeper. But I knew I had to end things before I spent my summer mourning what we could have had.

The thought of parting from Adam was unbearable, but I knew it would be much harder in the future.

I was a coward. It took me three agonising days to make this decision. It was time, though. Friday night. The lies were becoming too difficult, and I could see the hurt in his eyes every time I pulled away.

I stepped into the house with determination, my heart pounding. The sight of the kitchen beautifully set up. It was clear, I had to do it now, before we both got even more hurt.

"I want to end our arrangement," I said, forcing a professional tone.

"E-excuse me?" Adam stuttered, hurt washing over his face before confusion settled in.

"We should end things now," I said yet again and tried not to look at the bush of flowers in the kitchen. I couldn't be caught in his kindness at this moment.

"Why?" Adam asked, his demeanour shifting from joy to confusion.

"Because," I stated. I didn't expect him to question me about it.

"Because isn't a reason, Brooke, and you know that." Adam rolled his eyes and crossed his arms, his gaze narrowing on me, demanding a real answer.

"Adam, we agreed we could stop whenever we wanted," I reminded him, trying to ignore the pain flickering in his eyes. I was wrong. I wasn't ready for this conversation.

"That was before things changed between us." Adam stepped closer, his voice softening.

"Nothing changed between us," I insisted, looking up at him.

"Look me in the eyes and tell me that," Adam demanded.

I took a step closer. "Nothing has changed between us, Adam," I said, my voice steady, though my fingers nervously tugged at the ends of my shorts. I expected him to step aside, but instead, his gaze softened, and a small smile played on his lips.

"Nice try, Brooke, I know all your tells already, and it's clear you're lying," Adam said so calmly that it pissed me off.

Damn it. He always caught me when I rubbed my hand over my thigh.

"Adam, leave me alone." I tried to push past him, but he gently wrapped his hand around my wrist and pulled me to him.

"No, Brooklyn, I won't leave you until you can give me a solid reason," Adam requested and didn't let go of my hand. "One valid reason, and I'm letting all of this go, and I'll respect your wishes."

"I can't tell you, Adam," I said, trying to keep the sadness from consuming me. "Even if I could, it would be of no use," I muttered. "We can't be together."

"What do you mean?" Adam frowned.

I took a deep breath and told him everything about my current situation, how I wouldn't be able to stay here despite getting into the program I wanted. He'd understand then, who would remain friends with benefits when you lived on opposite ends of the country?

"I plan on moving back to my grandmother's home. My cousin and her husband are still there, covering the bills. I applied for a state master's program, and I got in. The costs are substantially lower, and it's doable for me," I said, repeating the plans I wished I didn't have to follow.

"No." Adam shook his head, his brows furrowing.

"What do you mean *no*?" I raised an eyebrow at him and tugged my hand out of his.

"I'm not letting you move back home where you would be unhappy when I can ensure a future where you're happy," he replied. I wasn't sure why he thought he could dictate my happiness or fix everything.

"Adam—" I warned, but he cut me off.

"Listen to me, please," he pleaded, his tone softer now. "I spoke to my parents already. They won't retire for another two years. I asked them if you could stay here—"

"Adam, no, I will not accept any of this." There was no way I could let him do more for me.

"For Christ's sake, Brooklyn, let someone do something for you for once." Adam's voice was filled with frustration, and it sure got me to shut up. I blinked at him several times, unable to say anything. "Why do you deny yourself happiness when it's right here in your reach?"

That simple scoff threw me off. Why did everything have to go his way?

"Why do you care so much?" I pushed back, expecting him to let me go finally.

"Because I fucking love you, Brooklyn," Adam confessed, anger and devotion entwined in his tone. "And I'll be damned if I let you move back to a place you referred to as your personal hellhole, especially when I know this is where you want to be. Attending DTU, doing that animal rights program you dreamed of, and being surrounded by your friends," he said, his eyes locked onto mine. "Let me do this for you, Brooklyn," he asked, and I wanted to defy my stubbornness for him.

My heart pounded in my chest as his words sank in. The sincerity, the raw emotion in his voice.

"You love me?" I whispered, still stuck on that part.

"I know we promised that it would only ever be casual." Adam shrugged helplessly. "But it hasn't been casual for me for a long time already."

I was blindsided for a moment, drowning in my own feelings.

"Adam, I truly appreciate it all, but I can't risk losing you." I caressed his face and pressed my lips together to stop them from quivering.

"You won't lose me," Adam assured me, placing his hand over mine and bringing it to his lips. "Give me a chance, let me love you, Brooklyn. I will spend every day giving you more than the last. My heart is yours, Brooklyn," he continued, and damn it, his eyes alone were convincing enough. "Let me prove to you how much you mean to me, and I won't ever take it for granted," Adam pleaded yet again. The sweetest man I've ever known.

"You've already proven yourself, Adam, I fear I won't be what you want," I confessed. He was beyond perfect, it was me who could fuck everything up.

"Brooklyn, you're all I ever wanted, and I wasn't even aware until you pulled me to dance in the rain with you," Adam said, a gentle smile playing on his lips as he tucked a stray curl behind my ear. "I want you by my side, Brooklyn. Nothing will ever change my mind about you."

"Adam, even if I accept your offer, you still have to move." My heart raced like I had just run a marathon. The initial excitement was quickly followed by fear. Was this the right decision?

"New York isn't that far," Adam replied confidently. "I checked my schedule. I'll be able to visit you while maintaining a long-distance relationship," he said, stepping closer and tilting my chin up so our eyes met. "It's going to be new for both of us, but I know we can get through this."

"Adam, this is too much." I let fear consume me. I had come to terms with the idea that none of this would happen.

I spent the past three days convincing myself it was okay to let go. Now, having him offer me everything on a silver platter felt like a trap, like a dream I'd wake up from, wishing it were real.

"If I took a shot every time you said that, my kidneys would have given up on me," Adam joked, his timing impeccable as ever.

"I'm being serious," I said, narrowing my eyes at him.

"As am I." Adam mimicked my behaviour. "I spoke to my parents first. They plan to work for two more years before retiring. They're happy there will be someone living here, you only have to take care of the yard and utilities," he explained. "You wanted into this program so badly, you want to be surrounded by your friends; all of that can happen, Brooklyn."

That program was my dream, it was a stepping stone to a future with more opportunities. I wanted it, I wanted to stay here in this exact house, I wanted to be with him. I wanted it all.

"And I can have you?" I asked. My heart thundered in my chest. The nerves piled up in my stomach, and I needed an answer ASAP or I might just throw up.

"Every fibre of my being will be yours." Adam took my hands in his. "All you have to do is ask." He laced our fingers together.

"Tell me those four letters again," I whispered. Those four letters he said before brought me such pride, I had to hear it once more, and I'd have all the courage in the world to ask him to be mine.

"I love you, Brooklyn," Adam said with devotion and let go of one of my hands to caress my face. His eyes trailed over every detail on my face as he smiled.

My turn, I guess.

"You awakened feelings within me I wasn't aware I was capable of. You slithered your way into my heart. Every second, every glance, every smile, they all whispered your love into existence. I'm done lying to myself that it's purely platonic because I love you too, Adam," I confessed, every word poured out of my soul. With each word, his smile only grew, and I only gained more confidence to finish my confession.

"You're incredible," Adam whispered, his gaze softened with adoration.

"Ask me to be your girlfriend, Adam." I pulled him closer.

"Will you be my gir—" I didn't let him finish that sentence.

I pressed my lips to his for a searing kiss. Rising onto my toes, I pressed my body against his, feeling the heat of his skin through his shirt. My fingers tangled in his hair while he settled firmly on my waist. The kiss grew heated with each passing second, and when we finally pulled away to breathe, his eyes found mine, and he simply raised a brow at me.

"You talk too much," I said breathlessly. "I'll be your girlfriend, yes."

Chapter twenty-nine

Brooklyn

I gazed into his eyes, drowning in their depths once more. I caressed the short strands at the nape of his neck, savouring his warmth. Adam admired every little detail of me, his thumb gently tracing my jawline, shooting a wave of pleasure through me. Our breaths mingled, the want was clear in the air between us, and yet all he did was stare.

The tension was unbearable, and my patience was thinning. I pulled him to me, crashing my lips against his in an intense kiss that sealed our new bond as girlfriend and boyfriend.

Adam moaned into the kiss as I nipped at his lip, a smirk forming on my lips. He responded by firmly planting his hands on my hips, pulling my body flush against his. Breaking the kiss, he swiftly removed my sundress and lifted me effortlessly, carrying me to the nearest surface—the dining table.

I pulled him down to me, locking our lips once more as my hands roamed over his muscular arms and back. I had familiarised myself with his perfect body over time, and still, I could not have enough of it, I would never have enough of him.

My foot traced a slow and teasing path up his inner thigh, grazing his hardened cock that was still restrained. Adam groaned against my lips. All he had to do was give in, but I think he was there to play games.

In an instant, he grabbed my legs and wrapped them around his waist, preventing any further teasing. Adam started kissing down the side of my neck, and I lifted my body to him, taking all I could get.

I tugged at his shirt and rose to my elbows, watching as he pulled his shirt over his head. I was about to lean back when something warm touched my arm, and I looked over to see a small glass bowl.

"What's that?" I frowned.

"Oh shit, I was making chocolate-covered strawberries for you, it's the leftover molten chocolate from that fancy brand you like." Adam reached for the bowl.

"So that's molten chocolate." I held his hand to stop him from walking away with it.

"It is," Adam confirmed and looked down at the bowl.

Tonight is about to become messy.

I dipped my finger into the chocolate and brought it to my lips, spreading it. Adam watched me with excitement and his eyes followed my hands as I dipped into the chocolate again. The sweet substance spread across my neck, down my breast, and around my nipple. I slowly drew a path down south, Adam wasn't the only one who could play games tonight. I drew the letter '*A*' on my lower abdomen, finishing the course for him.

"You'll be the end of me," Adam whispered as I pressed my two chocolate-coated fingers to his lips.

Adam held my hand, eyes locked on mine as he sucked my fingers clean. He swirled his tongue around them, then pressed a kiss to the tip of my fingers. He put the bowl away, then grabbed my hips and yanked me closer to him.

He kissed away the chocolate from my lips, the sweet and rich flavour danced between our kisses. Adam kissed down the path I laid out for him, each kiss and nip at my skin had me anticipating more. His tongue swirled around my nipple briefly, and he continued his path down while his fingers rolled over my nipple before tugging at it.

I moaned his name and buried my hands in his hair. He pressed warm kisses down my navel and stopped right underneath. His tongue danced across my pussy, and I couldn't wait any longer. I knew he was close to feasting on me, but I wanted more than that, I wanted him in me right now.

"Adam," I called sweetly and tried pulling him up by his shoulders before he'd go down on me. Adam looked up at me, kissing my inner thigh. "Take me to bed."

"Now? Are you sure?" he asked, brushing his fingers over my pussy.

"Yes, definitely now."

"As you wish."

We barely made it through the door, and he already rushed me to the bed. He threw me down and got rid of his clothes as fast as he could.

Adam hovered above me, and I dragged him down for a kiss. I traced down his back, loving the touch of his muscles under my touch. Adam slipped his tongue into my mouth, ensuing a passionate battle. His hand moved down my curves, touching every part of me he could.

Adam broke away from the kiss and reached for the nightstand. "No, I don't want that." I placed my hand on his when he grabbed his favourite toy. We had definitely been experimenting more, and tonight I felt ready for more.

"Tonight, I want you, all of you everywhere," I said and grabbed the lube instead and pushed it against his chest.

"Yeah?" Adam asked, surprised as he took the lube. I nodded.

"Sounds good to me," he muttered before kissing me yet again. I closed my eyes and caressed his face as I kissed him back with every bit of passion I could muster up.

Adam, without a warning, changed our position so I was on top now. He trailed his hands down my ass and looked up at me. "First, show me what you can do, Brooklyn," he said and delivered a spank. "Ride my cock and I'll fuck you how you please," he promised. Adam kept all his bedroom promises, and I was sure he wasn't planning to break them now.

I moved to straddle him, my hands planted on his chest as I looked down at him. He smiled at me and reached over to pull at the ribbon that held my hair back. He then carefully moved his fingers through my curls and let some cascade over my shoulders. "How are you real?" he asked in a whisper.

“Do you ever get tired of praising me?” I asked and leaned over to kiss his neck. I kissed, sucked, and nipped at his skin. Adam caressed my thighs and hummed softly.

“Never, and I don’t plan on stopping, ever.” He gripped my hips, pushing me against his hardened cock. “Now, please ride me, Brooklyn, I need that pussy wrapped around my cock,” he pleaded.

“I like it when you beg,” I teased and kissed his chest now. This time, I sucked long enough to leave my mark. Then another and another.

Perhaps I liked being on top, admiring my pretty art on his body and relishing in the adornment in his eyes.

I moved down to his cock and slowly lowered myself onto him. I moaned and tipped my head back. Adam moved one hand to my hip as the other slid up my side to my breast, where he squeezed me.

“That’s it, you look so gorgeous riding my cock.” He smirked as his fingers toyed with my nipple. I placed my hands over his, squeezing them as I started riding him. Adam continued to whisper sweet and dirty words as I took him deeper with each movement of mine.

As I moved faster, the coil of pleasure tightened within me, my moans growing louder with each movement as did Adam’s groans. Adam’s hands roamed over my body, claiming and caressing every inch of me.

I could feel my release approaching, the sweet sensation building at my core. Adam picked up on that and brought one hand down to my clit, rubbing me with a driven desire. I came closer and closer until Adam’s name left my lips as a sweet mantra of pleasure. Crashes of pure satisfaction consumed me whole. My body trembled as I fluttered around him and rode out my orgasm.

Adam’s fingers dug into my hips as he pulled me down completely, a loud groan of his filling the air as he tipped his head back and came. I leaned forward with my hands planted on his chest for support as he took what was his.

“That was perfect,” Adam said and kissed me hungrily. He barely moved me off him and was already kissing and caressing me as we lay together and attempted to calm down.

After a few minutes, Adam flipped me over to my stomach and raised my hips. His hands roamed over my curves, caressing my skin with a tender yet firm touch. He gently palmed my ass before parting my knees further.

He grabbed the lube, and I took a deep breath, anticipation clear in the air for me. I heard the bottle open and the squirt of the lube. Closing my eyes as excitement filled me.

"Do you still want this, Brooklyn? I don't mind if you say no." Adam's voice was soft, filled with concern and care.

"No, I want this, I want this with you," I replied, so quickly it made me sound a bit desperate, but I didn't care. I still haven't had enough of him.

His fingers circled me, gently probing and preparing. He started with one, moving it with a rhythm that made my body hum. Then came the second and the third, stretching and filling me in a way that was both more exhilarating than with the toys. "Look at how well you're taking me," he marvelled, his voice thick with admiration and desire. "Tell me how you feel, Brooklyn baby."

"It feels good, but I want more," I answered, pushing back against him, my need for him growing with each passing second. "But, I asked for your cock, Adam," I sassed and heard that sweet chuckle of his that meant trouble.

"Always so impatient." He spanked me. I jolted forward a little and bit back a whimper. "You better take every inch of me, I plan on stretching this pretty ass of yours." Another spank followed, and I gripped the sheets, my anticipation increasing.

I heard the squirting of more lube. I looked over my shoulder to see him stroking himself as he lathered it onto himself. He caught my eye and smirked at me. One hand anchored on my hip as he came closer to me. The tip nudged at my entrance, and I closed my eyes as he inserted me leisurely.

"Oh god, Adam," I gasped, feeling him. It was a foreign sensation, but my body responded, accommodating him as it had done before with the toys, though nothing compared to him.

"You sure do wonders for my ego, darling." Adam chuckled as he palmed my ass. "Now ease up, I'm only halfway in," he requested, and my jaw hung open.

"Fuck," I cursed as he pushed himself in fully. I closed my eyes and took deep breaths. Adam allowed me a moment to adjust, then started driving into me slowly.

When my body got used to him and this new sensation, he started picking up the pace. This was so worth everything.

"If you could see what I'm looking at, Brooke," he said, his tone heavy with lust. "So fucking marvellous," he added and spanked my ass, the stinging feeling soon soothed by his hand. "My cum leaking out of your pretty pussy while I'm fucking this perfect ass," he said as he continued to plunge into me, his fingers finding my clit, and all I could do was ride out this path to ecstasy he was taking me on.

"Tell me, Brooke, do you want me to cum in your ass too?" he asked, his thrusts becoming more urgent, his fingers toying with my clit.

"Yes, Adam, please, don't stop," I whimpered, my grip on the sheets tightening as I buried my face in the mattress. Adam spanked my ass yet again, pleasure spreading over the ache.

It was all-consuming, leaving me breathless and yearning for more. Adam knew every part of me so damn well.

"Come on, Brooklyn, I know you have another one for me." Adam rubbed my clit faster as his strokes became harder and deeper. He filled me in every way possible. "Let go for me." His voice was a mixture of command and plea.

His words were the final push I needed. The world around me blurred as the sensation overtook every last sense of me. An overwhelming wave of pleasure crashed over me, and every muscle of my body tightened as I chanted his name out of pure bliss. My nails dug into the mattress as I felt him everywhere inside me.

Adam moaned my name loudly as he came, his hands planted on my hips and fingers digging into my skin. He prolonged our release as he thrust slowly now, the waves of my orgasm slowly subsided, but I was still floating on a cloud of pleasure.

Adam leaned over and kissed from my shoulder to my ear. He gently stroked my hair aside with his calm and loving touches. "You're so fucking incredible," he whispered in my ear. Adam pulled out and gently palmed my ass. "The prettiest fucking sight," he muttered under his breath.

Adam came to lie down next to me and pulled me to his chest, wrapping his arms around me as we both caught our breath. I smiled, feeling an earnest connection to him, a bond that went beyond the physical. "I love you, Adam," I breathed, still basking in the afterglow.

"And I love you, Brooklyn," he replied, holding me close. "So, so much, words know no bounds to describe it." In his arms, I felt complete, every part of me was cherished and adored.

After a while of just lying in each other's arms, we finally got up and went to the bathroom. Luckily, we managed to actually shower and not do anything else... Beyond some touching and kissing.

"I'm hungry," I said as I began to apply my lotion.

"I made us taquitos and Mexican rice, I followed the recipe we found," Adam said, grabbing some of the lotion to do my back. "Oh, I also got you flowers and made the strawberry-covered chocolate." He snuck his arms around my waist and pulled me to his bare body.

"What exactly did you have planned?" I asked, looking at our reflection. I could tell he had been itching to touch me, hold me, love me like this, and frankly, now that I had a taste of it. I didn't want him to let go.

"I was going to tell you how much I love you and how I came up with a plan for you to stay and attend DTU," Adam said, looking into my eyes through the mirror. "But you just had to attempt a breakup." He rolled his eyes.

"Fuck," I gasped with realisation.

"What?"

"I never failed a breakup before," I realised.

"First time for everything." Adam laughed and let go of me so he could get dressed too. "I'll go put on some clothes, meet me downstairs so we can have the dinner I actually planned." He slapped my ass before leaving the room, his naked ass on full display as he walked away.

After a nice dinner and dessert, I admired the flowers for a few more seconds before planning to head to my room. It was safe to say today tired me out.

"You're not going anywhere." Adam grabbed my arm and pulled me back into his chest.

"Right, sorry, I forgot to thank you," I realised and reached to caress his face. "Thank you for everything tonight, Adam. The flowers, confession, food—literally everything."

No one ever did anything like this for me. Adam truly had won my heart in every way possible.

"I appreciate the words, but I didn't mean that." He smirked.

"Then?" I raised a brow at him.

"Boyfriend taxes," he said, then wrapped his arms around me in a tight embrace, "My rates are 15 percent cuddles and on rainy days 25 percent."

"I—"

"Don't you dare deny loving the cuddles, you wake up with your body draped over mine almost every night we've spent together," Adam whispered and squeezed me in a hug.

"Fine, you caught me," I teased, rolling my eyes with a smile.

It wasn't that bad—at all. I snuggled up to him, feeling the familiar safety of his embrace. Nestling my face into the crook of his neck, I draped one leg and arm over his torso. With my eyes closed, I let the warmth and comfort of Adam's presence envelop me.

My Adam, I didn't have any idea how much he'd change my life.

Chapter thirty

Adam

|The following week.|

The birds were chirping, tapping against my windows, even waking me up. I felt the warmth of Brooklyn nestled in my arms. Eyes closed, I pulled her closer, nuzzling my face into her neck. She loved this, she didn't pull away for a moment.

I tried to block out the birds' persistent songs, but Brooklyn began to stir in her sleep. She shifted around, eventually draping one leg over my waist and clutching my shirt with the fist her hand always formed when she slept.

I opened my eyes and gazed at Brooklyn. She looked angelic, her full lips forming a slight pout, wild dark curls framing her face. Gently, I brushed her hair aside and smiled at her. Holding her like this was a blissful sensation. Waking up next to her was going to be the thing I missed most when I moved.

I held onto Brooklyn until her alarm went off. We were forced to get up, even on our day off.

We had plans to hike the trail in the backyard to the grand oak tree.

We spread our blanket on the grass and unpacked our lunch, which featured my famous sandwiches, chips, and guarana soda. Brooklyn had prepared a mini cheese and cracker spread for us.

It had only been a week, but dating Brooklyn was already the best decision I'd ever made. I was forever grateful she'd given me a chance. Things were almost the same as before, except now I no longer had to hide my feelings or worry about them, they were fully reciprocated.

"The sandwich was really good," Brooklyn complimented, crumpling her paper towel.

"Thanks, I added extra sauce for you," I replied with a wink, knowing she preferred it that way. "I, uh, forgot to tell you something."

"What's wrong?" Brooklyn asked, her tone laced with concern.

"Do you remember that night we went clubbing during our junior year? We had tequila?" I asked. She had to know.

"Vaguely." She frowned.

"We kinda kissed that night... It wasn't meant to happen, and I swear I was as respectful as possible," I confessed and watched as the news surprised her.

"Really? You never said anything." She frowned.

"We were just becoming great friends, and I didn't want to make things awkward," I explained truthfully. Brooklyn was quiet at first.

"No, you're right, things would've been awkward. I'm really happy with how things turned out," Brooklyn confessed as she leaned back against the tree with me.

"Thank you for giving me a chance, Brooklyn," I said, lowering my bag of chips and looking into her eyes. "It's only been a week, and I know this might sound cheesy, but it's been one of the best weeks of my life."

"Definitely cheesy... but I feel the same way," she replied, her lips curling into a smile as she focused on her own bag of chips. "All our plans are set, right?" she asked, for what must have been the third time this week.

I knew she wasn't used to others handling major plans. Or perhaps she wasn't used to things going as planned, but she no longer had to worry about that. I would make sure everything went exactly how she wanted.

"Yes, Brooke, my parents are more than happy for you to stay here," I reassured her once again. They had never turned away someone in need, especially a friend of mine. "I've pencilled you in for all my free moments, and I'll spend my long weekends back here, or you can visit me." I already shared my agenda with her.

It would be my first year playing for Liberty FC, and I needed to prove to them that they made a good choice picking me. I had meticulously planned everything, dedicating all my free time to Brooklyn without jeopardizing my spot on the team.

"Okay, okay, it's only going to be a year," Brooklyn said, trying to reassure herself as much as me.

"Then you'll move in with me, right?" I asked, wrapping my arm around her. My back ached against the tree, but it was worth it for this moment.

"Mhm, AREP has an office in New York. It's further from where you'll be staying, but we'll be in the same place again," she said, nestling her head against my chest.

"I can survive a year," I replied, leaning closer to whisper in her ear, "As long as you promise to send me more photos."

"Don't be a perv," she said, playfully jabbing my stomach.

"Hey!" I groaned.

"Are you excited about this new chapter?" she asked, her tone softening.

"Of course I am," I said. "I've got my dream girl and my dream job. What more could a simple man like myself ask for?" My fingers traced along her jawline, gently turning her face to meet mine.

"You're right, what a lucky man you are." Brooklyn smiled.

In the bright midday sun, her hazel eyes sparkled with flecks of green. The sunlight played on her brown skin, giving her an ethereal glow. She looked vibrant and full of life, with the sun highlighting her natural beauty.

It wasn't her beauty that had me smitten, but I was well aware of what a lucky man I was to score someone as stunning as her.

"I love you," I whispered and leaned down to kiss her briefly.

"I love you too, Adam." Brooklyn smiled and closed her eyes as she relaxed against me.

I held her close, feeling grateful for every moment we shared along with the promised future ahead of us. This was all I needed.

Lately, everyone in the group had been busy, everyone had passed all their exams and was set to graduate. Tonight, we'd finally get together to celebrate at Alfonso's kitchen. Brooklyn and I planned to break the news about our relationship.

"You ready?" I asked as we stood outside the restaurant. Brooklyn looked at me with a soft smile and nodded.

"I'm ready to openly claim you," Brooklyn said, fixing her hair and giving me a subtle nod.

"Okay, alpha, settle down." I laughed, opening the door for her.

"I'm considering breaking up with you every day," she said, narrowing her eyes at me.

"And every night I remind you why you stick with me," I whispered in her ear as we walked towards our booth. My hand settled on her lower back. Making sure no one was watching, I slid my hand down to her ass and gave it a subtle squeeze.

"Adam—" She glared at me, but couldn't say much since we had arrived at the booth.

"Okay, that's everyone, perfect." Stella smiled and scooted over to make room for me and Brooklyn. "The food should be here in about ten minutes," she said, glancing at Carter's watch.

We were running late, but we texted Stella our order to save time.

"I'm so happy we all passed," Dante said, relieved.

"What would've happened if one of us didn't graduate?" Ibrahim asked curiously.

"You probably wouldn't be invited to the graduation trip." Darshini shrugged.

"I'm sure you could unbutton the first buttons of your shirt and try to seduce whoever you need to for some extra points," Dante suggested, his fingers playfully reaching for the top button of Ibrahim's shirt.

"Stop trying to pimp me out." Ibrahim slapped his hand away and glared at him. "And how dare you assume I'd even fail at something?"

"You failed to make me the dumpling soup," Zaira recalled, bringing up the latest laugh in the group chat.

"Well, he did make it," Carter pointed out the technicality.

"But it was super salty," Darshini butted in.

"Sounds like a murder attempt if I ever heard of one," Stella muttered with a wicker smirk.

"Okay, I was learning? Go pick on Adam instead or Brooklyn, they're late." Ibrahim jutted his chin towards us.

"You're sitting awfully close to each other," Dante remarked.

"Oh, so you're allowed to be glued by your girlfriend's side, but I'm not allowed to do the same?" I asked and pulled Brooklyn closer as my hand slid down her shoulder.

"Girlfriend?" Carter frowned, deepened with confusion.

"Are you guys actually dating or are you messing with us?" Zaira asked, excitement evident in her tone.

"Not messing with you, we're actually dating," I said proudly, meeting Brooklyn's smiling gaze.

"But the jock? The one you were—" Darshini started, confused until realisation dawned on her. "Oh... It's Adam—oh my god, wait, what you said about the jock—is about him?" Zaira asked, all eyes turning to Brooklyn. I raised an eyebrow at her, curious about what 'things' she had mentioned. I bet it's all the compliments on how great I treat her.

"I can neither confirm nor deny," Brooklyn quickly responded, avoiding eye contact.

"I, for one, love this. The group won't be expanding, it will just be us eight," Carter said, skilfully changing the subject.

We already struggled for a table of eight in some places, now we wouldn't have to worry. It would only be us.

"Didn't we try to set you guys up before?" Stella asked, raising an eyebrow at us.

"It wasn't the right time back then." I shrugged.

When they wanted us together, the circumstances were different. I would've fallen for Brooklyn regardless, but our schedules wouldn't have allowed it.

"What changed?" Darshini asked, sipping her drink.

"Oh, you know, he finally got a contract and is worth my time," Brooklyn joked, placing her hand on my chest and gazing into my eyes.

"She finally stopped bullying me," I said proudly, winking.

Not true she mouthed, but no one believed her.

"Aww, she softened up," Zaira teased.

"We're really happy for you," Stella said, smiling as she looked between the two of us. "You make a lovely couple."

Telling our friends went far better than we expected. They were all genuinely happy for us and only asked the basic questions. Then we moved on to more pressing topics, such as finalising the plans for our trip and debating who among the guys was the best at grilling. Personally, I thought it was me, but apparently, that's up for debate.

It was a night of fun and laughter with our friends, and I couldn't have asked for a happier night.

Brooklyn

|Two days until graduation|

Four years of relentless hard work, and finally, I'd be receiving my degree. My last graduation was decent; I was just eager to leave town and head to college. This time, it's different. I had amazing friends who were graduating alongside me.

I darted around the kitchen frantically, ensuring everything was flawless. Adam and I spent all day yesterday cleaning the house. His parents and grandmother were coming over and planned to stay with us for a few days.

Adam descended the stairs, looking as relaxed as ever. He was supposed to pick them up at the airport and seemed utterly carefree at the moment.

"Adam, I'm nervous," I confessed, walking over to him.

"I know, I know. Technically, it's too soon to meet the parents, way too soon, but given the circumstances, we have no choice." Adam sighed and reached to hold my hands in his.

"It's not that exactly." I watched as he laced our fingers together.

"Then what is it?" A frown formed on his face as he studied me.

"What if your parents meet me and decide to change their minds?" I asked, unable to bear the thought of their rejection, especially when I love their son so deeply.

"They won't change their minds." Adam smiled, his worries vanishing, unlike mine.

"How can you be so sure? What if they don't like me? Adam, all our plans will be ruined," I groaned, burying my face in his chest. Adam wrapped his arms around me in a warm, reassuring embrace.

"Nothing is ruined," Adam soothed, rubbing my back. "Vovó already likes you, so I doubt my parents will feel any different," he explained, kissing my forehead. "They aren't difficult people. They will love you—they already do based on what I've told them," he spoke gently, rubbing small circles on my back.

"Promise?" I tilted my head to look at him.

"I promise. I know my parents; they'll love you." He leaned down and kissed me softly. "Just be sure to call them Mr. and Mrs., it's considered disrespectful for them if people younger call them by their first names," he advised, booping my nose.

"Noted." I nodded.

"Are you okay now?" Adam asked, and I nodded. "Alright, I'll head to the airport then."

"Sounds good, drive safe." I walked him to the door.

"I will," he promised, kissing me briefly before leaving.

I leaned against the door, watching as he got into the car. He waved at me one last time before driving off. I headed back inside to finish up the food. Adam had actually helped me with most of it; he took care of the veggies, chicken, and salad. All I had to do was prepare the quinoa and desserts, my specialty.

I set the cheesecake in the fridge to cool. Then, I stacked the macarons in a tower, closing it carefully with a glass dome. I rushed upstairs to get ready, but when it came to picking clothes, I faced another dilemma.

Oh god. I need help.

"Okay, Stella, what did you wear when you met Carter's parents?" I asked, pacing the room in my underwear on a group call with the girls.

"Probably a pink swaddle? I'm not sure, but they did visit me in the hospital when I was born," Stella replied with a playful tone. Now was not the time for jokes, but I had forgotten they grew up together!

"You're no help!" I groaned and could hear the other girls chuckling.

Zaira met Ibrahim's during winter at a cabin, dressed from head to toe, being of no help to me whatsoever. Darshini met Dante's parents at the age of five, but when they dated and broke the news, it was a 'not too revealing' dress—once again being no help.

Maybe I won't go downstairs. I'll just stay here.

"Brooke, you'll be fine. Send us some photos," Stella said back. All the girls agreed.

I sent them photos of my outfit options, and after some debate, they settled on one. A pink dress with a sweetheart neckline and puffy sleeves. I thanked the girls and continued getting ready.

I heard the car pull into the garage and went to greet them. A middle-aged woman stepped out, laughing at something someone had said. She had a kind face with honey-brown eyes and blonde hair that matched Adam's. A man, Adam's dad, given their similar features, exited the car as well.

"Brooklyn, it's so lovely to meet you," Mrs. Serra Valle said, walking towards me with a warm smile. She rushed to hug me, her embrace washing away all my worries.

"Mrs. Serra Valle, it's great to meet you," I said. Her embrace washed away all my worries.

"Is my son keeping you hostage? Blink twice if you need help," Mr. Serra Valle joked as I stepped aside to help them with their bags.

"Seriously? What if she's the one keeping me hostage, hm? Ever thought of that?" Adam asked and rolled his eyes as he carried in more bags.

"No, Brooklyn is too sweet for that," a firm, familiar voice said. I turned around and saw a short woman, no taller than five feet, step inside. The grandmother! The woman who was always on my side on every phone call.

"Oh my god, it's so good to see you in person." I rushed to hug her. She hugged me instantly. Adam was right, she smelled like sugar cookies.

"I know I'm smaller than anticipated, but I can still act on all the threats I made." She swayed her finger and had her eyes focused on her grandson.

"Mãe, what did I tell you about making threats online? We have an image to keep up," Mr. Serra Valle groaned as he looked at his mother.

They got into some debate, Adam placed the last bags by the door and walked to me. He placed his hand on my back and held me to his side. He smiled at me and whispered, "See, not so bad, right?"

"What a lovely couple," his mother gushed as she looked at us, already taking out her phone to take pictures. "Started as friends?"

"Yeah, just friends and roommates," Adam said with a grin as he looked at me. "She's incredible—oh and she's allergic to nuts, so please nothing of that sort around."

"You told us twice already," his father groaned.

"I'm just making sure." Adam held his hands up defensively. "She just made macarons, they're the best things ever," Adam then said, pointing to the tower.

"It's made with coconut flour, so it's a bit different from your typical one, I assume," I informed them. I realised I hadn't taste-tested it. I only tasted the fillings, all of which were perfect for me. But I'm not sure what quality they're used to.

"Shh, they'll love it." Adam squeezed my side before letting go of me.

"I'm sure we can serve some with the cheesecake too after dinner," I offered and led the way to the dining room.

"After dinner? How about right now?" his grandmother scoffed, walking to the kitchen right away.

"Hmhm," both men hummed and followed right behind her. I stood there baffled, and Adam's mom nudged me.

"You can see where Adam has his sweet tooth from." She laughed.

"I can see, yeah." I smiled and watched as the three acted like little kids to get some dessert.

"You guys kept the place clean," his mother mentioned.

"Thank you," I replied.

"I hope you know what you're getting yourself into with that one," she told me as we both watched Adam and his father fight for a piece of cheesecake.

"I've lived with him for months, I think I know enough, right?" I assumed and looked at her.

"Have you experienced Christmas with him? He's a very festive guy," she replied, taking a seat at the table.

"Worse than on his birthday?" I frowned. He was a bit of a birthday boy, but I loved him regardless.

"About three times worse." She laughed.

"Oh dear," I muttered. Well, at least his birthday is on December 24th, so I'll only have to deal with the overly festive diva for a week.

We all gathered at the table, finally, and began to enjoy our dinner. Adam and I got complimented on the food, which made us both happy with our hard work being recognized.

"So, Adam mentioned you volunteer with animal shelters and are planning to further your studies in that field," Mr. Serra Valle said as he refilled his glass of passion fruit juice.

"Yes, I got accepted into an animal rights education program," I confirmed, and they all seemed genuinely thrilled.

"Tell us more," Adam's grandma asked excitedly. No one outside our friend group had ever shown such enthusiasm.

"Well, it's a national organisation dedicated to improving the lives of stray animals. Thanks to their efforts, they receive donations, which they use to offer scholarships for master's programs. In return, I'll have to complete a sixteen-month internship with them," I explained.

"It's a fantastic opportunity for your career. That's incredible. Is their focus national or international?" Adrianna gushed, her happiness unmistakable. These people, who had just met me, were genuinely excited for me.

"Nationally, but they often collaborate with international organisations," I answered, hoping to eventually work on a global level.

"That sounds amazing. How did you discover your passion for this work?" Matheus asked.

I shared the story of my grandmother, who introduced me to animal welfare work, and how I fell in love with volunteering at the shelter. I managed to avoid talking much about my parents, as they were only interested in my story.

"Seems like you and Adam both have super awesome grandmas," his grandma joked.

"Damn right," Adam confirmed with a proud grin.

"I think it's incredible what you're doing," Adrianna complimented with a soft smile. "Volunteering was the start of my journey too. Maybe one day, you'll work on an international level."

"I hope so. It would be a dream job," I admitted, gently placing my hand over Adam's when he snuck his hand to my thigh.

"So, you get to see cute animals all day? I always wanted to work in those penguin habitats." His grandma sighed lovingly.

"Mãe, you'd slide down the ice within seconds with your clumsy feet," Matheus teased, a smirk playing on his lips.

"Let's get some dessert before you two start bickering at my table," Adam said in a slightly authoritative tone as he stood up.

"Fine, but only because those macarons look so delicious," his father conceded, pointing to the tower of macarons.

We all got up to select our desserts. Adam, his grandmother, and his dad gathered around the tower of macarons. I watched as it slowly diminished while I savoured my strawberry cheesecake. Adam's mom sat next to me, devouring her slice of the cheesecake. Adam might have mentioned it was her favourite, hence why it was made.

"So, Adam told me you were a little worried about doing long distance," she mentioned, looking at me with a gentle expression.

"You guys talk about everything, huh?" I asked awkwardly, unsure of how this conversation would unfold.

"Not everything, just the important things." She shrugged, biting into a strawberry. Important things—of course, I was important to him.

"I see," I muttered, meeting her gaze.

"You know, long distance isn't as hard as some say, but that doesn't necessarily make it easy either. Matheus and I spent most of our youth together throughout college, but when we were recently engaged, he had this big job opportunity here in the US while we were both still in Brazil," she began. I listened attentively, curious about their history. Adam admired his parents' love story, and I wanted to know more.

"I told him to take the job. We were strong enough to survive it," she said, gesturing with her tiny spoon. "But then Matheus and I spent two years apart, one of which we couldn't visit at all. It was difficult—extremely difficult—because I missed him a lot. But it was worth it because we'd have a great future together. It worked out for us because we believed in each other and put in the effort," she continued, glancing lovingly at her husband across the room. "Now we've been married for over two decades, both work our dream job, and have an amazing son.

"I've heard how Adam talks about you and seen the way he looks at you. I know determination when I see it, and I know my son truly loves you and will do whatever he must to hold onto you," she said, patting my back reassuringly.

Matheus and Adrianna managed it across different continents. What's a year in different states? Adam had already printed out a schedule, weeks circled when we'd see each other. We could do this—I believed in us.

"I'll do whatever it takes. Thanks for the talk." I smiled, finishing the last of my cheesecake.

"Of course. Now show me some cute cat photos. I could never have one because first, it was my mother who was allergic to them, then Matheus." She scooted closer to me, glancing at her husband again.

I pulled out my phone and started showing her photos of the cats I had worked with. Her eyes lit up with each picture, and we laughed together over the adorable photos. Just like Adam, she reacted enthusiastically to every photo I had to show and kept asking about them. She was certainly his mother, they were quite alike.

"I forgot to ask, do you have a favourite flower?"

"No, why?" I frowned.

"Just making sure you get a bouquet you love," Mrs. Serra Valle dismissed casually.

"A bouquet?" I was still confused.

"For your graduation?" she replied as if it were common knowledge. "You're achieving something great, and we always treated Adam with flowers and a cupcake, so you'll get the same."

"Oh, I can't wait," his grandmother said as she walked over, the two men following behind her. "My sweet baby will graduate, he got into a football club, and he has an incredible girlfriend," she gushed.

"I told you they love you," Adam whispered to me as he joined my side.

"Should we get balloons with the flowers like high school?" Mr. Serra Valle asked as he leaned against his wife, planting his chin on her shoulder.

"Did you tell them to get me gifts?" I asked quietly.

My own parents weren't coming to my graduation, and here Adam's were, ready to bring gifts and celebrate the day with me when they had only just met me. Adrianna and Matheus welcomed me with open arms and brought warmth, filling a gap that had been in my life for a while.

"Nope, they made their own plans. Do you think I'd ask them for flowers at my graduation?" He shrugged and grabbed my hand. "Now come on board game time."

Sitting with Adam and his family made me realise this was exactly what I had wanted all my life. Finally, I was surrounded by people who treated me with love and respect. I wasn't sure how I got so lucky, but I knew for a fact that I'd be holding onto this happiness.

Epilogue

Adam

|Ten months later|

The video review meeting took longer than anticipated, but I finally bade goodbye to my teammates. Two months into my new job, I was thrust onto the field after the main left winger got injured. I felt bad for my teammate's injury, but it was a blessing for me. Over these past eight months, I'd been giving it my all, and it was paying off. I was garnering attention and recognition for my skills and hard work. I proved to the club that I deserved my spot on the team and on the field. I was here to stay, and they knew it.

I checked the time—only 6 PM— I was excited to go home, just to sleep. Brooklyn had three days off from work, and with some of her classes being online, she planned to visit me. Her flight was in the early AM tomorrow, and I was excited to pick her up. I missed her dearly.

The switch from seeing each other every day to only once a month had been hard on us. Most of our contact was digital, but it was worth it. Every morning starts with me longing for her, and every night ends with me loving her more than the night before.

I didn't like the long-distance aspect of our relationship, but I knew it wouldn't last forever. Soon, I'd be back at DTU, cheering for her as she received her master's, and she'd be transferring to join me in New York.

I just had to push through for a few more months, and I could handle it. For Brooklyn, I'd wait an eternity if it meant having her in my arms at the end.

Brooklyn was thriving and happy, which was most important to me. She loved the program she enrolled in and constantly talked about her job and how much she was learning from the organisation.

When I missed her and couldn't reach her, I liked to look at all the photos she had taken over the past few months. She was utterly happy in all of them and surrounded by our friends, people who loved her too. One of my favourite photos was when she and our friends surprised me at one of my games. They were all there to watch, and it warmed my heart to see all seven of them.

When I got home, I entered the apartment with a frown. Why were the lights on? I remembered turning them off before I left. This wasn't right. Looking down, I saw a pair of familiar sandals—Brooklyn's. I dropped my keys and immediately went to find her. The kitchen smelled like her famous brownies. She was definitely here.

My bedroom door opened, and Brooklyn emerged, wearing only a jersey of mine as she dried her hair. She instantly dropped her towel and launched herself at me. I caught her in my arms and held her tight as I told her how much I missed her constantly.

"How—when?" I tried asking her something, but my mind was overloaded with joy and unable to answer questions.

"There was an issue and I had to take an earlier flight, otherwise I'd have to wait till tomorrow afternoon," Brooklyn explained as her face was still nuzzled in my chest. "I couldn't wait to see you, and I was off from work already, so I came straight here to see my favourite centre forward."

"This is the best surprise ever." I cupped her face and kissed her.

Brooklyn's fingers found their way into my hair as our kiss deepened, pulling me closer with an urgency that matched my own. Our lips moved in a rhythm that showed just how much we missed this.

My hands slid down her curves and under her ass. With a swift movement, I lifted her off the ground and pressed her body to mine. She wrapped her legs around my waist as she kissed harder, her nails grazed my scalp all the way down to my nape. Shivers shot down my spine as I moaned into the kiss.

Oh, how I had craved the taste of her sweet kisses that always left me wanting more. Her hands roamed over my shoulders, down my back, as if memorising every contour of my body.

We only pulled away when we needed to breathe. I smiled as I gazed into her eyes and leaned forward to kiss her forehead.

"I see you made brownies," I said, still holding her close.

"Mhm, I had to get the ingredients myself because you don't have a single sweet thing at home," she said dramatically, walking over to grab a piece of her brownie. I playfully rolled my eyes at her statement. I had just finished the last of my sweets, the plan was to restock with her—I missed the mundane things like grocery shopping with her.

"You're the only sweet thing I need." I winked and moved closer to her.

"Ewww, I hate you." She scrunched her nose in mock annoyance. I wrapped my arms around her and kissed her cheek several times.

"Yeah?" I asked between kisses.

"Mhm," she murmured, letting out a soft moan as my lips trailed down her neck. "How much?"

"Oh, so much," she whispered, her fingers weaving through my hair, urging me on.

"That's the worst," I teased, pulling away and stealing the piece of brownie from her hand. Brooklyn rolled her eyes but didn't fight me for it.

"I have some great news for you," Brooklyn said, grabbing another piece for herself.

"Go ahead," I said, biting into my brownie and humming at the taste. It was just as perfect as always, with those little flakes of salt on top.

"I spoke to Mrs. Moore about the transfer, and it's official. After graduation, I'll be placed in their NY department, and I'll join a team that works internationally," she announced, her smile radiant.

"Wait, really? You got a promotion too?" I pulled her into a hug and kissed her cheek.

"Yep, being forced to learn French finally paid off," she joked.

"Brooklyn, that's amazing. You're incredible," I complimented her, smiling proudly.

"Thank you! I even checked the distance—it's less than thirty minutes away on the subway."

"I can't wait," I said, letting go of her to grab some water. "How are the others?"

"Med school is killing Zaira and Ibrahim, Dante and Darsh are as cute as buttons, and Carter and Stella are disgustingly adorable." Brooklyn shrugged.

"So everything's the same?"

"Basically." She smiled.

"I didn't know you were coming; I would've gotten you food," I said, staring at the fridge. It was mostly beverages. "I was planning to make fried ramen noodles," I said, pointing to the packs on the counter.

"Is that what you're feeding yourself as a professional athlete?" Brooklyn teased.

"Hey, I'll add chicken breasts and eggs for protein," I defended my poor choice of dinner. "I can have a day off, and nobody has to know."

"I know now... I wonder how the team's nutritionist is gonna feel about that," Brooklyn said in her sing-song voice, aka her blackmail voice.

"Name your price." I sighed, walking closer to her. Maybe I'll get lucky and she'll ask for a kiss.

"There's this black-tie event... I checked your schedule and you can make it, but you'll have to fly out the next morning," she said sweetly, trailing her finger down my chest. I tried not to show too much excitement, getting to show her off in public was more of a reward than a blackmailing price, but I didn't let it show on my face.

"Consider it done, now go sit that pretty ass down." I moved my hand down her back, then spanked her. "Dinner is in progress."

After dinner, we snuggled up on the couch, watching a random drama on TV. My eyes were glued to the screen, curious about the sister-in-law's scheming. Brooklyn held one of my hands on her stomach while she scrolled through her social media feed with the other.

"Hey, there's a new club that opened up nearby," Brooklyn said, moving her phone for me to see the screen. "Vibe Haven," she read aloud.

"What a ridiculous name," I replied, staring at the image. I vaguely remembered hearing some chatter about the place.

"I know, right?" Brooklyn muttered, and we both continued to study the image.

"Should we check it out?" I suggested. As much as I loved cuddling and staying home with her, I wanted to make the most of the little time we had together.

"It's been a while... I think we should," she mentioned, sitting up and taking my hand in hers. She gazed at me with the sweetest look, as if I'd ever declined her offer.

"Sounds good. But no tequila for either of us, okay?" I said, narrowing my eyes at her playfully.

"Nope, none of that," she promised. "I want to enjoy my night with you, not end up drunk on your couch with crackers and cheese," she joked, making me laugh.

I sat at the edge of my bed and watched as Brooklyn moved around to get ready. She wore a pretty little red dress, and I had a hard time peeling my eyes off her curves. Her makeup was spectacular, of course, and right now she was busy doing her hair.

It doesn't matter what I wore; she always outshined me.

"How are you real?" I asked as I moved behind her. I wrapped my arms around her waist and looked at our reflection. Brooklyn smiled and brought her hands to mine as she leaned against me.

"I could ask you the same thing." She turned around, placing both hands over my shoulders.

My hands rested on her hips loosely, swaying with her as I got lost in her eyes. She got on her toes and pressed a kiss to my neck, just above the collar of my shirt. Judging by the smirk on her face, I was pretty sure she just marked me and my shirt.

"There's no need to mark me, Brooklyn sweetheart. No one could ever stand beside you without dimming in your radiance." I gazed into her eyes as my fingers traced shapes on her lower back. Nothing but pure love dripped from my words as I stared at her.

Brooklyn's eyes softened at the words as she stared at me for a moment, her hand moved to caress my face. "Two drinks for me, a bit of dancing, then we come back home and you peel this dress off my body, okay?"

"What a perfect end to my night." I smiled and leaned down to kiss her, not caring if my lips would match the wine-red shade of hers.

I knew how incredibly lucky I was to have gotten the woman of my dreams. It might have been our arrangement that brought us together, but it was our love that kept us bound. She held my heart completely. Anything she wanted was hers without question.

If I had to describe our love in one word, it would be serendipitous. It had been a beautiful surprise that unfolded naturally for us like pieces of a puzzle falling into place.

Acknowledgement

Hey everyone!

Thank you so much for giving this book a chance! It's been bittersweet writing it, knowing it's the last in the series (apart from special scenes that will be released in the future hehe) I just want to say thank you, The Seasons of Love has been my first ever book I decided to publish and seeing it get loved makes it all worth it as an Indie author.

I truly hoped you enjoyed reading this as much as I enjoyed writing it. Brooklyn and Adam had such a unique dynamic.

My thanks go to Hannah, my editor, of course. She has been incredible with all four books and made sure to polish these with love and care.

Once again Dida will get her little spotlight. She supported me from the beginning, always pushed me to self-publish. If it wasn't for her, all my books would've still been archived, unseen by anyone but me.

Last but not least, my thanks go to Mama and Papa. They're still banned from reading my books (the dicktionary says it all) But as always, they support me in (almost) everything. Self-publishing is no cheap joke, but they never once tried to stop me and instead offered their support where they could.

To every reader, thank you for making this first series possible. With your support I managed to make these silly little ideas in my head turn to more, reach something real till the very last chapter. Your support has meant more to me than words could ever say.

More about the author

E.L. Deliza is a twenty-three-year-old author with a lifelong passion for storytelling. Her journey began at a young age, crafting plots for her dolls, which later evolved into writing stories on platforms like Episode and Wattpad by the time she was thirteen. Initially, her work was shared only with close friends or kept private, but her love for creating stories continued to grow.

With time and growing confidence, E.L. Deliza decided to expand her horizons, leading to the self-publication of her debut novel, It Happened One Fall and now It Happened One Winter.

Currently, she is a university student majoring in software engineering. While she enjoys her work in ICT and excels in her studies, writing remains her true passion, and she hopes to share many more stories with the world.

An introvert at heart, E.L. Deliza loves napping, indulging in chocolate chip cookies, and spending countless hours watching her favorite shows and movies.

Follow E.L Deliza for updates on future projects and sneak-peak into her character's life.

@ **el.deliza_author** on Instagram

www.ingramcontent.com/pod-product-compliance
Lightning Source LLC
LaVergne TN
LVHW100516110826
845146LV00002B/658
9789991487236